PRAISE FOR

THE DIARIES OF EMILIO RENZI

"Splendidly crafted and interspliced with essays and stories, this beguiling work is to a diary as Piglia is to 'Emilio Renzi': a lifelong alter ego, a highly self-conscious shadow volume that brings to bear all of Piglia's prowess as it illuminates his process of critical reading and the inevitable tensions between art and life. . . . No previous familiarity with Piglia's work is needed to appreciate these bibliophilic diaries, adroitly repurposed through a dexterous game of representation and masks that speaks volumes of the role of the artist in society, the artist in his time, the artist in his tradition. . . . Piglia's 'delusion of living in the third person' to 'avoid the illusion of an interior life' transmogrifies us as well, into the character of the reader, and 'that feeling is priceless.'"

MARA FAYE LETHEM, *THE NEW YORK TIMES BOOK REVIEW*

"When young Ricardo Piglia wrote the first pages of his diaries, which he would work on until the last years of his life, did he have any inkling that they would become a lesson in literary genius and the culmination of one of the greatest works of Argentine literature?"

SAMANTA SCHWEBLIN, AUTHOR OF *FEVER DREAM*

"A valediction from the noted Argentine writer, known for bringing the conventions of hard-boiled U.S. crime drama into Latin American literature. *L'ennui, c'est moi*. First-tier Argentine novelist Piglia's (*Money to Burn*, 2003, etc.) literary alter ego, Emilio Renzi, was a world-weary detective when he stepped into the spotlight in the claustrophobic novel *Artificial Respiration*, published in Argentina in 1981 and in the U.S. in 1994, a searching look at Buenos Aires during the reign of the generals. Here, in notebooks begun decades earlier but only shaped into a novel toward the end of Piglia's life, Renzi is struggling to forge a career as a writer. . . . The story takes a few detours into the meta—it's a nice turn that Renzi, himself a fictional writer, learns 'what I want to do from imaginary writers. Stephen Dedalus or Nick Adams, for example'—but is mostly straightforward, reading just like the diary it purports to be. Fans of Cortázar, Donoso, and Gabriel García Márquez will find these to be eminently worthy last words from Piglia, who died at the beginning of 2017."

KIRKUS REVIEWS, STARRED REVIEW

In this fictionalized autobiography, Piglia's ability to succinctly criticize and contextualize major writers from Kafka to Flannery O'Connor is astounding, and the scattering of those insights throughout this diary are a joy to read. This book is essential reading for writers."

PUBLISHERS WEEKLY

"Where others see oppositions, great writers see the possibility of intertwining forking paths. Like kids in front of a stereogram, they are able to shift their gaze in ways that allow them to read the history of literature *otherwise* and, in doing so, write beyond the dead end of tradition. Ricardo Piglia, the monumental Argentine writer whose recent death coincided with increasing recognition of his work in the English-speaking world, was without a doubt one of these great visionaries. . . . It was said that there lay hidden something more impressive than his transgressive novels or his brilliant critical essays, a secret work of even more transcendence: his diaries. . . . In the tradition of Pavese, Kafka, and Gombrowicz, the diaries were the culmination of a life dedicated to thinking of literature as a way of life."

CARLOS FONSECA, LITERARY HUB

"It almost seems as though Piglia has perfected the form of the literary author's diary, leaving in enough mundane life details to give a feeling of the messy, day-to-day livedness of a diary, but also providing this miscellany with something of a shape, and with a true intellectual heft. In these pages we see the formation of a formidable literary intelligence—the brief reflections on genre, Kafka, Beckett, Dashiell Hammett, Arlt, and Continental philosophy alone are worth the price of admission—but we also see heartbreak, familial drama, reflections on life, small moments of great beauty, the hopes and anxieties of a searching young man, the endless monetary woes of one dedicated to the literary craft, and the drift of a nation whose flirtation with fascism takes it on a dangerous course."

VERONICA ESPOSITO, *BOMB MAGAZINE*

"As a fictionalized autobiography, it is, like the work of Karl Ove Knausgaard, of *My Struggle* fame, part confession and part performance. Renzi meets and corresponds with literary luminaries like Borges, Cortázar, and Márquez, and offers insightful readings of Dostoevsky, Kafka, Faulkner, and Joyce. . . . Fans of W.G. Sebald and Roberto Bolaño will find the first installment in Piglia's trilogy to be a fascinating portrait of a writer's life."

ALEXANDER MORAN, *BOOKLIST*

"In the long history of novelists and their doubles, doppelgängers, and alter egos, few have given more delighted attention to the problem of multiplicity than the Argentine novelist Ricardo Emilio Piglia Renzi. . . . Under the name of Ricardo Piglia he published a sequence of acrobatic, dazzling novels and stories that consistently featured a novelist called Emilio Renzi. . . . The larger story of *Formative Years* reads something like a roman d'apprentissage: the romance of a writer's vocation, in all its hubris and innocent corruption. . . . [T]he book's real subject is more delicate and more moving than the simple story of a literary vocation. It is the process of textualization, of the stuttering, hesitant way a writer tries to convert life into literature. In these diaries, Piglia is dramatizing not only the writer's split between a public and private self, but also the time-consuming, exhausting, delicious, compromised effort to construct that textual self: the self that exists only in words. . . . *Formative Years* is one of the great novels of youth: its boredom, powerlessness, desperation, strategizing, delusion. . . . this journal impassively records not only a novelist's self-creation, but a society's unraveling."

ADAM THIRLWELL, *THE NEW YORK REVIEW OF BOOKS*

RICARDO PIGLIA

THE DIARIES OF EMILIO RENZI

A Day in the Life

Translated from the Spanish by Robert Croll

RESTLESS BOOKS
BROOKLYN, NEW YORK

Work published within the framework of the "Sur" Translation
Support Program of the Ministry of Foreign Affairs, International
Trade and Worship of the Argentine Republic.

Obra editada en el marco del Programa "Sur" de Apoyo a las
Traducciones del Ministerio de Relaciones Exteriores, Comercio
Internacional y Culto de la República Argentina.

This book is made possible by the New York State Council on the Arts with the
support of Governor Andrew M. Cuomo and the New York State Legislature.

First Restless Books paperback edition October 2020

Paperback ISBN: 9781632060471
Library of Congress Control Number: 2018956686

Cover design by Daniel Benneworth-Gray
Set in Garibaldi by Tetragon, London

Printed in Canada

1 3 5 7 9 10 8 6 4 2

Restless Books, Inc.
232 3rd Street, Suite A101
Brooklyn, NY 11215

restlessbooks.org
publisher@restlessbooks.org

CONTENTS

THE DIARIES OF
EMILIO RENZI

A DAY IN THE LIFE

I

THE PLAGUE YEARS

1

Sixty Seconds in Reality

He had spent several months, exactly from the beginning of April 2014 until the end of March 2015, working on his diaries, taking advantage of an illness, a passing one according to the doctors, which prevented him from going outside; as Renzi would say, joking with his friends, going outside was never a temptation for me, but I never had any interest in what we might call going inside either, or being inside, because inevitably, Renzi told his friends, one wonders, inside of what?, and so it turned out that, thanks to—or as an effect of—that passing illness, he could finally dedicate all of his time and energy to reviewing, rereading, revisiting his diaries, which he'd spoken of too much in another time, for he'd always been tempted—in another time—to talk about his life, although it wasn't quite that, but talking about his notebooks. Yet he'd never done it, and scarcely alluded to that personal, private, "confidential" work, although what he'd written in his notebooks had, so to speak, often passed unchanged into his novels and essays, into the short stories and narratives that he'd written over the course of the years.

But now, taking advantage of the illness that had suddenly befallen him, he could shut himself away in his study and dedicate himself to transcribing the hundreds and hundreds of pages written in his cursive scrawl inside notebooks with rubber covers. And so, when he found himself afflicted by a mysterious illness, which had visible signs—for example, he had difficulty moving his left hand—even though its diagnosis was uncertain, then, Renzi said, he began an interior work, something done inside, in other words, without venturing into the street. He hadn't read his diaries chronologically; I couldn't bear it, Renzi told his friends. Before, on several occasions, he had undertaken the task of reading them and trying to type them up, to make a "clean copy," but within a few days he would have deserted that horrible chronological succession and abandoned the project. Even so, Renzi intended to publish his private notes according to the order of the days because, after rejecting other forms of organization such as, for example, following one theme or person or place over the course of the years in his notebooks and giving his life an aleatory and serial order, he'd realized that the confusing, formless, and contingent experience of living was lost in the process, and so it was better to follow the successive arrangement of days and months. He had suddenly recognized that his work—but was it work?—of reading, investigating, tracing through his notebooks was one thing, and the published order of the notes that recorded his life was a very different matter. The conclusion: reading isn't the same as *giving to be read*. As he'd learned in college, the research is one thing and the exposition another; for a historian, the time spent searching blindly in the archives for things you imagine are there is antagonistic to the time required to present the results of the investigation. The same issue arises if you become a historian of yourself.

And so, he'd made up his mind to present his diaries in chronological order, dividing what was written into three large parts that observed the phases of his life, because, in reading the notebooks, he'd discovered that a fairly clear division into three eras or periods was possible. But, in April of the previous year, when faced with the task of rereading and copying the entries of his diaries, he realized it was unbearable to imagine his life as a continuous line and quickly decided to read through his notebooks at random. They were filed haphazardly in cardboard boxes of varying provenance and size; they'd been with him everywhere he went, those notebooks, and the disorder that came with each move had thus broken any illusion of continuity. He'd never attempted to file them in an orderly way. He would change their placement and position according to his mood, would stare at them without opening them, for example, strewn across the floor or piled on his desk, and be overwhelmed by the amount of physical space that his personal notes occupied. One afternoon, following his grandfather Emilio's example, he'd decided to set aside a room exclusively for his diaries. The fact that they would all be in a single place and, above all, that the door to them might be closed, even locked, reassured him. Yet he never did it. If he had wasted part of his life writing down events and thoughts in a notebook, he wasn't going to waste a room of his house on top of that, only to sit and spend entire nights reading and rereading the catastrophic stupidity of the way he lived, because it wasn't his life, it was the passage of days. And so he asked his friend, the shopkeeper on Calle Ayacucho, for some cardboard boxes, and he used these boxes that once held all manner of products to store them away, packing them in no order, and finally, so as not to be tempted, he decided he would turn his back to the notebooks, contained inside eight boxes, and then, not looking but feeling his way, he would take one out. In that way, Renzi told his friends, he had managed to completely dismantle his experience and move from his notes about months of loneliness and inactivity to another notebook in which he found himself active, lucid, conquering. In that way, he began to perceive that he was several people at the same time. At certain points he would encounter a failure, a good-for-nothing, but then, reading a notebook written five years later, he would discover a talented, inspired, and triumphant young man. Life must not be viewed as an organic continuum, but rather as a collage of contradictory emotions that do not at all obey the logic of cause and effect, not at all, Renzi repeated, there's no progression and of course there's no progress, no one ever learns from their experience, unless they've taken the rather deranged and unjustified precaution of writing and describing the succession of days, for then, in the future—and only in the future—the meaning will blaze like a fire on the plain, or rather, will burn within those pages. Unity is always retrospective, all is intensity and confusion in the present, but if we look at the present once it has already passed and situate ourselves in the future, in order to once again see the things we've lived through, then, according to Renzi, it could become somehow clearer.

He had spent those many months, from the beginning of April to the end of March, immersed in the abyss of his existence, sometimes murky, sometimes clear and transparent. Several times he'd become captivated by one writer or philosopher for a while and would spend months immersed in the mass of writings left by that single author—Malcolm Lowry or Jean-Paul Sartre, for example—and read everything they'd written and everything that had been written about them, but now, although the system, to think of it that way, was the same, everything was different because the subject of the investigation was himself, the self, he said, with a burst of laughter. The self, one's essence, and yet, since one isn't just one but rather another and then another still, in an open circle, it is understood that the form of expression must be faithful to contingency and disorder, and its only form of organization must be the flow of life itself.

Since April of the previous year he'd dedicated himself to that project, along with the invaluable and sarcastic help of his Mexican assistant, Luisa, and Renzi had dictated to her, just as he was dictating now, all of his notebooks, and they'd managed, amid jokes and laughter, to swim through that abyss of waters at once murky and transparent. That day, Monday, February 2, they had reached the shore and could look back at what they had done from a different perspective. Amid the mire of pages written, read, dictated, and amended, certain events, certain incidents or situations had shone out, things he'd captured or glimpsed while dictating to her, as though he were living through them once more. All experience is, so to speak, retrospective, an *après-coup*, a later revelation, save for two or three moments of life in which passion defines temporality and fixes its enduring sign upon the present. Passion, Renzi repeated, is always present; it is actuality, manifested in a pure present that lingers on through life like a diamond. If you return to it, you are not remembering but living through it now, once more, in the present, ever vivid and incandescent.

For example, back in that time, a meeting with a woman, alone and undefeated yet also aching and broken, at a modest apartment in Villa Urquiza, furnished in an anonymous style, its kitchen like so many kitchens in Buenos Aires, expansive, with a white wooden table where you could sit—as she and I did that day—and drink yerba mate. I saw only the kitchen and living room—the dinette, as it's called—with framed photographs and decorations that were almost invisible for being such ordinary sights, and I never saw the bathroom but can imagine it—the mirrored medicine cabinet, the white tiles—just as I can imagine the bedroom with the double bed, used for many years by only one spouse—the one who had survived. An apartment like any other, on the sixth floor, with a TV on a table to the left side of the living room, facing white armchairs. The truth shone out in such a common place. And that's why I remember that meeting so clearly; I need only shut my eyes to be right back there. There's barely more than a terse reference in my notebooks, the date and time and a note in passing so as not to say too much during a time when any word or gesture could bring harm to the person you mentioned and thus exposed. It was a precaution that did not guarantee anything or allow you to imagine you were safe but served only as a record that you'd lived in those dark days. At the time, I wrote: *Today I visited the Oracle at Delphi. I don't call her that because she—the wounded woman—presents herself that way, but because of the composed clarity of her speech. An oracle with no enigma; the confusion, at any rate, is on the part of the one who comes seeking advice.* I can remember it better and more vividly than if I'd written it all down, and, for me, that piece of evidence—every time I've come face to face with it or recalled it—has served as proof of a single moment in which life and meaning were joined together. But what was the cost?

That's why I've spoken of those as "the plague years." In Greek tragedy, it was a way to refer to social evil. A plague that devastated a community as a result of a crime perpetrated in the very site of state power. A state crime that—in the form of an epidemic—caused terror and death among the citizens. A metaphor, in short. Quite opposite to the metaphor, a familiar one in our time, of the despotic power associated with a surgeon who must operate without anesthesia and cut open the ailing body of the nation. The idea of surgery as a medical metaphor for state oppression is very common in my country's history. A doctor sees his obligation, as those bastards say, to act upon the body in order to cure the political disease that, so they claim, is afflicting the nation.

By contrast, in the Greek tradition, the calamity is seen as a result of the crime being perpetrated in the state; who murdered Laius, the king, at a cleft in the road? The plague, then, is the result of a crime that befalls the populace, and the plague years are the dark years during which the defenseless suffer under a social evil, or rather, a state evil, descending from the seat of power onto the innocent citizens. And so, in order to remedy the wrong or to find some relief or escape, I had to visit the Pythia, that woman, a cross between seer and bird, to face her and to hear her song. That lady, whom I met in secret, was compelled to be beyond reproach in her life and habits. And so she was, Antonia Cristina, whose powers I only glimpsed years after visiting her in her modest home, at Delphi, that is, in Villa Urquiza.

That too was the meaning behind the title of Camus's novel, *The Plague*, the first book I read "myself," which is to say, I used it so that I could tell a woman, a girl really, my version of what I'd read, and I don't remember what I told her but I do remember that night I spent reading the novel, furiously, as though the book were alive, inside me, even as I was reading it for her. And that's all I've done ever since, reading a book, or rather, giving a book to someone who's asked to read it. For Camus it is Nazism, the German occupation, which causes the epidemic that sweeps across Algeria. The other meaning of the plague is that it gives rise to a series of narratives for which it is the condition, not the subject, as is visible in Boccaccio's *Decameron*; always, amid the terror of death, there is a group of people who shut themselves off in order to tell, by turns, some stories. The danger, the terror, the curse of a reality with no escape is often transformed into tales, little stories that circulate in the middle of the night, relating imaginary versions of the lived experience of those dark days and making it possible to bear through them and survive. The telling of stories brings relief from the nightmare of History. For example, in the past I've related the anonymous story that began to circulate around Buenos Aires in those days. Someone said there was someone who had a friend who, one morning, at a railway station, in a suburb of the city, had seen a freight train passing, slow and silent, heading south with a load of empty coffins. That was the story that circulated by word of mouth in the midst of the military plague and the horror of Argentina. A perfect story that both said and did not say, that alluded, in its image, to the reality we were living in. For those empty caskets invoked the unburied bodies that had ravaged, and for years to come would ravage, the memory of the country. They were heading south, a brilliant detail that referred to the desert, but also, of course, to the Falklands War, which the murderers had been preparing for months as an escape route and which the story seemed to anticipate. How did they know the coffins were empty? It was, Renzi thought, the gravitational pull of fantastical literature, which had been, in our culture, a very original way of writing that allowed us to postulate unsettling realities that contain more truth than reality such as it is experienced. The other highly political detail in that story was the presence of a witness. There was always someone present who saw what happened and could recount it; there's always a witness at the scene of the event, an individual who sees and then goes on to spread the story. In this way, there is a certain poetic justice in the world that makes it possible for social crimes to be revealed and made known.

There is a witness who gives testimony and shares the things they have lived through and the things they have seen. Showing them and making them visible, for their account, said Renzi, does not judge, it only *implies* and, in that way, allows the things that History conceals to become known.

Thus, the plague, and we as witnesses describe what we lived through in those dark times; my notebooks are a stunned yet serene record of the experience of life in a state of emergency. Everything seems to go on in the same way, the people work, have fun, fall in love, amuse themselves, and there seem to be no visible signs of the horror. That's the most sinister thing; under an appearance of normalcy, the terror persists, and everyday reality remains there like a veil, but sometimes a breach allows the harsh truth to be seen. For example, the time I returned to Buenos Aires after spending several months teaching at the University of California, San Diego, in 1977; I didn't go into exile, even though I could have stayed and lived there, but decided instead to return to Buenos Aires because Iris Marrapodi, the woman I was living with at that time, didn't want to leave the country without her son, and his father, Javier Méndez, a professor of Greek and Latin, using the so-called *patria potestas*, refused to allow his ten-year-old boy to travel abroad. So I stayed with her, and maybe I would have gone on living here even without her, for I wasn't a well-known writer at that time, not even close, and I didn't suspect I was in any real danger and anyway struggled to imagine a life outside of Buenos Aires. And so, Renzi said, when I returned, just as I do whenever I've spent a while outside the country, I took to the streets and went through all of my places, so close to my heart and so filled with emotion; I ventured out in search of the world where I'd lived and been happy, and that afternoon I realized suddenly that the military had changed the system of signs in the city and, in place of the iconic poles, painted white, which indicated the bus stops, had installed notices that said *Zona de detención*. The entire city, I realized, said Renzi, was flooded with those ominous signs, which were there in order to say—and not say—that all of the inhabitants were eventual detainees, detainees and *desaparecidos* in waiting, at all times, permitted to walk the streets until they ordered us to line up and await transfer. The city divided into detainment zones. I stopped, paralyzed; it was as if I was reading that the people must stand here all night and line up to be taken to concentration camps, where they would be tortured and murdered. *Zona de detención*; there are many ways to indicate where buses stop, but labeling the stops with that name seemed to be a manifestation that made it clear what was going on. I suppose that, before choosing to name the stops that way, the military officers would have discussed it with urban planners and publicists until they found the phrase that squared best with their acts of kidnapping and detaining citizens. *Zona de detención*: a few of these notices still survive around the city. In my notebooks from those years, there's an account of how I lived during the plague, how I moved around the city like a ghost, how I earned my living, the things I was writing and doing.

The best example of the truth about that period, said Renzi, was my visit to Antonia. Both of her children had disappeared: Eleonora and Roberto had been kidnapped, tortured, and murdered. She was an activist in the Montoneros organization, and he was the leader of Vanguardia Comunista, a political group with Maoist leanings. I was friends with Roberto and saw him often, and our meetings are recorded, elliptically, in my diaries. But my visit that afternoon to their mother, who received me in her house in Villa Urquiza, was an epiphany; in the midst of the terror and despair and the terrible news that filtered in to us from hell, a miracle occurred, without histrionics, in calm conversation, in the midst of that woman's pain, there was a moment of clarity.

According to Junior, there was a video on YouTube in which Renzi spoke about the Mothers of the Plaza de Mayo and said that he'd visited one of them and that this mother, according to Renzi, Junior recalled, would argue with the TV every day because of the lies that emanated from it. He remembered her very clearly, Renzi said, and he began to dictate: in 1978 he'd gone to visit Antonia Cristina, the mother of Eleonora and Roberto, her two vanished children. She lived in a very modest apartment in Villa Urquiza, and indeed, Renzi said, she used to argue with the TV and refute its lies. She told me: I only ask God to grant me one minute on TV to set the record straight. Every night, she told me, I go over it, practicing what I could say in one minute, changing it, adjusting it. And the things that this woman, alone in the city, wanted to say are now accepted thought in Argentina. The truth of the vulnerable sometimes succeeds in making itself heard. That's something we must always remember.

Wasn't she the oracle? She was the oracle, a lone woman in the city who, each night, in the uncertain hour when the day was changing, before sleep, would memorize and review and sometimes recite the truth in a soft voice while, outside, the so-called spokesmen of the military power said thousands upon thousands of words, repeating their dirty lies, trying to erase the reality of their crimes, and the TV presenters and leading journalists repeated and extended their distorted version of events, while in a modest apartment in Villa Urquiza one woman kept thinking on and on about how to craft an account that was simple, true, frontal, and direct, one that could sum up and respond to the thousands of words spoken by those bastards. The seer must be a woman of integrity; so it was in classical Greece, and so too it was centuries later when, in a modest apartment in Villa Urquiza, Antonia took up that tradition, the same as Antigone, and appealed for justice and a dignified burial for her children. Renzi had tried to imagine those words, and the impact of her voice had helped him to survive and write. That woman's silence—the words that she thought but could not say, that no one was listening to—was the secret, the enigma, the thing that is known but never uttered, a speech awaiting its opportunity to transform into an action that would change reality. The Argentine military had gone to war in the Falklands so that this voice would be left unheard. And their attempt to silence it had led them to defeat and disaster.

And so Renzi had spent all of those months shut away inside his study, reading his notebooks in no order, before arriving finally at the years of his experience in those times, and that was what he now intended to divulge, that is, to reveal the confused, uncertain way that he'd written about those years while living through them. Not later, once everything had become clear, but on the march, in the field, or rather, at the psychological frontier of life, situated inside the no-man's-land that divided reality into two, on one side horror, on the other side insanity, the *locas* who repeated the truth of History at night like a prayer, the nightmare, the plague, their unburied children. Those women repeated, like a litany, the things that everyone knew yet none could bring themselves to say. That was what Renzi spoke of on that February afternoon, in his study, afflicted by a passing illness that prevented him from moving about freely and forced his friends to come and see him, to listen to his version of the events of his life, according to the way he'd recorded them inside his notebooks with rubber covers.

2

Diary 1976

January

A person writing in an alphabetical notebook and placing the emotions in order, the letters guiding the feelings (what syntax can resist the discovery of passion?).

Sunday 4

I'm reading *Madame Bovary* once again and am in the middle of the scene at the fair. Is the contrast too facile? Clumsy discourse, clumsy seduction: grand words. The same feeling since the beginning: too much emphasis on Charles Bovary's "stupid" world, opposed to Emma's sappy spirituality. I must apologize, Flaubert is a master, it's extraordinary how he sets up the adultery with Léon and then has it consummated with another man, remarkable.

Tuesday, January 20, 1976

The lecture hall at the College of Law, opposite the Panthéon, men and women crowding in, maintaining suave complicities. Lacan enters with a leather coat, plaid blazer, doctor's jacket, unlit cigarette; he speaks, sprawling and zigzagging, in an incomprehensible whisper: strangely aggressive. He makes his voice the object of desire, since they've come to listen to him, and twice repeats: "anyone who wants to hear me should read me." Then he introduces a clean-cut young man (Jacques Aubert), who expounds a correct reading of Joyce while Lacan acts as monitor, writing stray words on the blackboard with theatrical gestures: Dublin, father, Bloom.

We saw Barthes: insanity, he said, always lies in the syntax, for it is there that the subject seeks his place. A long wait beforehand, in the stairwell.

Sunday, February 1
In Buenos Aires, back at home by myself, I enter the apartment on Calle Canning, organized and clean: a strange peace. Playing the solitary man returning from a trip to Paris.

Saturday 14
I've spent a week sorting out my library. Packages upon packages of papers burned, accumulated over the course of years, in which I did nothing but write pointlessly. I trace back the line. How old was I? Papers upon papers now in transparent plastic bags, good only for trash.

I'm reading Nietzsche's final letters, the destruction of his mind, which, nevertheless, did not contaminate his style.

Rumors of a coup d'état. According to Rubén, it won't make it past this week.

Monday 16
I have fruit and milk for lunch. I don't start smoking until two in the afternoon.

Thursday 19
An unexpected call from Ulyses Petit de Murat in praise of *Assumed Name*. His reading seems to come from another world yet nevertheless goes against those that seem closer (Juan Carlos Martini, Enrique Molina, Osvaldo Soriano), who take my story about Arlt at face value and believe it is true.

Friday 27
The military coup is being discussed as something inevitable; Lorenzo Miguel supports Isabel, and the military, so it seems, has already put together a cabinet. The generalizations from the coup in 1955 are repeated: corruption, inefficiency, etc. The goal seems to be to break up the union movement in order to open the way for the liberal project.

Saturday 28
Sarmiento's memories are organized along an axis that I'd like to examine: the project of being a writer, the conditions that make it possible. In Sarmiento's case, I find a nucleus that I'll call "Arltian": an obsession with legitimacy due to his lack of academic titles, excessive reading, a search for recognition: he becomes a writer because of these shortcomings. Maybe it would be possible to start from these nodes as a way to reconstruct a trajectory—making a name for oneself through literature—that is present in Sarmiento but not in him alone.

In Arlt, rereading his *Aguafuertes*: the writer who sees, the seer (coming from the occult arts); this is the form: today I was walking down the street and I saw. He writes them for money, and the editor, therefore, has the right to cut his articles down. You're a genius, he says, explaining to him why the crossed-out fragments don't work.

For his part, Mansilla: the beginning of his writing is tied to his escape from prison after the attempted duel with José Mármol. He takes refuge in Santa Fe and is hired by the governor to describe things he didn't see under the name of the man paying him; he can't do it on demand and for money, he doesn't have the will ("how hunger made me a writer"). Inversion of his "ability" and his family fortune. After that he'll write only under his own name and only about things he has seen. Compare, then, Mansilla's *Causeries* and Arlt's *Aguafuertes*.

I'm rereading *Don Quixote*; I remember the first time I read the novel in 1959. The Quixote–Sancho opposition seems to be based on the legible, and the insanity–reason opposition depends on reading: Don Quixote says, "and this would have been clear to thee hadst thou read as many histories as I have," and Sancho answers him, "Pardon me, your worship, for I cannot read or write, as I said just now."

Monday, March 1
All in all, the old superstition that has been with me forever is clear: the precise beginnings that make it possible to start over again. Someone who goes away ("Wakerfield") and leaves everything behind to become "the other."

Tuesday 2
Sometimes I have the feeling that I'm moving forward with a ten-year delay: that would make me twenty-five years old now, and in that case I "could" have—or take—the time needed to do and understand everything I want. Why ten years? As if I'd awakened to life in 1950, that is, the year my brother was born, the sudden discovery of "reality," the emergency room, etc. Maybe that's the way to understand my ungoverned education: guided by the drifting of desire, only this diary connects and anchors the fragments. I was remembering former times similar to the last month: that summer in 1960, living in my parents' empty house near the port. I had written or was writing "Las actas del juicio" and was simultaneously immersing myself in an economic history of the Argentine Republic (the one by Ortiz? I wonder) and a strange (Soviet) book on dialectical logic. I was filling hardcover notebooks with feverish entries. I remember, finally, an immense reading of William Shakespeare in the kitchen of my house.

On Saturday a visit from Augusto Roa Bastos, alone and a bit removed from his emotional storms. He nearly died—he told me—while writing *I, the Supreme*. He's planning three books: one of them written using remnants from *I, the Supreme*, another on López; he'll spend what's left of the summer in a cabin on the outskirts, alone.

I'm fascinated, as always, by the idea of writers who isolate themselves. In my case, the fantasy was always tied to the presence of someone else waiting for me. I mean, being alone but having others aware of it. Which once again demonstrates the literary texture of my intention to live in solitude.

Saturday

A variety of successive trends have homogenized Argentine intellectuals: Cortázar (1963–1967), structuralism (1968–1971), populism (1972–1974), and today that fashion is exile. Everyone is leaving or wants to leave, to flee, and all of them make the same arguments. Yesterday a succession of meetings with José Sazbón, Néstor García Canclini, Eduardo Menéndez. Terrified, unable to sustain a project amid this darkness, they think only of leaving, of finding an academic structure that will sustain them. I resist exile as an alternative to life in hard times.

Saturday 13

Devoting this month to copying out the diaries (1958–1962) and writing in this notebook. Among the old days I find this comment, written on a typewriter on the first Saturday in July, 1970: "A good way to change the subject will be to start making a clean copy of these notebooks, finally become a reader of myself, view myself as if I were someone else, feel the roughness of a language forgotten, incidents not recorded in memory, which I clumsily rescue inside these volumes with their black covers, written too with the music of a secret conversation." Like today, as I walked back along Corrientes, going in and out of bookshops, the chill wind freezing my feet, before arriving here.

A meeting with Andrés at Ramos. According to him, there isn't going to be a military coup (he's mistaken). He speaks to me distantly about his family dramas and his father, who refuses to eat. He's resistant to pressing Corregidor to give him a publication date for his novel, so it's doubtful that it will come out in the next few months. I meet him because he's bringing me fragments from Brecht's diary.

Sunday
A productive reading of *Facundo*: the system of quotations and cultural references that come to authenticate the utterance. Errors, deviations, lapses, contradictions.

Another change: this isn't the right moment to type up the diary. It requires time that I can't allow myself. Transcribing it as if it were a novel—with what goal? I go back to the essay on Roberto Arlt.

Thursday 18
Extensive praise for "Homage . . ." in *La Nación*. "A story that will take its place in history."

Friday 19
The same thing that Shklovsky says of Shakespeare can be said about Brecht: "In Shakespeare, who didn't create his own plots, there is a reinvention of plot, revisualization and reclassification of methods for evaluating the action."

Novel. I'm writing the story of someone (Maggi) who is writing the lives of others (Enrique Osorio). With the right impulse, it could open up into a strange account with endless tones and anecdotes in the style of *One Thousand and One Nights*. Maybe the other could be imprisoned or insane. On the other hand, the writer is compelled to decipher the papers (letters, diaries) that the other left behind. But does a novel like that end? A detective intrigue, investigation. Osorio's papers come to Maggi by way of one of the nineteenth-century character's descendants.

Saturday
Dinner at Andrés's house: the neighbors monitor each another; Yrigoyenist radicalism—which no longer exists; the decline of social struggles and the exasperated militarism of guerrilla groups can be blamed on the far right, Andrés says. The patrol officers bring systems with them that allow them to verify anyone's criminal records in ten

minutes. They make you wait next to the car, your documents confiscated; Russian roulette.

Monday
Rumors of a military coup; attempts at alliances between radicalism and Peronism. Plan: a multiparty system with a path toward elections in December, intended to halt the coup. There are fewer and fewer supporters for this solution: certain sectors within radicalism (Perette, De la Rúa) and verticalist Peronism.

Tuesday 23
The military coup seems imminent. The radical legislators removed the bust of Yrigoyen that was in Congress. I'm outraged by the general attitude, a terror of violence, a hope that the military will bring "order."

Thursday 25
Yesterday, the coup. I stayed up that night, reading until early morning, and from the window I watched as the military cut off traffic; I heard commanding voices, saw buses blinded in the glare of an antiaircraft spotlight, saw officers patrolling the streets. The next morning, I went back to my rounds, listening to the radios in series broadcasting military marches. They're getting ready for a bloody campaign of repression. Martínez de Hoz is their economic adviser. On Wednesday I didn't venture outside; today I'm preparing to show myself in the city.

It would seem that I've always been waiting for something like this to happen.

Friday 26
The worst part is the sinister feeling of normalcy; the buses travel in their loops, the people go to the movies, they sit down at bars, leave their offices, go to restaurants, laugh, make jokes, and everything appears to go on as before, but you can hear sirens and there are armed police going past at top speed in unmarked cars.

Monday 29
On Saturday I visit Enrique Pezzoni, hospitalized after a car accident. I go there with Gusmán. I stay alone for a while with Enrique, who maintains his good spirits in a cast and everything. A while later comes Bioy Casares, a polite and tactful gentleman, and he—even he—criticizes the military coup.

Monday, April 5
On Friday in the bookshop, Marcelo Díaz tells me about the raid at Siglo XXI, armed men from the police, a shutdown by order of the military junta. The military will continue in this line; is exile the only way? In Buenos Aires, in short, a great atmosphere of uncertainty and terror.

Tuesday
At the moment, the novel I want to write is more of an indefinite desire. I'll have to make up my mind and focus myself on the project, whatever it may be, for the next six months. A rather abstract idea of the subject: the biography of a historical character written based on an archive.

"I find it difficult to describe the state I found myself in; it was a strange chaos of fear and impatience, dreading what I desired, and studying some civil pretext to evade my happiness," J.-J. Rousseau, *Confessions*, Book V.

Wednesday
Naked in the bathroom, I bang my foot into the door, my toes crunch with a sinister noise. I hop around on one foot and can't look at myself in the mirror, many fears: repression, the political situation.

Confusion yesterday; I gave terrible responses to Alberto Szpunberg, who's putting together a piece on new narrative and has selected my book as the best. In spite of that (or because of it) I think that I'm incapable of thinking and that whatever comes out in that feature will ruin me.

I wouldn't like to return to the prison of 1969–1970: wanting to write a novel but having nothing in hand (except for that desire), leaving everything behind, letting the days pass (one after the other).

Friday 9
Strange anxiety. For the first time, I'm living historically. Fears that go beyond the fluctuations of the soul. Arrests, raids. A bit of music in the house opposite is enough to make me peer out of the window and look to see where I can escape.

Along with that, everything seems to be going by normally: an offer from *El Cronista Comercial* for five hundred thousand pesos to write a six-page piece on Arlt. To convince me they say: no one has ever been paid that much in the newspaper's history.

At La Ópera I run into Roa Bastos, rather lost and pale, suffering from a variety of misfortunes. His marriage is broken, and his affair with the young literature student didn't even last more than a month, he complains mildly. We talk about the political situation; he's very pessimistic (so am I): he doesn't know whether to stay in Buenos Aires or travel to France. He offers me one thousand dollars to write a prologue on Rafael Barret for Biblioteca Ayacucho, which is managed by Rama in Venezuela. I don't accept. I make them a proposal, through him, that I could do a prologue for Roberto Arlt or Sarmiento's *Facundo* or *An Expedition to the Ranquel Indians*.

Thursday, April 29
For the novel, working with the same method as Dickens: recognitions, unexpected and numerous.

Wednesday, May 5
There's no more artful solace than thinking that we've chosen our misfortunes.

Yesterday at the Biblioteca del Congreso I returned to the pleasure of the reading rooms, the card catalogs. I lose myself there the same as I do when traveling. For that reason, I've thought that I would be able to endure three or four months of total solitude, my only course of action to leave home at five in the afternoon and go to the library until midnight. The remarkable thing is that a means of defense becomes an example of intellectual rigor. Or rather, it's remarkable that, in this kind of war, digging trenches could be a form of "intellectual escape."

Thursday 6
Several fears, the effects of a reality growing worse, becoming more complicated. Confusing news. Nostalgia for the days when I could write in peace without the fear of history (a nightmare from which I am trying to awake, as Stephen Dedalus said).

Tuesday 11
An offer from Ángel Rama (through Roa) seems to be confirmed: one thousand dollars to put together an edition of Roberto Arlt for Biblioteca Ayacucho in Venezuela. The kind of demand I need in order to put my life in order (aside from the fact that in this country you can live for a year on a thousand dollars).

Sometimes I've had the thought that if you chose a man at random and followed him along the streets of the city, that man (or any other) would lead the way to a crime.

Saturday 22
Videla's meeting with writers (Borges, Sabato, Castellani): being a bastard doesn't depend on the quality of the style. For my part, nothing to say, although they say Father Castellani asked about Haroldo Conti, missing for several weeks now. The Jesuit priest met Haroldo in the seminary.

Monday 24
At the bar on Córdoba and Callao where I run into Pablo Urbanyi, as if in an apparition or a Proustian memory, I remember the time I was talking on the phone in this bar and saw Julia crossing the avenue with her air of Egyptian beauty. A moral lesson: this memory has made me completely forget my conversation with Urbanyi.

Shklovsky wrote an admirable letter to Roman Jakobson, who was in Prague (included in *Third Factory*): "But you are an imitator. And you a redhead! So why be an academician? They are dull, celebrating their three-hundredth anniversary. They are continuous. Immortal."

Thursday 27
Yesterday I saw Carlos Altamirano; he left *Los Libros* (along with Beatriz) for the same reasons I did.

A variety of readings about Argentine history with *Facundo* as the central axis. Far removed from the writing, I make note cards as though putting together puzzles, empty games.

Bad times for lyric poetry, as Brecht said in the era of Hitler.

Saturday 5
A tourist, if not to say a prisoner; last night Stravinsky until early morning. It's raining now; I'm waiting for the hour when the course begins. I make yerba mate.

At the movie theater, yesterday, I saw the most beautiful woman in the city.

To make it out of this bind, maybe it would be best if I devoted my mornings to transcribing the diary. An exercise, or rather, an obsession.

I change the position of the lamp, and the desk now seems to have new space. That simple change was enough to make me happy.

Sunday 6

In the leather armchairs at the International Office, I imagine David in San Diego: I call him on the phone. I hear Beba's sleepy voice, and then he and I exchange a few muddled sentences. "Does my trip seem possible to you?" he asks me. That was why he wanted me to call him: "Things, essentially, haven't changed since you left." I go out into the city with a vague sense that I didn't tell him how happy I am that he's coming back and, at the same time, with the fear that I wasn't clear regarding the situation, the danger, and the futility of returning from exile.

Saturday, June 12

Two days go by with fluctuations that remind me of the year 1970. I read, study, try (unsuccessfully) to carry on with the novels. I have money but don't know how to spend it: I buy shoes, sweaters, books, two bottles of whiskey. There is nothing to say. This diary has fallen lower than ever before.

Wednesday, June 23

Let's call this a typical day in these times. I work all morning on the first draft of a novel, achieving some results after a couple of hours. Arocena, the censor who reads letters at random in a room at the Central Post Office.

At three I go to the National Library, readings on the nineteenth century, Tulio Halperín's book on Echeverría, Sarmiento's letters. At seven I stop by *El Cronista Comercial* to see Andrés, then we go to Querandí: taking stock, wandering. He gave me a short story ("El cruce de la cordillera"), rhetorical and disjointed. He hopes that Sudamericana or Seix Barral or Siglo XXI in Mexico will publish his novel. Then (yet again this week) I went to the Cinemateca, a good Czechoslovak film (*The Valley of the Bees*). When the lights come up, I see José Sazbón. Great joy. He, like me, is a solitary man seeking refuge in the screen and the darkness of a theater. We eat a pizza on Callao near Corrientes.

Saturday, July 3

I turn onto Arenales (because I wanted to get pills to relieve my throat, burning because of the cigarettes) and run into Eduardo Galeano; we say goodbye because he is leaving (for Mexico or Berlin).

Saturday, July 31

A terrible month. That same Saturday, the third, the day of my last note, soon after I get back home, a man's voice comes on the intercom, saying that they have to enter the apartment and that they've come on behalf of Sanitary Works. He mispronounces my last name: "Is this Señor Rienzi?" Immediately I went out to the Botanical Garden, and they came up by the other elevator. I spent two hours sitting under the trees, my mind a blank. Finally, I went back and talked to the porter: "They showed me army credentials," he said. Since then I've been moving from place to place, and I spent a while at Horacio's house in Adrogué. He knew perfectly well what was happening and didn't ask many questions. Even though he has three children, he risked sheltering me for a week. I moved into a back room and stayed there, reading a history of Nazism. In the evening, Horacio, my brother, would come to shoot the breeze with me. The harder and more despotic the political situation becomes, the more we talk about anything at all, as if we were repeating that line from Joyce: "We can't change the country. Let us change the subject."

Monday, August 9

The effort to keep my thoughts at a distance from reality reduces me to a mental age close to what mine was at twelve years old. Back then, I used to take shots at a bucket with a rubber ball and fantasize about being a great North American basketball player (some kind of Bill Russell). Now I'm reading a variety of books at the same time, about the Nazis, about the Middle Ages (yesterday, Sunday), and about pronominal formations. For the first time in my life I'm having insomnia every night.

Sunday, August 29
I spent two weeks at the home of one of Horacio's friends who's away on a trip; he got me the key and led me to an old building near Tribunales. Having no place, no future, I'm able to concentrate, inside this hideout filled with absurd rituals.

Mired in everyday life, I watch as several women pass by me (Amanda, Isabel, Lucia, Pola), but have no space to realize my fantasies. For the first time, the crises are objective. Maybe I should go into exile, but in the meantime I'm living hand to mouth. Conflicts by day, nightmares by night.

Monday 30
I recall my worst times with nostalgia in the midst of the torrents that are now laying this country to waste. Lost and without an anchor. Only made worse by the presence of S., who comes looking for me with the same eagerness as ever, though I resist considering it anything more than a fleeting passion. I've lost everything, I'm living in an enemy territory, mired in dirty contemplation.

Thursday, September 16
I walk around the city. How can this be happening to me? I think that I'll come out of this situation in one of two ways: destroyed or certain that I can be reborn. But I don't know what it is that I want to happen either.

Wednesday, September 22
I'm coming back along Callao and on the corner of Viamonte there are crowds of people and several patrol cars. Someone, a woman, says: "It's inside a house." I head back, turn down Tucumán, and on the corner of Riobamba a soldier is diverting traffic. I think: "It's a raid." The time is 15:30. I sit down at a bar, make a phone call home. No one picks up. I travel on the subway like a dead man, getting off at the intermediate stations to call home again from public telephones. No one picks up. I wait for the next subway car and pretend to get in but stay on the

platform, checking to see that no one is following me. I get on the next train and travel around the city from one end to the other. Scattered images. I end up at Plaza de Mayo. I don't know where to spend the night. I think: "We've lost everything." I decide to call Andrés and we meet at El Querandí. I tell him. He seems surprised. We go to a bar on Avenida Belgrano. He makes a call, and Iris picks up. The traffic had been diverted because of the Spring Day celebrations.

Tuesday, September 28
The descent into hell continues. Sinister news of raids and disappearances.

The story of a pessimistic man who spends the best years of his life awaiting catastrophe, and when the catastrophe comes it is worse than anything he had imagined.

Today Elías's friends surreptitiously moved my books and the few possessions I'd left behind when escaping from the apartment on Calle Canning.

In the middle of everything, the women. Last night it was Pola who wanted to spend the night with me, the same as S.

I can't even read, so the emptiness is complete.

Wednesday, September 29
Now I'm reading Kafka's diary. It's striking in the—ever precise—tone of his descriptions, at once algebraic and lyrical. Avoid the Kafkaesque (his subjects, that is) but court the intonation of his writing: distant, cold, cerebral. The opposite of my relationship with Borges, from whom I learned a great deal about how to articulate many different materials, though—unlike the majority of my contemporaries—I avoided the gesture of his style (which everyone copies). Kafka and Borges: two writers who are inimitable but easy to plagiarize.

Monday, October 18
I'm drinking alcohol to sustain myself, white wine since eleven in the morning, and I received a letter from David that brought me some relief in the midst of my solitude. As if I'd already lost my points of reference and no center existed. I am a hostage.

Thursday 28
"There is no man more different from another than from himself at different times," Pascal.

I will only change when I'm able to change the writing of this diary.

Luis Gusmán asks me for a short story for an anthology of new writers (new?). I would like to give them a text consisting of "Pages from a diary." Ten days: someone says goodbye to his friends, to his wife, he packs up his books as though he were going to die . . . During those ten days he finishes a translation of Malcolm Lowry's letters and gives a talk about Borges. He writes letters. Receives one . . .

I've never written so little in these notebooks, one year in fifty pages, and at the same time this year has been the most charged with events in history.

November
These days my trips outside are limited to the visits I make to Luis Gusmán every afternoon at the Martín Fierro bookshop. I've been alone ever since the exile of my friends (David, León, José Sazbón, the distance of Saer and Puig) and my estrangements (B. and N.), and now I'm cut off from old social circuits (the meetings at Galerna, the magazine, the publishing house) that have disbanded in this situation. I'm suffering the effects of political history in my private life (of course there's the loss of the apartment on Canning, my furniture and books in storage, the lack of work and money, the danger), but I attribute those catastrophes to myself. Today I went to the bookshop as usual and found Nabokov's *Speak, Memory* and Rilke's *Notebooks of Malte* to

motivate and justify the emptiness of that monotonous exploration. Sitting at a table in Banchero, on Corrientes and Talcahuano, I listen to Luis tell me news about the general state of Argentine literature and its young writers. He keeps going back to a roundtable with Asís, Rabanal, et al. I walk through the city without seeing it; the distance of those far-off years now lost, the city has ceased to interest me, but perhaps it's the other way around: the city, occupied, has forgotten about me.

One way to work orality into literature is to avoid description. In that sense, the mistakes in my narrative are visible with its overwritten tone and excess of descriptions.

It's clear that I've lost something more than an apartment. At the same time, it's clear that I shouldn't have left it, and if I did leave it, it was on the advice of my friends. But if they really were looking for me, why did they only go to the apartment? Maybe I was in someone's appointment book, maybe the neighbors reported me because young people used to come over. The porter said they showed credentials. Ever since that day, one month ago, I've been wandering the city, out in the elements.

And so it doesn't seem possible to admit that *everything* can be blamed on the political situation.

Tuesday
Precisely because I don't find myself in these notebooks except at intervals, I must value their writing. To write a diary is to write for no one, a coded language that only the one who has written it understands, for I have no reason to tell myself what I already know, no need to explain: the point is not to narrate, but to write. And, at the same time, to write as though that verb were an intransitive.

Conclude a text (this diary, any other) with the sentence: I have died.

You had decided to say goodbye without fully explaining it, or rather, without anyone fully realizing it. Furtive movements: organizing and boxing up the library, storing away the papers. (A desire to give away all of my books.)

Wednesday, November 10
A narrator telling the same story to different listeners. Or different people listening to the same story. An inversion of Conrad and Faulkner. Not different versions of a story but the same story for different people.

At noon I go to Martín Fierro and meet Luis. We get lunch at a bar on Calle Talcahuano. Luis wants to convince me to contribute to a book on Borges. I refuse, evasive, making general critiques: all the idiots write about Borges. I swore I'd never write a book about him.

Thursday 11
I'm starting to grow old. Here I am, flattened in a chair, buried in my own life, believing in nothing. I work, I wait, I had what I wanted. All as if in a dream.

I run into Andrés Rivera, we see each other at El Querandí, he's going back and forth about whether to publish his novel. I advise him to wait; the military leaders aren't going to last ten years . . . he laughs. In one sense, it brought me some peace to run into him, as though he was a lone survivor from the past that I could talk to. He has moved, anticipating the deaths of his parents.

Sunday, December 12, 1976
Yesterday a call from the United States. They're offering a place for both of us at the University of California, San Diego, for six thousand dollars from January to June. At the same time another option, two four-hundred-dollar doctoral fellowships for three years. We talked today and asked for eight thousand dollars plus travel. Leave and have six months' rest from this horror. Why not go?

My passport expired on December 5, and I have to renew it, request the visa. Fear of the identity checks.

3

Diary 1977

Wednesday, July 6, 1977
Back in Buenos Aires, entering the city under fog. I go to the Telefónica on Calle Maipú to call Joe in California and put him at ease: we made it back fine, the mole poblano came out perfectly—we used Mexican food as a coded message—then I walk back along Corrientes like someone living in a city occupied by an enemy army.

My reactions to coming back, the news from friends, and my difficulties in finding a place to live can be seen as a private version of political history.

Thursday, July 7
Zona de detención on the signs indicating bus stops. The truth is made visible by the change of the traffic signs in Buenos Aires.

Saturday, July 9
I'm reading an excellent novel by Peter Handke (*Short Letter, Long Farewell*): sedate tones of a writer traveling across the United States, "free of ties," solitary, with echoes of Fitzgerald and Chandler, it's in the tradition of the stories I want to write.

In California I stayed in La Jolla; incredibly, no one knew Raymond Chandler, who lived in that town for many years and died there.

Tuesday
Once again I make my way around Buenos Aires, get lunch with Germán García, Marcelo Pichon-Rivière, Luis Gusmán, María Moreno; we discuss the environmental conditions, the danger in the city's atmosphere.

I'm looking for an apartment. Shouldn't I invest all the money I have in that? A place to work, to break free of the cycle that began just one year ago.

Sunday
In the analysis of Sarmiento's *Facundo*, taking into account the change in the army after Napoleon: a people's army, not professional, voluntary conscription that for us defined the gaucho *montoneras*.

I reread my notebook from November to April; well written, a bit tragic: so trivial, however, when viewed from today. I think about a room in a hotel to solve things once and for all.

I'm working on an anthology of American writers who began publishing in the late fifties (T. Pynchon, J. Hawkes, J. Barth, D. Barthelme, J. Heller, P. Roth, J. Updike, G. Paley, W. Gass, J. Donleavy, J. Rechy, etc.).

Monday
A melancholy tour through the deserted places of the city: I'm back from looking at an apartment smaller than a shoebox, for which they were asking two and a half million a month with a fifteen percent increase every three months, apart from an advance of twelve million. Close to ten people were fighting over it when I arrived. I have to learn to work anywhere: bars, libraries, plazas, buses, trains, stations, hotels. I have six hundred dollars and a guaranteed income of three hundred dollars every month from now to December, and a few prospects for work on the horizon. Throughout my life I've put everything else aside for literature; I chose exposure to the elements to preserve the freedom of

the work. At least I must be sure that below that there's nothing left: I've never thought about money, there isn't enough to rent a cave, I let myself be guided by the metaphysics of economy.

At dinner on Tuesday with Beatriz S. and Carlos A., the idea resurfaces of running a magazine with the support of the boys (Rubén and Elías), working in the shadows on a publication devoted to rebuilding all that has been lost and connecting with friends in exile. No enthusiasm on my part, but I agree to the project because I understand its importance, etc.

Thursday
Dinner with Anita Barrenechea, E. Pezzoni, Tamara, and Libertella. I try to communicate my experience in California, a possible golden exile that we turned down because Iris's so-called husband won't give her his paternal consent to travel with their son. There's no bastard worse than the *bien-pensant* leftist. In any case, I'm secretly celebrating not leaving here: I'm on the second line, the ones who were at the front all died. Soon the bullets will reach this trench . . . Enrique asks me for the novel that I still haven't written (except for the first chapter).

Friday
I rent a room in a large house belonging to a woman who lives alone on Calle Azcuénaga, near Córdoba. She's a distant relative of a distant relative, and she goes off to work in the morning and comes back in the evening, so I have several hours to work in peace. I keep throwing books away; the libraries that I've lost (beginning with the ones I left at my two exes' houses) are no more than a "material metaphor" for the books I haven't read, an imaginary library, lost as well.

Closely related to the above, ever present, a project about reading in Argentina: Mariano Moreno, who dies translating a novel; Mansilla, who reads *The Social Contract* under a willow tree by the slaughter yard; General Paz, who falls prisoner and whom Estanislao López furnishes with Julius Caesar's *Commentaries on the Gallic War*; Hernández, who reads *Los tres gauchos orientales* in his room at the hotel where he has taken refuge; Borges, who reads the *Divine Comedy* for the first time on the tram that crosses the city each day and carries him to his job as a librarian in the shadows.

Saturday
I know no other feeling than nostalgia.

I admire those who struggle to write something in a tone that is irrefutable. It's a quality I find in Brecht, Kafka, Borges, Calvino.

Monday 25
To go back to the subject of the lost library, the memory of books that I was on the point of buying but did not: for example, the La Pléiade edition of Flaubert's novels, which I saw that day in the window display at the Hachette bookshop; I didn't stop, and by the time I came back looking for it a few hours later, repentant, they'd already sold it. A book on language and context by Coșeriu, the Romanian linguist, which I saw in the bookshop on Callao and Córdoba. Finally, the complete edition of Gramsci's *Prison Notebooks*, which I didn't buy at the Rizzoli bookshop in New York because I was thinking about going through customs, etc. Lost, unforgettable books, which I never had. An imaginary library: I remember those books more—their format, their typography—than many others I have with me. Write an essay about the books one remembers.

Thursday 28
To make some of the everyday fabric of my life known, I will say that in the next few days I have to get someone to come for the two boxes of books and move them out of the room where I'm thinking of setting up a table for work.

Friday
Certainty that I will never be able to write.

Saturday

Remembering the line I wrote down yesterday about being sure that writing is impossible for me, it's the only means of being able to start writing: from emptiness, from stupidity, a slow and clumsy progress.

"Let us propose, then, as a starting point, that art is not cut from the real but from the spirit—and that there exists no form from the formless." Pierre Francastel, *La Figure et le Lieu. L'ordre visuel du Quattrocento.*

Sunday

I keep going over a text by Saint Augustine, and the fact of my reading it is evidence of my present state. "Unhappy man that I am! Who will deliver me? From what will anyone deliver him? Tell me this. One says from freedom, another from prison, another from captivity among barbarians, another from fever and weakness; tell us, O Apostle, not where we are being cast or where we are being led, but what we carry within ourselves, what we ourselves are; tell us. From the body of this death. From the body of this death?" From the body—he says—of this death: work with this double enunciation, which speaks for another, and writes with another, for example in *Facundo*. Representation of delirium.

Monday

Unable to maintain any continuity in this notebook, I jump from one thing to another; that is my life. I read Auerbach, I see Bernardo Kordon, who is going to Nice, and he reminds me of the need to not believe in anything in order to be able to write. At night, dinner with Beatriz and Carlos; we move forward with the magazine project. How have we arrived at this situation? What is there in Argentine culture that can explain this moment? And, at the same time, what is there in Argentine culture that could enable us to build a way out?

I meet with Hugo V.: closer and closer to the Lacanian mode, determined to study with Sciarreta. I see a strange film by Coppola at San Martín: a woman traveling with a fool.

Friday
Being unable to write is hell. I'm in hell, and I know too that willpower isn't enough to overcome this inability. The strange paradox of a man who organizes his life according to something he cannot do. Of course, that is the writer's condition, since everyone in the world can write, except for him. For what does it mean to write but to escape from oneself and from language? Never confuse writing with drafting.

Monday 8
On Saturday at the IFT I see a filmed version of *Mother Courage* by the Berliner Ensemble, directed by Brecht. The songs, Helene Weigel's livid face, the scene when the prostitute Yvette appears with a tall lover, the cook who bears a strange resemblance to Brecht.

Tuesday 9
A wicked day; at nine o'clock my key breaks and I can't get in. Sitting in the stairwell, a laughingstock, my net bag full of food. I spend the day jumping through hoops with the locksmiths. At night Carlos Boccardo's show opens at the Carmen Waugh gallery, at midnight dinner and other digressions.

Friday 19
Last night I saw Oscar for the first time in years, always just as enthusiastic, the greatest enemy is the one who will not do battle.

The novel is advancing. It took me fifteen years to discover that a schedule really is necessary in order to write.

Last night an argument with Iris about David Viñas's intellectual merits, where to judge him from, etc. The finest critic, a writer with two books. Sartrean; he hates literature.

Friday 26
An almost metaphysical attack, choking episodes that last all day Wednesday: I end up at the Hospital Alemán at midnight. Artificial respiration, or nearly. My father's breathing problems, the known affinities. Now I'm in recovery with injections and sedatives. I had the first attack ten years ago when I went to my mother's house in Mar del Plata with Julia, and she, sarcastic, made the bed, oh Electra, I woke up that night unable to breathe. All so trivial.

Tuesday 30
I can't remember my dream, and yet it still seems close and well-defined: was I entering a theater and seeing the dream on the screen?

Friday 16
I attack Beatriz S., a bit too harshly, when she exposes her ideas about realism. Literature is as foreign to her as reality is to the realists.

Monday 19
I spent the last few days in the movie theater, as I always do when I want to run away. Thursday, Polanski's *The Tenant*. Friday, Fitzgerald's *The Last Tycoon*, with a script by Pinter, directed by E. Kazan. Saturday, Buñuel's *That Obscure Object of Desire*. Sunday, Ettore Scola's *A Special Day*, and I'll go to the theater tonight as well. I create my own private festivals.

Friday 30
The fact that critics must carry out social analysis doesn't mean they must read only works in which social issues are evident. Choosing Balzac over Baudelaire is a way to choose works in which the social analysis is more obvious and simpler for the critic to perform. (All of that because of my polemic with Beatriz S. about Lukács, I advise her to read Benjamin, etc.)

Living inside the cold dream of contempt that Mallarmé spoke of.

Optimism, a flaw that, as you will know, was not criticized, although, at this point, I prefer that flaw to the aristocratic renaissance of the virtues of nihilism (from the letter to José Sazbón).

Tuesday 11
I go to the theater in the afternoon and night to escape my own images.

I bought a kind of computer programmed to play chess. The machine learns as it plays. The people who programmed it saw that it made mistakes in the first game because they never told it that two pieces couldn't go in the same space. It is simultaneously idiotic—it must have everything explained to it—and very intelligent. It beat me in two games. I spend the night playing chess alone: an effect of the political situation.

Wednesday 12
At night I go to Beatriz and Carlos's house, the magazine project is advancing.

Wednesday 19
Today can serve as a model. I arrive at nine o'clock, read the newspaper (*La Opinión*), drink coffee, and start to revise the draft of the chapter about the senator. Then I write ten lines of a letter to María and Willy, my friends from California. At 14:00 I go out, buy *Clarín*, get lunch at the restaurant on Calle Córdoba, have fish with Roquefort and a bottle of white wine, pay the check, and now I don't know what to do, maybe take a walk around the city.

Thursday 20
Last night I saw Hugo V. Like all of my psychoanalyst friends, he tells me his stories. The seventeen-year-old girl, dressed in red, who fascinates him with her perverse adventures; she and her girlfriend in a triangle with interchangeable boyfriends.

Tuesday 25
Maybe I could go to the bookshop and visit Luis Gusmán, see if I can find a book for tonight, but to do that I'd have to change my shirt and it seems like too much. Very hot in the city.

Isn't it incredible (I suddenly think) that for twenty years, in spite of everything, I've found the drive to write these notebooks? These closed-off notes that mark out the present have, all the same, been faithful to me for years and years. They run through my life like nothing else, bad writing (in a moral sense) that has no use, that has no value, that one day will have to be thrown out. Or will I decide to type them up and run the risk of encountering my stupidity?

Wednesday 2
Last night an argument with Iris about my story "Tierna es la noche." She shows me the weakness of the structure and the artificial effect it produces. Maybe she's right, but for me the mistake—which I will not repeat in the novel I'm writing—is the excess of description. I am determined to narrate without describing.

Friday 4
Last night another argument about Lukács with Beatriz and Carlos: literature is a form of ideology and, therefore, reflects. Turn off the projector, I say.

The magazine is moving forward. This afternoon at the weekly Friday meeting, Susana Zanetti, Noemí Ulla, María Teresa Gramuglio, Josefina Delgado, Beatriz, and Carlos. Vague theoretical remarks that I argue without conviction. The only one I get along with at times is María Teresa because she, at least, knows how to read.

Wednesday 9
I finish a twenty-page draft of the chapter about Osorio in New York.

From the window, I see the balcony of the nuns' school below: gym class. I am the prisoner.

Iris is insistent in her critique of psychoanalysis: it's consolation for the middle class, she says, something that never amounts to anything more than going somewhere to complain. "In the future they'll laugh at us when they see what we wasted our money on."

One of the most striking characteristics of a diary is that it is written in order to be read in the future. That could be enough to define its technique. What will it mean for me to read today's entry in ten years? Now I'm going to make myself a hard-boiled egg.

Thursday 10
The (illiterate) deaf-mute who murders prostitutes: he has killed twice. He walks through the city, engulfed in an absolute silence.

I reread what I've written of the novel so far; I have a title that comes from Borges and alludes to death. *The Prolixity of the Real* (from the poem "La noche que en el sur lo velaron"). As always, I'm telling the story of someone encountering papers, letters, documents from someone else.

At the Premier bookshop Iris and I have a conversation with Germán García about one of Lacan's classes that deals with the woman's pleasure, only "named" in Catholic mysticism. Iris laughs.

I see a man I remember vaguely, he has a frank and "Argentine" face, and I gradually manage to identify him from the past, one afternoon at the call center, before I traveled to the United States, when I was making a call to California. The guy approaches, greets me. He's the brother of Juárez, a Montonero killed in those days. Now I see him on Corrientes, and I ask how he is, how things are going (casually). "They're hitting us hard; they've had it with us. A police officer came and told us my brother's wife died under suspicious circumstances in prison. We had a letter from her, she was optimistic, thought she'd be out by the end of the year. The kids are going to stay with my folks. They want us to say it was suicide."

Friday, November 11, 1977
The only way to return to the fascination of reading is to not write, two antagonistic modes. I remember my readings in La Plata in the year 1960; I was listening to jazz music on the patio, writing in these notebooks, sitting in the wicker armchairs in that house where I used to rent a room, I remember it very well. Sánchez, who came from Mar del Plata and also lived there, is dead. He was studying medicine, was his name Carlos? So fascinated by his mother, a beautiful teacher with formidable breasts, like a goddess out of Sacher-Masoch, just as proud and scornful. We stayed up all night studying, but I was only there to spy on his mother.

A distinctive feature of the uncertain discussions at Beatriz's new house: my lack of interest doesn't stop me from regularly attending meetings for the magazine. I go because that's what I have to do; after dinner, certain subjects persist. I'm an accumulation of anecdotes, and I find it harder to reflect than to tell.

Saturday, November 12
Every morning at nine I sit at this table covered with a brown cloth and repeat the oldest rituals of my life. Quiet happiness, doing nothing but thinking about the world until past two in the afternoon. Wonderfully building a time of my own in which the environment is already a form of literature, that is, the postulation of a free reality.

Sometimes an odd feeling of favorable destiny was with him; he'd come to believe that it was enough for him to desire something in order to possess it. This reinforced the duplicity of his life, the secrecy in which he experienced that certainty with its benevolent airs. As for misfortune, it seemed to come from someone else, as though someone were taking over living for him.

We had dinner with Tamara and Héctor; he brought his book on the avant-garde in Latin America. We talk about the success that *Assumed Name* has had, which hasn't ceased to amaze me. The conversation gets sidetracked and drifts toward the bad times when we were overwhelmed. The difficulty of survival, friends in danger, friends living in exile, literature to us is an island battered by typhoons (as in Conrad).

I work for a while, but it seems like the things I intend to bring into the essay (relationships between translation, originality, and literary ownership) will not come in, as if the text itself were resisting generalization.

Sunday
I'm always accused of being cold and distant (today, unexpectedly, by Iris). As if I were someone who doesn't know how to express his emotions. Cynicism, or rather irony, is the shield of oversensitive hearts. Isn't that as literary a theme as that of Don Juan? A passionate man, too passionate, accused by all of being insensitive and distant. He would be a lover, hiding the love letters he never manages to write.

In any case, the "theme" is evident: the man who believes that he feels, who even believes that he believes in love. The man who believes—and is waiting for—the opportunity. The belief, that is, the certainty, the credence that one is able to give it to another, that is the secret foundation of this thing we call love, passion; desire is something else, it is experienced in the body, it is immediate, experienced always in the present, there's nothing to wait for because everything is given there. But what happens with a man who experiences the present as if it has already passed? From a distance, isn't there a tragic theme in that as well? A story should be written about a Don Juan whom no one believes; all masks fall, seduction fails.

Monday 14

After two hours of work, if I'm very concentrated, I have to pull my head out like someone who dives into the sea and then rises up to break once more into broad daylight. Two hours to write one page, and then the rest of the time spent waiting for the next morning when it will again be possible, in two hours, to write another page.

Novel. I'm advancing blindly, but I know what I'm looking for, and I know which novel it is that I'd like to write. Maggi is hired—or entrusted—to write someone's biography. He needs another life to support himself on. He handles documents, letters, photographs. He meets Osorio every afternoon. Maggi reads him what he has written in the morning and at night. They live in an isolated house in a quiet neighborhood. The man whose life they want to find out about has disappeared, and only his papers, his secrets, remain; he wrote too much or left behind too many traces. Someone wants to prevent those recollections from being published. Interviews and searches in the historical archives of the people referenced in that biography.

My greatest difficulties in life stem from the fact that I do not have, so to speak, a model to identify myself with, or rather, a model to rely on (the meaning behind this is known in psychoanalysis). I've never been able to rely on received experience to know whether everything is going well. I very quickly broke my relationships with the family world; my father was always a counterexample for me, but all the same, thanks to that, I gained my liberty quickly, at least quite young, and was already living alone and not dependent on anyone before I turned eighteen. But that isn't to say that family history isn't the great theme of my life. My grandfather Emilio, my father's father, was also a father to me, but a serene and pensive father who did everything in order that I might understand why he was what he was. When he died, I felt, very vividly, that I was now alone in the world. Because of him, maybe, because of his way of speaking and seeing the world, I became a writer.

Novel. Trivial, paradoxical tension because the matter is an "assignment": Maggi is writing almost by dictation, but he takes part in transformations to the life he's trying to reconstruct. Where can "Argentineness" be found? That's what I can't guess. And why, after all, do I have that intuition, if I don't believe in anything of the kind? I think this can be my way of writing about the present, about these dark times. And so, I think that the best way will be to work on a historical biography (maybe of a real figure, an invisible and obscure hero from the nineteenth century). Avoiding the temptation to have that man be Witold Gombrowicz.

Tuesday, November 15
The evil noise of a compressor, the first cigarettes of the morning, the blind certainty with which I write in spite of everything. I have a ten-page draft done, a possible outline of the biography of a character who will be one of Osorio's ancestors.

Dialogue heard on Callao yesterday on the way back from classes. A newspaper hawker, with the six o'clock edition on his shoulder, asks two handsome and well-dressed young men to let him go past. "Excuse me, *compañero*, please," the paper seller says. "Compañero," one of the guys says. "Compañero," says the other, "we're going to erase all of you from the map." A clear verbal encapsulation of the current political situation.

Novel. How to find the plot for that life story? The man who left for the United States, drawn by the gold rush. He meets a woman from Martinique, and they become lovers. The woman is married to an industrialist. The lovers have a son whom the husband accepts as his own, the man sees him in secret, the son doesn't know that he's his father. The man, alone in New York, visits the woman as though he were her lover and maintains a friendly relationship with his son.

If I could assure myself that I'll be capable of writing four or five books in the next twenty years, that I'll be able to live on my work without too much economic distress, and that those books will meet with some approval, if I could assure myself of that, I'd have no reason to suffer the ills of an uncertain future.

I'm reading *Doctor Faustus* by Thomas Mann. I like the way he brings reflection into the book, the technique of narrating lectures and classes. However, the book has a certain naive quality that I don't think can be attributed solely to the ironic tone of the narrator. Very interested in the texture of music theory, a novel of "perverse" initiation, slight parody of the biography of a brilliant man, and very elegant handling of references, the fragments he uses without citing them. Excellent, the relationship between irony, coldness, intellectualism (as devilish details), and the always clear quality of Adrian's music. Besides that, it mustn't be forgotten that Mann was compelled, in the editions of the book after 1947, to confirm that the music theory attributed to Adrian had been copied from Schoenberg, via T. W. Adorno (whom he had often seen in California while he was writing the book). As for the deal with the devil, it's slightly ridiculous in this era and, as Brecht said well, it demonstrates the end of romanticism with its theory of genius. Today, in order to find a bit of inspiration, brilliant artists, the poor fellows, need . . . to make a deal with the devil! According to Brecht, they're so sterile that they have to call up hell on the phone when they want to write a sonnet.

These last few months, since I returned from the United States, I've been exercising in the pure gymnasium of work and, in that way, like a boxer training before a fight, acquiring "form and style."

Novel. After Maggi disappears, the narrator still receives a letter that his uncle sent him before being captured. Unrevealed facts about his life as a history professor at a secondary school in the interior.

Wednesday 16
See how I worked things out this morning to write a "historical" chapter (one about history), avoiding a tone that is descriptive and overloaded

with information. But the issue is how to dramatize the facts and the documents.

Thursday

Uncomfortable, as though scorned by my body, overweight, to my dismay. I weigh sixty-seven kilos now and will have to go back to some asceticism and see if it's possible to recover a more "romantic" figure.

I receive the proofs of my translation of *Hombres sin mujeres*; the prose seems fluid and efficient. I deliberately used the guideline of translating Hemingway's prose into Río de la Plata Spanish, in which the orality gains thrust and loses a "literary sparkle." It's more faithful to Hemingway's poetics. I have to remember that this project accompanied me through the most sinister months, defined by the horror of the military coup.

As always, the Thursday ritual, dinner at the restaurant on Primera Junta with Carlos and Beatriz, meeting to talk about what we're doing, to recognize that there are others amid this wasteland. Particularly striking is the case of Carlos, who seems very sure of his place in the intellectual world, a position at once humble and complex. An intellectual of a new type, in a time that refuses all reflection and quashes any will to work. For my part, I'm far removed from him, not personally, but just because of his mode of thought, which I feel is foreign to the issues of poetics that in my case determine all of my work. How can I do what I want to do if no one notices, etc.?

Friday 18

To corroborate the above, I'm attracted to Roa Bastos's offer to attend the Congress of Latin American Literature in Cluny (with Cortázar, Carlos Fuentes, or Paz and other self-appointed Mandarins), and then I could give a series of lectures at universities in France and Germany. It would be a basis for me to live in Europe. But is that what I want?

It has always been easier and more agreeable for me to write fiction than essays. One writes fiction while one writes; there's nothing prior, and you select and discard what works (or doesn't work) as you advance, there's nothing "to be said," whereas in the essay you have to try to make the prose support what you came to say, that is, the theories you're attempting to disclose. The prose is filled with knots, protuberances, ideas that belong in another register, etc. What is being written is what has been thought before, and that's always a problem because language is created for one to think while using it. Thus, before writing an essay, you must develop the ideas, have a plan. What you struggle most to write is what you "are clear about," whereas in fiction you set out from an uncertain nebula (for example, a man writing about someone else's life) and then progress toward clarity by writing. I must find a way to write my essays as though I were improvising them while having a conversation with a friend who knows something of what I'm talking about.

The young man, balding, dressed in a black suit with wide gray stripes, wearing various photographic apparatuses and devices across his chest, advanced through the city under the sun, intoning an aria in an affected voice.

Beatriz, who when speaking "in public" (even if it's a conversation with me) projects not her voice but rather her vocabulary, filling it with recherché words, foreign terms, expressions from old Spanish (today she said, for example, "*ora esto, ora lo otro*," sometimes the one, sometimes the other). She seems as if she's always speaking in front of a mirror.

Saturday 19
A dream. Someone, a woman, is talking to me about Pirandello. As for me, I'm finding pills on the ground, and at first I think they are . . . (and now, as I'm recalling it, I can't place the name for the tablets they use as a sugar substitute in coffee). There are many of them, all over the path, and I'm filling a bottle. Evidently, I want to lose weight. But

the most striking thing, however, is this forgetfulness, the word that comes to me is *Dulcinea* . . . *Edulcorante* is the word I was missing, it's horrible to think about an artificially sweetened reality. I think that some of my friends, not the closest, let's say some of my acquaintances and the public in general, are living through the political situation with artificial sweeteners . . .

I work on this afternoon's class. Echeverría's *The Slaughter House* doesn't situate the narrative in the future but rather in the past, that is, the narrator views the backwardness of brutality from the future. The asynchronous nature of reality is one of his themes: we are not in the present. Or the present, which is the time of Rosas, forces us to live in the past. As a result, the theme of the story is manifested above all in the few occasions when the present-tense verb is used. Especially in this sentence, which condenses the "moral" of the story: "All a representation in miniature of the savage ways in which individual and social conflicts are thrashed out in our country." The concentrated nucleus of the text is expressed there.

Sunday
The plan to look through old bookshops. In Dávalos I find an anthology of essays by Lukács and the facsimile edition of *Archivo americano* by Pedro de Angelis. In the book by Lukács, a remarkable essay on film from 1913. In it, he is already proposing his theory of how the cinematographic image's effect of reality begins to resolve the traditional opposition between fiction and reality. The illusion that everything seen on film is real implicitly creates an impression of ambiguity with respect to what is lived. One very clear experience of this is coming out of the theater at three in the afternoon and perceiving the sunlight as a vision, an apparent continuation of the light that comes up inside the darkness of the theater. The shock that the spectator suffers in moving from the shadows of the room to the brightness of the day is connected to the uncertainty that Lukács describes.

Monday 21

My confidence in being unique, which I built up as a child, causes dubious effects in the present. I'm always surprised to realize that there may be someone else occupying my place, although of course this place is imaginary. Today I saw Luis Gusmán, and he raised a few ideas about translation; Luis is thinking about publishing his essays of literary criticism in *La Opinión* this year. This series of examples and their consequences on my Robinson Crusoe island are very evident to me. As if I were the only writer writing in the world. Rather, I imagine I must be the only writer surviving in a world in ruins: the catastrophe rapidly shifts from being an image of the world deserted to a "private" but equally violent catastrophe. Only in total isolation, cultivating my fantasies, can I "sustain" my writing. The lone man . . .

I'm working on Foucault's *History of Sexuality* for my class with the psychoanalysts. The shift from inheritance as aristocratic legitimacy to inheritance as biological "defect": there is a continuity there as well as a permutation. Two ways of thinking about "blood" (as nobility and blue blood, or as sickness and tainted blood that is transmitted). Another issue: confession as a practice in which the truth is placed on the listener.

I stop by Fausto to pick up Thomas Wolfe's book *Death the Proud Brother*, which was just released as part of the American literature series that I'm doing for them. Manolo lets me know that Negro Díaz lost the jacket copy. So I now have to write new introductions for Hemingway and Fitzgerald. I try to remember what I'd written, but then I'm saved by one of my most consistent faults: I never throw anything away (that's why my bookcase and desk are a mess of old papers and useless scraps), and so I find a draft and can reconstruct them.

For the past few days I've been thinking again and again that I need to lose weight. It's unclear why I'm preoccupied with these things. Vanity? I don't think so, it's more that I can't stand to imagine myself as *un gordo*.

I weigh sixty-seven kilos, I'll have to lose the amount I gained after I stopped smoking (five kilos). So it must come from thinking about the imaginary figure of the writer that I attempt to present in society. More and more writers depend on their public image and the construction of an impactful figure and less on their books.

I go to the theater to watch *Patton* for the excellent script by Francis Coppola. Enclosed scenes that end with an effect and form a chain. The tiny theater on Calle Lavalle is full of single men, a place for fighting, a wicked atmosphere, an air of homosexual hookups. Soldiers, sailors, guys with manic looks. I walk back along Lavalle with the same calm I always have on these wanderings.

Tuesday, November 22
I'm working on the essay collection; the key is my theory about the forms of appropriation in literature. These are texts of a double enunciation, written by two hands: citation and plagiarism define the border of legal/illegal. Translation lies in the middle: the translator rewrites a book—copies it, in fact—so that it both belongs to them and to someone else (above all to someone else), and the translator's name—their property—is always invisible, or nearly so. They have written the entire book, yet it does not belong to them. In every case, it has to do with writing a single reading. In language there is no private property; the passage of ownership, that is, appropriation, in a sense defines literature. You have to think about what happens with the change of language: the writer writes the same book in another language (as Borges does with the quotations that he translates, turning them into texts that are always written "in the style of Borges," that is, he appropriates them, and so we always have a feeling that the quotes are his inventions or that he has attributed his own lines to an existing author). Must work on the relationship between legibility and property.

Argentine Novel. Of course, the national character of the genre arises in the autobiography. The "portraits" of the people whom the author addresses and is familiar with begin to define a novelistic use of personal narrative. For example, Cabo Gómez in Mansilla's work, the portraits in Sarmiento's *Facundo* (the tracker, the evil Gaucho). One should also pay attention to the transcription of letters, personal or from others, to analyze their (semi-fictional) narrative function. Devote oneself to reading and filing all those biographies that are integrated into the personal account. Also tempted by autobiographies from *The Man Without Qualities*. A man whom nothing special or historically revealing happens to, but who writes about his life in order to bear witness to something, which is always explained in the book (for example, how he was saved from a shipwreck or how he witnessed a fantastic swarm of locusts on the plains at the end of the nineteenth century). A narrator need not be a writer.

I press on, taking notes about the micro-story that has intrigued me for the last several months, in which I see something like the nucleus of the novel that I want to write: a man finds a trunk full of papers, letters, documents, and starting from there he reconstructs the life of a man he doesn't know. He finds a trunk or is provided with a file and is asked to write the life of a dead ancestor.

Wednesday 23
I work for three hours today and progress slowly on the second chapter. Each sentence takes me an eternity . . .

A curious metaphorical coincidence: the Minister of the Interior, General Harguindeguy, after praising Onganía, announces that the first phase of the National Reorganization Process will be initiated in 1979 and stretch until 1982, and then a second stage will come, spanning from 1983 to 1987, in order to arrive at the New Republic. "As I speak to you from here, in Comodoro Rivadavia, I want to tell you, listening here and all around the country, to once and for all stop heeding the siren songs and to forget about your immediate electoral conflicts" (strange for a military officer to make a reference—of course without realizing it—to Homer's sirens, and also amusing for a Minister of the Interior to decide, on his own account, the amount of time he will remain in power).

Likewise, the Minister of the Economy, Martínez de Hoz, also referring to the economic plan and the fight against inflation, stated that the armed forces are prepared to uphold the economic plan and that "it will happen in such a way that we do not fall into temptation and let ourselves by guided by the siren songs of those who, having private interests to defend, be they political, economic, or social, try to divert the course that we have devised in the general interests of the nation." Ulysses' sirens appear once more.

It would be possible to invent a story by imagining a man who writes all of these speeches—or corrects them for the ministers—so that, knowing him to be a single individual, it becomes possible to reconstruct his personality based on the allusions repeated (for he is doubtless an intellectual) and on the turns of phrase and grammatical forms. Starting there, it's possible to imagine the situation of constant danger that this scribe inhabits in the presence of arrogant and idiotic generals and militarist politicians. From time to time they will place him under house arrest for a few days, because they didn't like the speech he wrote for them.

Thursday, November 24
For twenty years I've been writing this date in my notebooks. It would be nice to say that that is my age.

Last night my mother—as always—came bearing the family stories, as if it is up to her to look after everyone's memories (since she is the youngest of twelve children): she's been storing away each of her siblings' stories and has ended up as the Scheherazade of the Maggi clan. For example, the epic account of Chiquito's project and the factory, his unexpected connections with the Soviets and with industrialists from countries in the East, whom he ended up doing business with after seeking funding all around the capitalist world, in Argentina or any country, in order to keep the empty factory afloat. He came from Poland with a patent for an electric car. The rights that are miraculously saved, the check that goes missing and reappears. At the same time, lucidness about the future of the automotive industry. My mother tells me that he told her that Gladis Espinoza is the great madam of luxury prostitution: you have to go and see her to get the women who escort the senior executives. The key is that the designated woman lets herself be seduced by the magnate, as though she weren't a whore but had fallen for the candidate's personal charm. Then Chiquito takes care of paying the woman the amount she charges for a night of intimacy. The amusing thing is that my mother relates these affairs with both a conspiratorial air and feigned innocence.

A letter from my brother with news of Helena D.'s death, and the first thing I thought was that she'd committed suicide. A beauty of excesses, always seeking death as a culmination, that was her. The great romantic theme of lives that are "not written" but are in some sense "read" by her. I should, nevertheless, write about my emotions, but what is coming back is the experience of my distant youth, when we began a passion that lasted nearly a year. Only the feeling of danger, that night when we traveled in the very car that she's been killed in now, on that very road, when she suddenly lost her way and we entered a stretch of dirt road, not knowing which direction we were going. A metaphor, or rather, a metaphorical woman to whom one could attribute all meanings. In any case, that gesture lingers, stepping out of the car the first time we saw each other, the way she touched my face.

Also in my brother's letter: a reference to Julio A., who now runs a wine business and is still clinging to his old fantasies (which were mine as well in those days). He's writing a book in two parts—from what he says, the first in English, a script he sent to Stanley Kubrick—and so he is living under the delusion of unseasonably becoming a famous man because he has written to a film director whom he admires. He isn't very different from me, as I too have written messages—with a bit more luck—to strangers and expected everything from them.

Some fear of proliferation prevents me from writing, I spend the greater part of my time in a struggle incarnated in words, paragraphs, periods, pages, chapters. I rewrite and reread, copy them and review them, but they do not progress, rather the prose has an effect that for me has always caused a sensation of well-being: I write so as not to think, but, then, what can I do to distance myself from the story and know where to find the ending?

The proof that something is known, said Aristotle, lies in the fact that it can be taught.

Disorganized readings of early Lukács. Fascinated with his *Theory of the Novel*. He tends to construct a theory of character by distinguishing the protagonist in the novel from the hero in tragedy. Must think about the shift from tragedy to the novel. Everyone's question is why tragedies are no longer written.

I'd like to record for myself the way in which today is becoming a typical day. I get up after reading the newspapers, bathe, have a large cup of black coffee with a piece of toast, and then come here, bringing several books that I expect to use in my work. I buy the Thursday *Clarín*, which comes with the literary supplement, and enter my office, a bit later than usual, drink the first yerba mate, and write in this notebook. At around ten I sit down to work, and five minutes after starting, I decide it is impossible, I'm not going to write, but I can't make up my mind to do anything else either; I'm inactive all morning and finally, out of pure boredom, I find a sentence that rings out inside my head like music, I write it down, and after that I don't stop again and work straight through until five in the afternoon. In a while I have to go meet with Beatriz and Boccardo to decide the graphic model for the magazine.

The news. "Early this morning, around four thirty, a Fiat 128, driven by Gustavo T., Argentine, unmarried, age twenty-three, crashed into a trailer on Avenida Peralta Ramos and Ortiz de Zárate. Assistance was immediately given to T. and his companion, but the intervention of firefighters was needed to rescue the wounded. In these circumstances, it was ascertained that a woman traveling in the car had died, while the driver showed multiple injuries. They were transferred to the Hospital Interzonal, where the fatal victim was identified as Helena D., age thirty-seven." (*El Atlántico* newspaper).

After noon I nap during siesta and have a dream. Someone says to me: "In Lukács, the relationship of essence–appearance is key to the theory of the reflection." The less I think about them, the more intelligent my dreams are.

Friday 25
I work on the first part of the essay on translation. Maybe it could begin with the analysis of the first page of *Facundo*. Just now I've more or less decided on the trajectory of the work; maybe the whole thing can be developed based on the sentence in French that Sarmiento wrote in 1840 when he went into exile.

Sunday 27
The results of the poll in the newspaper *La Opinión* come out. One hundred writers, critics, etc. were consulted; in fiction Asís, M. Briante, Rabanal, Lastra, Gusmán, Germán García were voted in (Saer isn't there, nor Puig). In criticism, Ludmer is ahead, followed by Gregorich, Pezzoni.

Monday 28
I'm working on this hypothesis: Europeanism is the condition and the form of struggle for intellectuals in the nineteenth century who seek an autonomy for literature. The connection to European thought serves to designate a literate group that continues in the tradition of the May Revolution, and this process advances and postulates the autonomy of

culture. Second issue: nineteenth-century Argentine literature faces two kinds of autonomy. On one side, literature must be made autonomous in relation to other social practices, politics in particular. The second issue is that Argentine literature must also be made autonomous from the Spanish tradition (and to that end it supports itself on French culture), which defines it and delimits it. In short, a process of double autonomy.

I prepare this afternoon's class on belief, magic, and superstition. An inversion of "good faith": black magic duplicates religion but brings in the other side of the good/evil dichotomy. An attempt to arrive automatically, by a mystical path, at the fulfillment of desire (deal with the devil); at the same time, I reflect on meaning and the search for significance in individual life (which replaces the idea of destiny). Magical thinking enables a new system of reference, into which previously irreconcilable information can be assimilated. Logic of randomness, chance, resemblance, and coincidence: things that occur by chance, or the repetition of certain coincidences, becomes a sign of good luck or of some mysterious order. A secret esoteric language that depends on initiation in order to be understood. Magical formulations are often worn out in being transmitted, ending up in a senseless cube (it's possible to view Lacan's language and the initiation rites that come with access to psychoanalysis as a structure of magical initiation). Also, the proper name is considered an extension of the person, and maybe that could be one of the origins of the alias, of the nickname, of designation according to kinship (brother, etc.). Nothing is entrusted to a stranger other than the face, considered an impersonal formula; by contrast, the name is hidden and circulates only among close friends. "If the gods do not grant this prayer, the men will rise up against the cult," Egyptian religious text from 2100 BC.

Tuesday, November 29
A dream last night: I'm talking on the phone with Mujica Láinez. I explain to him how I struggle to write essays: "I need three months to write ten pages."

It's a Frenchman, Paul Groussac, who first formulates the idea of style. And he is the first to speak of "writing well."

I'm working on the beginning of the second part. Analysis of the first page of *Facundo*: the opposition between civilization and barbarism is transformed into the opposition between those who can and those who cannot read a line in French.

One afternoon in 1963, talking with Pochi Francia opposite the university dining hall in La Plata, I defined the essay as the key to literary work. Why is it difficult to write them? Because I have a clear idea of what I don't want to do: I don't want to perform cultural journalism, but I also don't want to perform academic criticism; there is a jargon in each case. For my part, I try to find a way to do what I call "writer's criticism." Writers don't talk about their own work, they can't say anything about it, but the experience from their creative work gives them a unique perspective on literature made by others.

A diary is written as a way to say what cannot be written. Kafka, it's typical in his work. The amusing thing is how many pages are written in order to describe this subject.

It's true that my determination to write the essay is tied to the idea of getting a job (teaching classes, being an editor, giving lectures). The other reason comes down to what I write in these notebooks: private reflections on the forms of creating and reading literature. There would be no need to publish any of these theories if some sort of implicit demand didn't exist. I'm often asked to write essays and am paid to do so, but it's very difficult for someone to ask for a short story and pay for its publication. (At least in Buenos Aires.)

Thursday, December 1
An excellent story by Alan Pauls, who, at age eighteen, manages to achieve a *nouvelle* ("Anverso y reverso") on the subject of the lone man: one who is

locked away in a sanitarium after disfiguring himself in order to escape his pursuers. Alan is very intelligent and writes quite well. With him, I have the same feeling I had when I read the first works by Miguel Briante, who also displayed great skill and a remarkable style at that age. However, I think Alan Pauls has a greater future; Miguel ended up tangled in the myth of the precocious writer and struggled a great deal to go back to writing. Alan, on the other hand, is—or attempts to be, I think—more complete, more sophisticated, and great things may be expected of him.

What's most difficult for me is keeping momentum when my favorite writing and texts seem to be being written without my help, on their own. Usually, that "inspiration" (that is, for me, an extreme concentration) lasts for two hours at most . . .

Clearly this notebook progresses because I invariably write in it a series of motifs that I will call musical, a melody, a *ritornello* in which the same thing is always said over again but in a different register. The most visible change is chronological: I write the same thing, so to speak, but I write it on successive days, that is, there is a continuity in the repetition. I'll never know whether what exists here is a narrative, that is, an articulated series of events; if that were the case, the only way to confirm it would be to read all of these notes in a linear succession.

At an unexpected bookshop on Calle Lavalle I find *Culture and Society* by Raymond Williams, and I start to read it and encounter a variety of confirmations (originality, trade, etc.), a feeling of knowing this book, which, nevertheless, I had never seen before.

"A Child is the Best Investment," title of an advertisement that appeared today in *La Nación*.

Friday, December 2
From time to time, an awareness of the importance of the essay I'm writing on Sarmiento. How has no one seen it before? At the moment

I'm working on the quotations, paraphrases, cultural references. This essay and my story about Arlt are my contribution to Argentine culture, he said.

Paranoia, the tone of the times. I receive strange telephone calls.

Sunday 4
A peaceful weekend spent organizing the books in my bookcase. Once again I find an old subject that could possibly be the basis for a novel. A man taking out his diaries to read: he analyzes them and writes about them.

In the afternoon Anita Barrenechea comes over to talk to Iris, and I go to the movie theater. I come back and she's still there, and the conversation becomes slow and heavy.

I awake with a start in the night: fantasies of pursuit, dangerous noises.

Monday 5
Another unsettling call. Associations that create meaning. Everything might signify something. Especially faces in the street, or cars moving slowly, at walking speed. The experience of political terror is subtle and formless. This signification defines the context, that is, the era we live in.

I go to Fausto and select images for the Hemingway and Fitzgerald book covers. I teach my last class of the course on Mondays with the psychoanalysts, a primary source of income that I hope will continue next year. Then I go to the theater alone: Visconti's *Senso* at the Coliseo, surrounded by the "Italian community." Dinner late at night, also alone, at Arturito on Calle Corrientes.

Next year I'll put together a course for the architects, maybe it can begin with Mumford's *Culture of Cities* and W. Sombart's *Luxury and Capitalism*. Old books that I'd like to read again. And, of course, Benjamin's essays.

Tuesday, December 6

As always in the last few years, I work hard to finally have four or five months in the summer free, which I finance with the cash that I can draw up from a variety of sources. The feeling of having all of my time available allows room for happiness and writing.

Suddenly I remember Tristana, who used to light one cigarette from the butt of another. That early morning watching the sunrise in Plaza San Martín. A beautiful woman. Our last meeting, months after everything would have ended, when she came to the beginning of a seminar I was teaching in Philosophy and Letters. No one said anything that time, and there were three women all in the same place.

Wednesday 7

I'm making progress on my essay about Sarmiento. Europeanism as an autonomous function. The literati give themselves a place, an awareness of their social importance based on the difference supposed by their use of a foreign language. "The European acclimatized in El Plata," the great compliment that Sarmiento bestows on Alsina.

The woman (descended from a great poet) who made a note of each of her affairs in her agenda book, with her lover's name and a cross, like a strange pathway.

I meet Ricardo Zelarayán. Calmly paranoid, he is going to try (once more) to have his wife tried for insanity. He tells old stories of Peronism: Ramón Carrillo's lover became a popular poet at age seventy, thanks to a reference to her poems in a TV soap opera by Migré. Perón signs his name as Descartes, because Descartes had signed his name as Perón.

Friday 9

Writing is so difficult, it requires so much patience that, if I'd known, I would have chosen another path in 1960. But in choosing it I couldn't escape it, that is, one writes first and only later sees, at the end of the road, a book that one has managed to finish (and not the other way around).

A weekend reading Proust; there is an obscure origin of Benjamin's theory of mechanical reproduction: the narrator's aunt doesn't want photographs. A remarkable book, but at the same time, when one reads it again, everything seems too familiar already, almost trivial. There are books that can never be read for the first time.

On Saturday a long conversation at Beatriz's house, which I leave discontented. Conciliation.

The weight of things to be done is a constantly renewing obstacle: letters, articles, assignments, reader's reports, etc. Today, what's more, they notified me of the dinner tomorrow with other critics (Nicolás Rosa, M. T. Gramuglio, etc.): I never did like meals with the intellectuals.

Wednesday 14
The meeting last night, the dinner, the talk, the wine until three in the morning. Nothing to say. All the same, I'll say what I can remember: we gathered at the only restaurant in Boca, Lafforgue, Josefina Delgado, etc. The conversation drifted in no order: Joyce, Borges, the poll in *La Opinión*, Saer, my story about Arlt, actresses. Then we went to Los 36 Billares on Avenida de Mayo, and there, at the far end of the table with Lafforgue, Carlos, and Beatriz, we made a review of Argentine philosophers: Astrada, Mondolfo, Guerrero, Pucciarelli. We argued (they argued with me) over the advisability of including León Rozitchner on that list.

Thursday, December 15
I started working on the novel in August, but I got into the book seriously at the end of October, so I've spent two months immersed in *Artificial Respiration*.

I meet Rubén K. at the bar on Córdoba and Ayacucho. He comes to see me so I can tell him what I'm up to, what I'm writing. I summarize the subject of the novel for him and he, as always, seems attentive and interested in what I'm doing. He lives a clandestine life, carrying false documents, and always appears happy. A life at once humble and epic.

Friday 16
We have dinner with Tamara K. and Héctor L. A dark round discussing the books we are writing. Héctor has an avant-garde touch that I have lost or, at least, have replaced with a passion for experimentation that I prefer not to define. I get along well with him because he's a bit of a lunatic (not in the sense of one who is moonstruck, but rather in the poetic sense of a slightly esoteric type). The patio at Munich in Palermo, the food horrible and undercooked.

Novel. The period when Maggi frequently saw Witold Gombrowicz. He discusses with him the article that W. G. is putting together ("A testimony") to sell to a newspaper. The inability to detach himself from W. G. He gave him money, in exchange for what? Analyze certain central ideas: the adolescent who finds the letter.

Sunday
I meet Andrés R. at Tortoni. Fear for the future, the same arguments as usual when faced with his principled skepticism. I talk to him (without conviction) about the book I'm writing. He tells me a story in which his obsessions return. Apart from that, no one wants to publish his novels.

Monday 19
I never end relationships because of differences in ideas (today with Beatriz), I don't place importance on the people I argue with. All the same, I keep on repeating the points I made to her while we were arguing. She seems to have multiple internal conversations going on simultaneously and the things she says adjust to fit to each of those potential subjects.

Tuesday, December 20
Beautiful novels paralyzed. German cinema at the Goethe. Aging con-women in banks, ladies of a certain age. The young student at the Bauhaus who decorates her body.

Wednesday 21
For the first time in my life, I think fearfully about the time that will follow the end of the work. All I hope for is that the day will pass so that I can sleep and get up to write the next morning. I'm unable to read because I'm writing, I try not to think until the next day about the page that I left half finished. A few friends, Gusmán, Andrés. Carlos A. Too separate for one reason or another. Several letters pending, to Roa Bastos, to Jean Franco, to Osvaldo Tcherkaski, to a variety of publishers, to Arturo Cancela's heirs. I think I have the right spirit to be the protégé of a patron who would pay me to write . . .

There is an intrigue within this diary: what will have happened when all is said and done, with this certainty that, deep down, I have always had in my future as a writer. The blind and certain choice I made back in the days when I began to put everything else aside (first of all, escaping from any family ties) for "literature" (which was nothing to me, except that wager), where will it end? Others fear their old age, but I, on the other hand, have a kind of blind confidence about a future in which I will reach what I have sought (although I don't quite know what that is). The present presents itself poorly, and the near future as well, but those final years will be the ones that make room for the old hopes. Strange personal mythology.

Novel. I still think that the story is better and more open if Maggi is employed to write the biography of an ancestor for someone else. Maggi, an amateur historian, teaches classes in the secondary school (he is an attorney). If I can find the character he must write about, there will be no difficulty. I do have, on the other hand, the central idea: the disappearance, never stated.

Thursday, December 22
I work at intervals on Sarmiento. I go to the National Library and spend the afternoon there, under the shelter of history, reading history books.

Sunday 25
I write overdue letters. I tell Roa Bastos: to make gold from dirt, you have to use the ashes of the dead.

Monday 26
Once again I spend the morning trying to organize the beginning of the novel. From now on I have to write it as it comes, letting the prose define the things I still don't understand. I think about bringing my typewriter to Santa Fe, where we're going to spend fifteen days on vacation.

On the other hand, I'm trying to write the essay on Sarmiento using the structure of a short story: plot, intrigue, suspense, *raccontos*.

Tuesday 27
I work all morning and a bit more in the afternoon. Maggi, as his final wish, so to speak, facing the imminence of catastrophe, leaves his papers to his nephew. This must be the beginning, I'll see how the rest comes into it as I write.

Wednesday 28
To know the surface of my soul. Are these little meetings with intellectuals the cause of an apathy in me that lasts for days? As though after seeing them I thought it better to dedicate myself to something else. Last night, dinner with Anita Barrenechea, Pezzoni, Libertella, Tamara Kamenszain, and a woman with red hair who teaches in New York. Everyone eating at Claudio. For me, tedium and tension. I immediately forget whatever it was we talked about, as if I wasn't there, despite the fact that I like Anita and do appreciate Enrique and Héctor.

If I think about the effect of such superficial matters, I must say that a varied series of affinities appears: I tend to see my future in those "literary" exchanges (which I hate). The process is known; I need unreality, fantasy, magical affinities, writing with no presence other than the void so that I can advance through the snow or the desert without any orientation, guided only by words.

I've been working on the translation of Hemingway's stories for money, and for that reason I haven't made up my mind to suspend it. Manolo Mosquera just called, I thought I would make ten million, but he gets me twelve million; I thought I would get paid after the first, but he sorted it out for tomorrow. Friends are the best part of literature, as Paco Urondo said. On the other hand, I've worked out the classes with the psychoanalysts for next year (three hundred dollars per month), and in this way I can ensure the free time I need. And with that I have left a record of my summary of the year that is coming to an end.

Thursday 29
I spend the day working on an overview of the cultural situation (1955–1975): an intellectual autobiography. The story of my life interrupted—or defined—by the weight of politics. At night I have dinner with Carlos and Beatriz.

Friday 30
Everything is magically solved, and in that sense my economy is imaginary. I make six million at Tiempo Contemporáneo (that is one hundred dollars) and at Fausto I make two hundred dollars for the translation and fifty dollars as a bonus. So in December I'll have made almost five hundred dollars in total. As always, I don't really know what money is good for, except that I can use it in order not to work.

I buy books: Z. Medvedev, *Ten Years after Ivan Denisovich*. Solzhenitsyn, *One Day in the Life of Ivan Denisovich* and *In the First Circle*. J. J. Johnson,

The Military and Society in Latin America. T. Di Tella, *Argentina, sociedad de masas*. Vicente Fidel López, *Autobiografía*. Paul Groussac, *Relatos argentinos*, and J. B. Alberdi, *Cartas inéditas*. Then I had lunch alone at the bar on Calle Talcahuano where I used to go in the Jorge Álvarez days.

Dinner in the colonial house of my friends the Os. The excesses of money and art. Too much beauty: the bay window, the colorful tiles, the iron cover of a tank where cows would bathe, the garden and the river, the ravines, the paintings (Figari's *La muerte de Quiroga*), the objects (the little trunk where Güiraldes kept his manuscripts), the history of the house that once belonged to Le Blanc (the leader of the French fleet during the siege of 1832), the dinner with French champagne. Unreality à la Fitzgerald yet patronage at the same time: next year their psychoanalyst daughter will be the driving force of the group that I give classes to on Mondays (to finance my free time).

Saturday, December 31
No evaluations this time (the first trip to the United States, New York, California. The draft of the essay on Sarmiento. The beginning of *Artificial Respiration*).

Gombrowicz and Jimmy Carter. Differing versions of the speech that United States President J. Carter gave when he arrived in Warsaw. The translator, speaking in Polish with a strong American accent, made President Carter say things that were, more than shocking, inexcusable. For example, Carter had said: "I am happy to understand the Polish people's desires for the future." The interpreter translated: "I desire the Poles carnally." Even worse, in another passage, the translator made Carter say: "The Polish constitution, an object of ridicule" (a wire from ANSA in today's *La Nación*).

Just now, twenty years after I started writing in these notebooks, I have the feeling that I'm recording my everyday life with caution and efficiency.

Maybe one day I can read a published version of this novel, which is taking so much effort for me to write now. This notebook will also be read, sometime in the future, by someone who will not be this person I am today.

4

Diary 1978

Sunday, January 1
I enter the new year reading history with *The French Revolution* by G. Rudé and *The Age of Revolution* by Eric Hobsbawm. As though wanting to think of the end to that cycle of revolutions and counterrevolutions, I also read *One Day in the Life of Ivan Denisovich* by A. Solzhenitsyn. The current discussion, after the catastrophe, the horror and nightmare that we are living through in Argentina, seems to be a distorted reflection—as in a fun-house mirror—of that violent political reality.

Monday 2
Always threatened by dark melancholy.

I've been working since nine in the morning, with no great results. I organize the order of the texts. The amount of time (and the number of sheets of paper) that I throw away is incredible.

Wednesday 4
The novel is advancing, and now I'm imagining the censor reading letters at random in a gleaming office in the Central Post Office. They've told me that they act in the following way: they have a series of monitored correspondence that they open, read, extract information from, seal, and send. Most of all, the letters arriving from abroad; especially from the people they have under surveillance. But there is also another system, more sinister, that consists of selecting an increasingly large

number of random letters every day. They open them, preparing new compendia, sometimes drawn by phrases that they misunderstand (they usually believe that everything is a reference to what they're after). I think I've been able to find this out because of my friends, but at the same time I think they make it known so that the people will always feel threatened. So, the censor controls Maggi's correspondence but also reads a series of letters selected randomly. With a system of one out of every ten, or three out of every hundred, according to their mood and according to the political news.

Thursday 5

As anyone who works with a fragile material (and I myself am that material, my walls of glass behind which terror rears its head), should I, as so many have done, write with a coded language in these notebooks? My decision is in fact very pessimistic: if I am in danger, if they come looking for me, it will not be because I write or because of the books I have in my library, but instead because I've been marked by someone who confesses a name under hellish conditions; it could also happen that my phone number would be found in the appointment book of one of my friends gone missing after the coup. As we have decided not to go into exile, we live under always unstable conditions. (I'm putting it on the record that the father of Fernando—Iris's ten-year-old son—will not grant the essential paternal permission needed for the boy to leave the country.) In any case, I prefer not to go.

I've taken on some publishing work (I live off what I read, or what I report about what I read, or the translations I make of the texts I read), and now I have twenty million pesos in my pocket. A figure that doesn't impress me much, the greatest amount I've had in my life and yet, that said, in spite of all the zeroes it isn't much cash. Economic reality is as absurd as political life (or rather, economic and political non-life).

I'm absolutely immersed in Solzhenitsyn. He, in a "socialist country" and in the twentieth century, possesses the simultaneously heroic and fragile tone of the old ideologies and the old stories by the *maudit* writers who left their mark on nineteenth-century Russian literature. He is an undeniable testament to the terror of the Soviet system: arbitrary and absurd. And he has the same structure (as, let's say, Dostoevsky's *The House of the Dead*): the impossibility of publishing, and then "friendship," success, and recognition. His books were copied entirely by his friends on little pieces of paper and distributed in that way. As always, I read everything an author has written (today his *Memoirs* and, while still in the middle, *In the First Circle*), and I become inspired, though only once he's gone out of style.

Tuesday 10
Novel. Whose life? If I can resolve this, I will quickly find the materials to form the basis for the biography. I sift through information, letters, and documents from the nineteenth century before sitting down to write. It seems that this must be my system: not writing every day but in short streaks. That, of course, explains my "short-storyist" production and use of amphetamines.

Yesterday I met with Alberto Laiseca. A strange character, a Saxon version of David Viñas's face, but creating a mythological work, science fiction and delirium, he wants to go and live in the United States, write in English, be like Pynchon or Philip Dick or Vonnegut. But he is very poor, so poor that he counts his matches and not his cigarettes now, of course he doesn't know a word of English, and his readings are motley (as he would say, always using that kind of expression), what he writes is quite good, he has a very fluid and dour style, at times almost an idiolect. He lives under constant threat (like many of us in this period), though for other reasons, esoteric and private. He can't earn a living, in that sense he's very similar to us as well, but with him it is an almost majestic inability.

Wednesday, January 11
I'm totally blocked, not knowing what to do, as though afraid to think. Where is this coming from? Maybe the feeling of failure and of excessive

and empty effort in the face of what I'm writing. I trust that the fifteen days we are going to spend away from Buenos Aires will help me. In February I'm going to make clean copies of the two parts of the novel that I have written. For now, total indifference, a desire to do something else (go fishing, put together a puzzle, etc.).

I have to narrate this state with the utmost courtesy. Strange distance, unforeseen clarity, and a dull pain in my left side.

Constructing a character who invents fictions in his conversations with friends, incessantly, never stopping, especially about himself, because he forgets who he is but refuses to recognize that he's disoriented, and so he picks up the history of his life from any forgotten point and goes on ahead, trying to appear sane and happy.

Saturday 14
Yesterday a surprising meeting with Amanda on the corner of Córdoba and Pueyrredón. Much deteriorated, shall we say. Bound to her convictions of insanity. Strange stories about thinking with someone else's head, accounts of her experiences with LSD in the Fontana clinic. She tells me that she wanted to study with Ure, and then goes on to tell me in an incoherent way that she was in a car with him and opened the door and threw herself out while the car was moving to escape from something I couldn't understand. She is very beautiful (I do not want to write that sentence in the past tense), I loved her. Now, distance: a stranger.

I put together the papers that I'll bring to Santa Fe, fifteen days in the lands of Saer, and I'll write to him to say I'm going to visit Colastiné.

Wednesday, January 18
In Santa Fe. A country house with a pool, air conditioning inside, a stretch of time in a kind of neutral space. They are vaguely related to Iris. At night, they show us a pornographic film on a 16 mm projector

and then invite us to join them in the room upstairs. I'll pass, I said. Then they invited Iris, and she smiled with her most perverse air and said she'd rather not.

The next morning the hosts had breakfast with us, very relaxed; she is a dull, ungraceful blonde, and he is a country doctor. They're the worst! All the same, they are very friendly, they keep up the formality and leave the place to us while they go out, I imagine, to look for other companions to take to bed in the city of Santa Fe.

I buy new glasses but choose some terrible frames, which I already want to change again.

Thursday 19
Isolated and imprisoned, the citizen I used to be easily entered into a strange dialogue with distant or already dead friends. In that moment I was reading a biography of Gramsci and started up conversations with him in an almost oneiric way, while walking through the garden or swimming in the pool. I identified with him in his fight against fascism under conditions of extreme hardship, in a prison like mine, so to speak. Gramsci's position, "democratic" and broad-front, was opposed to the leftism of Bordiga. I think something of that these days, in the sun, in this pause, regarding the friends who years ago chose—wrongly, in my view, and in obedience to idiotic and provocative political leadership—the armed struggle.

Friday 20
For the new ideologies or ways of thinking—Lacanianism, post-structuralism, the linguistic turn, etc.—which are in fashion, the scandal—to use Marx's words—is that there is a world, that is, a history, a reality.

"The need for philosophy arises when the unifying power has disappeared from the life of men, when the opposites have lost the living tension of their relatedness and their mutual interdependence and have become autonomous," Hegel, on the origins of philosophy.

Some of my current hopes are simple, and I may be able to achieve them: to spend a year in the United States, in one of the university libraries, consulting all of the books necessary to write a work on Sarmiento that could at the same time be a history of the years spanning from 1838 to 1852. What left the greatest impression on me at the University of California library was that, one afternoon, browsing through the stacks, I could have all of the resources at hand that I would need to write on whatever subject occurred to me, whereas in Buenos Aires I need more than three months to get the materials I need in order to work.

Monday 23
I'm rereading the notebooks; only by means of a great number of hours of work will I be able to restructure and organize this accumulation of incidents, memories, ideas, feelings, conversations, and forgotten things. Someday I'll go off to a tranquil place like the one where I am now, far from the city, and will begin to transcribe what I've written over the course of these many years in my—as we will call them—personal diaries.

Tuesday 24
The American crime novel and its detective figure can be understood as a consequence of the crisis in '29: intimidation of the workers and industrial espionage. According to what the Report on Private Police System presents, the use of systems of private detectives led to "private usurpation of public authority, corruption of public officials; oppression of large groups of citizens under the authority of the State; and perversion of representative government," cf. M. Dobb, in his *Studies in the Development of Capitalism*, pg. 418.

Wednesday 25
Although it may seem incredible (though not so much after the dream I had the other night when I saw the number four every way I turned), I went to the casino in Paraná, Entre Ríos, and by betting everything on four and one chip on zero every time, I won four thousand dollars.

Thursday 26
I returned to the casino and lost two thousand dollars, even though I won two thousand dollars over the first three hours, but since I'd won last night, what I lost in the end was "only" two thousand dollars. That sentence is written with the numerical logic typical of compulsive gamblers.

Saturday, January 28
We're finally going back tonight. Fifteen days in a strange land, plenty of sun and plenty of tedium. If the polite and friendly couple had instead invited us to bed a few days ago, we would have accepted as an aphrodisiac effect of the boredom of this vacation.

Over the past several days I have read: the book by Dobb that I already referenced, *Industry and Empire: The Birth of the Industrial Revolution*, and *The Age of Revolution: 1789–1848*, and *The Age of Capital: 1848–1875*, all by E. Hobsbawm. Also, *Antonio Gramsci: Life of a Revolutionary* by G. Fiori. Readings that for me are tied, on one hand, to the current period and, on the other hand, incomprehensibly, to the novel I'm writing.

Sunday 29
I go to the theater with Iris to see *Annie Hall*, I bring my briefcase containing my documents and the keys to my office, I forget it in the theater, I go back looking for it, certain that it's lost, but a foreign woman—as they explain to me—has left it for me in the theater's cloakroom.

Wednesday, February 1
Last night I went to look for a copy of *Hombres sin mujeres*, my translation of Hemingway's short stories, which now, reread, seems harsh and stiff to me.

Saturday 4
Over three days I began editing the chapter about the censor in the novel. His name is Arocena, that passage is rewritten in third person. In a sense, the letters he has on his table form the central tension of the novel and the strongest mark of the context in which I am writing it. A book written at the same time as the history that motivated it.

In the library I find a biography of Einstein by chance and inside it encounter this note from A. E.: "When one's thought falls into despair, nothing serves him any longer, not his hours of work, not his past successes—nothing. All reassurance is gone. It is finished, I told myself, it is useless. There are no results. I must give it up."

Monday 6
Beautiful ideas about suicide. I can fall no lower. Never a crisis so deep, yet still, amid the darkness, I manage to write a draft of the Arocena chapter.

I'm writing about W. H. Hudson for *Punto de Vista*. I view Hudson as part of a pattern of Europeans acclimatized in El Plata (to use Sarmiento's expression); his novels are translated simultaneously with the rise of criollismo. In that sense, he's a kind of peer to Güiraldes. And, of course, he's an extraordinary writer, on the level of Conrad.

Monday
The story of the suicidal Colombian who locks himself in with a tape recorder: "This is my last recording. After this song, everything will be over." (He's listening to music.) This story could be used to write a short one-act play. A sort of more extreme version of Beckett's *Krapp*.

Now I'm going to improve the style of the piece on Hudson. I hope to be able to sign it with my name.

Novel. Always the story of a delusional criminal, locked away in an asylum, or a woman writing letters to the future.

This is the situation today. I get up at seven thirty to finish the article on Hudson for the magazine. It isn't well-written but it is well-considered (if that is possible). I don't have much money; I'll have to exchange one hundred dollars—out of the five hundred that comprises all of my capital. I have to answer a false and affected letter that Oscar T. sent me more than a week ago. I'm going to write a report for the project of an essay collection for Fausto. Now I'll go and bring the article to Beatriz.

Who would be able to reach the freezing point that consists of knowing oneself to have failed completely? Writing like a sick man describing his illness with the secret hope of remembering, afterward, the forgotten suffering.

I could earn my living "decently," doing translations, improving my work at the publishing house, making myself better known, teaching more courses, writing articles in the newspapers from time to time (though not in this era). Not imagining anything for myself. Reading, awaiting the future; I could, then, perhaps, be more peaceful. Curiously, that is the failure—or for me would be the failure—that I've sought for twenty years, making my life more difficult, as though that were the condition of art . . .

Tuesday 14

Unlike me, he had accepted the idea of failure. Some time had passed since he had abandoned all pretension of doing something that would go beyond his mere subsistence. He discovered in his lack of ambition a kind of confusing joy and felt an ironic amusement when he observed his contemporaries who had achieved some modest success.

He will never be able to find that compensation: he writes so as not to think.

I go to the publishing office. I present a report about a possible collection of essays, based on books or as a collection of articles on literature made by writers: Brecht, Pound, Valéry, Eliot, etc. In the bookshop is Luis Gusmán, who has returned from a trip to Brazil and brings news from Manuel Puig. I have lunch with him at Banchi: Manuel does not plan to return, and we have no plans to leave.

Thursday 16
One of the keys to modern literature in Argentina is the Frenchman Paul Groussac. He defined the notion of style that has come as far as Borges. And after that? There is no longer a single criterion to define what is usually called "writing well," meaning that there no longer exists a single site of literary power that defines what is excluded and included.

Punto de Vista is at the printers and will come out in March. Elías and Rubén are the basis of our economic support. We're trying to keep the magazine afloat in this cheerless era, in which everyone is being cautious and hiding: we must try to bring the intellectuals together and also keep ties with those in exile. We discuss vague plans for the second issue. We try to make old friends resurface, get them out from under their rocks. Nicolás Rosa, M. T. Gramuglio, Jorge Rivera. The dictatorship disheartens them. I'll see if I can ask for a story from Miguel Briante or Alberto Laiseca: those who are surviving within this terror.

I fervently work on the novel, and the notion of failure slowly reveals itself as a strange engine for the narrative. A kind of negative epic: those who have failed, what do they say, what do they talk about? A feeling of fatigue, that it would be better to let the time pass and wait. That "impression" holds some appeal for creating a character, a mixture of quixotism and weariness. Someone who stops when faced with the slightest difficulty. Fear of possibility: that is the evil of our era, to talk in that way. A sort of idiotic nihilism.

Friday 17
A dream. I was looking at my watch and saw that it incorrectly said Thursday 3; "the day didn't change," I thought. "Today is Friday." It seems like a transposition of the first meeting with Carlos and Beatriz to discuss the magazine: it was Thursday, February 2, but the meeting was scheduled for Friday the third. A day's residue: yesterday I went to see them, it was Thursday, but it wasn't the meeting day either. Now, in reality, I wrote the essay on Hudson and signed it with my other name. The fact that I must sign it that way remains a metaphor. Will I be able to accept anonymity, discretion, insecurity? It would seem that that is what I must do in this time. Praise from Beatriz, which I receive with irony. We are a group of snipers behind a scattered front line.

I'm a very individual man, he said. I get up at seven to go to work. When the sun goes down I return home. I have to go and find, he said, a vacuum at a store that closes at eighteen o'clock. Then I will go to the fair, he added, and have a night at the theater. The struggle against ideas rages on within me, he concluded.

Saturday 18
Last night at the theater, *Butley* by S. Gray, a rather conventional work, with a delirious character who gives a monologue without attending to the words of his friends' replies. I liked that situation, a character who exists in a play as though he were a visitor caught in a plot that he doesn't understand. He soliloquizes on that subject. I read a novel and want to write another by altering what I've read, for example, *The Heart of the Matter* by G. Greene, taking away all of its mode of being transcendent and religious, what would be left? In this case, I saw a play and imagined a different work that could be written. The virtues of non-empirical literature. This morning, while bathing, I imagined a work that I could write: "Gombrowicz in Buenos Aires," the ravings,

"the performances," the boarding house, etc. The man who says he is a brilliant writer and whom no one believes. The art of failing in style.

The general situation acts as an evil potion that produces an effect of general lethargy. Nothing interests me, he said. I can't stand myself. He responds that he mustn't confuse the world with his inner spirit. He laughs, and that is the beginning of what we call the negative epic.

Sunday
In the bathroom, as I was shaving—my face in the mirror—this morning, Gombrowicz once again. Write about him in *Artificial Respiration*. "The blond man who moved into the room today claims to be a count." A writer as protagonist once again? Better if Maggi is a historian and the other is a philosopher. Bouvard and Pécuchet. Maybe this is tied to what I thought today when I saw a story by Borges in *La Nación*. It seems like a collage of his previous stories. "He repeats himself," I thought, "but I will persist in difference."

Yesterday I received a letter from Manuel Puig; he has finished, he says, his fifth novel. He expects, he says, great things from me in the trajectory that I "have opened" with *Assumed Name*. He's doing well and remains calm, in love, never plans to return "to that country, horrible and spiteful." He complains with good reason about the stupid and negative criticism that he receives all the time from the "literary and like-minded journalists." I respond to him that I'm working with difficulty on a novel with a confusing outlook involving the temptation of failure.

Monday, February 20
In the last few days I have written a thirty-five-page draft; I've limited myself to developing the line of the epistolary novel. An ancient genre that has become fashionable again in the present world, friends scattered like a tribe ravaged by evil spirits. Many take refuge in the high mountains, others hide in the forest, and some remain under the elements.

Wednesday 22
Last night this dream. I am with Amanda. Someone is talking about guns. I ask them to put them away "in the closet at the back." She refuses, frightened. "It's for style," I say. Amanda has a brother who's a doctor, etc.

Novel. The man without qualities who reads letters in the post office and must censor them. He classifies them. Photocopies, transcriptions.

Curiosities. The refrigerator has been running constantly since yesterday: it is small, it stands against the wall facing the kitchenette, and it is broken. But it has broken in a particular way: instead of not running, it runs without stopping.

The test of a first-rate intelligence, said Fitzgerald, is the ability to hold two opposed ideas in the mind at the same time. Here, it isn't just two ideas; I wish there were only two: the proliferation persists so that one believes insanity is near. I write lists as if that were a way to erase the things I think, put them in writing so as to forget them, staying alone with the unhealthy drone of the broken refrigerator. How to create a system to erase memories? Write a story with a man who has been trained by the secret police in East Germany: a Soviet method, more or less Pavlovian, which allows the names, addresses, and details that might slip out under torture to be erased. The man, a guerrilla from the ERP, let's say, learns how to create oblivion and remembers nothing that he doesn't want to remember, etc.

Thursday 23
It seems that an analysis of the beginning of *Facundo* ("the first page") could be the nucleus of an essay on Sarmiento.

Sunday 26
I meet with Laiseca, he gives me his excellent interminable novel to read, written by hand. Paranoid fiction, the best part is its bizarre and very driven style.

All day yesterday in conversations about the sixties. Decades are meaningless, they do not provide a way of thinking, yet still you have to reflect on the years in which a vast group of people in different places saw change as imminent and possible. No one can imagine the happiness that this suggests.

On Friday I go back to *la Italiana*, a stranger yet also close and also decrepit (as I am). It was for her (not on her account), as though in a reality parallel to the one I cannot escape from, that I separated from Julia. She has that merit.

I wouldn't wish to turn these notebooks into a simple pad of sketches of the things I'm writing, but I don't want to forget the air of these times either. My friends in the city, faces exposed, we admire those few who persist in imagining that there secretly is an end to this, or in any case, that it obeys—said in quotes—a political logic that is classic in this country. At some point they will have to play politics, and then they will be out of time. Additionally, some difficulties with the books for Fausto, they resist approving my compensation (six million per month). They pay me tangentially. Meetings to establish the magazine and its environs: I always experience these things from the outside.

Tuesday 28
I finish working amid great personal anxieties. Last night I went to sleep at nine and was in bed for twelve hours. I have been working on the novel for eight months and the results still are not visible. Yesterday I met with Luis Gusmán at Los Galgos, a flowing conversation with him, a friend, I read him a few fragments from *The Prolixity of the Real* and he shows me the novel that he's just finished. We are always alone and isolated in these times, "bad times for lyric poetry," as B. B. said.

I have to go to the American embassy so that they can return the money from the taxes that they withheld when I was working at the University of California, last year. It seems they will return seven hundred fifty dollars to me.

Wednesday, March 1
I exchange one hundred dollars at Pocho Peña's place. They give me six and a half million pesos. I go through the bookshops on Florida and Avenida de Mayo. I move among the pedestrians like an invisible man. I buy Drieu La Rochelle's *Journal*. I sit down at the bar in Los 36 Billares. In the book I encounter a narrative method, the writer in another country who records everything as though he were an anthropologist. (Doing the same thing here.)

I spend the morning working at the Biblioteca del Congreso. Foreign language as a key to the autonomization of intellectuals in the Literary Salon. Europeanism, a method of autonomy.

Thursday, March 2
I spend the afternoon at the National Library. I take an A and work all night until eight in the morning.

Sunday
As I'm coming this way down Viamonte, a woman in the middle of the empty street approaches me with a piece of paper in her hand. I think she is going to attack me. May God bless you, she says, and help you achieve your desires. She hands me a brochure from the Pentecostal Holiness Church.

Tuesday 7
Midmorning I lie down to sleep. Will I have to give up the Dex for E? Too strong, they make me work for twelve hours but deplete me the next day.

I go out to eat at one thirty. When I come back, I lie down and sleep for three hours. It is five in the afternoon and, stupefied, almost dead, I look out at the city through the window.

I have dinner with Alan Pauls, who is back from Europe and brings me books by Tynyanov.

Thursday 9
The Diary of Anaïs Nin, a way to include in texts what one then wants to provoke in reality.

Friday 10
Now I'll go to the barbershop, and after that I'll see Andrés, and then I'll go on reading the novel by Semprún to kill the tedium.

Argument with Iris about *Punto de Vista*, which just came out. What she says is true and that's why I get furious. All too journalistic, she says.

Tuesday 14
Last night, returning from the cinema, in Plaza Lavalle, in one of those breaks in the middle of the street, a man, kneeling, holding a half-full bottle of wine as though it were a microphone, was praying aloud, in solitude. "He who was dead and buried and rose on the third day to save us from our sins." A vaguely Balkan face.

Thursday
Below, on the balcony of the school, the Jewish children in their capes make me think about Nazi brutality, the photo of a boy on his way to be executed; that image serves, paradoxically, to remind me which country I'm living in.

Saturday
In his house, Héctor Libertella receives Enrique Lihn. He drinks whiskey, and we talk about Chilean poetry.

Tuesday
Every once in a while, I go back to the family crisis of 1955—in this country, politics has a direct impact on private life.

A letter from Joseph Sommers arrives from the United States. Maybe I should leave once more.

I've been working on the novel for months. The pills allow me to concentrate and work for ten hours straight, and then I spend a day doing nothing before again shutting myself in for another ten hours. I try to write a first draft without backtracking or rereading. The letters that Arocena reads form a basic nucleus of the plot.

Monday, March 27
I go over the translation of Nabokov's *Despair*; I'm putting together a philosophy course for the psychoanalysts, in exchange for five hundred dollars per month.

Friday 31
On Wednesday night we meet to discuss the magazine, criticism and diversions that are prolonged until two in the morning.

Friday, April 14
The story of Marcelo Maggi is advancing. "For me, this story begins ten years ago. I had published my first book and he sent me a photograph and a letter."

The uncle only wants his situation to be known because the account of that life contains a secret, and he wants it to be exposed. He is in danger and disappears at the end of the novel.

Plan: the history, he writes letters to him, never meets him. He discovers a secret (he loved her or any other detail to uncover what he didn't want to say).

Tuesday 18
Why is he looking for him? To correct his history. Which? There's something that will not be said. Setting off from a single piece of information (insignificant) that the narrator tries to correct. It is that anecdote that I have to "discover."

I manage to create the anecdote (the fraud) and write two and a half pages. It is three in the afternoon, and I enter the second part of the long chapter: Maggi's "corrections" of the novel and the history of his life.

Wednesday 19
I spend all morning making a legible version of what I've written so far, because Iris wants to know what it is I'm writing. The draft is forty pages and is advancing, improving. Today: "Convicted and Confessed."

Thursday 20
Iris reads the first forty pages, and they work well for her.

There is a version of the novel published in April 1976 that Marcelo Maggi has corrected, filled with notes, insertions, even critiques on the style. This dialogue with the public novel from the autobiographical "truth" as a sign of a man who is in danger.

Friday 21
I rewrite the first letter. The character is becoming situated and the anecdote that will give the intersection of the letters is becoming defined.

The second part of the novel: trip to Concordia. He doesn't find him. He has left him a note in the hotel. A long conversation with the Polish chess player. He crosses the river and finds Coca, who raves on with another story.

Tuesday, April 25
I don't have a clear sense of how to continue after the first letter. I'll have to solve the technical problem, how to explain the succession of letters?

Bogged down. Maggi carries the story, but it's essential to find a hook. I don't like the succession of letters without motive.

Thursday
The novel is advancing, exasperating slowness. I write drafts of another two letters. The exile in the era of Rosas. The imprisoned man who does not see the political changes.

Tuesday, May 2
The Prolixity of the Real. 1. Family history, the novel already written. Expand Marcelo's biography and information about the family. 2. Letters. He sends it to various friends to look at. 3. Trip to Concordia. Marcelo "has gone away." Dinner with the Pole. 4. The Pole, sole heir. 5. The archive. Personal notes, historical documents. Letters from Maggi. Letters from Esperancita. 6. Crossing the river, Coca's monologue.

May 3
Marcelo Maggi is working on a biography of Enrique Lafuente. Secretary to Rosas: traitor. Grandfather of Esperancita. He leaves behind a trunk with unpublished documents that Esperancita's grandmother (Clara Lafuente) decides to keep in secret. When Clara passes away, the trunk passes into the hands of her oldest son, Marcos, the unforgettable blind man, Esperancita's father. No one ascribes any importance to those papers. For family reasons, the father makes Esperancita swear not to open the trunk until after his death. The papers spend thirty years in Marcos's control in his bedroom. Marcelo doesn't obey the vow and starts to work on those documents after his marriage. This would be the prologue that Marcelo Maggi writes.

May 12, Friday
Bogged down. I can't resolve Chapter II; what tone and what anecdotes do Marcelo's letter contain?

May 18
I have to learn how to wait. Let a solution come that will tie together this story, which began well and has come to a halt.

Wednesday, May 31
I resolve the chapter transitioning between the letters and the journey.

Wednesday, June 14
I put together a fragment of the beginning of the novel with the story of "my mother's brother" for *Punto de Vista*.

I watch the World Cup on television; nothing that happens makes sense, and it isn't worth remembering.

Monday 19
I remember a scene, on the corner of Rivadavia and Medrano, before entering the subway: I'm reading some praise for Doris Lessing in the literary supplement of the London *Times*. Why was that fixed in my memory? I should reread the diary from that year (1965) to see if it meant something in that moment. And that could be a method for writing the book of the diary (relationship between what I write and what I remember).

Friday 23
Meeting for the magazine, a chapter from the novel and a piece I wrote on Saer were published.

Multitudinous gatherings to celebrate Argentina's qualification for the finals of the World Cup. I walked alone among the multitude, like Robinson on his island.

Wednesday 28
Susana Appel from Editorial Pomaire called me last night, she read the chapter in *Punto de Vista* and expressed interest "in the novel I'm writing."

Tuesday, July 4
Quite a coup, I've just resolved the subject of the second letter (Genz and Maggi's conversations about philosophy and history; they avoid talking about personal matters). The same illumination a few days ago, when I wrote the transition from the first to the second part of the novel.

Thursday 20
Last night, a sudden appearance of paranoia. The hallway. I couldn't move forward or back. I hope I don't return to the nightmarish atmospheres of March and September.

Tuesday, July 25
I start to make a clean copy of the first half of the novel.

Only virtue, the cautious utilization of my own flaws. I am the one who couldn't be, etc.

Will I one day be able to create, from these "black" notebooks, a laboratory of my own life? Traces, references, experiences, short fictions.

Tuesday, August 1
A story. The man who cannot make up his mind to do anything and postpones everything. He spends his days sitting in a bar, or wandering around the city, or lying stretched out on his bed. Everything makes him struggle, and he lets himself go. Outside, a strange and intimidating reality (which isn't described) that he's the only one who seems to understand.

Another story. A man who lets himself be trapped in fantasy, imagining a life for himself, most of all when he walks alone in the street. In his imagination he has a very safe, bright apartment, and someone brings him five hundred dollars every month, which he lives on modestly. He lets himself live inside this invented and peaceful life, but gradually—first in his dreams and then in reality—he has a strong impression of having been betrayed, because this was not the life that he had imagined for himself, etc.

Wednesday 9
Monday and yesterday, unexpectedly, a crisis. Rosita wants to sell the apartment, and I have to give up the room that I rented from her to write in.

Monday 14
It's very cold. I went to the barbershop and got a haircut.

I'm reading Brecht's diary, he too had lost everything, but he wasn't afraid in the night, nor was he awakened by noises in the street. What can be learned in these situations? How to recognize determinations; life no longer depends on oneself. Exterior reality invades the initiative in such a way that it seems absurd to do anything, since nothing can be done that will solve the main problem. It isn't true that in these cases one values—as one must—liberty: the fear of losing it makes one prefer not to think about its virtues. Rather, one tends to think that life becomes so complicated and threatening that ultimately death would not be so serious (of course it isn't only about dying . . .). A strange relationship with time, the future (another political situation) seems too distant. Hard to make plans, living day by day. Memory is bound to the present: only the current situation is remembered. Nothing is known about the events that said it all; what will they be thinking about? What are they thinking of doing? The telephone, a perverse device. It only brings bad news. Except for hoping things will clear up, everything ceases to have importance. And so it becomes more and more difficult to act.

Another fact: I'm unable to reread these notebooks. Now I also distrust the past.

You have to know how to wait, to have the patience—the fortitude—of a stone that alters the course of the river. Something I thought after having leaned out on the balcony, over the ninth floor, with the secret illusion of "going on to a better life."

Tuesday 15
The class I taught turned out well, the study groups are an unexpected space of freedom and determination, the students seek to instruct themselves outside of the university, now taken over by the military. For months I taught a course on Sarmiento. I left home and went to the cinema and then had dinner at the old restaurant on Riobamba and Santa Fe.

Last night's dream is the best expression of my present state. Unexpectedly I was traveling to the Philippines, where Karpov and Korchnoi play for the world chess title. I was worried about the students and groups, which I hadn't been able to notify on the phone.

Friday, August 18
A meeting last night at Pezzoni's house with Bianco, Anita Barrenechea, Libertella, etc. Arguments, conversations, jokes.

Tuesday 22
Last night: I wake up at two in the morning. Terror. I look out the window, there are no cars in the street. I take a sleeping pill. The microscopic details of fear (the sounds of the elevator in the night).

Monday 28
Disappeared friends. Last night Andrés brings me the version, the details. Elías asked for some books to read when they came looking for him, Rubén said goodbye to his wife and two children. I discuss it with Andrés, walking down Florida. Then, later, intense nocturnal worrying. Alcohol. Sedatives. Awake since three in the morning. I think about them and can do nothing.

Monday, September 4
I travel to Mar del Plata. Two nights without sleeping (Wednesday and Thursday). The news comes in, one thing worse than the last. The waiting. The fear. The sedatives. All of the news is catastrophic.

None of my arrested friends said anything about the group's relationship with the magazine. During those days I walked, devastated and confused, through the city, but none of the ones who knew the relationship with the magazine said anything that compromised us, despite the horrors that I try not to imagine.

Friday 8
I spend three days at my family house in Adrogué. I'm alone in the back part of the house; in the front, my father rented the place to a printer and his wife. I hear them talking and laughing in the night. I sleep in the room that was my grandfather Emilio's central archive. There's a room next door with a desk, a kitchen, and a bathroom. For me, these are days of confinement and waiting. We will see what can be done.

Thursday 14
I remain in this house, that of my childhood, shutting myself away inside. The waiting persists. I come here to Adrogué every Tuesday in any case, confinement and solitude until Friday, and then I return to Buenos Aires (hotels, friends' houses).

Thursday 21
Since Tuesday, as always in this alien house, shut inside, reading. I don't want to write in these notebooks unless I can find a coded language that no one can understand.

Friday 22
I meet Beatriz Sarlo at the Biblioteca del Congreso, and after a brief and nervous chat we decide to return home, certain that our friends kept us safe. So the magazine will continue to be published.

Tuesday 3

I see several German films by Wim Wenders (*Alice in the Cities, Kings of the Road, The American Friend*), in which I find journeys, escapes, distance, American literature.

A short story. "Heroic Paysandú, I salute you." A good sentence for writing a final letter. He commits suicide. Alcoholic. Solitude in that corner of Buenos Aires. He doesn't know how to live, an effect of his political resolve. Solitude and asceticism for nothing. Total bankruptcy. He is thirty-seven years old. A useless life.

I work on the period of 1852–1874 for the course on Saturdays. Mansilla and Hernández. One wrote *An Expedition to the Ranquel Indians* when he was dismissed from the army, waiting for a military trial. The other wrote *Martín Fierro*, shut up in a hotel room, pursued, facing Avenida de Mayo, in Buenos Aires, yellow fever, tedium. As Rodolfo Walsh said to me a few years ago: "When bored, what is there to do but write." (The list of the dead.) So many things can be done . . .

Wednesday, October 25

I work on the novel. I'm back in Buenos Aires now. Tomorrow a lecture on the detective genre.

Tuesday, October 31

Once again in the family house, after the train ride that cleaves my life in two. On Thursday I gave the lecture; on Friday and Saturday I taught class; on Sunday I wrote a short piece on Barthes that Tamara requested for *Confirmado*; on Monday, a class on Deleuze with the psychoanalysts.

I'm reading a biography of Goebbels: "He once stated to the American journalist Edgar Ansel that it took him three days to come up with the two essential words for an effective poster."

I go back to the family myths. As in Elisa's house, the family is a machine for producing fiction about itself.

Wednesday, November 1
Today I visited the Oracle at Delphi. I don't call her that because she—the wounded woman—presents herself that way, but because of the composed clarity of her speech. An oracle with no enigma; the confusion, at any rate, is on the part of the one who comes seeking advice.

It's enough to talk with one of these women to perceive the other reality. These mothers live in a country occupied by an enemy army.

Tuesday 7
Back again in this house in the south. I'm reading a book on Nazism (Karl D. Bracher, *The German Dictatorship*). Hitler's trajectory, calling himself an artist ("the only work he did was an occasional copying of picture postcards"), various failures until he "arrived at the 'awareness' that the creative person—and he, being a painter, belonged to this category—gets cheated by the sly, worldly, aggressive Jewish merchant after he himself had an unpleasant experience with a Jewish art dealer." A strange antisocial root of the "artist" facing off against society, a fascist mold not at all foreign to other "creators": here, what Flaubert call the bourgeois is incarnated in the Jew (but this petit bourgeois wasn't a landlord).

At the same time, another detour from this reading: "Hitler's mysterious drifting, prolonged for more than five years. An abrupt and concealed disappearance." During those years (he reappears in 1913 in Munich), suppose Hitler meets Kafka. They walk together along the streets of Prague. "Antisemitism as occult science" (according to Hitler). Both, on the other hand, are marginalized "artists" who dream of great creations. Create, then, a story that would help to explain how and why Kafka anticipated the realities of Nazism in such a providential way. Hitler told him his plans, etc. Kafka, of course, was the only one (over time) not to take him for a lunatic. Another explanation, what's more, for his decision to have his writings burned. A portrait of Kafka painted by Hitler exists: a postcard and, in a corner, the gentle figure K. Apart from that, Hitler, let's say, was in Prague because he had eluded "the duty of military inspection and enlistment that was carried out between 1909 and 1910." A deserter, bound also to his "nostalgia for Munich, city of the arts."

"To the inquiries of the Austrian authorities, who even conducted his provisional arrest and transfer to Salzburg, he responded by quite submissively confessing his hardships. In fact, he was freed from enlistment and the corresponding punishment based only on his state of health. The extensive document of his deposition, which he wrote to the authorities in Linz [a Kafkaesque detail] is almost a draft for *Mein Kampf*, in which he feels sorry for himself (in 1914) in the following way: 'I have never known that word, so beautiful, which is youth.'" ("Artist, frequenter of cafés, incapable of normal human relationships.") ("He never drank, never smoked, was fond of candy.")

We were men of transition, living at the edge of reality.

Wednesday, November 8
Polemics about the thirty months of military dictatorship and the economic plans led by Martínez de Hoz. With respect to inflation and considering only the official facts, it is observed that during those thirty months the increase of the so-called "cost of living" has reached 1,354.3 percent. The participation of workers in the national income, which in 1974 reached 46.9 percent, has at present descended to an average of less than thirty percent. Taking as a basis the figures given by Martínez de Hoz for the GDP of fifty billion dollars, salaried earners have lost wages of 7.85 billion dollars (that is, more than 200 million lost per month). The current recession, based on its duration and depth, has no precedent since the crisis of '30. The official facts are the following: the GDP is 5.1 percent below that of last year, and lower than those of

1976, 1975, and 1974. The gross fixed investment, in the first half term of this year, is 13.7 percent lower than the same period in 1977 and 14.4 percent below 1974. The productivity of the industrial sector is 24.9 percent lower than 1974.

Within the frame of these developments we must take into account that the latest cabinet change meant absolute support for Martínez de Hoz and the Minister of the Interior, A. Harguindeguy. The crashes reached, in the first nine months of 1978, a historic record, being eight times greater than those of 1977 and eighteen times those of 1976. Everything makes us think that the crisis of the dictatorship will start to accelerate, I mean, we begin to glimpse the internal rupture and a new regrouping.

Difficult to foresee the course of events; upper military echelons are doubtless trying to change the class character of the State and reformulate the base of political power. Is it an expression of monopolistic financial capital? Hard to know. For the moment, Peronism and radicalism do not advance beyond an abstract critique; the working class seems unable to get out of the downturn. Nevertheless, you have to take into account the pressure from the United States, which proposes democratization and dialogue, and the "risks" of a war with Chile, which could have two effects:

1) Political backing of the dictatorship ("national unity against the aggressor") and its economic plan (the crisis will come to be explained as the effects of war).
2) A process of reconstituting military power, "coup d'état" against Videla and the effects of securing the effectiveness of military and political management in face of the war.

Thursday 16
Swamped: the confinement, the pills, the solitude. I don't make too much progress, but then again: I finish a very shaky draft of the second chapter.

Sunday 19
A short story. A man who lives with just enough money to get by rents a room in the house of a German woman, widowed and solitary. He writes a novel. Every night sitting in a bar, etc., trying to dissolve the effects that the writing and isolation have on his language: he writes fluidly but stutters when he speaks.

Wednesday, November 22
Railway strike. I'll drive to Adrogué with Horacio tomorrow. Is the process of growth finally beginning? The successive positions of opposition to the dictatorship by the political sectors, statements from Peronism, from radicalism, from the Christian People's Party. So that war with Chile appears to be the only possible counteroffensive against the dictatorship.

Wednesday 29
I decide to write a prologue for an edition of Sarmiento's *Facundo* that Lafforgue requested for the Centro Editor.

Wednesday, December 6
I'm working on *Facundo*. The prologue is progressing, but it's stretching on too long: it will reach thirty pages, and everything will be left only half said all the same. As always, I imagine myself dedicated to writing a book about Sarmiento that could include everything I've thought about his writing.

I worked for six hours, starting at eight. Now it's five in the afternoon, and I am at once bored and exhausted. Always alone, as in prison. I should keep writing but I no longer have the desire. Yesterday, on the other hand, I worked from nine in the morning until ten at night.

Thursday 14
I finish a twenty-page draft: introduction to *Facundo*.

Tuesday, December 19
Over the last few days I have written a prologue for an anthology of detective stories.

Tuesday, December 26
Between yesterday and today I finished a version of the prologue for *Facundo* condensed to twelve—fairly good—pages. Apart from that, I finished teaching my courses. I'm reading Freud.

5

Diary 1979

Thursday, January 11
I'm back in the house "of my birth." I live in the wing that opens onto the interior patio, isolated, far from the buzz of the family that rents the area in front. The ladies talk to themselves; the air is very hot. I return to fiction again and again. Where does this novel end?

Monday, January 22
I'm not interested in writing essays without finding a specific form that allows for a personal view. I try to convey "the writer's reading": I see three steps, or three fields.

1. Analyzing the structure, a technical reading, shall we say, centered around the method.
2. A strategic reading, which consists of looking at the territory in its totality and orienting oneself there. On one hand, a struggle of poetics; on the other hand, what is the place of literature in society? And not the other way around.
3. An imaginary history of literature. Defining the way in which fiction narrates different spheres of literary life. History of imaginary writers.

Saturday 27
At Tortoni, a meeting for the magazine. Various articles are read, among them my essay on Borges.

On Friday at the Centro Editor I earn thirteen million pesos for the detective anthology and the prologue.

I finish a draft of the response about *Sur* for the poll in *La Opinión*. I have a very critical interpretation of the current wisdom, which attributes "the modernization" of Argentine literature to Victoria Ocampo and her group. Translation became institutionalized on its own, as well as the systems of cultural legitimacy. What angers me is the obsequiousness of all the intellectuals, who do not take into account the dictatorship's use of Victoria Ocampo as a model of the Argentine intellectual.

For my part, I recover from chemical attractions at the expense of a kind of stupor that seems perpetual.

As it has always been, I've never desired anything other than immortal glory and to be a great writer, but now it's plain to see how much those hopes have diminished.

They tell me about an apartment that could be rented for twenty-five million (two hundred dollars), on Maipú and Viamonte. Temptations; I won't have much money this year, but I could find some way to pay for it.

I still don't quite know what I'm going to write in this month that I have free, before the classes start up again. In the last few months I have read *Capital*, trying once again to confirm old ideas about the concept of "unproductive labor" (it isn't that nothing is produced; it is unproductive for capital because it produces no profit) as a field for reflecting on art in this society. Along those lines it is possible to analyze the social place of literature, that is, the place of literature in the social sphere (which interests me more than the inverse, or rather, the place of society in literature). The key is that art cannot be measured with the criterion of abstract, general labor, which serves to measure or calculate profit. How many hours are required to produce a Borges story? It's a ridiculous question and does not, of course, serve to calculate any price. Books have value, as objects, because of the socially necessary work time (or abstract labor) that is required to create them. (The base is the price of paper, which is calculated in the same way.)

Friday 16
I also work on this year's course amid distractions. How to think about the origins of the Argentine novel? Several readings and notes on the period of 1870–1916. Now I return to Mansilla, who was at one point a possible thesis subject for me, such that I even went as far as talking about him with my teacher Enrique Barba.

In any event, next week I will once again seclude myself in the house in Adrogué for three or four days to make some progress on the novel I'm writing.

Monday, February 19
I came, once again, to this house where I lived for many years, to withdraw for three days. Trying to write the story of the censor who reads letters. The story relocated to a town on the border. All in view of advancing on *The Prolixity of the Real*, finding a way to advance on Enrique Lafuente's history.

Nevertheless, something will have to happen. I've been writing in these notebooks for twenty years and for that same span of time have been resorting to "speed" pills: a closed process. Now it's 17:00, I've had three cups of tea and eaten, over six hours of work, two ham sandwiches, a peach, and two pears. I smoked almost an entire pack of cigarettes and my mouth is burning. What is the cost of a writer's hour of labor? And what's more, how much does he spend during his hours of work?

Tuesday, February 20
Romanticism then was like a necessary sickness, which consisted of spending the night, if possible, helped along by the drugs, in a state

of sweet literary intonation, worn down by old unachievable projects. Alone and with no contact with the real, that was how I conceived of happiness back then (and I could continue, but with Lafuente, recounting his life as if it were my own).

Wednesday 21

When I return to Buenos Aires, I find a letter from Sazbón: he has written a fifteen-page essay on *The Prolixity of the Real*, that is, on the first chapter of the novel I'm writing. Very intelligent, very exhaustive, with several derivations, but at the same time superfluous. It helps to accentuate my skepticism regarding criticism. He includes in the letter vague references to a possible invitation to teach courses in Venezuela.

Thursday 22

While writing, one imagines a book that does not yet exist. One even views it as a physical object, with a cover, title, and quantity of pages. It reminds me of my abstemious times, when a glass of whiskey would suddenly appear to me in the air. Desire produces images, but it's difficult to sustain an empty fantasy day after day. Neither do I clearly see what novel I'm going to write, I let myself be guided by intuition and I make decisions, carry the story forward, understanding it better as I write it.

Friday

I'm accompanying Crist L., a student who attended my seminar in California and came here on a year-long fellowship to study Roberto Mariani. With that ability that American academics have for creating in the void: Latin Americanists study what they imagine is not being studied, but do not study what might really interest them.

Wednesday 28

I'm writing the novel, a second chapter of the novel. The one who reads letters in secret. Alone in an empty house, at the end of summer, listening to Telerman.

On Monday I meet Andrés. Casual conversation, he is very generous in his friendship as always. An apartment might be secured for fifty dollars. Silvia Coppola is traveling to Paris, making her home in Europe. She would leave me the furnished apartment on Bartolomé Mitre, number 1500, close to Pasaje de La Piedad. Starting in April. I trust (have always trusted) in my lucky star and this time I have faith just as in times past.

I write a couple of pages and then the chapter stalls. Possibilities: analyze a single letter in detail or work on several letters, varied subjects. The situation in Buenos Aires in this period, expressed through the letters that are written from exile and from here, alluding rather than speaking clearly, and elliptically describing the horror of the political situation.

I've been working for ten hours and the chapter is now starting to work. There are several letters, read by the censor. A fresco, so to speak, of Argentina today, or rather, of the relationship between exile and permanence.

Thursday, March 1
The chapter progresses, I already wrote a few letters, two and a half letters in fact, and another three remain. One, by the narrator; another, by a woman, maybe from Puerto Rico; another, by an Argentine man who travels to New York. After that the difficulty will be in weaving them together and creating a structure with the mosaic or collage of censored letters. For me it is about women, and outraged, conscious men who are unable to say what they mean directly and so disguise it, hide it. For his part, Arocena, the censor, reads too much, interprets excessively, sees signs of danger in any phrase. At the same time, I'll try to find a way to make the voices of the mothers circulate, starting from a charm on a bracelet. The charm: that is the true utterance. I'd include a line from Shakespeare that I recall from memory and translate like this: "A greater storm indeed, to clean away so black a cloud."

Monday 5

A rather auspicious succession. Andrés calls me; he will, it seems, get the apartment. We'll meet on Thursday. Bernardo Kordon calls, more prodding from China to have me make a second trip to Peking. Contacts. A long stay in Europe (before returning). Esther Aráoz calls (from the IPA), the course on Mondays with the psychoanalysts is confirmed for this year. Yesterday, Sunday, my position on *Sur* magazine was published in *La Opinión*. Highly critical, highly ironic: all elites are self-appointed, that's the hypothesis. Victoria Ocampo, an intellectual from the generation of '80 who lives fifty years behind. The first one to call me in excitement is José Bianco (the same one who ran the magazine in its finest era), Borges might have called as well, he thought the same about Victoria Ocampo as I do (and sometimes said as much). A very provincial magazine, according to him.

Tuesday 6

I dreamed that *pajamas* was an anagram of Hegel. I'm in my childhood home once again, in the south. I only see Horacio, my cousin, my brother. He promises to take me to El Soviet, that's what they call the club where they always go to play poker.

I worked for ten hours, smoked a pack of cigarettes, but I finished the first draft of the second chapter. It's twelve pages but will end up being twenty or twenty-five because the ending and one of the letters (which is in code) still have to be done. At the end, Arocena meets with his father and then returns to the Central Post Office.

Arocena is the one who writes Maggi's archive, after he has been kidnapped. His reading of and commentary on those documents would close the novel.

Novel. 1. Uncle Maggi. 2. Arocena. 3. The narrator's trip to Concordia. Maggi has disappeared. He talks to Tardewski and goes to see Coca. 4. Coca's monologue. 5. The archive.

Wednesday 7
In one of the letters, a fantastic story that I hadn't anticipated arises. I close the chapter, which I still need to write an ending for, in this way: the father finds out about the work that Arocena is doing and breaks ties with him. Arocena, in the street, turns to diagrams and decryptions. He finds another coded message and returns to the Post Office.

Thursday 9
Iris reads the chapter, suggests ending it without the meeting with the father. She's right.

I go to look at Silvia Coppola's apartment, it's perfect. A studio with a kitchen and bathroom, furnished. The window has a view over Plaza Congreso. But I'll have to pay one hundred twenty dollars a month for it.

Saturday
Issue 5 of *Punto de Vista* comes out with my piece on Borges. Carlos and Beatriz tell me about a "Glossary of Sociology in Literature" that they're writing together. (They place too much importance on sociology and too little on literature.) In the magazine meeting at Tortoni, a variety of arguments and plans. Praise for my critical statement about *Sur* magazine. It wouldn't have been possible to publish it in a paper a couple of years ago. The political situation remains complicated, but we have a crisis in place once again: the military will have to start seeking alliances to be able to govern, and that will bury them (Peronism is in the opposition and won't compromise. Impossible to govern without them).

Monday, March 12
Everything was going well, but there is a small conflict in the Monday group of psychoanalysts. Julia C. withdraws, for professional reasons. The difficulty with private groups is always contingency; of course I need the money to handle the rent for the new apartment.

Tuesday

I come to Adrogué, alone in the house, as always, without interruptions. I rewrite the end of the chapter. Arocena's delirious interpretation. I finish it and now start work on the continuation of the novel. Things are going along well, I have great confidence in this book. Of course, the economic situation is always precarious.

Saturday, March 24

Catastrophic anniversary. The military has been in power for three years and has destroyed all the best parts of this country.

I'm reading Pynchon, always striking and unexpected. In the German submarine during the Second World War, he places a discussion typical of Argentine nationalism about Hernández's *Martín Fierro* (Pynchon seems to be well informed; he's probably taken some course on Argentine literature at Cornell). It validates me in the draft I wrote a year ago with a conversation on literature at a bar, which lasts all night. The novel, for me, aspires to integrate the essay, that is, it aspires to narrative interpretation.

I go to the book fair (I've never been) anonymously, only to meet Juan Rulfo. He is there, as though distanced from everything, drinking Coca-Cola ceaselessly and signing books. I can't make up my mind to talk to him, I stay for a while and just observe him.

As I advance on the novel, the issue of publication appears. It may be that I have to publish it abroad. Not thinking about the future has been my life's motto.

Monday 26

What is the reason for the state of things? Problems in outer space. Sorrow, a lack of concentration, with no precise origin. It isn't about my economic situation, I'm doing better than ever, earning some thousand dollars per month. The political situation is oppressive, but it is at a standstill, and the military has gone on the defensive. Ridiculous to talk like this, being alone in an eighth-floor apartment in the occupied city. Through the window I see the pathetic ceremonies of the Advisory Council, which the military has created in order to replace the Congress. They roll out a red carpet so that their accomplices can come up amid the general indifference, and in the plaza even the retirees withdrew on the day the members of the military cabinet took over.

Sunday, April 1
Tristana sends me two boxes of amphetamines, via her doctor husband. She lives in Concordia and I'll set the action of the book there in her honor. After a morning interview, I hire a woman who will come to handle the cooking and cleaning for my office.

I read *The Interpretation of Dreams* once again (maybe because I'm dreaming less and less).

Schedule for the study groups. Monday night, the psychoanalysts. Saturday afternoon, the second literature group. Friday, the first literature group.

Wednesday 4
Interview for a Spanish magazine. Three hours talking about myself, impossible to reflect on "that subject." A tape recorder to capture my stupidity. The trivial (so as not to say personal) myths: the diary, North American literature, the detective genre. I can't say anything that goes beyond the situation itself: there I am, obliged to refer to the one who is speaking. In order to think or write, I have to be absent.

Thursday 5
The classes will be: Mondays from 19:00 to 20:30, the subject philosophy for psychoanalysts. This year I'll begin with Freud (self-analysis, his relationship with philosophical introspection. Socrates' "know thyself"). Fridays from 10:00 to 12:00, poetics of the novel today. Saturdays from

14:30 to 16:30, history of the Argentine novel (1880–1916). I have to prepare for the courses, so I'll have three free days per week.

I continue writing the novel. Trip to Concordia. Meeting with Tardewski.

I have three tasks: an article on Arlt for the fiftieth anniversary of *The Seven Madmen*, an essay on "the reversal of *The Return of Martín Fierro*," with Hernández's warning announcing "foreign books" in his book-shop. An introduction to *Facundo* for the Centro Editor in exchange for seventy-five million pesos (seven hundred fifty dollars). Apart from that, two public courses (one set of four classes on Arlt and another of four classes on Borges). Plenty of work, too much work.

Friday, April 6
Today I signed the lease for the apartment (utopia of the last three years). I pay six hundred dollars for six months in advance. I receive the key. The study groups have formed themselves on their own, and I now have thirty students; that is, three groups, and I won't admit any more students. We meet in rotating houses, the students very generously offer up their own homes despite the potential risk. The students, what's more, put together the money to support the work. In these times, the university students, and recently graduated young people, form private groups to solve the deficiency of the university taken over by the military. The first group is formed by young psychoanalysts, the second group by literature students, and the third group by a combination of young writers, architects, film students, etc. From what I know, there are five of these private universities in the city.

Investigating the history of Moreau, the communist and morphine-addicted painter who lived in José Mármol, the town next to Adrogué.

Wednesday 11
Yesterday, photos in a plaza. I "disguise" myself in my detective's trench coat to endure the images. Have to live in third person.

Tuesday 17
I spend the day in the apartment on Bartolomé Mitre for the first time.
I arrange my books, place the table by the window, begin writing the
chapter about the trip to Concordia. Is it halfway there?

Wednesday 25
Chiquito, my cousin from Tandil, shows up. He remains standing on
his own, stubbornly, in the empty factory that belonged to the family
until a disagreement between the brothers caused a rift that he refuses
to acknowledge. As always, he comes to see me without warning, rings
on the intercom, and starts talking as soon as he sees me. Cosmic forces.
Maria Theresa of Austria. An Arltian, a family version of President
Schreber: the same illusions (rays, lights, religion, the system, being a
woman, pictures, passion) translated into Lunfardo. He calls Jesus "el
Flaco." He tells me explicitly that I will be the one to write his truth. We
go out to eat at the restaurant on the corner and he speaks forcefully
and, because everyone stares at him, lowers his voice and says: "You can
see I have an aura." I'm the only one who takes him seriously because
deep down he is speaking the truth. He has spent money that he doesn't
have to obtain some satellite images of the factory and the neighboring areas because he wants to establish an Institute of Agro-industrial
Development. I listen to him and remember him in the summers of my
childhood when he would make mechanical, semi-robotic toys for me,
which worked perfectly. He would build them in the workshop that he
had set up at the back of his house.

Thursday 26
One element to take into account in relation to literature is the end
of the morality of the work, the end of craftsmanship as a virtue that
gives meaning (one example is my cousin Chiquito, who does everything with his hands). The craftsman has been set aside for the world
of art, but there too he is losing his value: art utilizes more and more
techniques and instruments or concepts that do not take manual skill
into account. The labor is disappearing from the ethical and specific

horizon. The writer uses the language that belongs to everyone and, nevertheless, receives the profits.

Tuesday 1
Too busy with classes. All the same I try to advance with the novel. Tardewski's account: the disappearance of Maggi. A journey.

Wednesday 2
I begin, with great difficulty, to write the novel starting with Tardewski. Two pages in six hours, close to the right tone. I see what is coming in the book fairly clearly, although it's no more than a vague intuition of the form.

1   Contact with Maggi (still have to expand the letter).
2.   The censor.
3.   Maggi's police record.
4.   Tardewski tells of his meeting with the narrator.
5.   Coca's monologue.
6.   The narrator recapitulates and introduces the archive.
7.   Maggi's archive and notes.

Monday 7
I just turned down a request from *La Opinión* to write about Arlt. I don't like to enter into contact with the party-line scribes (Luis G., etc.). I wrote about *Sur* because I was saying what no one would say and was the only one to cast doubt on Victoria Ocampo amid the celebrations and military tributes. On the other hand, I have no time, the classes keep me very busy, I can't even bring my correspondence up to date.

Wednesday 9
I'm working on the lunch scene and Magdalena's visit. Will I be able to set up the meeting with the narrator? The chapter is justified in that. I struggle to find the way out and write their conversation.

I am tired, shut away in here since morning, it's already three in the afternoon. I manage to advance a bit on the scene and write for a couple of hours in the right tone.

Thursday 10

I am so tired and so overloaded from literary criticism that I don't understand how I was able to spend a few months writing about Arlt and Borges. It makes no sense. Only by changing the style of the work can writing about literature be justified. So I don't intend to perform academic criticism. I made the decision to abandon the university in 1966 (then, as now, it was taken over by the military) and set aside my academic career. I will hold firm in that, despite the reasonable advice from Iris, who subordinates her writing to the academic standard. She is fully entitled to that, but it is not my case.

Tuesday, May 15

I work for ten hours, take amphetamines, don't want to sleep, feel urged on, and want to finish the novel that I've now been working on for a couple of months (or more). I write the first version of the dialogue with Tardewski that lasts all night, but it isn't convincing to me, too flat. I have to rewrite it. Nevertheless, Iris reads it and thinks it works. I'm going to write it over again from the beginning.

Wednesday 16

In a sense, the Concordia chapter is written, but I'll have to work on it a great deal to reach what I still do not know. I have to manage it without saying what is central, the whole conversation revolves around what they are not saying, they're waiting for Maggi, even though Tardewski knows he will not come. I must be able to bear a reading without the support of Maggi's history. It is the nerve center of the book. I went around in circles and wrote something after noon but without any major results.

Saturday 19

So Lafforgue calls to tell me that Spivakov is rejecting the prologue I wrote about *Facundo*. I can't believe it. Put better, I can believe it perfectly, because the Centro Editor practices a type of criticism and dissemination of literature that is exactly the inverse of my own thinking. They combine common sociology with journalistic dissemination. It's the first time that someone has turned down one of my texts. Of course, I won't say it is for political motives (I don't like to play the victim or put history on my side, in Viñas's style). We simply live in different worlds. According to Spivakov, the people want rump steak and I'm offering them viper's tail (a metaphor meaning that my dish is for few . . .).

Thursday, May 31

I finish a twenty-page chapter narrated by Tardewski after ten hours of work. I lost all of last week because I was in bed with the flu. I worked on Friday and changed the tone; on Tuesday and Wednesday I wrote a nearly final draft.

Friday, June 8

Good news, vague invitations to give lectures in the United States starting in September of next year. I hope to finish the novel before I go traveling. Meanwhile, I move around like a typical Argentine writer, earning a freelance living. I do many things, teach many classes, and struggle to gain a couple of free days per week and maintain some discipline of working in the mornings, without letting myself be overwhelmed by the effort of earning my living. It has always been that way, and I don't see why it should be any different for me. It's enough to think about Borges, who did all of the things we do (he taught classes, gave lectures, did translations, wrote pieces in the newspapers, directed collections, made anthologies); we aren't American or European writers, though we are now on the same level.

Monday 11

He thinks about suicide once more, it's a way to pass the time like any other, he said. He does not think about death but rather about the form of dying: drowning in a river, hanging from his belt in the bathroom, hurling himself into the void from the balcony of the building. Avoiding pills or the thunder of a revolver. The thought that follows is about the preliminary moments of that final act. He quickly gives up the plan. "Before I killed myself, I'd go and get a haircut," says Iris.

For a while I've been avoiding writing in these notebooks; superstitious thoughts but also the effort not to think. I turn over an idea that isn't worth naming. I have set a deadline and have seen how many ways there are of doing the thing I sometimes imagine as an escape. It's comical, but I've gone up to the balcony and looked down and decided that I can't jump. So I'm going to wait it out until I can find a quiet way to muddle through.

I don't want to reread these notebooks, sometimes they are an assessment that I don't want to face. Sensation of extreme precariousness. Continuous present.

Tuesday 12

I make no progress on the monologue by Coca, Marcelo Maggi's ex-wife who lives on the other side of the river, in Uruguay. I reject, without much certainty, the possibility of everything being related by the narrator. Maybe, then, ravings by Coca, talking to herself.

Wednesday 13

I don't know what story I have to tell and can't find the right tone either. Coca's "spoken" monologue, a voice recording? The narrator is there with a tape recorder. Is there another way to write it? I can't find the path, there's no plotline.

After several hours of work, I write a draft of Coca's monologue, six pages that I reread just now. It doesn't seem bad at all, maybe she's the only one who tells the story of Marcelo's kidnapping.

What did I learn in these long years? That no plots exist until one begins to write, there is nothing before.

Saturday 16
Can Coca's monologue be Chapter II of the novel? In that case, the narrator's trip to see her will have been anticipated and the first part could close in that way, before entering the archive. Then it could go something like this:

1. The narrator talks with Maggi.
2. Coca.
3. Censor.
4. Tardewski.
5. The narrator synthesizes.

Tuesday 19
If, as Iris suggests, Coca's monologue doesn't work, or, as I think, it has no narrative function because it reiterates what is already known and only shows that she is delirious without advancing the story, then I need to find another ending, but I still don't know what it is. Maybe a final summary by the narrator, who has already read the archives and has a conversation with Coca about all of it. But isn't that reiterating the conversation with Tardewski?

Thursday 20
The narrator tells the story once again after the trip, the reading of the archive, and the meeting with Maggi, who refuses to recognize him and be recognized. But what story is it that is being told over again? I don't want what already happened to me twice with two different novels to happen again. I have to find the plotline before I continue.

Saturday

Last night a lecture on Arlt in the series for the magazine on Calle Jean Jaurés. My father slept here, his stories from childhood. Lots of work with the courses. I hold myself up on the novel like a castaway on his lifesaver.

Tuesday 26

The novel is bogged down. By not writing Coca's monologue, I don't know what the narrator is going to do in Concordia. If I don't want to repeat old mistakes, I have to wait: and not write until I have the story more clear.

Wednesday 27

Last night a dream: an American woman asks me to write about her life. She is a prisoner in Sing Sing. I think: how can I switch languages?, etc.

There is another dream: a young man who wins the short story competition. Praise from Macedonio Fernández, at the beginning of a story. It doesn't seem that good to me. The young man dies before the book is released, yet is certain of his glory.

I'll try to organize and write the archive, and then I'll see what happens with the ending of the first part (the narrator's journey). The problem is how to create interest in that story from the nineteenth century. Weeks of uncertainty await me.

Thursday 28

I am a foreigner. I am less and less able to talk to people, less and less able to think. I spend the day struggling against "bad thoughts."

Monday, July 2

I prepare today's class about the notion of crisis in Walter Benjamin. An appropriate subject for me. The state of emergency is the norm in my life. Isn't the crisis at age forty what helps most people to understand that the hopes of youth haven't been achieved? I don't see much of a way out for myself and, all the same, "the way out" doesn't seem so difficult: I have to finish the novel. Historicize personal misfortune (subject of the sentimental novel).

A quote that seems as if I wrote it. "The meditation on death as the final defeat is as natural for men in the Middle Ages as the meditation on one's own life as a frustration of the ambitions of their youth might be for our contemporaries when they turn forty," E. Le Roy Ladurie.

Tuesday 3
I work in the National Library (letters and documents from Lafuente) without ambition, trying to define the material before I write.

Isolated, without friends, without future.

Thursday, July 12
At Fausto, they offer to have me direct the publishing house's magazine in exchange for five hundred dollars per month.

Friday 13
I believe I've discovered a system for writing the archive. As Lafuente's work in progress. Notes, letters in no chronological order. After four hours of effort, the archive started to work.

Saturday 14
I wrote seven pages yesterday, but when I reread them today they seem too watered down. I still haven't found the axis to organize the archive around. At the moment, I think that the "absence" of the narrator (in this case, Maggi) complicates things; I have a tendency above all to think of the beginning of the novel as a succession of documents.

Wednesday 25

I have tried, without success but not without dedication, to write the following failed novels. The "true" novel; the story of the attack on the bank truck, four criminals' flight, and their confinement inside an apartment in Montevideo where they hold out from the police all night and, before dying, burn the money. Use of the tape recorder and a technique to convey the orality of the characters as a real document. A short novel centered around Pavese, which takes place in Italy and revolves around personal diaries.

How can I believe that I'll be able to write this novel in which I'm bogged down once again?

Monday, July 30

"Let us reflect in another way, and we shall see that there is great reason to hope that death is a good, for one of two things: either death is a state of nothingness and utter unconsciousness, or, as men say, there is a change and migration of the soul from this world to another. Now if you suppose that there is no consciousness, but a sleep like the sleep of him who is undisturbed even by the sight of dreams, death will be an unspeakable gain. For if a person were to select the night in which his sleep was undisturbed even by dreams, and were to compare with this the other days and nights of his life, and then were to tell us how many days and nights he had passed in the course of his life better and more pleasantly than this one, I think that any man, I will not say a private man, but even the great king, will not find many such days or nights, when compared with the others." Plato, *Apology of Socrates.*

Wednesday, August 8

The day before I wrote what can be read above about suicide, Silvia Ahumada, a student from my Saturday group, killed herself. She didn't say anything, none of her friends or acquaintances could have predicted it. In the meeting on the Saturday before her death, she gave a very intelligent presentation on Felisberto Hernández. She threw herself out of the window, leaving no note or letter. She was twenty-seven years old.

Friday 10
Lafuente's life. I try to avoid biography. As a result, I decide to make a change, to arrange it in small blocks, a mosaic, a kind of ensemble with no order. He too is a victim of suicide.

Friday 17
The Faulknerian machine. I finally read the Snopes trilogy (*The Hamlet, The Town, The Mansion*) and before that the unabridged version of *Sartoris*. He is telling a single story in his work.

Tuesday, August 21
Classes. Monotony. I'm not writing, but I can't think either. Last night I dreamed that I was committing suicide by injecting venom into a vein in my left hand, which is my good hand.

Monday 27
We've arrived at the end that we should have reached fifteen years ago, and so everything will conclude, unless I manage to solve the writing of this novel so that, perhaps, things might really improve for the first time.

Tuesday 28
I'm not even capable of analyzing the collapse, selling everything once and for all (and that can be a source of relief, the small misfortunes don't seem to be a "historical" catastrophe), and I will still be here. A strange feeling of unreality, as though I could know my fate.

I'm reading *The Golden Notebook* by Doris Lessing.

The strangest and most difficult thing to consider is this: although things are going very badly, as badly as one can imagine, it doesn't mean they can't get even worse. There is no logic and no equilibrium. History and the political situation directly affect private life.

The alcohol, the alcohol.

Wednesday, September 26
Last night with Miguel Briante until early in the morning. I went to his literary workshop and read a chapter from the novel. Then we went around to all the bars in the city. A question from Miguel, very wise: "Why do you live shut up inside, if you aren't writing anyway?"

Wednesday, October 3
How did I get here? It was always the same thing, and what melts is the exception. Now that not even delusions are left, what must a man do to kill himself? I think: a window, etc. I think I'll hold out until I turn forty.

Thursday, October 18
I'm going to kill myself. I only have to decide the way and the date, he said. He was in the bar and appeared content; the things he was saying didn't seem to be spoken by him. Then he added, smiling: as of now, I can think that I've lived with better luck than I could have hoped for. What is to come will not bring my ruin. He finished the glass of whiskey and ordered another with a gesture, passing a hand over his neck as though slitting his throat, but the waiter understood what he was asking for and brought him another whiskey. I should put it like this: I hope to have no fear and be able to do what I've decided to. I need a high window and enough courage to not think for an instant; he stared out through the window. It's a beautiful afternoon, he said. I have no future now, not a single hope. I no longer can nor want to live like this. The issue, then, is to make up my mind and to act. It will be a way to end with dignity. What can I do between now and that moment? He looked at the waiter who was moving away with the bottle of whiskey, as though expecting him to respond. I've decided to kill myself for various reasons that I prefer not to explain. We all have good reasons

for killing ourselves, he continued, euphoric. For my part, the reasons are several, but basically I am very tired. It's clear that I can no longer establish fluid relationships with the world and grow ever more alone and isolated. The waiter had returned to the table and was listening to him with a preoccupied air, supporting his tray on one hand. It's clear that nothing interests me anymore and that I lack faith in my own projects. Now I only have to find the courage to kill myself. The bar was empty at that hour, but an older woman, sitting at a nearby table, was listening to what he was saying with some interest. He looked over at her and said: the key will be to decide on a date and not postpone it, don't you think so, *señora*? he asked her, smiling toward the neighboring table. The only issue is jumping from the window, that seems difficult, but it's essential to choose a place high enough to ensure that I won't end up only crippled. I've been thinking, he said, about going to that place, opening the window, hanging my legs over the other side, and casting myself into the void. He lifted the glass of whiskey and saluted the woman with a gesture, as though toasting with her. Can I do it? What do you think? If I can't, the decline will be complete. I have to think of a way that's infallible, *señora mía*.

Tuesday, October 30
Beatriz brings the articles for *Punto de Vista*. We talk about the magazine and the future. We're getting what we had imagined. Beatriz ran into Luis G. on the bus, and he made a comment to her, scornfully, that it doesn't make sense to publish "those magazines." (Because he writes at the newspaper taken over by the military.)

Monday, November 5
I'm working on Kantian morality. "The moral man knows that the most valuable of his possessions is not life but the preservation of his own dignity."

Decided. Maybe in twenty days, birthday, etc. The only problem is how. And if he couldn't bring himself to do it? He was thinking of giving some meaning to what he planned to do, for example a suicidal attack on the military officers who come once a month and gather in the Congress. He saw them from his window. He could dedicate himself to preparing one act, for example using a high-precision weapon from there (talk to someone from the armed groups).

Tuesday 13

"Once again the idea of suicide," he wrote. "There's no way out, for a variety of simultaneous reasons. I speak and am someone else, distanced from myself, someone annotating the things I write. A feeling of being split into two."

Wednesday 14

Waiting is hell and has the structure of paranoia, everything fills with signs, reality doesn't help me, sometimes I think that all of the people I pass in the city are potential assassins. Bad thoughts prevent me from thinking clearly. Pure waiting: I hear the elevator and think they are coming for me. It seems unbearable to me, the idea that everything has gone astray. Or will there be a delay? I can't see any reason. I lean out of the window, look at Plaza del Congreso, there are pigeons, men and women walking slowly.

Thursday 15

Last night I dreamed a kind of perfect solution for the book: I saw a man and heard his voice. A little while ago I transcribed what he said to me or what I remembered, an almost elegiac tone.

Now he knows why, to what are owed his intentions to end things once and for all. We will see how all of that came about, why he sees in it an example of the inner linings of his heart. Death announces itself. The following day he thinks he must choose a date. All week he does nothing but wait, not knowing what for. Last night he had a dream in which he was talking with someone and awoke with a feeling of being set free.

He weighs sixty-four kilos.

Monday 19
I suspend all of my classes, leave the week open until next Monday. I isolate myself here, determined to resume the novel and find the tone I heard in the dream.

Saturday 24
I start to understand that the novel must develop based on Maggi's correspondence with the narrator. Marcelo asks him to take charge of the archive.

Thursday 29
The dream helped me to define the character of old Lafuente. He is the one who has given his ancestor's documents to Maggi. He is, in addition, the father of Esperancita, Marcelo's ex-wife.

Tuesday 4
I work on the chapter of the narrator's meeting with old Lafuente. There, they talk about Enrique Lafuente, and another version of Maggi's past appears. But now, what is the key to this chapter? Enrique Lafuente, who must come into the novel in this way. Putting together Maggi's letter, in which the story will expand.

Friday 23
Last class with the groups. I don't know how I managed to write a novel without a plot, or how I managed to live without the money necessary. These practical questions have taken me out of, or rather, rescued me from, the ideas of suicide, which form a confusing conglomerate of real and imaginary situations. Between two worlds, equally near and distant: my meetings with Elías and Rubén, victims of the dictatorship, and a novel written on a desert island.

6

Diary 1980

Tuesday, January 1
I'm doing everything in my power to finish this novel. For the first time
I can say that Chapter I has started working.

Thursday 3
I worked very well today and finished a draft of the first chapter, more
than twenty pages, which I'll have to revise.

Saturday 5
Satisfied with the chapter, a hellish effort for me that I'd already
attempted to write a year before.

Chapter II. It will be the censor. Maybe one more letter can be added in
order to broaden the panorama of Argentina in 1976. Also a letter from
the narrator, maybe a letter from Maggi, and a file card from Lafuente.
Apart from that, I edited the letter from the adolescent.

Monday 7
Today I worked on the chapter with the censor, now determined to
get into Chapter III, which will be one of the keys to the novel. Old
Lafuente's monologue. I hope to write it in less than a month.

I managed to write it in six hours, almost in one sitting. Seven pages of monologue from old Lafuente, who will come to be called the Senator. In spite of the heat, the style and tone are quite good. I'm going to leave things as they are now.

Tuesday 8
Advancing slowly. I'll have to write twenty pages, because the trip must be the ending. I'll make it to eighty pages within a month. In that case I'd be able to dedicate myself to the archive. What I have left is the following:

1. Expand Maggi's reflections on Lafuente, and perhaps include some other references from Maggi's correspondence. Expand the final letter.
2. Change the beginning of the third chapter. Possibly include one more letter. Expand the nucleus of the Maggi–narrator relationship, monitored by the censor. Another letter from the narrator. Half of a letter from Maggi. Maybe a letter from someone else to Maggi. Police report about Maggi.
3. Carry the Senator's monologue as far as possible, at least twenty pages.
4. Rewrite the story that he presents to the Pole. Expand the conversation, which *lasts all night*. At the end, pass on the story to the narrator; in the early morning there's an hour left before the train departs. A prisoner approaches, spoken account. The narrator gets on the train, begins to read the file.
5. File. Beginning with the texts from Lafuente. Later they include the interpretations and biographical account, written by Maggi. Maggi's personal notes at the end. In Chapter IV the account must be rewritten in first person: Tardewski narrates something of his life. Expand the final dialogue.

Work plan.

1. The Senator.
2. Censor.
3. Tardewski.
4. Maggi–Renzi.
5. Make a clean copy of everything.

If things progress well, I'll be able to finish the first part before I travel. And the archive will require one month more. Therefore, I have to put in the effort and write that part in January.

Wednesday 9
Okay, in ten uninterrupted hours of work and in thirty-eight-degree heat, sitting at the typewriter from eight in the morning until six in the evening, I wrote twenty pages of Chapter II.

Friday 11
Over three days I've written nearly forty pages of Chapter II, completing it. I haven't reread what emerged, but I have my hopes. Then the chapter with the Pole is still left to be written.

Saturday 19
We'll see what to do with Chapter IV, which closes the novel before the archive. The Pole and the narrator, a dialogue that lasts all night. The speaker is initially Tardewski, then comes the dialogue, the account passes on to the narrator, who is also the one who concludes it (this chapter has a resemblance to *Ulysses*: Bloom, Dedalus).

Wednesday 23
In a sense, I can say that I just finished the third part of the novel. Chapter IV occupies almost seventy pages, which I wrote in three days and will start to clean up tomorrow.

I've managed, then, to write one hundred fifty pages in a month and a half of work. Chapter IV goes from pages 78 to 164. I can't believe it myself.

Friday 25
An argument last night with Iris, who read what I've written for the main part of the chapter, about the woman who writes beautifully but is very ugly, as if it were a personal reference. Marconi is in fact distantly inspired by Osvaldo Lamborghini.

Monday 28
On Sunday night I dreamed a poem, which I then included in the novel. The tightrope walker treading slowly on a string of barbed wire.

Tuesday
I edit and make a clean copy up to page 127 of the first draft, and so the chapter makes it to page 146.

I decide, then, to divide the novel in this way:

> First Part. *If I Were the Dark Winter*. Chapters I to III, eighty pages.
> Second Part. *What we cannot speak about we must pass over in silence*. Chapter IV, close to one hundred pages.

Friday, February 1
I finished the novel. It reached page 210. Yesterday I solved the structure of the final chapter. I close with Kafka–Hitler.

Saturday 2
So, can it be possible? The most intimate of dreams. To write a novel in two months. After resolving Chapter I, I wrote at an incredible speed, two hundred pages in less than forty days. A decision not to include the file as an appendix. Too easy. Better to use this month to

expand, edit, and clean up the text as it is. Lafuente must be as elusive as Maggi.

Can this novel be published in Argentina?

I will, however, say the following: what happened over these past weeks is what I always dreamed must happen in my life. To write a novel that I'm really satisfied with.

The text, then, will come out like this:

> *The Prolixity of the Real*
>> First Part. If I Were the Dark Winter
>>> 1. Maggi–narrator
>>> 2. Censor
>>> 3. Senator
>> Second Part. What we cannot speak about we must pass over in silence.
>>> 4. The Pole

At the end, on the last page, I will write: Buenos Aires, 1976–1980.

I'll go on my trip with the book complete. What more could I ask for?

When I was turning over the idea of killing myself, he said, and after several days of useless preparations and planning, I gave up on it and thought: "Well, now I'll have to see what things I live through, beginning at the moment when, theoretically, I should have been dead." In that way, I'll be able to see if it made sense to keep going, don't you think so, *señorita*?

The novel is sixty thousand words.

Monday, February 25
A variety of avatars, intense correction of Chapter III with Lafuente, who takes the place of the censor. Then the final task of revising and

copying the draft, which I'll finish cleaning up today. Then reality begins. Will I be able to publish it? I just called Pezzoni with the idea of bringing him the novel tomorrow.

Tuesday 26
I leave the novel with Pezzoni at Sudamericana. I make photocopies of the original and give Carlos Altamirano a copy to read.

Wednesday 27
I also bring the novel to Pomaire, where Oscar Molina offers me an advance of three thousand dollars, to publish fifteen thousand copies. Obviously he hasn't yet read this mixture of political allusions and discursive accounts.

In any event, I can go to Mexico and, if it doesn't get published here, release it with Siglo XXI.

I just reread the essay "Notes on *Facundo*" that I wrote for the Centro Editor, which was rejected. I'll publish it in *Punto de Vista*, and the honorable public will judge it.

Tuesday, March 4
Novel read by Carlos and Beatriz, Andrés Rivera. Praise, relief.

Thursday 6
Last night Pezzoni called, excessive praise. "The best novel since *Hopscotch.*"

Saturday 8
A call from Pomaire. We'll see. I ask them for an advance of five thousand dollars.

Good readings from Andrés and Gusmán. Everyone tells me it's the most important novel in recent years, etc.

Tuesday, March 11
Pezzoni continues with his praise and spreads propaganda for the novel all around the city. He will publish it this year. We can sign the contract on Thursday.

On March 15 I'm leaving for Mexico, New York, Mexico. I return on May 15.

Monday, May 19
Last night a slow walk along Corrientes, as if I were one of my exiled friends returning home. I look at the city through their eyes. The streets seem too dark to me. I seem like a newly arrived tourist. I haven't called anyone yet. Now I'm waiting to resolve the matter of the courses and the publication of the novel.

I talk with Pomaire; they offer me four thousand dollars, I ask for five. Molina, the publisher, tells me on the phone that it's the best novel he's read in years.

Tuesday 20
I reenter circulation. I visit Gusmán at his new bookshop, I call Andrés. I go to the office on Bartolomé Mitre; the window still opens over Plaza Congreso, which no longer seems the same. The groups are working. Contemporary philosophy with the analysts. Reading Brecht's prose with the Saturday group.

Thursday 22
I spend all day reading Brecht. Iris is still away. The solitude is like a journey. I can't change the style of these notebooks.

I'm at La Ópera bar and a woman comes up; she's bought *Assumed Name*. You're the author?, etc.

Subject. A man whose phone isn't working. He waits pointlessly for a call. He spends all day waiting.

At Pomaire they offer me a five-thousand-dollar advance and publication in December. So I'm going to accept.

Saturday, May 24
After the novel comes out with Pomaire, I'm going to propose that I oversee a collection of Argentine novels for them. Now I'm working on preparing the courses.

1. Contemporary philosophy with the psychoanalysts (Husserl, Heidegger, Wittgenstein). Before that, we'll look at what we discussed last year (up to Hegel) and find the transition via Nietzsche.
2. Brecht, study of literature, diaries, *Me-Ti*.

Wednesday 28
A letter from Iris. She has an intelligence as clear as crystal (and she doesn't realize it?). Since Sunday I've been trying to reach her on the phone, with no success.

I sort things out with Pomaire. They'll pay me two thousand dollars now and three thousand in September.

Saturday 31
In a sense, I'm reading the novel for the last time. I try to improve it, but there's nothing to be done now, only wait. Enrique Lafuente became Enrique Osorio. The Senator is Eugenio Osorio. The title isn't convincing to me. (I don't want to use a poem by Borges.) Possibilities: *Marcelo Maggi*. Another option: *Letters from Hereafter*.

Sunday, June 1
A subject. Airport. A woman says goodbye, crosses the hallway, and her boarding pass (or ticket) slips out. The man selling coffee at the bar observes the situation but doesn't warn her. After a while, one of the airport employees picks up the ticket. The woman is unable to travel.

The experience of teaching in the United States. He falls in love with a woman, a colleague, she doesn't speak Spanish. Transcribing the classes. An interview with Tillie Orsen?

I get dinner with Anita Barrenechea. She's staying for a week; she's in her manic, entertaining phase.

Monday 2
I teach the class on Husserl. After I leave, I stop to see Luis. I get the apartment wrong, call him on the phone. A total inability to participate in a social conversation. Great efforts. More and more confined within my own solitude. I have dinner alone at the restaurant on Córdoba and Ayacucho. I read Nietzsche's letters.

Thursday 5
The novel is going to be called *Artificial Respiration*. I find the epigraph for the novel in an Eliot poem that I almost know from memory, back from the days in La Plata. "We had the experience but missed the meaning . . ." etc.

How else could someone survive in these cheerless times?

Friday, June 6
So, I signed the contract with Pomaire today. Then I stopped to see Luis Gusmán. I bought shoes. I'll go and see Wenders's film *The Goalie's Anxiety at the Penalty Kick*, based on the Peter Handke novel.

For what's left of the year I'll be occupied with the courses. I'm working on the project of a novel about Alberdi, *The Last Days of J. B. A.*

Subjects. Write a story that consists of the indecision of a travel book by an outsider in Buenos Aires. He arrives, alienation. He describes everything as though seeing it for the first time. He doesn't speak Spanish. He meets a woman who doesn't speak English. He has a constant feeling of danger.

Write a book that consists in the adventure of reading my own diary. An anonymous narrator. He is investigating the causes of failure (or suicide).

Write a short story with the imaginary biography of Madame Bovary's daughter. Working in a textile factory.

Write a story based on my stay in the United States. At the beginning, the narrator is abandoned by his wife and decides not to return to Argentina. A woman who reminds him of another woman. He falls in love, etc.

Sunday 8
I'm perceiving a certain racism in Buenos Aires, and also, in some people, a defense of Martínez de Hoz. Minds invaded by television, which indicates what must be talked about: color TV. Heart transplants. Maradona's pass. No one reads the paper, but they all present themselves as very well informed. The journalists occupy the stage and have become the intellectual authorities of the moment.

For my part, I'm realizing some of my most intimate desires, which have been with me for more than twenty years. The novel has realized them and, in that sense, completes a cycle that began in 1957.

I want to buy: a rug, a floor lamp, another pair of glasses.

Sometimes I try to imagine the novel already published, the object itself.

Tuesday 10
I have two two-hour classes every Tuesday and two two-hour classes every Thursday; I'll have to live alone for three months in the middle of the desert.

To cheer myself up when thinking about the essays I want to write, I have to remember Michel Butor and Bertolt Brecht. A "subsidiary" work, for which I must find the form.

The death of J. B. A. The last will and testament, he is delirious before death and bequeaths things he doesn't have to friends already dead.

Wednesday 11
I live in a strange way, working, teaching classes, talking on the phone, going to the theater, visiting friends or being visited by them. Everything should be united or linked by my writing. Very particular conditions. Unreality. How can it be that I survive?

Thursday 12
I come out of a meeting with the design department at Pomaire, where we discussed the cover for the novel. We aren't in agreement.

I wire three hundred francs to Silvia Coppola for three months' rent.

Sunday 15
Yesterday a meeting with my Saturday group. Localizations in the novel, the autobiographical prose of Cambaceres.

Under what circumstance can I be certain that the thing thought of is real? The reality of the thing depends on the same circumstances as the truth of the proposition (that designates it), Husserl.

Dinner last night with Carlos and Beatriz. Conversations about the future of the magazine (auspicious), the alliances are growing; the intellectuals have started to come out of their caves and approach us.

Tuesday
Wide-ranging distress. Realities of my tendency toward indiscriminate entanglements. I tend toward fluid positions, pointlessly seeking

unlikely affirmations. This is a period I will return to many times in the future.

My current position in Argentine literature is minor or secondary. I like this place, on the margins. Behind, for the moment, Asís, Medina, Lastra, Rabanal. We'll see what happens after the novel is published.

This year, in what's left of this year, I'll work like this:

> Sunday/Monday: philosophy course for psychoanalysts.
> Tuesday/Wednesday: course on Brecht.
> Friday/Saturday: Cambaceres and the origins of the novel.
> For all of that, I'll earn three hundred million pesos per month (fifteen hundred dollars).

Tuesday 24
I get to my office at nine and sit down to work (without first reading the newspapers that I buy on the way here, *La Nación* and *La Prensa*). I work until one. At ten thirty I make tea and start smoking. After four hours' work, I go out to buy food at the restaurant downstairs or cook myself something for lunch. I read the newspapers and sleep until three. Then I try to keep working until seven.

I'm analyzing Brecht's narrative writings. Two directions. Some are rewritings of certain famous lives (Socrates, Julius Caesar, Bacon, G. Bruno), to which Brecht adds his individual viewpoint, selecting certain situations from those biographies. On the other hand, there's his "Confucian" prose, constructed as apologues, parables, or proverbs (*Me-Ti, Keuner*).

I stop by the publishing house to see the cover design for the book. I like it. As always, there's no landscape for me but the vision of the city. *Artificial Respiration*: I've dreamed of seeing a cover like this since 1970.

Wednesday 25
Working on Brecht, I read the notes from Benjamin's diary. Could I write a story consisting of the narrator's diary during the days he spends in someone's house? But whose? Astrada's? The character is Argentine and lives in Buenos Aires. He wants to write his memoirs and hires the narrator, who for his part is writing a diary.

Anita Barrenechea and Enrique Pezzoni talk to Iris about the novel; "excessive" praise. Pezzoni says he should have turned in his resignation at Sudamericana to make them publish it. "But five thousand dollars, they don't even pay Mujica Láinez that much."

At Pomaire, I try to get tickets to go to Venezuela and Mexico to launch the novel; everything depends on how the book does in the first three months.

This month I saved one thousand dollars, spent five hundred on rent, and gave four hundred for debts (from the magazine) to Beatriz Sarlo.

The novel was a stroke of luck; I wrote it in a few short months, they paid me five thousand dollars, I'll be able to publish it in Buenos Aires in spite the odds, and it will be published three months after submission.

Saturday
"I was unable to enter into the usual relations of life and I therefore concluded that my task was extraordinary," S. Kierkegaard. That quotation as a way to summarize my impressions from last night's meeting, a multitude, to inaugurate Gusmán's bookshop. The usual circus of erudition: Briante, Di Paola, O'Donnell, Gregorich, Lafforgue. I myself recognize that I am only able to live on my own.

Dream. Someone says to me: "You're exactly the same as your father" (physically). "He looks like your double." Another says: "But he (referring to my father) has a ruddy face."

A dream. My grandfather married Regina Olsen when Kierkegaard left her.

I prepare for the classes and await the moment when I can read my published novel.

I have to write the jacket copy and come up with a line for the back cover of my book. Mission impossible.

In the manner of Stendhal, I will note here my three desires:

1. That my novel will be a success.
2. That they hire me at Princeton.
3. That I can live alone.

Friday
A strange sorrow, hard to identify. External demands are weighing me down. Apart from that, uncertainty about having the novel published in these politically sinister times. It is a response to and a description of the state of things: at heart, it's a book about exile and failure, by which many of us are defined. Beyond a certain emptiness that I know in myself, I've never been able to celebrate my accomplishments, not even during this period, one I will recall with nostalgia in a few years' time.

The philosophical trajectory of my course with the psychoanalysts comes to this: Kierkegaard, Nietzsche, Heidegger, Sartre. Wittgenstein. In reality, it's a course about fiction and personal truth.

Monday, July 7
Insomnia. A variety of sorrows. Domestic matters, monotony, too much pressure from obligations. An empty life. I can only forget about all of that if I'm free, that is, under conditions so exceptional that they allow me to "occupy" time without any external pressure or obligations.

Thursday
At Pomaire, I receive two thousand dollars (four hundred seventy thousand pesos). I pay back the amount I owe and manage to put away fifteen hundred dollars.

Monday 14
A speech by Martínez de Hoz, which can be analyzed.

1. Exchange rate control. The dollar very low, 50% below its value.
2. Growth rate, the lowest since 1950.
3. High inflation. Retail: 5.2% in June. Wholesale: 71.3%.
4. Treasury deficit; over five months in 1980 it dropped 50% more than in all of 1979. Attempts being made to contain the loss of reserves that the Banco Central is suffering due to the very low dollar and possible devaluation.
5. Duplication of debt. Very short-term borrowing. The international bank benefits, having a direct connection with the regime.
6. Deepening of economic openness, and in particular the capital market, which is now deeply linked to the international financial market.

July 17
A theoretical autobiography. The history of one man's thoughts, of his annotated readings. A model life.

The novel narrates the history of those who have no history.

A long argument with Iris. Where should readings begin? With the text or with the world? How to read without prior knowledge?

Friday 18
A debate with Beatriz Sarlo and Altamirano about *Punto de Vista*. I don't agree to join the editorial board. Why? Differences in our

conceptions of literature. I feel no guarantee of its quality. A judgment that I don't make explicit. Instead, I said I didn't want to appear there because of differences that, nevertheless, needn't prevent us from working together.

Saturday 19
Perhaps growing old, for me, doesn't mean thinking more and more about the future? A strange inversion: the past is condensed into a long series of coincidences, something that's not advisable to consider as a logic for the future.

In the last few days I've been reading in succession: a book on Nietzsche by Deleuze, *Stories of Mr. Keuner* by B. Brecht, essays by Lukács that are contemporaneous with his *Theory of the Novel*, and a work on populism by Laclau. When I'm writing fiction, I read less literature, or rather, each time I write I move further away from "literature," and yet, nevertheless, my life is scanned ("programmed") by literary writing. Brecht's stories are perfect: Confucian parables in which the protagonist is a wise man whose only action is good thinking.

I wait for *Artificial Respiration* to be published, I mean, these days are nothing more than a preparation (though I don't quite know what for). What will happen afterward? I'll have to write another book.

Sunday 20
A spontaneous tendency toward isolation as a means of producing a sense of loss (a feeling that has always been at the root of my literature, since my most distant youth).

The sophist Hippias confronted Socrates with a marvelous question: "Who is the essence of the being?" The question *who* is the greatest of all questions, he said, the most apt in determining the meaning of the world (the meaning for whom?). Asking "who is right" and not "what is right" was, then, the result of an elaborate method that entailed a conception of the subject and an entire sophist art in opposition to Socratic maieutics. An art of concrete cases, empirical and plural, said Tardewski.

For years I've practiced a sophisticated intellectual activity that consisted of not thinking and not knowing. It has to do with a system of thought that I've started to envisage as being tragic, one that develops in spite of me, or rather, in spite of the "objective" situation. Removing ideas from circulation takes me three hours: otherwise, all will lead to evil.

If I think about the prior stages of my life, I can see a "social" period from 1963 to 1975, during which I circulated in a variety of places and had many responsibilities (magazines, newspapers, publishing houses, discussions, roundtables, public speeches), and then there came a phase of confinement associated with the political situation, and finally, in recent times, the moral obligations once again (*Punto de Vista*, meetings and discussions in the catacombs). In a sense, the novel I've written synthesizes all of these moments.

Monday 21
A meeting of writers convened by Pacho O'Donnell at his house. Everyone or almost everyone attends (myself included). What am I doing there? Rebuilding what isn't there. A degraded debate, in the tone of the times. The loneliness of the long-distance runner. The allies are somewhere else, in exile. I suggest including the matter of the disappeared in a letter with our signatures. I dispute the issue of the schism that Gregorich suggested a while ago, saying that the Argentine writers in exile would lose their language. Impossible to go anywhere with these people.

A long conversation with Andrés about Bloch's *Principle of Hope* and utopia.

I'm reading Hermann Broch. Isn't there a kind of difficulty that I can't resolve myself to face? Inventing a kind of story that progresses toward abstraction.

Stories. She is like a place that can never be reached. He is there. A strange temptation. He sees her around the city. A nubile woman walks past, looks at him, smiles, etc. The little courtesan was nothing like that. A woman seeks a man with the same name as her husband so as not to make a mistake. She says: I looked for him because he was the same as the one who died.

Crossing paths with Onetti. Jorge's wife gave him *Artificial Respiration*; he read your novel, Dolly tells me, he liked the Senator and Tardewski very much.

Tuesday 22
A certain "idea" once again: I don't want to write a book of criticism, I want to write a book in which conversations, notes, readings circulate. The book of a writer with certain ideas; really, the best thing would be to write a book that would take on the form of a theoretical diary. In order to prevent this from becoming only a project, it would be a good idea to apply a bit of order into the strategy of my essayistic writings, thus far always incidental and direct. Seeking an avant-garde reading and a writing that would forever remain a personal experiment.

I sit down to work on Brecht's *Me-Ti* at eight in the morning. The act in itself doesn't matter as much as the (rather childish) satisfaction of recording it here.

It's striking to see the novelistic effect caused by reconstructing certain chains that occur in "life." For example, the death of Roland Barthes. Susan Sontag tells of how Barthes, in New York, confessed to her his desire to write a novel. That, he said, would mean abandoning teaching, and in the end he never worked up the nerve to do it because he feared poverty. A while later, as he is leaving after teaching class at the Collège de France, a van hits him. And so, if he had abandoned teaching in order to write a novel (amid poverty), he wouldn't have died.

Maybe one part (the third part) of the essay could be a diary of thinking, which might combine still unthought ideas, or ideas on the point of being thought, or ideas that can only be thought in writing.

A day in the life. I wake up at seven thirty and have two cups of black coffee with two pieces of toast. I look at the headlines in the newspapers. I take the bus that follows Callao and get off at Bartolomé Mitre. I buy a pack of cigarettes and another two newspapers. At nine I sit down to work and stop working at one. I have lunch, read the papers, lie down to sleep a while for siesta. Around two thirty I make tea (I'd already had one in midmorning) and work until six. I walk back home along Callao, and now I do nothing at all until it's time to sleep, apart from eating dinner, drinking wine, passing my gaze over a variety of books without getting to the point of reading them. I go to bed at twelve thirty.

Write the biography of Madame Bovary's daughter as a textile worker. "When everything had been sold, twelve francs seventy-five centimes remained, that served to pay for Mademoiselle Bovary's going to her grandmother. The good woman died the same year; old Rouault was paralyzed, and it was an aunt who took charge of her. She is poor, and sends her to a cotton-factory to earn a living."

Write the biography of Lucia, Joyce's daughter, who died in the fifties inside a psychiatric clinic where she'd lived for twenty years. When Joyce explains to Jung that Lucia wrote just like he did (by that point he was working on *Finnegans Wake*), Jung told him: Yes, but where you swim, she drowns.

This month I finished a ten-class course on Brecht in which I analyzed the following texts: *The Caucasian Chalk Circle*, *The Exception and the*

Rule, Fear and Misery of the Third Reich. The stories "The Heretic's Coat," "Socrates Wounded," and "The Experiment." *The Business Affairs of Mr. Julius Caesar, Stories of Mr. Keuner, Me-Ti: Book of Interventions in the Flow of Things*, and an extensive series of essays and theoretical works.

Wednesday, July 23

I'll say something here for the amusement of future generations: I have a precise certainty that my intelligence functions almost perfectly, I can understand anything I need to, and my ideas proliferate, yet I still haven't found a form in which to write the essays I want to write. This intelligence is private and manifests itself, such as it is, under certain conditions (in solitude, as long as it's one I've been able to choose).

Thursday

I see Héctor Lastra at Gusmán's bookshop. Enrique Pezzoni, he tells me, praised your novel very highly in a meeting with Girri and Pepe Bianco; then he tells me that their conversation that night drifted toward Jorge Asís, whom everyone criticizes for reacting (but, as Iris suggested: "Do we have to accept that whatever the narrator says in first person is direct ideological content, or is the narrator a symptom as well?"), and toward the newspaper *La Nación*, a central concern (this last) for Lastra. His subjective description of the newspaper does not at any point consider that this newspaper consolidates conservative thinking (as much in art as in politics); he tends to explain the issue in terms of personal relationships (enmity, chance encounters, friendships). This notion allows him to perform "cultural politics," just as it is cultural politics that excludes me from those networks.

Monday

I'm slow. It took me a very long time to understand that I can only work in the mornings; after two in the afternoon I get scattered and lose myself amid stupid daydreams and vast conspiracies.

Also, write the biography of Marx's illegitimate son (he had him with the maid), who dies in London in 1924 having lived in obscurity as a textile worker. In turn, Marx's son has a son who comes to Buenos Aires in 1915. I would have to imagine his life.

Tuesday 29
Crossing paths with Onetti, who circles and is summoned like a ghost in recent days. Osvaldo Tcherkaski writes to me from Washington: Onetti read his story collection, one insomniac night in Paris, and then sent him his judgment, part derogatory and part fallacious. On Sunday, at Tortoni, Andrés tells me that Onetti's last book sold fifty thousand copies. Yesterday Dolly Muhr, his wife, called the house: "Juan has insomnia, he writes fragments that he'll never publish. We went to the sea."

Turn non-thought into a form of narration. For example, the struggle to erase certain ideas that seem to conceal threats. The fixed idea returns again and again; it isn't just an idea, for it drags along with it a variety of feelings and memories, as if a single idea could contain chains and webs of ache and affliction. At the same time, an interesting theory on narrative temporality: everything goes well (for the hero) in a particular space, in the pure present, but, for example, is there a way to stop fearing for the future? If I had a subject, I would try to write a story; for me, the methods are always the first part to appear.

I keep going with Brecht, planning to read all of his essays one more time.

Thursday, July 31
It's striking to see the way that Brecht displaces the origins of his theory of alienation: in 1923, he meets the Russian actress and theater director Asja Lācis, and it is she who introduces him to the positions and theories of the Soviet avant-garde (among them the process of *ostranenie*). Being Brechtian, he will say that his discovery of the effect of alienation comes

from 1926, when she, Asja Lācis, is performing in Edward II; she has a Russian accent, and that "produces the alienation effect."

August 1
Last night I dreamed of Perón; he was alive, and I was visiting him and trying to convince him to push Balbín toward a clearer opposition. In the dream I thought: how can they fail to realize the importance of the fact that Perón is alive, as a way to confront the dictatorship? These are my political dreams: the dead turn up alive, and from time to time I find myself with Elías, Rubén, or Rodolfo W.

Monday 4
In an unimportant book, which I look through while looking for material for today's class, I find this excellent—I think—definition of politics today. It asserts that, in face of the ongoing participation of the masses in political and economic life, a model has been designed: "the crises can be solved not by expansion but, on the contrary, by regression. Given that the offer is insufficient, it is asked, instead of contributing so as to increase it, why not contribute so as to decrease the demand? From here, the moral is quite clear: we need to impede the participation of the masses in all sectors in which they are manifested." The book is titled *Introducción a la política* and is more than twenty years old, yet Martínez de Hoz's program can be seen plainly in it all the same. Civil society must first be intimidated (as Portantiero said, "interpreting" the plan) and then it will be possible to impose the model of development and the type of accumulation. That explicit project of "cutting back" and "reducing" society is the refrain of old right-wing politics everywhere. "To distance a population from political life in order to impede it from reclaiming its share of the national income, a method that ends up being unsuitable in countries where the masses have a perfect awareness of their importance and their strength" (which is what is happening in Argentina with the union movement).

Tuesday, August 5
The worst part of life is the prison of insomnia. The ignored pains in my left side, what does it all mean? The novel is on the verge of being published, and yet it continues, passing through the mesh that I myself have woven. Will I need a transformation now as well? There was a metamorphosis in 1963 and in 1972. Is one necessary every ten years? There's something that prevents me from living: it settles me perfectly into the solitude of the month of June, but that is not the way I must get out of this.

Wednesday
At the Picadero theater I see a confusing stage adaptation of *The Seven Madmen*; in spite of everything, the lofty echoes of Arlt resound. On the way in I run into Jorge Asís himself; we get coffee at La Academia and, as always happens to me with "young writers," I sit there for his rounds of autobiography and self-praise. It seems as though he is writing for Buenos Aires and nothing else matters to him (this means he isn't being translated). He runs through the list of his previous books and sinks into political cynicism.

Monday
Private utopia: living without obligations, writing out of obligation (that, for me, is the formula for happiness). Tempted by the allure of the man who lives alone and isolated, I must force myself to socialize all the same.

I'm reading Heidegger. I encounter a relation, which is the following: the Being is not time, the Being is temporalized in the *Dasein* (the being there) and becomes nothingness. Aren't we close to Plato, for whom time is the moving, finite image of Eternity? The Eternity (of the Being) is made visible in time (through the *Dasein*) and dies with it (finitude: nothingness). Was it Wittgenstein who said that all of philosophy was a series of footnotes to Plato's thought? No, it wasn't Wittgenstein.

Tuesday, August 12
At Editorial Pomaire, I receive the remaining twenty-five hundred dollars, completing the advance of five thousand. The novel won't come out in September but in October, a local, accelerated, and reduced edition (three thousand copies).

Wednesday 13
Personal economy. How to manage those five thousand dollars? Basically, by paying rent for the apartment and buying a "uniform" (a blazer, an overcoat) in which I can feel comfortable—in other words very expensive.

Thursday 14
An unexpected appearance from José Sazbón, who comes from the distant past; he's the only friend whose friendship with me has now lasted twenty years. He's as shy as he is lucid, progressing with his stunning theories about English historians. We go out to eat at La Americana, fugazza with cheese and a bottle of wine.

He's the first one to have read *Artificial Respiration*, and if what I write can pass the rigorous customs office of José, it doesn't matter to me what others say. All the same, there are some tensions with him, obsessive over my novel, or slightly pedantic and at the same time passionate about literature. José is too bound to Borges, to his rhetoric, and to fashion as well (for example, history as fiction). He thinks things are novelties that I believed ten years ago.

Friday
I give a lecture on Sarmiento. Afterward, in a bar, a debate about the law of value between Sazbón, Dotti, Carlos Altamirano.

Monday
"I cannot read what I have written—but, surely, we do not require many signs in order to understand each other," letter from Heine to Marx (1844).

At the Premier movie theater, I attend the first tiebreak game of the match between Korchnoi and Polugaevsky; Russian KGB agents watching over Avenida Corrientes. Korchnoi physically resembles Nabokov, but on top of that he has the same ardent and daring intelligence. The game is brutal. Each move is a suicidal attack; Korchnoi wins in the end.

Wednesday
I read a biography of Janis Joplin while listening to her records.

Friday
"I have finished the worst novel in the English language," Virginia Woolf wrote in her diary after finishing *The Waves* . . .

At noon I go to the movies and watch a documentary history of French cinema in the Lugones room; at six in the evening I go to the Libertador theater and watch *The Touch* by Bergman; at nine at night I go to Cosmos with Iris and we watch *Muriel* by Resnais. (Cinema is the poor man's divan, as Deleuze said.)

Saturday 23
At times, my life takes on the pure form of that common dream that Freud defined as the "exam situation."

Monday
I talk with Pomaire; the novel won't come out in October but instead in November.

In any case, I manage to concentrate and prepare for the class on Heidegger that I'm teaching for a group of psychoanalysts tonight. (For the last several months I've been living on philosophy.)

Tuesday 26
Bad thoughts with respect to the novel, the postponing, the incompetence that circulates at Pomaire, where they only know how to pay in dollars.

Wednesday

I'm going to give a lecture—Borges in Argentine literature—for the series that *Punto de Vista* is organizing in homage to Jaime Rest.

Friday

José's reticence regarding the novel is of a wide range: an excess of certain techniques, an absence of characters, an intellectual story. Except for the observation about the characters, which to me seems mistaken (Tardewski, the Senator, Marcelo Maggi), the rest of his objections seem like virtues to me, but his opinion serves to rid me of any illusions as to the book's future. If he thinks like that, I can imagine the reaction from the multitude of idiots who populate Argentine literature today. Expect nothing, then, but rather be happy that the novel has been published in Argentina during these cheerless times.

Wednesday, September 3

"Any kind of polemics fails from the outset to assume the attitude of thinking. The opponent's role is not the thinking role. Thinking is only thinking when it pursues whatever speaks *for* a subject. Everything said here defensively is always intended exclusively to protect the subject," Heidegger.

José Sazbón demonstrates his reticence and his overly punctilious view of my novel for three hours. He critiques the Hitler–Descartes identification and various secondary matters and issues of detail. As if to him the novel seemed at once too experimental and not Borgesian enough.

I visit Grete Stern. We look at her photographs, her collages about dreams.

A letter.

> *The novel will come out in October, maybe November. This anticipation is a bad situation. I'm trying to write an autobiographical*

story about my father but not making any progress. I guess I'll keep struggling to write again until the book has been published. Your letter proves that you've apprehended a certain state that has lately been circling around my life. I'm irritated, discontented, nothing too real, or nothing tied to real events (though I don't know . . .). I think there are ruptures, transformations approaching. It usually happens to me every five or six years, and in general I latch onto something else. There are no motives this time, but the motives don't matter so much. When I was twenty years old, I thought happiness consisted of having written a good book and living in the days prior to its appearance. Now that I am, shall we say, going through something of the kind, I realize that happiness does not depend on the imminence of something already known.

A hug.

P.S My letters are getting shorter and shorter, considering how exciting it is to receive long letters. Don't forget about me.

Friday 5
I will say, with Wittgenstein: "The strange experience of feeling absolutely safe. I mean the state of mind in which one is inclined to say 'I am safe, nothing can injure me whatever happens'" (. . . except for myself).

I'm reading portrayals of Wittgenstein by B. Russell, by Von Wright, by N. Malcolm; Brecht's *Diaries*.

Monday 8
We could imagine that all of humanity has forever spoken the same language, but the language has been different in each era, as if Aramaic, Greek, Latin, Italian, English had been spoken in sequence. Each era would have its own language, which would be universal. Let us now suppose that this language is not fixed: it is necessary to find the word

each time one wants to define an object. That definition may change if someone demonstrates that his or her new expression is better suited to the object. That situation produces a certain chaos. Philosophers construct explanations. Plato, for example, says that the true designations of real objects exist in the Hyperuranion: everything has its corresponding name there. Then someone says that, in fact, God is the only one who knows the correct designation for all things and that faith alone permits access to the true names. For his part, Hegel will say that the Absolute Spirit develops through History in a process of becoming, the illustration of which is the uncertainty of names. On the other hand, scientists decide that in order to avoid uncertainty it is necessary to enumerate all things in existence, and the mathematical nomenclature must then come to be the language. In this way, they forget about common language and invent an artificial and true language. That is all very well, but who speaks it?

A register of my hideaways.

> 1966–1967: Pasaje del Carmen.
> 1968–1971: Sarmiento and Montevideo.
> 1972–1975: Canning and Santa Fe.

> And then here, on Mitre and Montevideo.

Monday 15
Yesterday a social day, a discussion with Pico, Carlos, Beatriz that ended up at Dotti's place, and the whole time I had an absolute feeling of idiocy; I could barely speak because, as I was speaking, I recognized the nonsense of whatever I said, the oversights, mistakes, assertions that weren't my own. What then? A serious crisis, a tendency toward isolation, inaction, I struggle even to read the newspaper.

What fiction could I write if I were able to work setting out from this state?

Wednesday 17
Tomorrow—finally—I'll have proofs of the novel.

Monday, September 22
I use the morning to correct the novel, which is going to the printer today. A violent argument yesterday afternoon with Molina about the book's cover. There's no way to stop the novel from having a debased presentation; on the cover it will advertise that they paid me five thousand dollars.

Facundo. The diversity of the audience explains the heterogeneous quality of the prose (he's writing simultaneously for Europe, for Alsina, for Rosas, and for Chile).

Is there a Borgesian economy? You'd have to consider it in multiple senses. A system of exchanges and evaluations as a key register in his fiction. Money in his stories (for example, "Emma Zunz," "The Zahir"). Literary property.

Tuesday
I work on my Borges lecture in the morning. In the afternoon at Pomaire: a mock-up of the cover design, relatively acceptable now after discussions. I'll try to get them to use a darker shade of red and have only one color. I write out my responses for a profile in a newspaper from Azul. At night, Pacho O'Donnell calls and invites me to a roundtable on new Argentine writers at the Sha along with Asís, Rabanal, Gusmán. I decline, I'd rather not. I go to the movies for a series of French screenings at the San Martín. On the way back, I see Luis at his bookshop, and he tells me about the betrayals of G. and F. I pick up a book by Brassaï: *Conversations with Picasso.*

Wednesday 24
Some disappointment, too, on (finally) seeing the first pages of the book now composed; they'll be enlarged, etc. But so far nothing has

managed to erase the distance between the actual book and the book as I imagined it (issues with the cover, the date, the likely errors in the correction of the galley proofs).

Friday
These days I go to the movie theater often in order to forget reality. Today *The Dirty Dozen* by Robert Aldrich.

At Pomaire, arguments about requirements with respect to my public appearances in promoting the book. Hoping for the book to have "a great reverberation" (according to the words my mother dreamed).

Tuesday 30
I work on my Borges lecture.

I go to Pomaire, where everyone's misgivings about my novel are growing (the title, the price of the book). For my part, I can't get myself to be interested in anything.

I spend five hours playing chess against a computer.

Thursday
Tomorrow the entire completed book will be here (280 pages), and I'll use the weekend to correct the proofs.

I'm advancing in a disorganized way on my Borges lecture. Borges and gaucho literature; Borges's fiction as action in reality (Scharlach, Acevedo Bandeiras, "Emma Zunz," "Theme of the Traitor and the Hero," "Tlön," etc.).

I finally see the typeset pages of the novel and read the Senator's monologue.

Saturday, October 4
A multitude at my lecture (more than 250 people), with several notable appearances, Lafforgue, Nicolás Rosa, Gregorich, Noemí Ulla, etc. A feeling of failure while I expound. Afterward, everyone congratulates me, and it feels like fraud. A horrible experience. I will remember this lecture in ten years, but with nostalgia then.

Monday
I work all morning and finish the page proofs. What do I think of reading the novel? I see only the flaws.

Tuesday
I buy three more notebooks like this one and another seven for the future; five years?

I'm reading Mailer's novel about Gary Gilmore.

Tuesday
An opening for a Juan Pablo Renzi exhibition. I run into Jacoby and Miguel Briante.

Wednesday
Wittgenstein's theory of linguistic games: determinative function of the extraverbal context. The variety of ways in which words acquire their meanings can be seen in the variety of their uses. A strange coincidence, incidentally, between Wittgenstein and Bakhtin: what do we do with words? We must remember Wittgenstein's suggestion that we look not for the things that correspond to words and phrases, but instead for their functions in social life.

Monday 27
Copies of the novel will be here as soon as Wednesday of next week. Under an imaginary canopy of glass, I witness events, undaunted.

Monday, November 3
I spend all weekend preparing my classes on Wittgenstein.

The thing one must remain silent about is ethical experience; the meaning of life can't be expressed with the language of events (that space is occupied by fiction and particularly the novel as a post-tragic genre). We can only name things that happen to other people; our own lived experience, our existence, our sensation of the passage of time are too close for us to view in an external manner (thus the impossibility and fascination of personal diaries like this one); that world constitutes the preferential object of the novel, the narrative coincides with the evocation of those incomparable experiences. They can only be shown—in the sense of Wittgenstein, but also of Henry James— because lived experience is incommunicable. Thus Brecht's premise, to live in third person.

"It is obvious," Wittgenstein wrote in the *Tractatus*, "that an imagined world, however different it may be from the real one, must have something—a form—in common with it."

Positivism maintains (and this is its essence) that the things we are able to talk about are all that matters in life. Whereas Wittgenstein believes ardently that all that really matters in life are the things about which we must keep silent.

Wittgenstein: "My work consists of two parts: of the one which is here, and of everything which I have not written. And precisely this second part is the important one." A good definition for the novel I'm about to publish: in this situation, politics is what cannot be said.

Wednesday
A person for whom Reagan's victory, which confirms the general process of a shift toward the right, has the same impact as the fact that his glasses slide down the bridge of his nose.

There must be no confusion, said Tardewski, between Husserl's coat and Gogol's overcoat; nor between B. Russell's theory of types and Lukács typicality.

Saturday, November 8
Dinner with Beatriz Lavandera. A brilliant career as a linguist in the United States, abandoned after the horrible experience of torture. Absurdly arrested while aimlessly taking photos with a friend around the city and accused of having photographed a secret detention center. She is tortured and sees others die. From that point onward, no more interest in linguistics even though she's one of Chomsky's favorite disciples. She becomes a crusader for human rights, and this action is supported by the activist Chomsky.

Thursday, November 13, 1980
At the publishing house they give me ten copies of the novel. I walk back home along Callao, just as I did in those years when I was writing it.

Friday
I sign copies that will be sent out to a variety of people. Plans for a trip to Misiones next Friday and a release in Buenos Aires on the twenty-seventh. I meet Héctor Lastra, give him a copy of the book, and immediately regret it.

I resist reading the novel, because the errors can no longer be corrected.

Tuesday, December 2
If, as at other times in his life, he has reached the point of sleeping for eighteen hours straight, it is because here, in the middle of this tunnel, he can find no sense in moving forward: he sits, then, in darkness, seeing neither the light of the exit or the light of the entrance.

7

Diary 1981

Monday, January 5
It makes less and less sense to write in this diary, maybe because I make less and less sense myself.

Saturday
Forge a new way out in another direction. The train crossing in the middle of the night. I read Robert Lowell, travel to Adrogué, always escaping in the same direction. Pointless to say that it's been years since I've wanted to go anywhere. Nostalgia in the empty house, walking around naked, talking to myself. Hours going through papers.

Monday, January 12
I persist here; I write the beginning of a story in which someone shuts himself away in a house much like this one to read his own life. We are sinister animals, etc. Maybe I could split my life into two, occupy two places, be someone else in each of them; could have two lives, at least two lives, symmetrical, concentric, coming and going, back and forth, always on the train at six in the evening.

On the street, whenever I go out to buy meat or wine, I always run into people whom I vaguely know yet can't quite identify. In their turn, they've known me since I was a boy and greet me effusively, smiling, as in a dream.

Wednesday, January 14
Tristana comes and goes. She undresses when she gets off the train, then she puts on her garters and stockings. She carries them in her purse the way someone might carry a souvenir. That part excites her more than anything; I travel to disguise myself, she tells me. In my turn, I watch her sitting in the wicker chair that belonged to my grandfather Emilio.

I talk on the phone, write letters; I'm going back tomorrow. Living like a traveler, a person always arriving at places for the first time, knowing no one there.

Thursday, January 15
How to write immediacy, to translate the experience of the present. Improvisation in music, for example, everything occurring in real time. A standard tune exists, a prior melody upon which the harmony of the instant is woven.

Inspiration. Inspiration is like respiration. It has to do with immediate thinking, separated from mediate thought, which is discursive (by means of language). Inspired knowledge: coming to know by seeing. It has a peculiar quality: it is apprehending the object immediately (the way vision works). It isn't an inference but rather an immediate vision.

Experience. It splits off from what is lived. Man would be the being for which truth appears in the present moment. "There is nothing entirely in our power," he said, "except our thoughts. Kept safe."

Monday, January 19
Remnants and memories without form: voices coming from the past. A second night without sleeping; sitting on the floor, I watch as the same shades as ever pass by: the girl lying stretched on velvet pillows caresses her breasts. Interested? she asked me. No, I tell her, I already imagined everything in advance.

On Saturday we went to the boxing match, and in Luna Park I thought about Madison Square Garden: the harsh report of leather gloves on skin.

In the two years that I've been here so far, what have I seen? Or rather, what can I remember? A sheepdog pacing on a tiny balcony, back and forth, back and forth. Once, I saw a man talking on the phone under a lamp that cast a strange blue light. Once, I saw a woman cutting her toenails while leaning against a windowsill on the tenth floor. Once, I saw a TV playing in an empty room, and it took me a while to realize that there was someone watching, stretched out on the floor. Once, I saw two women smoking brown cigarettes and playing cards; it looked like a simple game, only using a few cards.

Wednesday, January 21
I'm the kind of person who conceives of his style in this way: Here is what I am, I tell B., my bones fleshless, dry, as if abandoned for years under the elements. The skeleton of passions.

Thursday, January 22
I went there once again. The entryway, the patio, that ever surprising whiteness. I'm going to see what I can imagine: one nestles her head between the thighs of the other, who bites her lower lip ever so slightly. When I leave, three hours later, the city seems too brightly lit. For such tender lovers so enthralled . . .

Saturday, January 24
I'm working on two texts, the biography of Madame Bovary's daughter; that night, lost in New York.

I dream about her; I'm dreaming about her every night. A strange form of possession.

Tuesday, January 27

Just now I remember crossing paths with John Barth in Berkeley. A conversation in which I tend to remember what I said to him and not what Barth said to me. We talked about Borges and Joyce. I said: *Ulysses* shows the temporal form of the avant-garde; every hour of the day is related using a different technique. I also said something about style, something along these lines: In terms of style, a writer only has style inasmuch as he has conviction of having a style, no more. I recalled this conversation because I was going through some papers and found a kind of summary that I'd made at a restaurant in San Francisco some time later.

Thursday, January 29

The writer as critic. Criticism has not assimilated the work of writers (especially from the nineteenth century onward).

Literary criticism is bound to external knowledge (for that reason it ages). Criticism as suppressed knowledge: linguistics, psychoanalysis, sociology.

An unexplored territory (in the well-worn field of literary investigation): writers' contributions to theory and their reflections on literature. Writers have nothing to say about their own work but a great deal to say about literature.

My list is extensive: Pound, Brecht, Borges, Valéry, Gombrowicz, Auden, Eliot, Calvino, Pasolini. I've already quoted the line from Faulkner: "With *The Sound and the Fury* I learned to read." Writing changes one's way of reading.

What category of reading is this?

A form of intervention. The variety of intervention defines the form.

Often it is personal (diaries, notebooks, lectures, prologues). Often it is pedagogical: Nabokov's classes, Valéry's course in poetics, Pound's guides. Often it is polemical: discussions, manifestos, debates, letters. Often it is present in fictional texts: we need look no further than *Don Quixote*—we could devote a lecture to the analysis of that novel alone.

Characteristics: technical reading (constructivist, as Pound calls it). Fictional reading. Strategic reading.

1. Construction/interpretation. How it has been made, before what it means.

    Poe: "The Philosophy of Composition."

    Valéry: The Chair of Poetics.

    Henry James: considered to be the finest literary critic of the nineteenth century by Wellek and described by Kermode as: "The great master of investigation into the formal possibilities of narrative fiction" (*The Genesis of Secrecy*).

    Forster: *Aspects of the Novel*, contemporary with Lukács's *Theory of the Novel*, Bakhtin's book on Dostoevsky, Benjamin's essays on narrative, and Shklovsky's *Theory of Prose*.

2. Fictional reading.

    Imaginary history of literature. *El mal metafísico/Mad Toy*/"The Aleph"/"Marta Riquelme"/*Los ídolos*/Cortázar's "Footsteps in the Footprints"/"Shadows on Jeweled Glass"/*The Buenos Aires Affair*/*Aventuras de un novelista atonal*.

    Histories of the imaginary writer. Monsieur Teste, non-empirical literature. The conceptual writer. Stephen Dedalus.

    Henry James's *nouvelles* about writers.

3. Strategic. Situated reading. Reading from a position within and not from above.

    Its determinations. Family novel.

    Strategy of reading: even in his first known critical text, on *Don Quixote* ("Don Quijote Today"), in 1935, Gombrowicz defines his poetics of reading. That initial work contains everything of the future, all of his poetics.

He reads based on what he wants to write. His review of *Don Quixote* defines his future work. To each writer his world, to each world its language. "To create a language is to create a world," L. W.

"Here is a book that, even today, expresses an idea of a present for us that is at once stunning and threatening, namely that each man possesses his own, distinct reality, and that the universe is refracted in the spirit of each of us in a different way. To express this idea is the essential task of literature. To represent the millions of worlds known by millions of minds, to express that 'something else' that transforms either windmills into geniuses, or geniuses into windmills," W. Gombrowicz, *Varia* (trans. Allan Kosko), Paris, Christian Bourgois, 1978, pg. 11.

Friday, January 30
Only out of love for the desperate do we maintain hope, said W. B.

Wednesday, February 4
K. Gödel's hypothesis. It's impossible to demonstrate that a logical system is non-contradictory using only the means offered by the system itself. Mathematics is a series of infinite systems, logically distinct from one another, each of which contains a problem for which it offers no solution.

Thursday, February 5
I wake up at eight. Drink two cups of black coffee. Read the newspapers. Write letters. I recognize the sign of death each time I look at myself in the mirror. I need to get out of here. To move, to be in motion. Back and forth, back and forth.

Friday, February 6
The experience of living within occupied territory. The right to violence. That ethics, is it possible?

According to Kant, there is no aim, however lofty it may be, for which it may be said that all rational beings, in all moments of their laboring, must undertake and accomplish it. Every aim turns out worthy of being desired only under certain circumstances, whether it is a conditional obligation, a relative need, or a de facto situation that may or may not be. Morality does not order what must be desired but rather how what is desired must be desired. Not the content but the form.

Saturday, February 7
Early morning, sitting on a bench in Plaza San Martín. He's been up all night talking and his eyes are empty. They start up again. "Only utopia permits thought"; that's the direction he's moving in. Otherwise, what is left? Resignation, skepticism.

Friday, February 8
Working in such a way that the situation cannot be identified. There's never a real moment (as least as a way out): a narrator lost in time and language. There's no piece of information ensuring that, in that moment, he isn't buried in the past as well. I've done the same thing for years.

I spend a week in Buenos Aires with little to do. A narrative situation. Interviews in which I respond mechanically.

Wednesday 11
The notion of the destructive character in Benjamin: "The destructive character sees nothing permanent. But for this very reason he sees ways everywhere . . . What exists he reduces to rubble—not for the sake of rubble, but for that of the way leading through it."

Saturday, February 14
José Sazbón gives me his essay on my novel to read. The reading that I wasn't looking for, an excessive interpretation of things that are allusive and deliberately cryptic in the novel.

Monday 16
Interior exile: the "life" written in the diary (1959–1979), treated as the history of a generation.

February 17
A clear feeling of having no place. Excessive, excluded, eccentric exile. The stateless figure. Difficulty talking to anyone; I practice a language that no one now speaks. A personal language, private language. Nocturnal discoveries; has literature grown distant from me? Reflection too. I only read biographies, others' lives as travel journals. Disoriented. If they take from me what I have read, what is left to me?

A note on culture in Argentina. A society condemned to forget. There is no critical authority. Economy as space of meaning. Unmediated. Terror.

Is it possible to understand those already gone? A discussion with no way out.

Wednesday 18
We invent our dreams, said Tolstoy. We get up in the morning and create dreams that we later tell ourselves.

Friday 20
Being faithful to old discoveries. The detective investigating a case, rejecting all of the strange elements in the drama to which he is a witness. Couldn't that technique be used in an autobiography?

Thursday 26
The Polish crisis, that is, the presence of the workers' movement (Solidarity) amid the wasteland of the international situation, is accompanied, for me, by Gombrowicz, whose diaries I am reading.

Friday, March 24
I return to the same project as always, going through the diaries, transcribing them, finding a title for them, *Diaries (1957–1981)*. Publish: pages from a diary. Revise, reduce. Twenty-five years of writing, the prolixity of the real.

The fiction in my private life is always an unwritten fiction. The opposite of dreams. It captures an object, an incident, and creates a story of destruction.

The diaries of Pavese, Connolly, Gide, Camus, Musil, Kafka, Max Frisch, Jünger, J. Green, Michel Butor.

Use the genre and its truth (lived material) to write a novel.

Monday 30
An attempt on Reagan's life. The television sequence produces a narrative and fictional effect, with a real hero. The information in the media is totally exhaustive.

A hypothesis. Facing all politics that takes the form of social delirium, the isolated madman. Influenced by movies (*Taxi Driver*), he becomes fascinated with Jodie Foster (who plays the young prostitute in the film). He writes letters to the actress who, in the film, accompanies the psychopath. A new version of *Don Quixote*; his own books of chivalry are "hardcore" films and television series. In the letters he writes in roadside motels (which he never sends), he tells the actress that, if she responds to him, he won't kill the president. He only hopes for a single word from her, he says.

Thursday, April 16
One correlative to John Hinckley, who attempted to assassinate Reagan following an example that comes from the movies (*Taxi Driver*), is the case of the journalist Janet Cooke, who wins the Pulitzer for a true account (later discovered to be invented) that was published in the *Washington Post*: a portrait of an eight-year-old black boy addicted to drugs (he becomes addicted through breastfeeding, his mother a heroin addict). If the attempt against Reagan (who is an actor) seems like a television series when viewed on the news, it is logical that fiction—in disguise—is invading journalism. They revoked the Pulitzer from the journalist who wrote the piece, making her the villain because she revealed the manipulated nature of the information.

Sunday, April 26
I meet Andrés R. He has hopes about General Viola, from what they say, confronting Videla.

Monday
At Pomaire, figures about the novel that I look through with an uncomfortable sensation I know well, a strange mixture of anxiety and happiness. Five thousand copies sold so far, three hundred copies sold per month, the book is on the bestseller list in *Clarín*. It was impossible to predict that this novel might interest readers outside my circle of friends.

Friday, May 1
Years ago, in the very same area, the boarding house room on Riobamba near Paraguay, on a day like today, wandering alone though the empty city, everything closed, the bar on Callao, narrow as a hallway. How long has it been?

The novel's impact hasn't changed anything in me, since I am the writer and not the publisher.

RICARDO PIGLIA

I meet Luis Gusmán, "anxious" about Sazbón's reading of the novel, which was published in *Punto de Vista*. He opposes the political reading of the book. He sees opportunism there, right where he is the opportunist.

Wednesday
I'm traveling to Mar del Plata. They're operating on my father. Desolation and the past.

In the bus terminal I run into Osvaldo Lamborghini, and we go for a drink at the bar, he orders cognac and I a glass of white wine. He's coming from Pringles, from Arturo Carrera's house. He tells me, in his conspiratorial tone, that Gabriela Massuh asked him to write a piece on Asís and me; everyone is setting us against each other, so it seems, as opposing sides in literature today. But really, he says in his wicked little tone, he should be writing about you and me. He may write it. He's tied up with *Vigencia* magazine, which performs the cultural politics of the dictatorship and publishes abominable pieces by Marta Lynch exalting Massera's manhood. We chatted for a while and then each went our own way.

Tuesday, May 12
I've become more recognized as a writer, and so that draws, among other things, new students. I have, this year, three groups; thirty students from a wide range of backgrounds (aspiring to be writers, researchers, psychoanalysts, architects), and I'm teaching them how to read, so to speak. The work takes up three days of my week.

Monday, May 17
Isolated, in the ravine, in the study; below, the city. Frozen distance. One minute more is necessary to relate the things they tell me, one minute that will be used to define the situation as it develops, thinking that I'm going to relate it, one minute? Maybe less. If that time were prolonged, I could know what madness is.

Tuesday
Man thinks only of relationships, or rather, is only able to think of relationships.

Friday 29
I'm writing less and less in these notebooks because—paradoxically—I fear they will be read.

Receipts and sums, the chaos centers around my own basic weakness, a strange emphasis on waiting, or rather, not wanting to leave the present, not ruin it with obligations. No precautions, then; I'm not a cautious man.

Friday, June 5
I've spent the last few days resolving practical matters, renewing the lease for my apartment at seventy-six million (two hundred dollars), an effect of devaluation.

Tuesday, June 9
Many rumors in *Punto de Vista*; the steering committee is expanding.

Tuesday 23
I'm working an enormous amount, Lugones, I'm writing about Arlt's complete works. They've given me originals to read, Andrés Rivera, Marcelo Pichon-Rivière, Pacho O'Donnell, Diego Angelino.

Tuesday, July 14
Several meetings for the magazine, a steering committee is formed (adding María Teresa Gramuglio and Hugo Vezzetti). I try to politicize the issue but find no support.

Saturday, July 18
I can never get a photographer to take a photograph of me in which the face of the one who writes can be seen—or sensed.

I have several formulas:

1. Work in the morning.
2. Never have wine with lunch.
3. Always have several books I'm interested in to read at night. (Right now, for example, I'm reading a Samuel Beckett biography.)

Wednesday 22
Determination is a curious narrative situation, everything must be "forgotten," any thought causes pain. Not seeing anything, not remembering. Where does it come from? An unfolding; "professional" fulfillment is accomplished in exchange for personal uncertainty.

Saturday 25
If I think about the things that have been happening over the past few days, as always happens to me, I can't imagine the cause behind this slow and persistent indolence.

Monday 27
To move past this state of affairs I must resort to interior processes and try to get caught up in something else, as they say. "I don't want to know anything" is a phrase that follows me, and it means "I'm not at all interested," but also means what it says, to get away from knowing, to refuse it, to wish not to know the things I already know and am unable to forget.

Wednesday
I meet with Rabanal and Martini Real to write a statement. I say: an open letter from writers must address the disappeared. They don't agree. At least, I say, we have to talk about Walsh, Conti, Urondo, Santoro, Diana Guerrero, Bustos. If not, why write it.

Thursday
The dark temptation to die young (. . . but I'm no longer young).

Saturday, July 31
Dark hours, I cling to objects as a castaway to his red lifesaver, also desiring a revenge that has no object. From one object to another.

A meeting of writers, they make a statement. I remained alone in my position on what cannot be left unsaid. The others don't even want to talk about the disappeared.

Sunday, August 2
Circulation of phone calls. Rabanal, Martini, Moledo. Cultural developmentalism wants to put out a statement at all costs. The text written by Martini seems "excessive" to them (it speaks of the disappeared). Now we'll see how they "lighten it up" (they know that, if they do, I won't sign).

Monday 3
Also preparing for the philosophy course in the morning. Reading the newspapers. Calls. A certain disquiet that builds with the advancing afternoon. At four I go to Galerna on Calle Talcahuano. Someone brings me a letter from Ricardo Nudelman with news from Mexico. They're going to stop publishing *Controversias*. Are they, like everything in these times, placing themselves in relation with the summons from the "democrats" of the regime? In California, Portantiero—who'd come to give a talk at the University in Santa Cruz—spoke to me, inspired, about Viola.

Tuesday 4
A commotion around my article on Arlt that was published today. The bleak packaging, etc.

Too much presence of exterior space; distant voices speak to me inside my head. Calls, offers. I work on the classes with neither interest nor time. Today Lugones, the space of fiction via the occult sciences. Nervous, with a kind of secret angst. I struggle to concentrate. Tension.

I weigh sixty-four kilos. I go to the dentist; my teeth are in perfect condition.

Wednesday 5
I get to my office at nine, set up the chairs that the students will occupy, change the position of the table and the lamp. Through the window I can always see the changing image of Plaza Congreso. Rabanal calls me, intrigued by the echoes of an article about narrative today, written by a servant of O. L. in the official culture magazine *Vigencia*, working for the new consensus of General Viola.

I buy a bottle of Ballantine's whisky. I watch soccer on TV. I start to work on Bellow's *Herzog* for the course.

Thursday 6
An erratic conversation with Ludmer, who wants to write an article about the criticism of Hernández in order to "get into" the writing and be able to sit down and work on *Martín Fierro*.

Last night an attack against El Picadero, where Teatro Abierto was being developed. We gather in the ravine, an angry and confused group.

I go downtown and exchange pesos for five hundred dollars, thinking about my trip to Europe. I run into Ariel Badaraco, a sales agent for Pomaire, the son of a legendary anarchist intellectual. I meet him at El Ateneo, the bookshop on Calle Florida, where I'd gone to look for another book by Bellow for the course. The manager tells me: "Your novel is selling well." Badaraco is the optimistic version of the world.

I'll have to remember the conversation today at El Molino café, the ones who've come back from hell. The despondent air, an unreasonable experience, the story that arises on its own and continues; the events repeated many times, the names of streets, as if trying to get their bearings. Osvaldo B., who turns traitor and names people on the phone. "I have to give you some bad news," he tells them before they too enter the mob that surrounds him. "I'm doing this," he says, "because Roberto prevented my literary career." Wasn't that what I'd perceived in him when we worked together at the newspaper? The stupid narcissism of a writer in his case turned pathetic and conceited. Now it's clear that he harbored hatred and resentment for years, and then betrayed and sent to death all of the political leaders. He can't be judged because nothing can be said about someone who's been tortured. In any case, his "explanation" is an example of the *maudit* writer who turns wickedness into a poetics and a design. He stayed in the organization, like many, because he was a "professional revolutionary" and they paid him a salary for his political work. I need only recall his conversations with me and his insistence that I read his stories to find there an ambition to climb and become part of the pathetic literary life of Buenos Aires. He could belong to the sinister series of imaginary writers; his maliciousness too resembles the atmosphere circulating among "us" these days. There's something in it of the story "Failed Writer" by Roberto Arlt.

A long phone conversation with Martini Real. There in that tenement atmosphere. Gregorich, in a sinister article, attempted to erase the writers in exile with the argument that they're going to lose their contact with the Argentine language (the target, Saer). And now, in *Vigencia* magazine, where the rod of Editorial de Belgrano attempts to erase the writers who've written here, nominating themselves as the new culture—cynical and parodic—that has arisen in the plague years (I'm the target, remembering my talk with O. L. in the terminal). In an interview, Cesar A. said I had the face of a cop. Of course it's nonsense; accusations, the costumbrist maneuvers of hypervigilant literature, only appeasing the clowns from the "Coca-Cola Prize in Arts and Letters" awarded to Enrique F., promoted by the official culture to present to the new generation.

Friday, August 7
Facing off with the "avant-garde" from the Universidad de Belgrano Press (!) and the "realists" of the Centro Editor, I move in an unstable territory but maintain the war of opinions and my own ground. Two systems appear, which I would summarize as public and journalistic oppositions. Of course, I'm not the one touting these conflicts; I have nothing to do with the invention of rivalries that I neither advocate nor have any interest in.

The issue is always the same. What kind of people are able to resist social pressure, and in what moment? Maintaining style in the midst of conflict, grace under pressure.

Altamirano appears. A discussion about the general situation. He's very critical of Peronism and remains a skeptic. I see Peronism as the most solid pole in opposition to the military government. Interested in socialism à la Juan B. Justo (that is, opposing the Peronist masses and their tradition), against which I hold up the prospect of utopia as a critique of the present. I remember an unexpected and brilliant illumination by Sartre, who, in discussing Faulkner, says that his narrative world is buried in the past because he speaks of a society in which there is no hope in revolution.

I run into José Sazbón. A Kafkaesque quality, theoretical ravings, overly interested in structuralism. We walk along Corrientes and get dinner on Sarmiento and Montevideo. He brings me news of León R. and other friends exiled in Venezuela.

Saturday 8
I'm working on short stories and early North American narrative. I'm thinking of writing an overview of the Argentine short story. I put together a class on Saul Bellow.

This month is packed with difficulties. I think this way in order to create a deadline and imagine a way out; everything will be different next month . . .

Sunday 9

I spend the day reading Potash's book on the military and politics in Argentina between 1945 and 1962. A strange review of my own autobiography, the years 1955 to 1959. I encounter the exterior and historical context of my private life.

Monday, August 10

As has kept happening these past few weeks, the chain of misfortune continues. Calls from Paris; Molina, from Pomaire, hasn't sent the translation contract for the novel. Everything is delayed and complicated. Anxious, absentminded. I "hope," superstitiously, that this bad streak will only last for a month. Magical thinking, psychotic periodization, everything will be different next month, etc. Four courses per week, I hope to be more at ease once the classes end. Meanwhile I'm going around in circles like a dog about to lie down. I do nothing because there's nothing I can do but wait.

Almost a year ago I received the first copies of *Artificial Respiration*; Molina calls me, seventy-five hundred copies have been sold.

I meet José Bianco at his house. Though ill, he maintains what dignity he can. Praise for the novel; he read it to Borges. He apologizes for the run-down state of his home and recalls with clarity and nostalgia the lost places—because of the currency devaluation—of his childhood and youth. The anti-Proust, very Proustian. An arduously ironic conversation about Gombrowicz and Mastronardi.

Tuesday 11

At peace today. Maybe because I've suspended my night class. Maybe because I'm awakened by a call from Antoine Berman in Paris; his interest in my novel makes up for the difficulties with the literary atmosphere around here.

A visit from Daniel B., who is progressing on his English translation of the novel. *How to live in Argentina?* is one of his themes. For my part, I wonder: how is it possible to construct an intellectual project inside North American universities? The atmosphere here is so hostile, it's so difficult to earn a living in Buenos Aires, that the possibility of working in academia seems like one possible way out.

Wednesday 12
I work on *Herzog* (the Europeanized intellectual in crisis does not write letters to the dead and the unknown) and give a good class. I buy some records, hot jazz, Bessie Smith, Louis Armstrong, and Django Reinhardt. The sounds of adolescence can never be recovered.

I run into Leonardo M. The developmentalists are making special concessions for me and accepting the inclusion of a paragraph on the *desaparecidos* in the writers' statement.

Thursday 13
I arrive with the intention of preparing a class for my course on literary history, but I decide that I can't keep loading myself down with work. No interest in "sustaining" a critical discourse around issues that interest me less and less. A writer's reading must not take the form of an academic procedure but rather seek ways of thinking about literature from an unstable position. I put aside two hundred million per month and hope I can begin to do a bit of thinking or writing. Why should I start worrying about money?

The situation is becoming clear; my relationship with the group of writers I've driven to make a statement gets me bound up in alliances I don't like, but it does define a critical position. I don't have to—nor do I plan to—write in to *Clarín* in order to clear up any confusion. I don't like *Punto de Vista*, but that's "where I am," and it's all there is, it's a way to get out of isolation. All the same, I have nostalgia for solitude, for not having anyone watching out for me in the coming months. The novel has created a social space for me that I do not enjoy. I don't want to write criticism; it doesn't interest me as specific work. I'll try to think about a *nouvelle* based on the diary.

Lunch with Aníbal Ford. He invites me to the Centro CLACSO, creating an alternative space, hoping that things will change. Interested in the issue of writers who gather together; he doesn't see how it can work. Names too far devalued. He's thinking of a space tied to popular national thought. That is, to Peronism.

A summary of the current tendencies and perspective of a post-dictatorship culture. Socialists à la Juan B. Justo. Populists adjacent to Peronism. A frivolous and vaguely cynical avant-garde. Developmentalists practicing entryism.

Friday
Last night a call from Marcelo Pichon-Rivière, who alludes to the group connected to *Vigencia* magazine and the pathetic Universidad de Belgrano Press, who hold me up as their ideal enemy. They want to get me out of the way, but they won't succeed, he said, beyond the wounds inflicted in combat. What's more, I don't like having to face the women in the group, which I'm going to turn down in four hours. An uncomfortable situation that will be resolved if I can, once and for all, stop worrying about the opinions of others. "Let them think what they like about me," that must be the motto by which I can get out of this distracting situation. Maybe it's coming to a blind spot, and tomorrow, let's say, things will start to get better. I'm always cultivating the fantasy of a single change that will solve everything.

Saturday 15
Last night a long meeting about the writers' statement. It came out well, better than I expected when I posed the issue of the *desaparecidos*.

My novel has placed me in the sights of Argentine literature. I have to go back to a position apart from the tumult, back to being unpublished and unknown; I don't plan to publish anything in the next five or six years. Get out of there.

I'm becoming interested in the reconstruction of the context around Payró: the national theater, the articles, the *Pago chico* novels and, especially, *El casamiento de Laucha*.

José comes over, worried about the criticism aimed at his "sophisticated" method of critical writing.

Tuesday 18
Let's set aside this chronological idiocy. Conflict with Iris both last night and today, always the same. Wouldn't it be better to live alone? The emptiness comes from me; I've been repeating the same thing since 1963.

Saturday 22
A meeting to rectify the writers' text following Belgrano Rawson's (failed) attempts. Then, in the elevator, Lili Marleen. The walk at sunrise. The same fantasies as ever, yesterday realized as far as my [*illegible*].

I meet with Roger Pla, author of the magnificent *Las brújulas muertas*. A friend of Gombrowicz, whom we talk about for a while. He criticizes the essayistic quality of my novel. It's the best thing you've got, I said, and he smiled with resignation. I'll go to his workshop, to speak and give a short story reading. The old writer who doesn't sell his books, whom no one is talking about.

Sunday 23

A terrible month, my neighbor is leaving (just as I'd foreseen). She's renting out the apartment (from what I can tell), so I won't be able to live with the same absence of life entailed by not always having someone on the other side. Today I woke up preoccupied with that issue. Why haven't I ever felt at ease in this apartment, where I've been living for more than two years? As if I were living on borrowed money, precariously. Will I be able to resolve it now (cork-lined walls like Proust), or will I have to move? This is the year to do it because I have money.

As always, I discover that I myself am the center of this crisis, the bound man. Will I have to go back to psychoanalysis? If I don't travel to Europe? If I don't switch apartments?

An incredible feeling of unreality. Removed from everything. Having no place. Obligations, impossible to fulfill, overwhelm me. I always put them off. It's obvious that I'm unable to work. I'm about to read a novel by John Barth for this week's class.

Monday 24

In the usual sense, an ailing body. Physical malaise. I advance at an exasperatingly slow pace.

Friday

Lili Marleen, all night. In the morning I decide not to leave. The married woman. Facing up to whatever may come because, she says, she's seen something in me . . .

Argument about the novel; she isn't convinced either. Conceptual narrative is best, I tell her, because it produces greater incomprehension.

Monday, August 31

Isn't that what happened, in brief, this month? It was another place, one I hadn't foreseen, when I resolved to write down day after day.

Some cause (at last emotional) for the pain. Absence and nostalgia.

Sunday
While waiting for the change of seasons, I write. One pain in place of another, he said, and added: "She comes and goes. She dresses up for me." She said: "We'll see each other tomorrow." He answered: "No. There's no need now." Why should it be that way? he thought. No one can say. She cries, he sleeps. She sleeps, he leaves.

Monday
Remnants or memories without form: voices coming from the past. A second sleepless night. The house on Calle Sarmiento. Sitting on the floor, I watch the same shadows as ever pass.

Saturday 8
I've spent several weeks reading Tolstoy, whom I find very close to Wittgenstein. "It is harder to follow one rule of conduct than to write twenty volumes of philosophy." Tolstoy's individualistic anarchism is an extreme response to the capitalist mentality but also to Lenin's revolutionary violence. His ideas seem to reawaken in the face of the inclemency of an era in where no alternatives to the state of things appear—because they've been destroyed. On the other hand, with his use of defamiliarization as a way to view society in another manner, and with his rejection of art as false religion and his progression toward praxis, he anticipated the great currents of debate on the relationship between art and life. The artistic life before the art (Russian avant-garde and Duchamp) and personal engagement in society before the social impact of the work (engagement à la Sartre and aesthetic populism).

8

Diary 1982

Monday, January 4
I'm writing an autobiographical story about my father. Moving forward blindly.

January 21
One is what one is, and that causes a strange sensation of distance.

Friday 22
Fewer and fewer experiences in the old sense, transgressions? A feeling today of being outside the world, in the pharmacy on Paraná and Corrientes, which is always open, twenty-four hours a day.

Friday 29
I am one who moves forward and is transformed following catastrophes: 1955 was, in that sense, the initial form. Everything comes from there, my father's prison sentence, the move, the writing of this diary.

Saturday 30
Reading on temporality and private life written in a diary.

1. Spinoza distinguishes between eternity and duration. Eternity is the attribute through which we conceive of infinite existence. Duration is the attribute through which

we conceive of the existence of things insofar as they per-
severe in their existence.

2. Bergson. Pure, concrete, or real duration exists in real time,
   in opposition to the spatialization to which it is submitted
   (by means of mathematics). Material time and physico-
   mathematical time are the result of the need to control
   reality pragmatically. Duration is reality itself, beyond
   spatial schemes. What is experienced intuitively and not
   simply comprehended or understood by the understanding.

3. Leibniz. Time without things does not exist. Time is the
   order of existence of things that are not simultaneous. It
   is a form of relation.

Tuesday, February 2
Solitude in the midst of afflictions that persist and grow. Isolated,
seeing no way out.

Failure is the secret history of my life; that is the diary I've been writing for the past twenty-five years. Is all of life a process of demolition?
Externally (if that could be said), there exist incidents that aren't enough
to mitigate the lucid perception of the impending collapse. Suicide
would be the logical close to that life. Because I've never experienced
anything with as much intensity as the certainty of failure. Everything
has been precarious (inside), beyond what is visible on the surface.

I had made up my mind to kill myself (and it's idiotic to write that sentence) in 1955 and in 1979. Maybe now I could attempt another path,
change my life, my identity, my work, escape.

At the same time, I'm thinking about going to Adrogué to look for my
diaries; I'll start to make a clean copy of them so that, perhaps, I can
find a way out by that route. The relationship between suicide and
writing a diary is an intimate one (see: Pavese, Kafka, etc.).

Tuesday 9
To transcribe the diary would be to write my own version of *In Search of Lost Time*.

Wednesday, February 17
Notes for a course on Brecht's prose. "For those who practice superfluous thought, to assert that the grand intellectual systems depend on economics is equivalent to slandering them. Disregarding the fact that, here, 'economics' is the object of the disdain that in our time it doubtless deserves. In that disdain is exposed, in a totally unconscious manner, a profound discontentment with economics, not accepted by thought, as it cannot be altered by thought."

"The theory of knowledge must before all else be a critique of language."

"Philosophy teaches proper conduct" (it has always had a "practical aspect"). "Certain forms of activity and certain modes of conduct were always defined as philosophical" (in the form of gestures or "responses").

Thinking two thoughts at the same time. "The test of a first-rate intelligence is the ability to hold two opposed ideas in mind at the same time and still retain the ability to function," Scott Fitzgerald.

"And so by contrast I have kept my two thoughts together and neither detached myself from unease nor prudence: I didn't want to pause too long over inevitability or declare something to be inevitable too soon" (*Political and Social Writings*, p. 17). See the examples of double thinking in the story of Keuner. The truth is variable and comparative, things are relationships.

Thursday, February 18
Last night a persistent nightmare. As always, the idea of suicide.

Friday, February 19
Notes for a course on Brecht's prose. Mr. Keuner: short or incredibly short stories (designated by the name of the character, who always figures as narrator or protagonist), "represents an attempt to make *gestures quotable.*"

Notion of gesture: the node of a story. *Gesture* could correspond to a version of the English *gist*, "the main point or essence of an issue or argument." For example: "Richard Gloucester asks the widow of the victim for her hand in marriage." Or: "God makes a wager with the Devil for the soul of Doctor Faustus." Or: "Woyzeck buys a cheap knife to kill his wife." *Gist* designates the basic nucleus of the story, exhibited as a display of an ensemble of figures of basically social intention, in which a purely social interpretation—at least in the case of *Faustus*—would naturally be an error.

The *gestus* designates a figure [of the body] that expresses a state of social connection and translates in a singular way the link of determination between an individual and the community.

Modes of alienation in empirical experience. To make personal reflection "quotable" is to convert it into an experience that is transferable (transmittable) to others (quotable). The only thing that Mr. K said about style is: "It should be quotable. A quotation is impersonal." The word becomes gesture.

"Description of thought such as it presents itself through social conduct" (gesture).

"He thought about other minds and in their minds they thought about others as well. That is correct thinking."

Monday, March 1
A grave situation. Paralysis. How to break out of this stasis that began exactly two years ago? Immediate tasks: organize the library and the papers, write an essay on Arlt, prepare for the course on Brecht, make a clean copy of the diary as a mnemonic exercise.

Friday, March 19
Prose as utopia. The time lost is the time of the future. Proust seeks the past in order to extract himself, in the coincidences of lived time—concordance or correspondence are effects of the open syntax and the subordinate clauses of his analytical prose—and of the future above all. In certain isolated scenes, Proust recognizes the anticipatory signs.

Saturday, March 20
I try to submerge myself so as to magically rise to the surface. Months of despair and silence. I barely read, empty days, what am I waiting for? She comes on Fridays like a ghost desired; on Tuesdays I listen to myself teach class. It's raining now, and beyond a conflict with the English, Falkland Islands, will it turn for the worse? Surely yes, the military has no way out but murky nationalism.

Wednesday, May 26
In the midst of everything, a sinister and psychotic war with England. All of my friends have turned into military strategists. We read the English newspapers, which arrive with some delay, so that the things they predict are being enacted as we read them. The most incredible part was learning that soldiers carry infrared glasses that allow them to see enemy targets in the dark. We assembled at *Punto de Vista* to make a statement against the war, which Carlos Altamirano wrote. There are only five or six of us who look upon the horror with calm. The manipulation of information and the triumphalist headlines in the papers and the invented news on television create a sad, euphoric atmosphere. The Argentines in exile, in their vast majority, supported the position of the genocidal dictatorship. The military went to war, seeing a political escape route; defeat must be hailed as a political triumph. As always, the tyrants in this country—at least in the twentieth century—never last for more than five years.

Wednesday, August 25
The disenchanted exiles have been here for a month. They've become "realist" and democratic, all of the illusions they cultivated in youth now dead. For my part, hearing them and perceiving some degree of truth in what they say (beneath the rationalizations and the cynicism), I decide that my political position is utopia. And so, I declare myself a utopian socialist.

Friday 27
Erratic conversations with José Sazbón, a single talk, really, that has gone on for twenty years now. He offers me his apartment on Marcelo T. de Alvear and Ayacucho, and we may come to an agreement.

I'm planning a novel about Alberdi. The story would take place between 1879, when he returns to Buenos Aires after thirty years in exile, and 1881, when, defeated by the political situation, he returns to Paris and dies there, in 1884—and would concentrate on the final days of his life.

Monday, August 30
I visit Andrés in the hospital, just after the operation. I write letters concerning the English translation of *Artificial Respiration*.

I'm not interested in the false heroism of those who seek only the favor of the mass media.

Tuesday, September 14
On Friday I get lunch with Saer at Claudio. He's come looking for me here, on the way from the Centro Editor, where he sold all of his books in exchange for nothing; they'll be republished in that circuit that doesn't deserve him. He needed money because, according to him, he lost five thousand dollars that he was bringing with him on a plane. Of course, he must have lost it playing poker in the airport.

9

Endings

At some moment, on an afternoon like any other, he realized, Renzi told his personal physician, that his passing illness was the result of the months and months he'd dedicated to reading and writing his diaries; there are many ways to become afflicted and to grow ill, and he was certain that this prolonged exposure to the incandescent light of his style had caused a slight discomfort at first, but, as he continued onward, the persistent exposure of his body to the incomparable brilliance of the Argentine language must, he told the doctor, have caused unwanted side effects. The Argentine language, like any remedy or *pharmacon* or magic potion, had its contraindications. He wasn't the only one, doctor, Renzi told his physician, who'd suffered in his body the presence of his style when writing; he knew of other cases, Borges, for example, who became blind. Roberto Arlt, for example, who died of syncope at age forty-two. He was only forty-two, but when they did the autopsy, the specialists claimed it was impossible that the man could have been that age; his body was that of a person at age seventy, the specialists said after looking over the dead body of Roberto Arlt. There were other cases that confirmed this character, or the destructive quality of the national language, in which someone submits to that incandescent light for long periods of time without using protection to shield against the Argentine syntax. Saer, serious pulmonary lesions. Puig, general sepsis. Mediocre writers set out to write in space suits, in diving suits, their hands and arms covered with protective fabric; some write with helmets and tinted goggles, and I've seen many writing in bars with gas masks on their faces, and that's the way their writing turns out, aseptic, sterilized, and their style, to call it that, is a cautious and prophylactic style. They move away from the incandescence of the language of these provinces to shield themselves, so their writing becomes inoffensive. And so, Renzi told his family doctor that afternoon, the illness afflicting me is directly related to the years I've spent under the deadly light from above of the national grammar. You must be very careful with words and sentences, doctor, when you write.

Since my father was a doctor, a consulting room was a familiar place for me; I felt comfortable beside a stretcher, the scale that my father used to weigh his patients naked, the lights and equipment, the X-ray machines, the radiographs, and so I felt at ease in this consulting room, conversing with my family doctor about literature and illness. Doctor Andrade was a great clinician, that is, he examined the sick personally and didn't burden them with analysis all the time, computing tomographies and other scientific superstitions and the like, which serve only to extract money from the patients and, above all, to get rid of them. He, on the other hand, conversed with the sick, listened to them, read the signs of illness in their bodies. "The best medical instrument is the chair, because that's where the patient can sit and talk," he would say. And so I told my life to him, told him about my notebooks, about the years I'd spent exposed to the disruptive brilliance of the mother tongue, that's how we spoke one afternoon in his consulting room. The condition had first manifested in his left hand, and then his left leg was affected, and his physician, Doctor Andrade, after listening to him attentively, advised him to abandon his notebooks and notes for a while and go out walking in the open air and live a healthier life.

By that stage, Renzi had already transcribed twenty-five years of his existence and thought he could pause his march there, take a break midway down the road and rest under the shadow of the trees in a dark wood. On one hand, he thought, looking at the countryside, leaning against the trunk of a poplar tree and chewing on the stem of a shrub, he'd come to a final point, or rather, a place of a closing and changing of eras, 1982 or *The Eve*, he thought, because reality and the state of things had changed drastically at that point. And so it did not only concern the chapters of his own life but rather a shift that came about in reality. An end had come to an era in which a better reality was possible, an era in which he and his friends had lived in a parallel society, a world of their own, unconnected to the main current of Argentine culture. They had triumphed, because they remained alive, fighting on, but they'd also been defeated; they had scars and marks on their bodies, they were survivors, they were casualties of war. Their illusions *now*, he emphasized, were more illusive than ever, but social and political life *now* was more benign than ever.

Now, he emphasized, after defeat, they had all returned to the fold, *now* they were all official, recognized writers; they received prizes and were interviewed on television and put their names on editorial columns in the major newspapers, and their photos appeared frequently in magazines and periodicals. *Now*, he furiously emphasized once again, writers were decorative; they were received in salons, in embassies; they traveled from place to place, gave talks, and were insignificant but well-regarded; the most important cultural slogan in the new era was "be visible or be dead," and everyone wanted to show up, as they say, wanted to make themselves seen, and authors *now* were more important than their books, which was certain because their books were so insignificant that one photo in the cultural supplement of a local newspaper was worth more than three or four of their published books. Things being so, Emilio had perceived with clarity that one era had ended and a culture had been destroyed. Before, thought Renzi, we could circulate in the margins, attached to counterculture, to the underground world of art and literature, but *now* we're all little figures on an impoverished stage and must play the game that has dominated the world. He had no hope or will or courage to change things or, at least, to run the risk of living on illusions. And so he thought that this season of his life had ended and his twenty-five years devoted to becoming a writer had concluded. And what came after was predictable and mundane and wasn't a part of the history of how his personal spirit had been formed.

On the other hand, he was in a bit of a bad way with his health, as Renzi told his friends after the consultation with his family doctor; nothing serious, he had no pain, was in good spirits, and was working as always (which of course was not a value judgment). He didn't feel ill, rather he felt that his body was foreign to him, as if it were someone else's body, while his spirit or his soul remained intact. The problem was that his doctor had recommended that he stop running through his life such as it was written in his notebooks. That was the cause of his illness, he told the doctor, and because of that, as he left the consulting room with prescriptions for medications and the recommendation to walk and do calisthenics, Renzi understood that he must take some time off from the work of transcribing his notebooks and spending days and weeks shut up in his study with his diaries, the pages upon pages written, which, according to the doctor, were poisonous to his body. He could not travel with impunity—like a sleepwalker—in the time machine of his private notebooks, passing through the days of his life, or rather, the notes written feverishly with the aim of registering his experience. And so he decided to pause on that first cycle, which revealed the truth of his destiny better than anything, which revealed his project of becoming a good writer; it had taken him twenty-five years to find a way out, a narrow door through which meaning, so to speak, could pass.

Then he thought it would be best to pause, to break out of the incessant flow of personal duration and concentrate on one day of his life. One day, let's say twenty-four hours, a distillation, a demonstration of the passage of time. He would exchange the long duration for the micro-history. He had several references, several examples that he'd always intended to improve upon; he'd been very ambitious and, on nights of insomnia, crazed with panic, haunted by failure and impossibility, he'd confronted other ways of synthesizing an entire life into one day, for his model was always imaginary. He was interested in the literary construction of an artist's life. For example, one day in the life of Stephen Dedalus, one day in the life of the Consul, or one day in the life of Quentin Compson. That idea excited him; he would concentrate all his future years into one day. He was glad to be able to work in a reduced space; he would take one day as it appeared in different notebooks, or rather, would keep the notebooks in the cardboard boxes and take them to a storage facility as he'd done with the papers from his grandfather Emilio and his uncle Marcelo Maggi, he didn't understand why the men in his family left traces behind them, writings on paper that could reveal the misfortunes of their lives (and I did the same thing).

Then he imagined his life without the notebooks, *without the notebooks*, he emphasized, without the weight of the written record of the things he did, desired, thought, or believed. He must do well in choosing the one day to which he would devote the coming weeks. It must be a day like any other, a day within which he could reconstruct the essential moments. He'd read a book by Israel Mattuck, *The Thought of The Prophets*, a series of Biblical analyses on physical temporality, and it had left him thinking, as they say, of a commentary, which he'd jotted down immediately in one of his little books of reading notes: "It is hard to believe that the Prophet Isaiah went naked for three years . . . The Hebrew word for hours might easily be mistaken for the word which means years." That had been a revelation, to write a single day of his life in the coming years, forget about his diaries and, above all, remember the moments that repeated day after day; that is, since he'd been unable to learn the art of forgetting, despite having done those Russian exercises intended to voluntarily erase the events of his life, he would concentrate his energy on one point, a moment almost without time, eighteen hours, shall we say, of my life, a window through which other identical days could be imagined and it would be possible to pause over the microscopic fragments of experience. And that is what he'd done, or that *was* what he'd done. He spent the entire month of February, working for hours and hours, registering the span of one day in his life.

Was there an ending? Or was it only a change in rhythm? He'd thought about how, at the end of the novel, as the great post-tragic genre, in this world deserted by the gods, the hero would change or die, that is, he would commit suicide (like Quentin Compson) or come to his senses (like Alonso Quijano at the end of his life), while he, by contrast, would never consider compromise; and, with regard to suicide, he'd gone that way many times without success, and so it was better to leave the history of his life at this point, early, because his later life was too public, so that the things he'd recorded in his diaries weren't pertinent to include in this version of his experience. I stopped in 1982 because, up to that point, I had neither abdicated nor committed suicide, and later, like the Prophet Isaiah, I would confuse the years and the days; the span of one whole day would enclose, within its hours, many times.

II

A DAY IN THE LIFE

For in a minute there are many days.

WILLIAM SHAKESPEARE

He had reached Constitución on a train at dawn, confused, having slept badly, and continued downtown by taxi, leaning back into the crisp air of the window, smoking, sleepless, clearheaded, sadder than he might have wished, the night's memories like bolts of lightning in a pale sky, the images clear, the ideas so unsettling, so vile, a killer returning to his hideout but unable to stop seeing the body he's left behind, now rigid, pale, the terrifying pallor of the first night in death. *Horacio*, Emilio said in his mind, *there are more precious memories in the world than* . . . That wasn't it, the meeting had changed, the time of the meeting, he looked at his watch again, the hour, yes, but the name was real, and the dead man too, watched in vigil until the day began to grow light, so near, the deceased—he said it to himself, one more time, to inure himself to it—the one who died, the one who was dead, the deceased, so close to him, a brotherly bond. It was seven in the morning, and the way into Buenos Aires, from the south, let him view the city as if in a frieze, and it stirred in him the same feeling as ever, the certainty that he could conquer it, make a name for himself, so that people would speak of him and his deeds and his books, just as he'd plotted so many times in the old days, with his friends, with Horacio, with Junior, with Miguel, with Cacho Carpatos, leaving the bars and walking circles around the streets all night in pursuit of adventure, fame, life itself. And this may be the reason he decides to keep moving and not go to bed, not return home, but go instead to his place, his cave, his lair, to change course, not think, hide himself away, and—for once—not record the things he's lived through that night.

Horacio had arrived unexpectedly at the cabin outside the city that they were renting that summer along with Gerardo and Ana, and other friends who came and went, including Juani, who'd come from France at the end of March and stayed with them for a few days, and there was a photo showing Emilio with him and Alan and Marcelo Cohen, all half-naked in swimming trunks except for Saer, who smiled with a certain air of resignation but wore a coat and tie, like a banker—"in baccarat" he'd explained, cheerful and on horseback—although, on the day when Horacio parked his car on the other side of the fence, they'd all already returned to the city and Emilio was left there alone on that afternoon in April or early May of the year before.

"I came to see you," Horacio said as he got out of the car, wearing that familiar smile.

He arrived without warning and came alone, without Sofía . . . strange, no? But he didn't say anything, didn't explain why he'd come, seemed more silent than usual, intimidated perhaps, thought Renzi, who loved him more than anyone; he was his double, or had once been.

There was no need for talk between the two of them; they were brothers, or very nearly so, first cousins, and they'd been born in the same month of the same year, were physically identical, had grown up together, had gone to the same schools and fallen in love with the same women. Emilio was certain that, if he'd stayed in Adrogué, if destiny—the paternal oracle—hadn't uprooted him from there at age sixteen, his life would have been what Horacio's was—he would have studied to become a doctor, would have married his high school girlfriend, would have had children, would still be living in the family house where he was born—he was his double, his mirror, he was what Emilio might have been: a quiet man who stayed in shape by playing tennis at the same club where he'd learned to swim as a boy, while Emilio was a wanderer with no children, no home, no anchor, bound only to a dark conviction—a ridiculous one, clearly—which he'd taken on as a mandate—from no one—and on which he'd gambled his life, written words, and life, experienced obliquely, in order to write about it . . .

All of this he had thought that night as he entered the funeral home, Casa Lasalle, at the end of Calle Mitre, the same funeral parlor where they'd mourned his grandparents and his aunts and uncles, where they'd taken him as a boy and lifted him up so he could kiss an ashen face, which seemed made of wax; the same room, the same white light, the same people speaking in low voices, relatives, friends, neighbors, standing in a circle, like ghosts, dear faces that he couldn't identify greeting him ceremoniously, as if they'd come back from the past, he thought, and so he felt himself a stranger once more as he went in and made uncomfortable greetings, said the things people say, embraced the parents and children of the deceased, and saw Sofía, on her own, isolated, off against a wall to one side as if they'd built a ring of silence around her alone.

Through the window of the taxi he saw fleeting scenes pass by, memories fixed in the streets, the golden cupola on one corner, the Ferretería Francesa, the little white Eugenio Diez house, illuminated, high above. The city as a mnemonic device, as a kaleidoscope of emotion. He had once heard Horacio say: "Living in the past makes the hours turn slow, the years fast." Lentov, the Russian neuropsychiatrist, had done experiments with soldiers suffering from shock after the war. It wasn't the River Lethe but a technique to erase memories. Mutilated bodies, songs, stray words. Oblivion is a job like any other.

He walked over to her, he loved her, she'd studied Philosophy in La Plata, that was how Horacio had met her. Sofía had left him for a woman. She left, taking nothing, asking for nothing; their children were young adults now, independent, and she was leaving nothing behind but the pain and the memories. The world for Horacio, Horacio's world, he corrected himself, was in ruins; the young woman, his rival, was tall and strong-willed; she came to the house three times a week and Horacio could hear her laughing from the consulting room, an honest laughter, like a kind of music. Sofía suffered physically from the loneliness and monotony, the identical days, empty of desire, and this girl was her yoga instructor. When he came to the cabin that afternoon Horacio was broken, but he said nothing. They walked over to the house; he'd brought a couple bottles of white wine and got them out of the trunk of the car, from the Styrofoam cooler where he'd stored them, engulfed in dry ice, to arrive chilled at the large house in Pilar that Emilio had rented for the summer. It was a Swiss wine, Joyce's favorite, and Horacio summoned strength from some secret place in his soul to make a few jokes about that aristocratic ambrosia and the paradoxical quality of Swiss wines, so literary, Horacio had added, after they'd gone into the kitchen and put the bottles of white wine in the refrigerator.

The car has now turned down Córdoba, moving away from the river, and he once more sees like signs up ahead the places where he's been and has been young—el Pasaje del Carmen, the bar on the corner, the restaurant where he ate every night—and then they turn onto Callao, skirt around the Plaza, end up on Charcas—ex-Charcas—and head toward Ayacucho.

Renzi walked up to her that night as she stood alone, isolated, in the mourning room, with the coffin nearby, lying open, behind a glass divider; she hadn't hidden herself in a corner to go unnoticed, as they say; she was a brave woman, still young, and had stationed herself in the place where a widow would stand to receive the condolences, but no one had approached her, alone, then, in the middle of the mortuary chapel. No one bears the guilt for anyone's death, that was what Emilio wanted to say to her, though the phrase sounded inaccurate to him, but he said it all the same because he had no words that night, and ideas or thoughts were appearing to him in isolated blocks; he saw them somewhere before his eyes; writings, vivid slogans that he alone could see.

Emilio, dear, grand words are no use now, she said, not crying. I lived with Horacio for twenty-five years, and I've known him better than anyone. She wasn't crying, her eyes were dark, clear, serene. She wasn't crying for him. Too late for tears, she said, and that was his epitaph. To put it better, Emilio thinks now, getting out of the taxi, the epitaph for any death.

He opens the glass door of the building, takes the elevator up to the eleventh floor, and feels once more the same certainty as on each arrival, that everything would still be there, suspended, the newspapers from the previous day on the floor, on the mat, and today's paper as well, June 16, 1983, which he picks up and reads, on the front page, *Weather Forecast. Variable cloudiness with a slight increase in temperature. Slight wind from the north. Minimum and maximum for the urban and suburban area: approximately 7 and 15 degrees. Pope John Paul II begins his trip in Poland today. He is set to meet with labor leader Lech Wałęsa*, a swift glance as he enters the dark bedroom and walks over to the blinds, letting the sunlight flood into the room, and everything is the same, but nothing is the same now; the table with books and papers, an open notebook, the window to one side, the patio down below. What happened? What had happened?

He approached the telephone table; there was a fax in the tray, and he picked it up to read it against the light. Standing with his side to the window, he read. *Emilio, I'm faxing you the prescription. I hope they accept it at the pharmacy. Best, Dr. Alidio. Lotrial 20 mg.* One large box of sixty tablets. Pressure high, high pressure. And he saw it there before him, in the air, as if on a luminous screen, written in *his handwriting*; he could read his thoughts, or rather, his hallucinations. He was slightly alarmed. I haven't slept, he managed to say, mentally, before his mind deposited the words, which seemed to burn, meaninglessly, in the air. *There was a crime that, at times, like in a dream, is never identified, no one knows what it is, it's similar to HCE's crime in* Finnegans Wake, *or Karl Rossmann's crime in* Amerika, *or Erdosain's unnameable crime in* The Seven Madmen, *or it's the crime that Sofía Loria de Maggi commits for the love of a woman. But is it that way because of the mark of Cain or an ability to erase one's footprints and lose oneself in the crowd?*

More and more often he would imagine sentences and see them written, like birds or newspaper headlines, hallucinatory inscriptions, graffiti on the walls of the heart. He was uneasy; it was exhaustion and it was boredom and it was uncertainty and it was sorrow. The greatest sorrow, he repeated aloud as he pressed play on the answering machine. One call, another, and the voice:

"How's it going, *campeón*, it's Junior . . . I wish I could've gone with you, but we got caught up in this mess with the assumption, we'll see each other tomorrow in the bar. Anything you need, call me at the newspaper."

Then there was a beep and another missed call, and a voice appeared:

"Hello, yes, it's Enriqueta Loayza, I'm sending you a fax . . . " The voice moved away. "Okay, I hope you pick up, what do you think . . . ?"

Noise, a silence, then another call:

"Dear, it's Clara . . . are you there? Emilio . . . you already left . . . Emilio . . . well . . . give me a call."

He wouldn't call now, it was so early; he imagined the park, the house with its colorful tiles, the balcony, the living room, and, in the bedroom, Clara, naked in bed? Best to work in order not to think; he would make some coffee. His wife would still be at the cabin with

Gerardo and Marga, who knows. He'd left off what he was writing, on the typewriter, and he was trying to connect once again, to remember; he put the water on to boil, three large scoops of coffee in the glass coffee maker, and from down below came the harsh rumor of the city, ambulance sirens, Hospital de Clínicas, state of emergency, the wounded, the desperate.

†

Best to work for a while; he would erase the bad memories, the worries, as though diving into a lake of clear water and feeling the mud below, on his feet, the arborescent growths, the brushes in the depths, but overhead the clean light shining; he'd drunk two cups of coffee already and, sitting at his desk beside the window, began to read what he'd written the day before and went along, altering it with swift little touches [a few swift touches], almost without thinking, by pure instinct [pure intuition], like [cut 'like'] a hunter firing at his prey as it leaps [from the scrubland] or [and] the bird as it flies [takes wing] toward the sky, changing words, crossing them out, writing new sentences by hand, in the margins, in tiny letters, with arrows, circles, and brackets, trying to find the rhythm, the harmony, following the movement of the prose, so that what was written was reborn, actualized, became present, written in the present and narrated in the past, on the shore, a hallucination, she, the future Eva, *sleepless*. Then he put a page into the machine's roller, centered it, wrote 32 at the top and kept going, his fingers on the keyboard, a mechanical sound, the curved typebars rising, one letter, another letter, against the black ribbon, one word and another word and another, a phrase, *that was all*, a tone, capturing the submerged rumor of the iceberg, plunging and plunging into that transparent whiteness, a window into dream, seeing what remains in that frozen whiteness below, under the distant sunlight that filters in through the water, plunging into such white silence, what lay down there?, dark shadows faintly visible within the high walls of ice, static figures, lichens, a harpoon of carved bone, a wooden vessel, a kayak, a woman with long white hair, one foot clothed in a sealskin moccasin and the other foot naked as a fish, within a circle of blue amid the whiteness of the glacier, not only observing the iceberg's elegant visible silhouette but making its sunken gravity felt, moving with the mass itself, entering its chiseled caverns, the stalactites, entering the depths, not suggesting but naming the things he imagined he would see [find] [discover], and there he paused, distracted by the sound of a siren moving away down Calle Charcas (ex-Charcas), the ambulance heading toward the emergency room at Clínicas, ambulances bearing the wounded at all hours of day and night toward the hospitals at the College of Medicine, the alarms, the red lights, as if he were awakening, and he realized that he'd been away for an interval he couldn't calculate, had disappeared from the world, forgotten everything, the stubs crushed in the ashtray, a page per day, and he paused and once more saw through the window the glare of the sun and the buildings on Avenida Santa Fe, the parking lot, the church on Ayacucho, the dove on a wire, as if the world had been reborn, and with the passing of years his immersion was deeper but more fleeting, and when he returned he could continue no longer, he would have the whole day and night ahead before he would go back to writing, and that was all, he lived for those moments, to reach them, no matter how long they lasted, he used to take amphetamines to sustain this drive for a span of hours, but no longer, he only moved toward it, and it would last however long it lasted, but he made it further with each time, casting his pail into the underground river and drawing up a few lines, a thousand words, or some image, and I never know if I'll be able to swim in that river once more, the next day, more of a swimmer than a writer, he didn't like using that word to think about himself, a job, day after day, was it a job?, resumed day after day with no guarantee; he's gone half of his life with no company beyond the will to write, and he wouldn't use that word except with irony, a writer, and for decades he'd lived by setting out alone toward the things he wanted to write.

He left the table and went over to the leather armchair, the pages he'd written in hand, and sat down to read. First Eva saw a white gleam in the night, an eclipse in the middle of the plain. She acted without thinking, with natural and instinctive movements; the safety rules were like second nature. She was lost, cornered. She was eighteen years old. They were enlisting more and more young people. From ghettos and slums and high schools. She was eighteen but looked sixteen and was already a *histórica*, a founder of the movement in its third reincarnation. The daughter of exiles, she was born in Madrid and had grown up with her brother in Paris. They lived high up in the attics, did whatever work came their way, and had been made to return in the wave of '79. The strategic counteroffensive took refuge in the analysis of external leadership. They were dying like sparrows, although dying isn't the word: they were being snared in the traps of the city. Her brother Luca had gotten out in Ezeiza and was murdered. His body displayed on the outskirts of the city as both lesson and punishment. She'd come for his burial and got caught up in the clandestine networks of the organization. She didn't believe any of the information they gave her; the political situation was entirely different from what they claimed, and she had an idea that their leadership employed false information as well; she spent time among the cells and saw that their credo was an illusion. None of her reports reached the Executive Committee. She'd survived two campaigns of siege and extermination and had retreated until she was cornered in Almagro.

She needed to get new papers once again; safety would last ten or twelve hours and then she'd have to change her identity, for the losses never ceased, and the raids, unseen, dismantled the cells before they could begin to act. She remembered her childhood but couldn't be sure of what she'd done in the past week. She had notes of the fragments she did manage to rescue from oblivion. A meeting in the cathedral. She knew she'd been affected but didn't realize how much. Gone was her sense of direction, her judgment of reality; she recognized the city as though once more seeing it for the first time. She knew the fourth memorandum by heart (the second-in-command's name was Perdía, Lost!): "The key element that allows the enemy to complete their cycle of repression is a percentage of traitors upon which it perpetually regenerates its cycles. The existence of these traitors is linked directly to the morale of the forces with respect to their greater or lesser confidence in final victory." Garbage, Eva said furiously, pure garbage, it's destructive, demented, delirious. Criminal, that's what *La Orga*'s directives were. She had to think, find an escape route, an exit, but where? She had a wine-red stain on her face, a mark that she would sometimes conceal for a few hours with makeup. Some days she went into the street wearing a black tulle veil over her face as if she were a young widow.

†

He went out to the street, the porter didn't greet him, he didn't greet him?, the man was from Chile, he should have greeted him, was that a question?, should he have greeted him?, this question was the key to his current state, was it the key?, but the unanswered question, what would that be? . . . up ahead was the travel agency, one could always escape, flee. The expiatory goat runs away to the deserted countryside, he thought, a meeting this early was unusual, he saw his friends after two, that had been his only rule, but now, was he in trouble?, it was ten in the morning, it was another world, unknown to him, and what were all the people doing in the street this early?, he felt tired, but the crisp air of the city revived him and he decided to walk a few blocks to kill time, to kill time? It seems like more than a year must have passed, he would think, further ahead, but time doesn't matter to me, I already lost it, he'd thought then, he didn't want to go in search of any lost time, we have enough with the present, he said aloud, and the girl in the kiosk smiled at him even though he was talking to himself, she seemed used to it, the kid, whose customers blurted their thoughts to her aloud, and she wasn't perturbed, she had a scar on her hand, perhaps from a burn, and she had sky-blue eyes and was only interested in the change, do you have any coins?, you don't have anything smaller?, that was her question, and she gave Emilio the pack of Kents without his asking for it, he used to smoke Colorados, was there a difference?, only the price, sometimes he fantasized about taking her to bed, he had a history with a cashier from a supermarket on Calle Junín, beautiful women, strangers, connected to him in life by absolute contingency. The girl from the market was embarrassed about a tattoo with a man's name at the edge of her pubis, she'd been fifteen at the time, that was all she said for an explanation, and he'd kissed her there. I don't think it's going to rain, said the girl from the kiosk; he hadn't asked her name, didn't want to know it, that way he wouldn't get involved, he thought. Everything seemed dangerous to him in those days. Is the person her name?, there's no answer, he'd prefer to live among strangers, anonymous people, defined by their roles; him, for example, to the girl he was the young man, would she say *the young man* in her thoughts?, he'd be the man with the imported cigarettes, Señor Kent . . . On the same sidewalk, the copy shop was closed, it opened later on, would there be a later on in his life?, he was from Santa Fe, the young man, he'd gone into exile in Mexico, though now he'd come back to the democracy, he was separated from his daughter, who lived in Cuernavaca, he had seventy pages to photocopy, the manuscript. We go onward, Don Emilio, one step forward and another back, he told him, those clandestine references formed their complicity, irony and patience are the principal qualities of the revolutionary, Lenin once said. What remained from all that leftist culture?, references, some references were sung, as they say, were marked, and the armed activists dropped like flies. He crossed Callao, skirted around the plaza, and took Rodríguez Peña toward Paraguay; there were many men living on the street, beggars, vagabonds, and exiles were waiting in the plaza for the consulate to open its doors, which country's?, he couldn't remember, a little state in the Balkans that had changed its name several times, a theocratic state of the Muslim faith, it followed the religious norms of the Qur'an and gave food to the hungry, so that, in the morning, an assistant from the consulate would come out with a tray and serve breakfast, for free, to the disinherited of the world, but only to ten of them per day, this was the tithe to be divided among the poor, but why only breakfast?, and in what order? Renzi didn't know, but the mendicants, the vagrants, the poor were there. He entered the Post Office branch on Calle Paraguay, a narrow and bright shop to the left of the Pizzurno Palace, was this what they called a *palace* in Buenos Aires?, the pretension made him laugh; in 1974, when he spent a month in Italy with a fellowship to study Pavese, Pavese's diary, he'd taken a train, had crossed the North sea by ferry just to visit the palace of Elsinore near Copenhagen, the high walls, the drawbridge, the corridors and terraces paced by Hamlet and the ghost of his father, and mine, he thought, who'd put a bullet in his head that same year, but he was more Horacio's father than my father, why, why?, because Horacio had lived the kind of life my father could understand, he thought about Copenhagen, about the palace of the Prince of Denmark. He was a reader, Hamlet, he walks the passageways of the castle with a book in his hand. In the leather bag he was carrying two letters, one for his friend Jean Franco in New York and another for his brother in Ontario, *Dear Marcos, I don't think I'll be traveling for now* . . . he went up to the little window to send the two letters, express by air, and chatted for a while with the employee with the green visor and white-cloth elbow patches, he could only see his hands, refined, and part of the green reflection from the visor. It's been a while since I've seen you here, he said. I don't come in the morning anymore, Emilio answered, and they chatted a while about the weather and the movements of the economy, and then he went to his post office box. He never gave his home address, he'd maintained this habit since the dictatorship era, he opened the little wooden door and found a letter from Tristana, a covert relationship, CC 1224, there was also a package with a copy of a magazine, *El poeta y su trabajo*, which came from Mexico, and he walked across Callao.

At that moment he was seized by remorse over Horacio's death; he had the feeling that time had stopped with that death, as if a double . . . he'd read in the Bible about the miracle of the loaves and the fishes, Jesus Christ had performed it at his mother's request, it was the first one recorded in the Gospels, give food to the hungry, it was the Marriage at Cana . . . He'd sat down on a bench opposite, in the plaza, to kill time? The peaceful trees, a soft rumor, a green foliage in decline, first to darkness, then a Nile green, greenish pale, the beautiful streetlamps of Thays were lit, a faint light, beneath a tree. He'd sat here, once, unable to write?, and had read, on this very bench?, an interview with Gustavo Sainz in *Mundo Nuevo*, back then he was living on Pasaje del Carmen. In order to continue thinking, he must once more capture—by reading what he's written?—the old circumstances of his life, described well in other times, but must he repeat them?, he thinks, an experiment, not an experience. If it can be narrated, one is saved. *You must repeat so as not to remember*. Not to remember (Horacio's death?); forgetting is an art like any other. There was a leader high up in the ERP, he'd learned how to do it with the German services in Berlin, a neurological technique to erase names and places from memory; the Soviets employed it with their secret agents, it was useless to torture them. *They didn't remember*. They used the well-known interference theory, a theory that regards forgetting as the result of the interference of some memories over others. Lentov, the Russian neuropsychiatrist, had experimented with soldiers suffering shock from the war, it wasn't just the River Lethe but a mnemonics of forgetting. Emilio had attempted to learn the technique of erasing memories; Argentine guerrillas had the option to learn this brainwashing, which allowed them not to remember references or else, if they fell prisoner, if they were captured, to take the cyanide pill—where did they manufacture them?—in clandestine field hospitals, the Montonero doctors, or maybe chemistry students, they manufactured hundreds and hundreds of pills in underground labs, to stop from speaking in the interrogations; his friend had taught him the first steps, you have to sit in the open air and think about a name and replace the letters with even numbers, it's not just the river of forgetting, it's a Russian technique, invented by Pavlov's favorite disciple. To forget the women he had lost, forgetting first their names, their addresses, their beloved faces, so brief is love and so long the forgetting. With that method to erase memory, the nostalgia could not have existed, he thought, smiling mentally.

Facing the plaza, in the Pizzurno building, stands the Biblioteca del Maestro, once directed by the poet Leopoldo Lugones. The reading room was empty, it was very early, they were just opening, they already know me, Lugones was the director, he thought they were going to name him minister, but no, he fell in love with a teacher and killed himself in '38, he hated tango music and dedicated himself to collecting the songs and underlining the lyrics, *there's bound to be a fight when a poor man has his fun*. He hated that anarchist music, that reptile from the brothels. They know me, I go to the lounge, on the right side of the hallway, he killed himself for love, *three hopes I had within my life, and two were white and one blood red*, underlined, that watchful reading, blood red, he was a communist. Every month he wrote a column in a comic magazine, Renzi, and he was putting together an adaptation of the tango "La gayola." *Long years they kept me locked away in a squalid cage . . .* it was prison, down on the lower level he photocopied a few articles that he needed, he'd collected a bibliography on Buenos Aires, was going to write about the city, a novel that would also be a secret guide to the streets and the houses and the histories, all localized here. *It seems like more than a year must have passed*, he thought, but time didn't matter to him, I've already lost it, he only lived remembering.

†

I saw him come, looking as if he hadn't slept in a week, he'd paused in the door of the bar, half blinded by the noonday sun, and then headed toward the same table as always, in the chamfered corner, by the window; he doesn't write anymore or writes so little that he gets to the bar earlier and earlier, and he stays there, waits for a friend, writes in a notebook, orders coffee, reads a little, orders another coffee, looks out through the window, I call him the writer and he laughs as if I'd offended him, he doesn't like that crowd, he says, those imbeciles always follow the same routine, they say, at the border, when they have to fill out forms, they say, at immigration, faced with the little box demanding *profession*, the idiots will all tell you, proudly, so that everyone will know the certainty that accompanies them, they tell you how one day they plunge into the water and write: *writer*. Profession, writer, those bastards say, they make it known that they are, according to them, writers. They self-appoint, betraying the fact that it isn't true, since they say it, and they write it in the box at immigration, *in printed letters*, they're arrogant and idiotic to say it, whereas I, in the box at immigration, put *businessman* or *unemployed*, or *doctor*. Sometimes I put *doctor* to satisfy the ghost of my father, who wanted me to follow in his footsteps, and he was so upstanding, my father, that sometimes, in order to satisfy him, even though he's dead, I write on the form, in printed letters, *doctor*. No one goes to the trouble to verify those stated professions, a policeman doesn't say to those idiots, let's see, write a poem, define free indirect discourse in a few words, what is an image, no, but by contrast for me, if I say, as I've sometimes done, at border checkpoints or in airports, I am a doctor, it might happen that the captain of the plane will ask over the intercom mid-flight, for a doctor!, because someone is, as they say, indisposed and must be put right.

I would tell Renzi some stories if he came up to the bar; he'd stop there to talk to me while I was occupying myself, as they say, with keeping the tables at bay. He was interested in knowing how orders were called up from memory without being written down. One afternoon he confessed to me, sorrowfully, that if he, Emilio, didn't take notes, he would forget everything, and it seemed to him that he hadn't lived the days that weren't recorded in his notebooks. By contrast, a bar is run from memory, and running a bar, I tell him, is a mnemonic exercise, it involves the spatial arrangement of people; one doesn't remember the regular customers, one remembers their positions and makes a mental map of the bar, of each of the tables, and the arrangement of each customer at each table. The placement is remembered, the customer at the middle table, sitting at the end, in a northeast orientation, factoring in the entry door as a reference for this scheme to aid memory. On the contrary, he was interested in forgetting, he told me, in being blank, without recollection; he wants to live in the pure present, without memory, but he's very observant, nothing escapes him, he asks for detailed explanations on the workings of the bar, wants to know why I've come back, if I speak Swedish, if I'm a citizen without a homeland, and if the Uruguayan government can extradite me. He curses his social democrat friends, he says, they conform, they write speeches for the authorities and speak as if they were ministers, he says, they've sold their convictions to the press, he says, they're converts, they've become what they used to hate, they indeed have no memory, they know that in betraying one's ideals one forgets everything he or she has thought, has written, has desired, and that is an anti-mnemonic exercise that I despise and never want to employ; my friends now defend the things they hated in their youth, they've grown old and believe that they've matured, are prudent, they conform, they aren't even cynical, they change their beliefs, remain dogmatic, I've been left alone, Liber, he tells me, and asks me for the telephone. It's Emilio, he says, once the call connects, sometimes they call him here, at the bar, always the same woman, she lives somewhere else or is elsewhere in the summer and he stays, to write in his study, so he says, but he comes here earlier and earlier, today it was, I don't know, eleven or eleven thirty, he comes in defeat. I don't write anymore, he says, I only transcribe, he says, I only record.

I'm a bartender, I don't know the customers except through the things they tell me, and one day he started talking to me as if I both were and were not there; there's nothing better than talking to a stranger, "coming clean" to someone who appears to be listening and understanding but is in fact a stranger. The bartender at a bar is an essential figure in these anonymous confessions, and on that day Emilio began to tell me a story that I didn't quite understand, that I've forgotten, about a change of residence, by force, I remember he used that expression, *forced change of residence*, but I've forgotten all the rest, and maybe he told me about it because he happened to find out that I'd been exiled in Sweden, and then he goes and asks me about the Tupamaros, we took Pando, I tell him, we got in by the main street, we were in a funeral procession, if you have the money it's easy to hire a funeral service and go out with the black cars even though the coffin is empty, so we took over the police station, the telephone exchange, and the bank, but actually, I tell him, I always wanted to be a bartender and live in Buenos Aires. Two or three times a week he meets a friend, a young man with curly hair whose name I still don't know; he comes with a tape recorder and records their conversations, or really the things Emilio says. I only listen to fragments when I go to pour them a glass of wine; I listen because they go on talking as if I weren't there, so that bursts reach me, stray sentences, lost words, today for example I heard his friend say to him: "You're crazy, Emilio, you think you killed him. He came to see you and you didn't help him, you think you're responsible." "If I'd said something, I could have saved him from death, I could have said: Horacio, stay here with me at the cabin, I could have said: just think of it like you were widowed, she died, *c'est fini*, forget about her, time erases regret . . . " I listened, from the bar, to fragments, and based on these fragments I imagined or believed that I knew what they were talking about. Someone called Horacio had died, something fishy happened with his wife, it seems to me, she became a Buddhist and left him to devote herself to yoga. Something like that. You end up imagining the lives of the customers so that you can humor them when they come up the bar for a drink. If you talk to them personally, they come back and become habitués.

However, today, suddenly, a chime of silence occurred, as happens sometimes, there weren't many people in the bar and by chance they were arranged in a semicircle, their tables surrounding the chamfered corner, and in that way they isolated Renzi, and, because the windows were closed, Emilio's voice reached me clearly, it happens sometimes, there's an interval of silence in the bar and you can listen, clearly, to what they're talking about at one of the tables, it seems like there's a woman in Europe and Emilio is waiting for her, but she doesn't know. She writes him furious and passionate letters and he's almost petrified, from what he says. I heard the word *petrified* and looked up in surprise, and he was laughing, so petrified seems to be an agreeable state. I'm saying what I heard, he was laughing and then took a pause and went on talking. It seems that, on a trip to Germany, invited there with other South American writers, he met a woman on the subway. She wasn't German, she was an old friend. That's what I could make out.

Now I recall that the other day, when I went over to serve the table, Renzi was in conversation with a journalist, I think. The truth is that, since I had my antennae out to record their order correctly, I listened to what he was saying, and it was etched into me as if it had been a complicated order, like at a table with ten or twelve diners all saying what they'll have, I memorize it by looking fixedly at the place from which each of them speaks to me. What happened here is that Renzi stayed still, and I was the one moving around the table, and, because of those strange qualities memory has, I haven't forgotten what Renzi said as I was cleaning the table and serving him a glass of wine and a plate of Gruyère cheese. I say it as I remember it, just so.

"Compared with music, literature is a crude instrument. I always admired Gerardo Gandini, but when I met him personally (in March last year), he turned to be out much better than I might have imagined a musician to be. He works with constant inspiration and doesn't play the artist. One night I heard him play all of Schoenberg's pieces for piano at the Goethe and go out with the same smile and jokes as always. He does the extraordinary as if it were simple and turns the simple into the extraordinary."

If I have to make a summary, I'd say he's a fairly well-known writer, has published several books, is always reading, comes to the bar every day, writes down lines in a notebook, and spends a lot of time looking out the window until something occurs to him and then goes back to writing. It might be memories that he's writing down, because he writes for a while and then looks off into the air as though following the flight of some invisible fly, and then he leans over the notebook and furiously writes two or three words. And he goes on like that all morning. At twelve, he orders a glass of white wine and a plate of green olives.

His friend, the one who comes to see him in the bar two or three times a week, seems to be writing a biography of Renzi, because he questions him and asks him for details, asks him for information, he poses questions and they sometimes spend the whole afternoon together. But today his friend left early, he must have been in an hour and then left. Emilio stayed a while reading the newspapers, he always says that he comes to this bar because it has the day's papers and because he can get very pure white wine here, made in Switzerland. There are several cases of that wine downstairs, and I'm convinced that he's going to drink his way through all of them and that, once he's done with them, he won't come back to El Cervatillo.

†

He went down Callao, walking along the sidewalk in the sun, the bookshop on the corner of the Universidad del Salvador, and on crossing Córdoba, the funeral home. One afternoon in '67, when he was living in an apartment in the cul-de-sac of El Carmen, he'd found the beginning for the novel he'd been working on for months, the criminals had kidnapped a journalist, and during the siege he had recorded their stories on a portable tape recorder, he was trying to register the rhythms of their speech, could remember the first paragraph from memory, it had taken him two months to write those twenty lines and he remained faithful to that tone, the characters in the novel alternated, he had the newspapers from that period, the assault on the bank truck, the flight to Uruguay, the police blockade, the suicidal resistance until the end, when they decide to burn the money, but first they set the journalist free so he can tell their story. On that day he had seen, like an apparition, clearly, the image of the tall man, pallid, smothered by the smoke and gas, coming out of the apartment in ruins and passing among the ash and bodies with the tape recorder held high, like a soldier carrying his rifle overhead while crossing a river.

He knew that section of the city well, he'd lived in the area for almost twenty years, never moving outside a radius of twenty blocks, from Santa Fe to Rivadavia and from Cerrito until Ayacucho. If he used a compass to trace an imaginary circle on the map, he could see the places where he'd lived and mark them with a cross, and then he could draw the routes and movements of his life, the bars, the nocturnal walks, the bookshops, Hotel Callao, the endless conversations, the cinemas, Lorraine, Premier, the Lugones room at Teatro San Martín, the restaurants he would go to, the old market with its tin roof and incandescent murmuring, filled with life. And so that was his territory, the publishing houses where he'd worked, the women he'd loved, the magazines he'd been part of, the large newspaper kiosks on the corners with books, pamphlets, music records, posters, offerings of booklets on the history of painting. That was his world, his territory, and memory was fixed in every part of this unforgettable zone where he'd set up his camp, his tents, his precarious hospitals, he'd lived there, bought drugs in the pharmacies that stayed open all night, and if he wanted to tell his life, or, put better, if he had already told his life in the notebooks he carried from place to place, the key was the cartography of the space of his mind. The map as autobiography.

He reached Corrientes. He'd always felt a stroke of euphoria when he turned down Callao toward Corrientes, and in the times he spent abroad, the most vivid memory, the clear feeling, like a gentle breeze, was the emotion at turning the corner and seeing Calle Corrientes appear before him, that was the thing that he missed and could never forget and would return to him as a dream. "As in a dream," he thought, it wasn't about the content of the dream, a few times he'd dreamed of the city in the years when he'd lived in another country, or on his journeys abroad, as he said, New York, Mexico, San Francisco, Paris, Montevideo, Beijing, it was another map, as personal as the diagram of his days in Buenos Aires; he didn't dream of the map, but in his memory, in the lived images of the place itself, he had the same certainty that is felt in dreams, the conviction of the truth that lies beyond real life and is more real, it is the real, he repeated aloud. The emotional gravity of the images—the certainty of feeling, of being inside the feeling, to put it like that, which is felt in a dream, brought on by a minute detail, its consequences unforgettable: the feeling of terror or shame or surprise that exists in a dream—that's what was repeated in remembering, or rather seeing himself, in different periods of his life, entering Calle Corrientes from Callao. Turning to the left, on the corner of La Ópera bar, and going on without crossing, toward the river, but first, in a fragile instant that the memory records like painless fire in the blood, the change in direction, the precise moment in which one is no longer walking from north to south but heading east, toward the river. At that crossroads, between the horizontal line ahead and the vertical cut toward Corrientes, in that angle, was the memory that came back when he was abroad and lived as an outsider. Only in that image, where he sees himself entering the city, was happiness. The feeling that everything was possible, in the space that opened—as if someone had pulled aside a curtain of thick cloth to let the sunlight enter the room—before him, was there, ever since his distant youth, when he patrolled the streets with the violence of a lone wolf, until today, forty years now gone by, when he turns down Callao toward Corrientes and feels the same euphoria and the same sense of risk he once felt with Cacho Carpatos, Horacio, Junior, David, registering the city at night and seeking adventure, or a rendezvous with a woman with red hair, the intent of conquest that had forever marked his life.

It was not, then, the harsh feeling of entering combat, that situation wasn't the subject of the dreams, but rather it was the surety itself, the certainty about one's emotions that is felt in a dream, that had persisted within him over the course of the years, conquering his apathy and coldness. "It's been the only passion that has remained identical to itself until today, since long-distant times." That is to say that his autobiography, if he one day decided to write it based on his diaries, would revolve around the blue light of his truest emotion. A friend of his, whose friend had gone away, had spoken to him, the night before, in a dream. "You had come and given a lecture on Seminar V at the College, and Karla was with me," she'd told him. But her other friends were there as well, and all together, after commenting on the talk ("although I couldn't listen to the commentary in the dream, it wouldn't let itself be heard"), they made a fire on the dirt patio, and fire was at once the signal of an orgy, but, to Emilio's disappointment, the party, the get together, his friend commented, "had not entered the oneiric material." But now, Emilio thought as he advanced along the street, the meaning of dreams is an enigma that everyone solves as they can, but the synthetic truth of the feelings, which arises within us when dreaming, is unique and unforgettable. That same certainty and truth of emotion is what literature—when done well—transmits to us.

He sat at a table by the window in La Paz bar, yet another bar and another table looking out onto the street, the repetition had become his hallmark, maybe it meant something, that monotonous succession of identical actions over the course of the day. He ordered a coffee and took a letter out of his bag and began to read it with the same attention, a slightly comical kind, at least when viewed from the outside, using a pencil to underline words, phrases, and even a few paragraphs; it would seem that if he doesn't mark what he reads he remains detached, but when he reads with a pencil in hand, he manages, or attempts, to draw out the personal meaning that the text holds for him. This is a kind of reading that spans his entire life, reading with a pencil in hand, taking notes, focusing a kind of attention so as to be able to say something, later, about what he has read; the markings already form a commentary and are also a guide for transcribing the paragraphs or sentences in a quotation. But for novels and poems, he doesn't underline while reading, and at most he annotates in a microscopic script on the last page of the book, on the blank sheet, the number of a page, thus indicating his will to come back and read that moment of the story or poem again. That morning, he'd placed the typewritten page on the table in a space set aside for it, and went along reading with special care as if that sheet of paper contained explosive mines, as if the letter were, to put it that way, a minefield. *Dear Emilio: I have so many things to tell you that I don't know where to begin. The "company" of others doesn't exist. I can't understand any language. I put on my mask and go on without understanding. Something is clear to me, which is that I don't want to see you, and that the things in my life, the details, are impossible to explain. Those who speak too much grow weary. That's why I'm writing to you.* It was Tristana, they had a love affair more than fifteen years ago, and because of it, without seeking it, as an unwanted consequence, he'd lost Julia, they'd separated because Julia couldn't bear his having a special friendship with a woman who'd been a very close friend of hers. During that time, was it in '71 or '72?, they had to abandon the apartment on Calle Sarmiento because of an army inspection, a search operation, typical in those years; they were looking for a young couple, the porter had told him, and so he and Julia had packed up and fled overnight. They stayed in various hotels and borrowed houses until Julia told him about an apartment that a friend of hers could lend them for a couple of months, a stately building on Calle Uriburu near Avenida Santa Fe, and there, to conceal the anxiety caused by abandoning their home with nothing but the clothes on their backs, as they say, he began, almost without realizing it, a romance with Tristana, which in the end Julia discovered (by reading his notebook!). It had been idiotic, the affair itself and, above all, to have written the truth in his notebook, which he'd always left in plain sight because he didn't want to hide anything from the woman he loved, trusting in the pact of loyalty that is established, implicitly, between two people who live together. They aren't going to go spying on each other, yet that's what happens. Julia had read his notebook and, enraged, had written in it as well: *I want a word*, she'd written, *you knew I would be your first reader*. She wasn't the only one, others before her had done the same. (*It wasn't like that, it never was*, Amanda, for example, had written.) Tristana was a wonderful woman, and they remained friends even now, and she, who had lived in Entre Ríos, used to write him a letter every now and then, like the friend she was.

†

Letters from a friend who writes. That's what it would have to be called, thought Renzi. She would write to him every now and then; friendship with a woman lay in the words, he thought. Sitting there in La Paz bar, like so many times before, he killed some time, took a few detours, before reading Tristana's letter. One would arrive for him in his post office box, every now and then; it wasn't a covert or compromising correspondence, but he preferred to keep certain areas of his life hidden. Tristana's husband was a doctor, and she would contrive to forge his prescriptions from time to time and send Emilio, through a commission agent, a package with a couple boxes of Dexamyl spansules; the women in his life had been the providers of drugs, Circe, in the *Odyssey*, the lotus-eaters nearly capture Ulysses and his crew in the goodness of their wicked alchemy. *I get up at six in the morning, drink yerba mate, talk to the girls, then they leave for school at seven, and I leave at seven fifteen to go to the Civil Registry; I sought out that job (the only one I found) as a way to keep myself active and because there are days when we don't have enough for food.* The girls, the daughters, one of them, was she his?, could she be his?, a natural child, why not, the dates could always line up, and Emilio would receive an emotional and compromising letter many years later. "I'm your daughter, Papá!" He hadn't laughed at that news, but Tristana was very discreet, and one afternoon she told him: Emilio,

I love you but we're going to stop seeing each other; Tristana was going to get married, to a doctor, another doctor, because Emilio was out of the running. "You're never going to make, or establish," she said, smiling, "a family." *One of my old man's sisters, a widow of one of the Illias, got it for me, and she thinks I'm deeply radical as a result of the book on Alvear, which Nosiglia wrote when all is said and done (I, drunk, limited myself to gathering information from* Plus Ultra *magazine and the eminent Félix Luna). That book earned me some respect on the part of my parents and my daughters, who at that time viewed me as an amoeba. I was an amoeba, really, sleeping tirelessly and drinking tirelessly as well, telling myself that I drank because I had low blood pressure and depression. My will was absolutely ravaged.* So it was, so it might have been, it was a time of a great deal of alcohol, all a bit promiscuous, so to speak, for we were living in the imminence of a change in era, in the anticipation of being present for a change in civilization. *One thing is real: when I gave up the bottle, there came to me a desire to do things.* It was noon, and so, inspired by what he read, he called the waiter over and ordered a whiskey on the rocks. He had underlined or rather drawn a circle around the word *bottle*. The bottle, he thought, a synecdoche, rhetoric, or rather rhetorical figures, they'd helped him to escape from pain many times, as focusing on the form of an expression instantly put him at a remove. He had a very fine ear for figures of speech; the way a woman used the subjunctive, for example, could give rise to a sentimental passion in him. She, on the other hand, never joked around, although she didn't take herself too seriously and had a great deal of ironic elegance. *The job above ends at three in the afternoon. I could've encountered a hostile environment, considering that I came in like any gust of summer wind and with the same salary conditions as the girls who've been stuck there for fifteen or twenty years. But that's not what I found. The situation, morally speaking, doesn't give me any comfort, but I try as much as possible not to think about that. It's coming to an end, the thing you knew to call "a beautiful love story with a man who was in jail."* There was a series of repetitions in his life that he couldn't avoid, and they became visible in his notebooks because he could reread and not just recall them. For example, a woman who has a man in prison:

one series. Alcira, Bimba, Tristana. A woman who studies theater and sells her body so as not to betray her artistic calling; there were, even if no one will believe it, two in his life (Constanza and Amanda). There was an extraordinary succession of coincidences and replicas and figures that repeated in his life, that is, in his notebooks, which for him signified proof that what was written in his diary was life itself, with its chaotic repetitions. For example, some time ago he'd read a novel by Burgess (*Earthly Powers*, 340): "Mrs. Killigrew, whose husband played bridge all the time, discovered a passion for a man whose face was covered with warts. Why was this? In a story you had to find a reason, but real life gets on very well without even Freudian motivations." In life the ending isn't elegant, nor does it make sense, whereas in the novel, on the other hand, the ending must be energetic and electric and elegiac. He'd become distracted and resumed reading, he was on topic. *Do all love stories end? It would seem so, and that really doesn't affect me.* Tristana, before separating from her doctor husband, had lived in Concordia, Entre Ríos. That was why Renzi had set the ending of his novel *Artificial Respiration* there. In homage to his friend, and also because he liked the place, and, above all, the name of the town sounded good to him. Tristana had moved to Buenos Aires with her two daughters and had started to decline; she shouldn't have separated from the doctor, but she was too forthright and intelligent to go on living with a man she no longer loved, despite the very high price that—she knew—she would pay. *The present was the glass of gin and the future didn't exist. I was living in the past then, and there, fumbling around, I found this man, a ring on his finger because he too lived on memories. I tend to think that, if alcohol hadn't existed on the earth, I might have ended up on a desert island or raining bullets on people from some box seat, during some event. I'll never know if it tempered my imbalance with reality or increased it. Never ever. Better that way.* He hadn't spoken to her for a long time; both, in a sense, were convalescents, recovering addicts of different magical substances, in recovery, in home care, so to speak. *For the first two months (of not drinking), reality presented itself to me as something unbearable and cruel. I only felt safe here, with the girls, or there, with the drunks. That was my only venture outside, to those people. Little by little my introduction into society came about, and here I am, walking slowly, a bit tentatively.* He could say the same thing, with the same words. *It calmed me enormously to write you this letter.* Renzi underlined the sentence as proof of his recognition of her endless generosity, she, the friend he'd cared for, not loved, Renzi used that word very little. But he had cared for her, felt close to her, like so many comrades in life, injured, gravely injured, fallen in combat, hospitalized, high-quality losers, battered by the gale-force wind of the times. Horacio, for example, he was always thinking about him these days, there wasn't a day when he didn't remember him. And Tristana, so dear, the same thing happened with her ("With me," he thought). *Call me when you have time, so we can see each other. My congenital shyness, so well disguised by gin in other times, has reappeared. Today, May 17, it's exactly six months since I've had a drink.* He was going to call her, was he going to call her? He could get up and ask for the telephone at the bar, or call her from the public phone on the back wall, next to the door that opened onto Corrientes, beside the Premier bookshop, where he always went when he was in the area. He liked the epilogue to Tristana's letter. *I'm rereading this letter at the Registry, around ten in the morning. It seems like I entered a kind of dry drunkenness at dusk (yesterday, Sunday, in this case);* (he liked the expression, dry drunkenness, and underlined it and marked it with an arrow in the margin), *I seem to have written so many crazy ideas to you. Look what makes me content (and makes me happy, makes me well) in this moment: something as simple as seeing the sun through the windows (I spent a long time with the shutters down, as in a freezer). We can only find salvation (what an old word) in irony and humor (the sense of). Association; my sister-in-law from Mar del Plata said to me: "To my mind, you're giving your daughter a very liberal education," can you believe that? Liberal, she said. While her daughter (her own) at age fifteen runs off to dance at Gigoló and tells her that she's going to the theater to watch* Snow White. *A hug, Tristana.*

He was going to go to the Premier bookshop, the door that went through the bar, his friend Vicente Almagro was there, he looked after the place but was actually a secret leader of the community of friends excluded from the fever of Alfonsinismo, which was in fashion in those days, and so Emilio could meet Peronists of a different breed there, ones who reminded him, for better or worse, of his father, both in their way of speaking and because the Peronists are on the decline, they're in low spirits when they aren't ruling or holding onto a bit of power, Renzi thought, letting himself drift off with stray thoughts as he called to the waiter, who as usual seemed unable to see him and ignored him in spite of his gestures, having other things to do; waiters, even if they knew him well, wouldn't think of attending to him until they felt like it, thought Emilio. Thought? He thought less and less, was struggling more and more to think, he thought now.

†

The bookshop was a refuge, and he could spend hours there, conversing with friends as they came and went. "A basic unit," Emilio defined it. The Peronists used to gather there, and Emilio recalled his father's friends, always hoping for a political miracle; there was something like superstition in Peronism, as if being inside could grant safety to the desperate, a kind of irrational guarantee, a sentiment that assured their continuity. The Premier bookshop was in the best part of the city, right in the middle of Calle Corrientes, next to La Paz bar, to the side of the Lorraine cinema and opposite the San Martín theater. "El hoyo del queque," the heart of the matter, David used to say, always abstruse, with his esoteric language that superimposed geological layers of the city's forgotten words.

That afternoon, Emilio was—as he said more and more frequently—killing time, looking for a book on the First World War, and Vicente, his friend, who was in charge of the bookshop, suddenly asked him about the story of his grandfather, who had initially been in love with his wife because she had, for a period of time in Turin, been an opera singer, not a *prima donna*, a background character, but she viewed herself—in her dreams, Emilio clarified—as a diva, and even though she'd already lost her voice in her youth and so had participated only in the performance of *Tosca*, in a secondary role, she did have a few lines as a child prodigy, a goodbye to her brother who was going off to war. The fragment, which consisted of twelve words, which she'd sung on her own within the scene, off to one side, illuminated for seven seconds by a white light and dressed in period clothing, had been enough for her to go the rest of her life considering herself to be an opera singer who'd lost her voice. And sometimes, on Sundays, when the family was gathered together, all contented and slightly tipsy from the wine and champagne they'd drunk, she, my grandmother Rosa, would get up from the long trestle table on the patio at the family house, a bit red in the face, and, her hands resting on the tablecloth, would sing, in a low but very heartfelt voice, an aria from Aida, and everyone would applaud, moved by the sad story of my grandmother's triumphant career through the opera theaters of the whole world. It was also said that she'd abandoned the *bel canto* out of love for my grandfather Emilio; in that version, she was the disconsolate diva who left behind her art to come to America with him.

Linguistic constants and variations, continuous variation. Music and the relationship between the voice and the music (opera) fulfill a larger role than literature in defining the limits of language, thought Emilio. "Compared to music, literature is a crude instrument," he repeated. Opera was part of my family tradition, first due to the reverential respect stirred up by my grandmother Rosa, who—according to myth—had left the opera for my grandfather Emilio. And second because all of the tragedies and everyday life of my family were lived out in the melodramatic tone of an opera. If life had background music, like a film, my father used to say, opera would be the accompaniment to the peripeteias of your mother's family, the Maggis, he'd say, as if wanting to distance himself from those excessive passions and sentiments.

That afternoon at the Premier bookshop, Renzi began telling this story to his friend Vicente, the bookseller, but also to the bystanders and the regular customers in the bookshop, all of them embittered and self-sacrificing Peronist activists who met there in search of conversation and friendship among comrades from the movement. My father told me the story about his father one afternoon walking along the beach. My grandfather came to Argentina and settled in alone as station chief at a stop on the Southern Railway in the middle of the countryside, in a town with no houses that was called Martín Fierro! The country folk thought highly of my grandfather because he was an extraordinary craftsman and made astonishing miniatures. They were always asking him to make them a little horse with a gaucho dressed in Sunday clothes, the size of a thimble, carved out of balsa wood. If you blew into it, the little gaucho would fly right out. The locals, my father recounted, used to come up to the houses on holidays to listen to Puccini's operas.

My grandfather built a wooden scale model of the station and the houses in town. And the locals came to see how the place where they lived was reproduced in the replica. The roofs of the houses could be lifted up to reveal the interiors, just as they were. Only the bedrooms, the furniture, the meticulously reproduced objects, but not a single human figure: an empty town, in perfect condition, in the middle of the plain. The structure, which weighed nothing because it was made with such fine wood, was kept, for part of my childhood, in a shed where tools were stored, as if everyone thought ill of the way my grandfather had captured in a model the place where a beloved woman had lived. (Maybe, I think now, the diva who lost her voice blamed my grandfather for that misfortune, and for that reason, I think sometimes, the whole family tragedy was wrong.) In the end, an American collector bought it from my mother, and she was able to take a trip to Europe (in 1970) with the money. It was from there that the idea came to me for a man who loses a woman and builds himself a microscopic, alternative world (a museum). I remember even now how my grandfather was always listening to opera (preferably by Puccini, whom he considered a one-of-a-kind musician). My grandfather listened and never found out whether his wife, that is, my grandmother Rosa, was one of the singers on the recording. Maybe he only listened to the opera that she'd sung in as a way to hold onto the voice of the woman lost in the chorus. On that side I always associated opera with a family sorrow. I mean to say a pain that can't be expressed in words, something beyond language. I've already said once before that, when I saw Claude Lanzmann's documentary *Shoah* (a Jewish barber, forced to cut the hair of the prisoners in the doorway to the bathrooms where they were going to be killed with gas, discovered a nephew in line, and in telling it he broke down in tears, the emotion took away his language), I realized that there is a point at which feelings can't be expressed and people, then, stop talking and simply cry. In opera, the situations are so extreme that pain is expressed in song; the people can no longer speak, and it becomes natural for them to sing. The other experience connected to opera is an idea from Gramsci that always seems fantastic to me. *The Italians*, Gramsci says, *do not have the popular novel, but we did have the opera.* Italian opera as an exaggerated form of the nineteenth-century popular melodrama: like a version of Dumas or Dickens or Dostoevsky. It was the same story from the serial novel but in another register: in a sharper register, we might say, causing the sentiments that exist in life to stand out in an explicit way. A man is afraid of losing the woman he loves and can't imagine the world without her and makes a Faustian pact; my father, as a good Peronist, thought that my grandfather had gone off to war to settle his debts with Lucifer. Speaking figuratively, Renzi explained to the surprised customers of the Premier bookshop who'd come there in search of their political line because they were very disoriented, these Peronists, flattened by the social democracy, and they thought that Horacio González or Chacho Álvarez would be able to throw them a rope to climb out of the historical bog they'd sunk into, but they found themselves with Renzi, who, standing by the counter, was very enthusiastically telling the story of his grandfather Emilio's life, before, he emphasized, long before he volunteered in the War of '14.

Every now and then Gandini called me up, and I'd go to his apartment on Calle Chacabuco (which had once been Guillermo Saavedra's), and I'd tell him the story of my grandfather, and he, on the piano that took up all of a diminutive room, would play a fragment that he'd just composed and would sing to me, not articulating words, just a melodic and operatic murmur that reminded me of the way my family used to accompany the singing of the operas they listened to on the record player. A very musical family, Renzi said, looking at his engrossed listeners, how's everything going, boys? Is Peronism coming back to power or what?

Without waiting for the response, he said goodbye to Vicente and his cohort. He had a meeting with his students and the lost souls of the city at another bar, and, as he went out to the street and walked west, either because of that change in direction and because of his conversation about opera, his friend the musician Gerardo Gandini returned in his memory, and then, like a home movie on Super 8, images came back to him from that endless summer when they decided to spend a month together on a beach in Uruguay, in a rural town overlooking the sea, where the Surrealist poets Molina and Madariaga, and also Edgar Bayley before he died, always used to spend long periods of time. "We rented a few houses and went there with other friends (Rozitchner, Carlos Altamirano) and spent the night drinking wine with Freddy, Madariaga, and other companions. We talked all night, until dawn on those luminous January days; Gandini had taken over the house that used to be Edgar Bayley's, and Edgar's ghost appeared to him to console him and keep him company when he had insomnia." ("Infinite these riches abandoned.") In those days he told his friends over and over about his grandfather Emilio's passion and the story of his love with the singer who'd lost her voice because of him.

†

He stationed himself in La Ópera bar every afternoon to "receive" his friends, lovers, students, colleagues, and an ambivalent set of regulars, drifters, and bystanders from the fauna that gathered on that corner and hung around his table to take part in the conversation. Each corner in the city, especially if there's a subway stop, has its own local color and ways of surviving. He wrote down those details in his diary, imagining he would make a detailed survey of the city. The subject of the day, for each day had a distinct subject that captured the interest of the table where Renzi sat to receive his acquaintances, was cybernetics.

That afternoon, everyone was talking about the virtues and dangers of using word processors and computers. These were the great novelties that his friends broadcast with enthusiasm. One was writing, very inspired, but a power outage or a wrong keystroke would sink him to the depths of the sea. "I had five pages written, they'd taken me all night, and they were erased, bang, just like that," said fat Soriano, who was now a daring expert on writing about artificial intelligence. You have to print it, the fat man advised. You turn on the printer, he said, and click, out comes the page with its impeccable writing; he also propagandized the use of backup. You have to make a backup, every half hour, so that you don't lose everything and get caught up a creek with no paddle.

Renzi used WordPerfect and felt comfortable with his Macintosh computer, which he'd bought in New York on the advice of his youngest friends, who lived glued to their video games and computers with special programs. He has the benefit of using a mouse and being able to work without using the keyboard to start the programs, the documents and files can be viewed in windows, icons, just click and you're off. One advantage, quickly discovered, was the ability to correct a sentence while it was being written, without having to retype the entire corrected page once it was ready, the way it was on his Lettera 22, which he didn't want to abandon because he'd written everything on it ever since his grandfather Emilio gave it to him as a gift in 1959.

Renzi had learned, he said, during the months when he was work-ing on an opera with Gandini. Musicians have a private language, a pure form that allows them to phrase and modulate very sophis-ticated thoughts, which are made out of quotations and the voices of others as well. Just look at the way Gandini plays the piano, the notion of rehearsal scarcely exists for him, the music is absolute immediacy, the notes are there and he always performs them as if he'd written them. He reads from memory, if I can be permitted the echo of Macedonio in the definition, and that way of reading the music while he is playing, as if composing or as if improvising every-thing he plays, is something extraordinary. Music functions like an imaginary language; it is a language made of pure forms, and in that way, of course, it resembles mathematics. Literature aspires to that language but never reaches it, not even Joyce could attain that purity. It seems to me, he improvised, that the computer too has a rhythm of its own that must be searched for and discovered. When I trave-led to the United States for the first time, in 1977, at the University of California, San Diego, they were experimenting with the large computers of Palo Alto. They'd taken one of those enormous IBMs with eighty light bulbs and paper reels and loaded it with Melville's *Moby Dick*, hoping that the program would produce literature based on the combination of words from the novel. The harpoon has fallen out of use in life, but it sounds just right for hunting whales in the book. That, said Renzi, was the idea; get it? The hope is that the machines will be able to write on their own, preferably huge best-sellers, although the truth is that the machine from Palo Alto only produced unintelligible texts.

He took a pause, Renzi, excited by the interest that he was causing among the girls at a table in the bar and also by the fascination sparked in him by a beggar he'd seen on the sidewalk at the bar on Callao, talking on a mobile phone, made of wood, as big as a shoe. He was pretending to be talking with a client on the phone-like device, which reproduced what he'd seen around the city being used by executives from large corporations. The panhandler, dressed in rags, thought, with good reason, that using a mobile phone would bring him some status, and so he'd crafted a wooden replica and was talking with it in his hand, even now, at the table, commenting on what Renzi was saying and relating it to a friend somewhere below, in the subway station. "Here the gentleman is explaining the issue of artificial intelligence, a machine he saw in North America, it's a kind of giant telephone that talks to itself and runs on batteries."

In 1987, Renzi had spent a semester at Princeton University as a Senior Fellow in the Humanities Council and, taking advantage of the university library, had conducted the final studies for his research into artificial literature, produced directly by computer. In reality, the whole thing had begun some years before with an unexpected visit from his cousin Luca, whom he must thank here for being the first one to call his attention to the danger that all cybernetic devices could be disabled suddenly by an attack.

Renzi lived in the professors' neighborhood close to the lake, in a two-story Tudor-style house. My neighbor, Hans Kruster, would speak of his time as head researcher at the Institute for Advanced Study here at Princeton as if referring to a time at once immediate and distant. Hans abandoned theoretical physics at age twenty-three, or it abandoned him, as he often says with a smile, the same as someone who's lost a woman, and at age thirty, after a deep depression, he devoted himself to teaching and accepted the position. Hans speaks of theorists like telepaths who've lost their powers. Brilliant young people who turn useless at age twenty-five and survive like zombies until their deaths. We're veterans, or any class of subject who's had a sufficiently powerful and heinous experience to make everything else seem idiotic afterward, he told me one day. There exists an agility in youth that only musicians and mathematicians know: the velocity and purity of the forms fades with the years and lives only in extreme youth. We're old at age twenty-five; Einstein vegetated all his life as a mythical half-idiot devoted to performing the figure of the wise man in front of the mass media, while everyone knew, he most of all, that he was liquidated. Kurt Gödel created his theorem like a flash of lightning at age twenty and then did nothing more for the rest of his life. In reality, the great universities recruit us like we're a group of recovering alcoholics who have to instruct the newest generations of drunks; they put us in contact with absorbed and ambitious young people so that we might initiate them into the perverse game of artificial intelligence. He, now retired, had dedicated his nights to creating and thinking up a diabolical experiment right in front of them, in a lab that he'd set up in the basement of his house, intended to send creative writers and individual producers of literature to the landfill.

One night, at last, he showed it to me; he was waiting for me in the doorway and we went to his underground office as soon as I arrived. Onto a white Formica table he'd placed a cardboard box and, when he opened it, the machine appeared. It was a nickel-plated prototype the size of a standard toaster (possibly he'd used the structure of a toaster as a base). It had two red buttons and a roll of ticker tape that came out of a slot in the middle of the upper part. Now look, said Hans. He pressed one of the buttons and inserted a set of little cards that reproduced the letters of the alphabet. Close to twenty seconds went by before anything happened. Hans was calm and serious and drank beer from a can; through the window, in the setting sun, we could see the frozen gleam of the lake. Suddenly the machine began working with an electronic clickety-clack. Hans took the tape and read it, backlit, with a powerful magnifying glass. His eye looked like the Andromeda galaxy. He lowered the glass and smiled. A ghost story, he told me, as it should be. He placed the perforated tape on a black cardboard box and handed me the magnifying glass. The story was called "The Nightmare." "An aunt I've cared for very much goes crazy and becomes telepathic and in the dream won't let me wake." A twenty-word story. The most extensive microscopic novel in the world, said Hans. He was content. He'd created the prototype based on my explanation and a few books about cybernetics that can be found in the Firestone Library.

Experience is accumulative. On one hand, an enigma is an experiment. It is a diminutive verbal machine, double-sided and contradictory in form, created by a pair of opposing decisions: "we catch fish / we don't catch fish," "we leave / we take," which are joined in contradiction to what could naturally be expected, that is, in a way that is inverse to the formula "whatever fish we catch, we take; what we don't catch, we leave." An enigma is the formulation of a rational impossibility that does, all the same, describe a real object. (Whereas a scientific experiment, said Hans, creates an impossible event in order to express a rational object.) The wise man must know how to decipher the truth implicit in the false example. The enigma takes the form of a contradiction that is concealed in a story. (Whereas an experiment is an artificial reproduction of experience that serves to narratively imagine a world that doesn't yet exist.) When I say narratively, said Hans, I mean in the course of time. Enigmas always have to do with the future, with what isn't known, with the tension between old age and youth. The animal that walks on four feet and then on two feet and then on three feet. Everything must be viewed in an unfamiliar light even if it costs us our lives. Therein lies the art of narrative.

He was an unexpected friend, one of the closest and doubtless last ones in my life. At the beginning of 1990, when I relocated to Cambridge, Massachusetts to teach a course on paranoid fiction at Harvard, he caught pneumonia. I took a plane that night and spent two nights and two days with Hans. He was lucid, certain of his imminent death. In today's world no one believes in science anymore, he told me from his bed at the hospital, and everyone accepts superstitions and stories from TV and therefore novels are secondary. Then he began to rave. "They show us at once that they're much faster than us and can think with the lightness and focus with which a spider spins its thread. The teacher is the fly," he said from his sickbed, "who opens way to the icy world of perfect forms." Like an archaeologist of himself, he is living proof that it was once possible to think. He's certain that the same thing happens with writers, and, since I've come here to teach, he takes me for a retired novelist and of course is right. We're all retired writers. (His other model is of the great boxers of the past, rather muddled from all their old fights, who teach their tricks to the juniors. In that part he's right: I've always thought that it's more about training young writers than teaching them anything.)

We were alone, each in his own large, two-story house in the middle of the freezing woods, and we'd ended up becoming friends. This, Hans says, is like living in a large convalescent home in the Swiss Alps. I'm not familiar with any, but I can imagine them from having read *Tender Is the Night*. (Scott Fitzgerald paid two thousand a week when Zelda went insane, based on what I was able to see in his private papers, which are held at the Firestone Library. I even found bills from the old motel in Ohio where he took refuge in *The Crack-Up*). By the time you reach ninety, you're already insane. Everything is a copy of something you've lived through before. The best thing to do is act deliberately and transform obsessions into a style. Women, for example, become charitable and spend their time in clubs devoted to the poor. At least that's what Ana, my wife, did until the day she died. She was Russian and had witnessed the revolution and had known Trotsky and thought that the poor alone knew the truth. (A centrally anti-German theory; I fell in love with a Russian populist who carried a cyanide pill in her purse all her life so the police could never take her alive.) For me, on the other hand, truth is a temporary quality. The only interesting part of old age is that it allows the passage of time to be understood; after a certain age, the future ceases to be an enigma and becomes an experience. That's why the young hate the old; we live in what for them will be the future. Old age has the structure of a prophecy. It says something about the future that no one can recognize clearly. Once you cross the reasonable time limit and live too long, you exist in a zone of shadows that the ancients associated with forbidden knowledge.

†

Having returned to his study, he went through the calls on his answering machine, spoke to his wife and a few friends, and then made himself a ham sandwich and some tea and sat down in front of the computer. He'd transcribed his diary entries from 1987 and adjusted and revised them; he was going to publish them in an anthology of autobiographical prose for a Spanish publisher because there was a trend of what cultural journalists and manufacturers of academic papers called "writing the Self," which was based on the well-known temptation to reveal the secrets of one's own life, previously accommodated as part of general common sense. This novelty, according to those imbeciles, consisted of the author becoming the star by using the method of calling a character by his or her own name. Everyone immediately accepted that as true, since the personal name and the figure of the author was, he'd thought while walking toward his den, the guarantee of contemporary culture. For that reason he'd chosen a fragment of his diaries from 1987 in which he wrote about himself in the third person and revealed his secret passion—yet one that had accompanied him all of his life—for his cousin—his little cousin—whose name he'd changed so as not to disrupt her brilliant academic and emotional career. And so he opened the file on his computer in which he'd transcribed a few periods of his life, entirely based on his own experience and his own private diaries, which he'd been keeping since long before the so-called "cultural journalists" or explorers of the depths, of the underworlds in the spiral of the spirit, had spoken of "writing the Self." And so he started to read and revise in order to send it as an email attachment to the publisher in Barcelona, who'd created a collection devoted to airing out the idiocies in the domestic lives of the domesticated men of letters from the new—and also the old—generations. In short, he wanted to read it first, and as he was reading it, he recalled once more, vividly, the events and the words said during those months in 1987. He would call that fragment of his life "Cousin Érica."

Tuesday
Érica says that the diary is an idiotic prayer book, a mystical guide; he writes it, she says, "the way someone would pray." She says that he lives like a tourist in an unfamiliar station, opening a map and trying to find his bearings in that foreign territory. She also says he wants to fix the meaning in place before falling into melancholy. It's a catalog of the microscopic knowledge of a castaway, clinging onto words before he sinks once and for all into madness. He imagines that these notebooks are a compendium, a starting point from which it will be possible to start over; in the future, he can combine the words and extract the complete history of a life or several possible histories or the same life repeated in different registers. She compares the diary to a clock: it is a mechanism that classifies what is lived (what is lively, he jokes) the way a clock classifies time. (He practices the art of classifying experience.) Samuel Johnson compared the dictionary to a watch: it serves to divide what is known, uses fixed forms (the hours, the letters), and thus avoids the uncertain flow of events. A diary is a machine for classification.

Sunday 4
The fixed idea; it never changes. A fixed point. Remaining fixed onto a scene. Érica turned her face slightly and looked at him with a smile. Her small, high breasts gleamed in the clear air, the damp blonde hairs of her pubis, her smooth hips, her fine skin: she wasn't startled (she reacted with the ease of an experienced woman) while he, by contrast, loved her from that moment until the moment of his death. She was naked, fifteen years old, on the patio at the house, in a

tub in the shape of a throne, and she was bathing in rainwater. He'd returned unexpectedly and, as he entered, saw her body, which he would now never forget. She was sitting, her breasts bare, and stood, surprised, and turned her face toward him slightly, and she smiled at him like someone inviting a stranger at a party to step away into the dark of the gardens. He understood that the image moved him away from being someone falsely romantic, a sentimental fool, and that was the case because he'd drawn near to embrace her, as she wished.

Wednesday

Érica is now living precariously at her house on Calle Mansilla, her suitcases packed and the files from her research on microfilm because she's accepted an offer from Princeton University to teach in the United States beginning in September. She wants to disappear into the artificial stillness of these new medieval monasteries, to shut herself away forever in an endless and perfect library (Firestone Library, Floor C). She imagines that she can always return to Buenos Aires, where she has her house and a friend to look after her cat and water the plants. She imagines, Érica, that keeping her house ready to come back to is proof of liberty and self-control. She wants to live two lives. A possible one in Buenos Aires and another real one in Princeton (234 South Stanworth Drive). She calls it having two destinies, being two. In reality, she's fleeing from her first cousin and seeking a lab where she can investigate her theory of expressions in peace.

Thursday

Diffraction. A form that life acquires in being narrated in a private diary. In optics, a phenomenon characteristic of the wave properties of the material. The first reference to diffraction appears in the works of Leonardo da Vinci. According to his observation of the lake in Dei Fiori under the noonday sun, the light, when entering the water, spreads out diffusely and its radiance undulates in a system of concentric light and dark rings, all the way to the muddy bed. It isn't an optical illusion, it's a miracle. The days play out and are lost in the brightness of childhood and the sun barely illuminates the memories.

Monday

She says her name is Érica Turner. She was naked, fifteen years old, on the patio of the house, in a tub in the shape of a high-backed chair, and she was bathing in rainwater (fallen water that let itself be warmed in the sunlight of that siesta in summer). He'd returned unexpectedly that afternoon and, as he came in, he saw his cousin's unforgettable naked body and stood there transfixed, and no woman after would ever have that skin or that golden cross between her legs. She was sitting there in the rainwater, her small breasts bare, but then she stood, surprised, not moving her hands over her chest, her damp body, just turning her face toward him slightly and smiling at him like someone in a dream accepting a mistaken invitation from a stranger.

Thursday

One afternoon, years later, she (Érica) was informed that she must "look after" an ERP activist, hide her for a week because she was being pursued intensely. The girl had pale eyes and a birthmark on the left side of her face. This made her easily identifiable; she was the military leader of the *columna norte* in Santa Fe. Érica noticed that, when she was speaking, she tended to position herself to the left so as to hide her blemished profile. She arrived, accompanied by a distant friend of Érica's who was in charge of security for the organization. The girl brought with her a small leather suitcase and installed herself in the back room. She took over one of the wardrobes, and Érica saw her leave her Thompson submachine gun on the top shelf and saw her breasts when the girl took off the knit jacket she wore over her naked body and put on a light shirt. It was hot in that room because the heater ran all the time. Clandestine politics had always attracted her; living a secret life, moving through the city with plastic explosives inside a stroller with a doll, like a young mother walking her baby. The guerrilla (let's call her Elisa) was silent and calm; she hardly ever left the room, didn't open the windows, remained motionless, lit by the artificial light. Twice she took the risk of taking a walk around the neighborhood, in the evening, when people are returning from work and there is movement in the streets; she went out dressed in Érica's clothes, perhaps because the easy disguise gave her the fragile security that she wouldn't be recognized. Her photograph was on street corners, on newspaper stands, and on mail collection boxes along with the description of the birthmark on the left side of her face. In the two weeks she lived with Érica, they became fairly close and would speak for hours at a stretch, at first only about politics but later about their emotional lives and their private projects. She'd been with several men, but she could never start a relationship because she had to be constantly on the move, because she couldn't put the organization at risk with a long-term relationship. This gave her an air that was at once cynical and sympathetic, like a little boy describing his adventures and thinking that one day, in the future, he would settle down and start a family. She wanted to have two or three children and, for reasons Érica never understood, was certain that her first children would be redheaded twins. She had a secret fear that they would be born with marks on their faces, and she imagined (imagined Érica) that if two were born the risk would be minimal, or else the mark, divided between two faces, would be insignificant. She also thought that if the children were redheads the marks would be part of their fiery expression. The girl was an optimist, and she thought that within two or three years the ERP would have triumphed; her brother and father had disappeared, and her mother was a clandestine activist. Finally, a week later, when the danger had passed, Érica's friend came to get her. Érica and the girl, deeply moved, embraced and looked into each other's faces and kissed. The guerrilla had forgotten her mark and rested her wine-red cheek in the palm of Érica's hand. Her skin was both rough and smooth, like red velvet. Érica watched her from the window as she went down to the street and got into a black car with a license plate from Rosario. Three days later a man with a strong accent called Érica on the phone to let her know that the girl had been killed while resisting a raid in the Barrio Clínicas in Córdoba. She had died fighting. In a corner of the closet, Érica discovered a white handkerchief that the girl had left behind, and at the hem, someone (maybe her, maybe her mother) had embroidered the initials R. L. along with a tiny five-pointed star. Érica never found out the girl's name, but sometimes she'd see an image of her breasts as she was slipping her jacket over her head. That night Érica made a couple of calls, and a few days later she abandoned Buenos Aires and accepted the position as a researcher at the Institute for Advanced Study at Princeton. For years she kept the girl's handkerchief as a tribute to the injustice and senseless violence that dominated the history of her country. The soft handkerchief was a kind of tiny flag from the girl with the mark on her face whose name she would never know.

Tuesday
Everyone is speaking in low voices, no one is crying for him. A man respected and feared. The funeral room is empty,

and the dead man rests on a bed, dressed in black, lying on the woven bedspread. They've placed a portrait of Perón and an Argentine flag on the back wall. They say he used to set homemade bombs using round bell alarm clocks, and sometimes, as a way to rest amid the clandestine struggle (shut away in an anonymous room at a comrade's house in Villa Urquiza), he would take apart pocket watches (round, lidded ones) to build, using their tiny gears, microscopic (aerial) machines that worked away forever and served no purpose. Celestial, fictive circuits that participated in the daytime (and therefore invisible) movement of the stars. In the center of the pulley, at a slight angle, is the axis joining the gears that determine the variations in the repetition. He was a watchmaker by profession.

Saturday

A forbidden woman, you mustn't let another have her, not even one. She laughs: have what? she said to him, have? Nothing is preventing it, although he is suffering and she is not. They've paused on the patio, standing face to face, serious, serene. Oh my dear, do not suffer.

Érica came to visit him, excited about her new discoveries. There's something fishy here, *hay gato encerrado*, Érica says (reading from her note cards in the sunlit room): *gatos* refer to "money pouches made from [cat] pelts, skinned whole and unopened." The greedy rich are often called "atagatos." And by the Golden Age the word *gato* was already defined as "a purse or waist pouch or leather bag." They were given this name (she says) because they were typically made from the pelts of cats, skinned without making any openings except at the feet and head. In this way they took on the shape of a bag for storing and protecting money. So the origin, Érica says, isn't found with the cat but with the money, well-guarded and concealed. It's from there, she says, that streetwalkers in cities today say that they're going to *hacerse un gato*, turn a trick. Woman-cat: the call girl who makes love for money with a circumstantial man who's called a *gato* because of the way they slip along the rooftops at night, and, by displacement, (Érica says), they now become *un gato*. I'm clear, she says, I don't have secrets, I'll do it for cash if I feel like it (money expropriated from the bourgeoisie in order to pursue my studies into their morality).

He was there when the telephone rang. (It was her.) In a hotel room, a phone sounds like salvation. He delayed, of course, in answering. It was her, she'd come looking for him on her own initiative. Worried about the situation of her first cousin, who was worse and worse, more worn down. He thought he understood that, for her, *there's nothing left that he can say about himself.*

†

He stopped by Junior's place, an apartment with high ceilings above the Confitería del Molino on Rivadavia, close to Congreso. They were having a meeting, and Emilio didn't quite understand the goal of this gathering of the band of bandits who always went from place to place with Junior, enchanted by the oratory ability of El Inglés, the Englishman, as his oldest friends sometimes called him, having known Junior in the days when he studied at the Newman high school and played rugby at the San Isidro Club.

"Oh Emilio, the bard, our Virgil, you're finally poking your Italian nose into these lower latitudes," said Junior, and went along introducing him to his lifelong friends, saying their names even though Emilio already knew them from other civic and alcoholic events. "From here," said Junior, opening the large picture windows and stepping out onto the wide and sunlit fifth-floor balcony, which overlooked the Palacio

Legislativo, as Junior called it, "from here," he repeated, raising his hands in a bombastic gesture, "I can survey the temple of Peronist democracy."

Indeed, the plaza and El Congreso were visible down below, and also the white tent that the teachers had erected in protest of cutbacks to the education budget, decided arbitrarily by the Justicialist caudillo from Rioja who rules the nation with great popular support.

Several of Junior's friends, regular attendees at the Premier bookshop, had decided to publicly renounce Peronism, considering it a movement with no future that had betrayed the old rallying cries. And so El Inglés and his followers were in permanent assembly because they planned to publish a letter to the nation, in which they would state why the twenty of them—for there were twenty—had, after long years of struggle for the cause of Juan and Eva Perón, made the sad—in some versions of the letter they said "tragic," and in another draft they'd said "unavoid-able"—decision to renounce their allegiance to the Peronist movement.

"Unavoidable seems better to me," Emilio had commented, "because that way, you can take back the unavoidable renunciation card at any moment."

He didn't take them seriously, those parochial avatars of public policy; he'd come there because he liked to chat with Junior, to shoot the breeze ("but, after all, why were they shooting, and why the breeze?") and discuss literature, because his friend was the only person with whom he could stay up all night debating, for example, about the narrative poetry by the high priests of Argentine simplism, but these days politics and women were Junior's favorite topics and Renzi felt he'd lost his primary interlocutor.

The apartment was spacious and adorned with a large Argentine flag that took up an entire wall, which (Junior's) companions looked at with admiration and respect as if the very homeland had been founded there, and that afternoon the living room was filled to the brim with young men and women who spoke forcefully, all at the same time, and they smoked and drank beer and from time to time snorted a few lines of cocaine, arranged on a sheet of glass on a coffee table, watched over by a skinny woman in black who handled the papers. Emilio kept himself apart because he had to teach class, and it seemed improper to him to teach the young people while on drugs, although coke was circulating everywhere in those days as if it were an effect of the transformation of Peronism into an organism destined to finish the country off (with the help of large popular majorities). When the Peronists cease to believe in and participate in the popular national *feeling*, they turn into junkies, Renzi said to himself, addicted to any junk they can use to keep their heads occupied. Renzi knew this first-hand from the experience of his father, who, disenchanted by Peronism and everything he'd once loved, had shot himself, plunging Emilio into perplexity and a pain so deep that it took him nearly ten years to heal the wound, even though he and his father had a generally hostile and very fraught relationship, although—as Julia had told him—that, of course, was proof of how much he'd loved him. Private motivations, thought Renzi that afternoon in Junior's apartment, allow us to explain any state of the world and its opposite. Emilio had recounted his father's suicide in an (autobiographical!) story, which he'd finished on the very night of the death, yet the sorrow had gone on for many years, and the melancholy didn't begin at once, it appeared suddenly, several months later, when Emilio saw his father coming toward him, down a tree-lined sidewalk, limping, and that image had made him weep. He went into a brutal crisis and for a while, to keep afloat, got hooked on cocaine, and he stayed high for months until one day it ignited a pain in his face; he looked in the mirror and saw nothing, everything was clouded, and in the emergency room at the Hospital de Clínicas they told him that he had to quit alcohol and drugs because he had very high blood pressure and had only been saved from a stroke by a miracle. Had he been saved? Skepticism and lack of hope had killed his father. And now he saw coke circulating as an effect of the end of politics. In any case, in those days, in every corner, cocaine, hyperactivity, and cynicism reigned. He saw Junior lean over the table and snort the stardust with the blue tube of a ballpoint pen that he'd emptied of its contents.

"You used to use the pen for better things," Renzi said, and El Inglés smiled with resignation.

"Do you know old One-Eye?" he said, and indicated an aged, one-eyed man with a black patch over his left eye that gave him the look of a buccaneer. He'd lost the eye during torture and was a legendary political cadre in the Peronist resistance. He spoke in a very soft voice, an incomprehensible whisper, but some friends, Junior explained, care for him so much that they understand him and translate for him.

"You have to hold firm, in these dark times," the man said, as if talking to himself or as if dreaming. Our friend says that you have to go onward, full steam ahead, not give in, follow the path marked out by Chacho, and support this group of the twenty dissident lawmakers, a blond man in black glasses translated.

The one-eyed man shook his head, saying this wasn't what he'd said, but no one paid any attention. Peronism is like that, thought Renzi, someone says two lines and all the others understand it however they want and repeat it like sacred words. The same had happened when Perón was far away; everyone listened to his sententious and hollow words and translated them into political slogans that benefited their own portions.

The conversation continued, very intense and confusing; they listened attentively to what their guest, the one-eyed man, said that afternoon and then went on talking about the subject that was keeping them up: the renunciation of Peronist identity. They went in circles around the issue; was there any precedent for a moral decision of that caliber in the movement? they said, while the one-eyed man repeated his fighting slogans in a soft voice. "The true Peronism isn't the Peronism of that turncoat who usurped power." At this stage they were no longer translating him, and the only one who was listening to him attentively, leaning toward him with a hand cupped to his ear, was Renzi, nodding his head in a sign of assent because it pained him to see the old militant, a hero of so many battles, talking to himself.

It was easier to become a Peronist than to stop being one, thought Renzi, as he listened, compassionately, to the inaudible monologue of the old one-eyed man. Emilio had seen with astonishment the instantaneous and euphoric way in which people had joined with Peronism after fighting against it their whole lives, ready, from one day to the next, to give their lives for Perón. Great people with political experience, many of them former members of the Communist Party, poets, journalists, actresses, professors, they turned into Peronists but later, now, were trying to take off that shirt, as they say. His father and the one-eyed man who spoke in a soft voice were Peronists from '45; few of them were left, and the ones that were left no one heard.

Renzi managed to isolate himself with Junior in the kitchen, taking advantage of his friend's having separated from the group to eat some green olives that he kept in the refrigerator.

"How's everything going, *hermanito*? What are you up to? They told me at the newspaper that you're writing for films and teaching classes at the university. The two deadliest activities for a writer."

"Junior, listen to what I'm about to tell you," said Renzi, not paying attention to his friend's words. "I can't get my cousin Horacio out of my head, you know he came to see me, and I didn't do anything to help him. I let him go without throwing him a rope to save him from the water." Junior listened with a serious expression while he placed an olive in his mouth and then turned to spit the pit into the kitchen sink. He was at the bottom of the sea.

"Why don't you take a few days and go to the Tigre, a bit of peace? I'll give you the keys to my house and you can set yourself up like a king."

"He came alone, in the car, to see me at the cabin . . . his wife, you know her, Sofía. She took everything and left."

"With another woman," Junior interrupted him, "I already know, Horacio also stopped by the newspaper office one day, and he said he wanted to go traveling and asked if I had a reliable friend in Río de Janeiro, it seemed strange to me . . . "

"He came to see you?" He paused. "At the paper? And why didn't you say anything to me?"

"I did tell you, *querido*, but it was already too late. And why are you carrying that around in your head now?"

"Because I was looking in my notebooks from that time, before he came to see me, and I found a note mentioning a very strange phone call from Horacio one week before."

"And now you're worried about that? How many years has it been? Stop mucking around with those notebooks; who has the bright idea to write down every blunder in their lives?"

"So he came to see you, and what did he say?"

"Nothing, he wanted to go fishing with me in Mar Chiquita, but I didn't go, so he went on his own."

"Was that before or after his wife left him?"

"Before, I think, I don't remember the date, I don't go around writing down everything I live through like an amnesiac."

Renzi stood thinking and Junior placed a hand on his shoulder.

"I told you that Pelusa explained to me how, one night at the ERP, a Russian man taught them a method for forgetting whatever they wanted so that they wouldn't compromise anyone if they fell and were tortured."

"Apparently they forgot the method, since they, the military, broke up the organization in three months."

"It was a guy from the Soviet services, and the technique was infallible. The technology of forgetting."

"That's enough, Emilio. I can see you tomorrow if you want, I have to go back to the assembly now. Forget about those ideas."

"That's just it, I can't, I remember everything."

"And whatever you don't remember you have written down. You're a hopeless case. Come on, let's go."

And the two left the kitchen and returned to the living room, where the discussion was still going, intensely, on the same point they'd left it. Is it possible to stop being a Peronist, or is it an identity with no retreat?

You have to forget, thought Renzi, that's the way out, he told himself as he turned toward the door, trying not to disrupt the speakers.

†

Forgetting. It is one of the great themes of literature, Renzi said as he began his class. To be forgotten; the tragedy of the abandoned lover who knows he is lost to the memory of the one he loves. And then the inability to forget, another grand theme, memories as a condemnation, remorse.

I'd like to open this subject toward three linguistic points that may perhaps allow us to advance a little. Let's begin with the distinction between enigma, mystery, and secret, three forms in which information is typically coded inside stories.

The enigma, as we know, even through its etymology,* would be the existence of some element—it may be a text, a situation—that contains a meaning that is not understood but can be deciphered. *Enigma*, etymologically, means "to imply."

The mystery, on the other hand, is an element that is not understood because it has no explanation, or at least none within the logic of reason or the concept of reality as it is given, and within which we conduct ourselves.

As for the secret, it also has to do with a void of signification, a forgetting, something desired to be known that is not known, like the

---

* Enigma. Lat. *aenigma*. Taken from the Gr. *áinigma*, -*atos*. Mistaken or obscure phrase, derived from *ainíssomai*, "to make understood."

enigma and the mystery, but in this case, it refers to a thing that some-one has and does not say. That is, the secret is a meaning subtracted by someone. The text, then, revolves around the void of that which is unsaid; within the series that I've been discussing, it has the distinctive quality of referring us toward something that is guarded—and here once again the etymology of the word *secret** is pertinent—so that it immediately produces a well-known series, resembling gossip, where different versions of the same story are circulating: who knows what, who doesn't know . . .

Within this series, I would like to pick up on the notion of forget-ting. Something is forgotten because it's indecipherable or because it's incomprehensible or because someone has erased it. But the question, for us, is whether forgetting can be deliberate, and what class of strategy that would be; what is it that provokes or produces oblivion, that is, the forgetting of something.

Inside the third-floor lecture hall there were close to three hundred students crowded in, filling the benches but also sitting on the floor, in the aisles, many of them taking notes and smoking and others aiming their recorders toward the platform from which Emilio was speaking, now and then turning to write words on the blackboard and then, chalk still in hand, stepping down from the platform and pacing from one end of the room to the other, making use of the free space between the wall and the first row of desks to follow a horizontal line.

The word for forgetting, *oblivion*, is formed from Latin roots. Its lexical components are the prefix *ob-* (over) and *levis* (light). The verb *oblivi-ate* comes from the Latin *oblitare*, derived from *oblitus*, which is the participle of the verb *oblivisci* (to forget), formed from *ob-* (against, facing, opposition) and *livisci*, from the Proto-Indo-European root *lei* (viscous, smooth), which gave *lima*, file, an instrument for polishing,

---

* Secret. Lat. *secretum*, "separate, isolated, remote," participle of *secernere*, "to separate, to isolate," derived from *cernere*, "to distinguish, to sift."

and *liniment*. The original idea was the slipping away of memory, the slide toward oblivion.

Now let's turn to Greek words; and he wrote on the blackboard, using the vague memories that he had from Greek III, which he'd taken as a student, at the College, *αλήθεια*/alitheia (= *truth*) and *λήθη*/lethe (= *oblivion*). The meaning of the word *αλήθεια*, in Greek, derives from the state in which things are not in the domain of oblivion, that is, they are known and apparent and are, for that reason, essentially true. Furthermore, the Greek word *λάθος*/lathos (= *error*) is related to the words *αλήθεια* and *λήθη*, he said as he copied them out on the blackboard, since all of these words take their root from the verb *λανθάνω*/lanthano (= to escape someone's notice, to be latent, to not be manifested).

Indeed, when something escapes our perspective, perception, or attention, we tend to fall into error. Following the same line of thought, *memory* (*μνήμη*/mnimi in Greek) is a very important tool for defending the truth, for defending ourselves, I should say, said Renzi. In the Greek tradition, then, oblivion is antagonistic to truth as well as to memory, that is, it can be assimilated with the creation of an illusory and fragile world. It doesn't have to do with *doxa* or error but an empty class of entity, or rather, it belongs to a category of objects that are at once absent and latent. You all already know that, in the seminar, we defined fiction as a particular form of utterance, defined, as I've told you, in the following way: "The speaker does not exist." The one who speaks and narrates in a story doesn't exist, that is the truth of fiction; regardless of whether or not everything that is said in the story may be real and verifiable, fiction does not depend on the true or false content of what is related but on the position of the one who utters it, whom we define as a forgotten subject.

Now and then the door would open, and another late student would enter, looking for a place to slip in, but Renzi paid not the slightest attention to the interruption. Forgetting, he said, is an action, in principle, involuntary, which consists of ceasing to store acquired information in memory. Often, forgetting is caused by "interfering learning," learning that replaces a memory that hasn't been cemented in memory, making it "disappear," to put it one way, from consciousness. We must remember that one does remember having forgotten something, which is to say that one is aware of having certain knowledge that is no longer there, that is, there is a consciousness of having had it. Thus, forgotten memories do not disappear but rather are buried somewhere. We'll call this transition the *amnesiac archive*, that is, the place or site or space where the faces, the words, the facts, the people we've forgotten are accumulated. It's a kind of limbo where lost memories persist, invisible. In the Argentine countryside, in the desert, beyond the frontier, in *a strange land*, as Fierro says, the forgotten memories are manifested and appear as a glow, as evil lights, *luces malas*, as they're called in our Pampas.

Martín Fierro sings so as not to forget, and Facundo, according to Sarmiento, has a prodigious memory, he remembers all of his soldiers' names. Rosas recognizes which ranch in the province he's in by the taste of the grass. There's something barbarous in excessive memory. Borges's Funes is a primitive man, and even Plato had opposed writing to memory. Nevertheless, in one of the great narratives of Argentine literature, Martínez Estrada tells the story of a man who remembers an entire book that has been lost and writes the prologue to the absent work on the basis of his photographic memory. In Onetti's *Goodbyes*, the narrator "forgets" some letters, which reappear at the end of the story and are decisive for deciphering the enigma of the story and which, in being remembered out of place, make another truth possible. I'd like you all to keep track of the moments of oblivion that are narrated in the fictional texts by Onetti and Felisberto Hernández and Rulfo, places where they narrate act of forgetting or the loss of the memory of an event.

For us, the *nouvelle* form is structured around the narration of something forgotten that becomes the center of the plot. Why? Because if it were remembered, then it would have to be written as a novel. The concentration of the *nouvelle* form is founded upon forgetting. But not any forgetting, rather a void that arises and circles around the frame of the story, that is, among those who tell the story. They are the ones who are unable to remember something—a face, an address, a name—and that is the reason they narrate. The narrative is woven together with the fabric of oblivion. Example: Conrad's *Heart of Darkness* or Melville's *Bartleby* and Kafka's great short novels.

In Greek mythology, *Lethe* (*Λήθη*), literally "oblivion," or *Leteo* (from the Latin *Lethæus*) was one of the rivers of Hades. Drinking from its waters caused complete oblivion. Some ancient Greeks believed that souls were made to drink from that river before being reincarnated so that they wouldn't remember their past lives. And there's something of that in Rulfo's *Pedro Páramo* and in the specters of Cortázar's short stories and in José Bianco's *Shadow Play*. *Lethe* was also a naiad, a daughter of Eris ("Discordia" in Hesiod's *Theogony*), although probably a separate personification of forgetting rather than a reference to the river that bears her name. Some private mystery cults taught the existence of another river, the Mnemosyne, whose waters, when drunk, made one remember everything and attain omniscience. The initiates were taught that they would be given a choice of which river to drink from after death and must drink from the Mnemosyne instead of the Lethe. These two rivers appear within several verses inscribed on gold plaques from the fourth century BC and onward, located in Thurii, in southern Italy, and throughout the Greek world. The myth of Er, at the end of Plato's *Republic*, tells of the dead arriving at the "plain of Lethe," which is crossed by the river Ameles ("neglected"). There were two rivers, then, called Lethe and Mnemosyne, on the altar of Trophonius in Boeotia, from which the worshipers drank before making oracular consultations with their gods. Among ancient authors, it was said that the little river Limia, close to Xinzo de Limia (Ourense), possessed the same memory-erasing properties as the legendary Lethe. In 138 BC, the Roman general Decimus Junius Brutus Callaicus attempted to dispel the myth, which was impeding military campaigns in the area. It is said that he crossed the Limia and then called his soldiers from the other side, one by one, by name. Astonished that their general could remember their names, they too crossed the river without fear, thus bringing an end to its reputation for danger.

In the *Divine Comedy*, the current of the Lethe flows to the center of the earth from its surface, but its source is situated in the Earthly Paradise, located on the top of the mountain of Purgatory. And then Renzi, from memory and with an elegiac tone in his perfect Italian and his usual pedantry, cited the verses in which the reference to the miraculous river appears for the first time:

> E io ancor: "Maestro, ove si trova
> Flegetonta e Letè? ché dell' un taci,
> e l'altro di' che si fa d'esta piova."
> "In tutte tue question certo mi piaci,"
> rispuose; "ma 'l bollor dell'acqua rossa
> dovea ben solver l'una che tu faci.
> Letè vedrai, ma fuor di questa fossa,
> là dove vanno l'anime a lavarsi
> quando la colpa pentuta è rimossa."
> Poi disse: "Omai è tempo da scostarsi
> dal bosco; fa che di retro a me vegne:
> li margini fan via, che non son arsi,
> e sopra loro ogne vapor si spegne."

In a lost and nameless work of theater about Eurydice, of which only seven fragments remain, quoted by Herodotus, all of the shades must drink from the Lethe and become something resembling stones, speaking in their inaudible language and forgetting everything of the world. Likewise, a mention is made of the river Lethe in William Shakespeare's *Hamlet*, and it is the ghost of the father who recalls the river of forgetting. Then, once again from memory (he'd memorized it the night before, repeating the verses in front of a mirror), he quoted, in his Elizabethan English learned from Miss Jackson:

Ghost, he said, with a voice from beyond the grave, and then clarified, changing his tone: *The ghost of the father is speaking.*

I find thee apt;
And duller shouldst thou be than the fat weed
That roots itself in ease on Lethe wharf,
Wouldst thou not stir in this. Now, Hamlet, hear:
'Tis given out that, sleeping in my orchard,
A serpent stung me; so the whole ear of Denmark
Is by a forged process of my death
Rankly abused: but know, thou noble youth,
The serpent that did sting thy father's life
Now wears his crown.

A reference is made to the waters of the river Lethe in poem number LXXVII, "Spleen," from Charles Baudelaire's *The Flowers of Evil.* And in his macaronic French, holding a photocopy of the paragraph in his hand, he recited the verses with an air of mystery:

Le savant qui lui fait de l'or n'a jamais pu
De son être extirper l'élément corrompu,
Et dans ses bains de sang qui des Romains nous viennent,
Et dont sur leurs vieux jours les puissants se souviennent,
Il n'a su réchauffer son cadavre hébété
Où coule au lieu de sang l'eau verte du Léthé.

On the other hand, he added, reading his notes, the waters of forgetting are referenced in John Keats's "Ode on Melancholy" as well, and he repeated the unforgettable verses in his English learned in childhood:

No, no, go not to Lethe, neither twist
Wolf's-bane, tight-rooted, for its poisonous wine;

Poisonous wine, *venenoso vino*, he translated with irony; Borges liked that figure, and indeed, recall his poem "To Wine," which also alludes to the river of forgetting; and after a rather theatrical pause he recited two verses from the poem in the weary intonation of Borges:

> Que otros en tu Leteo beban un triste olvido;
> yo busco en ti las fiestas del fervor compartido.

After illustrating those references and others, he asked the students to look for the context of the verses referenced, that is, to read the poems completely. Thus, Renzi brought the class to an end and asked the students to write, for next time, a twenty-line summary of the plot of *Sad as She*, Onetti's *nouvelle*. Please, he said, as he moved away, typewrite it, I mean, on the computer, double-spaced, without corrections, and try to be clear and not to interpret the story but narrate it over again. I will analyze what you've forgotten from the plot in retelling it. See you next time, he said, stepping down from the stage to be immediately surrounded by a group of students, all talking at the same time.

†

Renzi went down the stairs of the College, surrounded by a mob of students who were talking to him, asking him questions, consulting him, proposing topics for their final projects or trying to give him short stories to read, books of poems, chapters of novels; they were intelligent, quick, likable; they were daring and combative, the students of letters from UBA who followed him on the way out of his class among posters, banners, slogans written on the walls with various leftist political positions, raised by the groups and combative movements. The names of certain groups called his attention, with titles like La Walsh or La Mariátegui, which seemed to claim drag identities, he imagined one that might be called La chica Che Guevara, but when

253

he made the joke none of the activists made any response and instead looked at him with some disgust. Propaganda saturated the place, and Renzi and his students advanced into a jungle of words and announcements, a forest adorned with graffiti and photos and banners, all very critical and euphoric, announcing marches, picket lines, actions, street blockades, strikes, and mobilizations. Even the stairs were taken over with sentences written in black spray paint, so that as he descended, he could read a fragmented summons, announcing a repudiation of the house dean. As in a film, images were superimposed onto Emilio of the college in his days as a student; he remembered the assemblies, the strikes, the marches, and he could see the posters and graffiti in his memory like permanent photos from his youth. It was the same, except for a certain discursive rage that now turned those legends into orders, counterorders, categorical imperatives intended to awaken the student masses from the ideological dream. He remembered his student years, which, in the memory—as they had been in reality— were incandescent, unforgettable, invincible, and serene, above all when compared to this current activism, marked by skepticism and the memory of the terror of the military dictatorship's repression. Socialism was now a ghost, deader than ever, and these revendications and struggles were, above all, negative and savage critiques of the political situation.

When he reached the entrance hall, the panorama was the same but they'd moved the tables together to sell books by Trotsky, John William Cooke, Jauretche, and Karl Marx; there were students out on the floor selling trinkets and crafts, and also music CDs and plates of homemade food. He made it across the market where political illusions were bought and sold and went out to the street, accompanied by his work team, the students who made up a research group—from the UBACYT—led by Renzi, which was called Colectivo 12 because there were twelve of them, because he liked the concept of work collectives, and also because the girls—who were an absolute majority, ten women and only two boys—took the Colectivo 12 bus to come to his office on Marcelo T. de

Alvear, where they met with him once a week to discuss, debate, and expound on possibilities within the topic of "Form and function of oblivion in the cultural tradition." They were working on the remnants, documents, and monuments that were erased, scratched out, rejected in cultural history, something they'd decided to call "the recollection of what has been forgotten." For example, they considered the charred scrolls from the library of Herculaneum, a town that had been burned in the eruption of Vesuvius in year 79 of our era, the only library that was preserved, intact though scorched, and also the deliberate arson of the Santa Fe province historical archive, which was burned by soldiers from the Unitarianist army at the command of General Juan Lavalle following the defeat of the caudillo Estanislao López and the occupation of the city; they'd used the papers, documents, and records of the province's memory to ignite the stoves they used to heat water for yerba mate. They were working on all of that and putting together a dictionary of oblivion; that is, instead of submitting papers, they were going to write, as a group, the alphabetical entries for a *catalogue raisonné* of what had been lost, burned, and destroyed in the past. They called it, as well, a dictionary of anti-memory.

They went out to the street and walked down Puán to Pedro Goyena and then installed themselves at two tables pushed together at the Sócrates bar, so that there was room for all twelve (thirteen, counting Renzi) of the conspirators who made up this amnesiac plot, as Emilio called it, but really, as one of the girls clarified, anti-amnesiac. The meeting was in disarray, with everyone talking at the same time, having conversations among themselves, not following or paying attention to the topic of the day, which was to prepare a public exhibition in Rosario, with a presentation of the group work in its current state. There were, as always, some gate-crashers as well; two students from Philosophy had sat down at the table and begun a chat in tandem about writing and oblivion in Plato. Writing was an erasure of memory, said one, dressed in a leather jacket. Oblivion lies at the origin of written literature, claimed the other young man, who had rings in his ears and large bags under his eyes. But no one paid them any mind; instead, the table's interest was drawn to an older man, very elegantly dressed in a suit and vest, whom none of them knew but who knew enough to guide the conversation toward the Stalinist practice of erasing Trotsky from the photos where he'd appeared alongside Lenin at actions and meetings, also making him disappear from the history of the Russian Revolution despite his having been the founder of the Red Army. The man was a Trotskyist and therefore wielded grand theories without too much substantiation, although— as Renzi pointed out—he was right. Investigation into photographic material must be a field of study in the coming months, he said, for example, keeping track of photographs from dinners and banquets of Argentine writers over the course of the twentieth century in order to see who was there and who didn't appear or ceased to be present. The talk turned general, they'd ordered finger sandwiches and beer and the atmosphere was relaxed. Renzi was very tired, which always happened to him after teaching class, his head was empty, blank, and he was drifting away from the place mentally; unfocused, rather downcast, he was listening to the murmur of the conversation but without fixing on any point.

He would have to cross the city to go back, and he could see himself in the taxi—he lived in taxis—and sometimes calculated how much time he'd wasted, time lost and never recovered, waiting at intersections for the traffic light to change. He calculated one minute of waiting at red, facing the red light, let's say fifty seconds, and in one day he might go through five hundred (that many?) traffic lights, approximately one minute each time, how many hours was that?, how many minutes?, the sums weren't coming to him, he'd have to bring up the topic with a taxi driver, see if they'd calculated it; a taxi driver, he thought, must spend, on average, two hours per day stopped in front of traffic lights, and that's why taxi drivers were always embittered and were all half Nazis, they were likable and entertaining, but very right-wing, and that, Renzi deduced, was due to the time they spent stopped in front of red lights, even I would turn into an outraged conservative populist if I had to sit waiting for so much time at traffic lights, because the first question that comes to mind is who is controlling them?, and it would be easy to shift from there into anti-political skepticism.

He was distracted for a while, thinking about the opposition of memory/ oblivion and its consequences in Argentine history. For example, he thought, forgetting was condemned by the left and defended by the right, but the issue was *involuntary* forgetting. Was forgetting always involuntary? As for the memory/oblivion dichotomy, perhaps a term could be added as a synthesis . . . He was thinking about all of that when he realized they were speaking to him.

"And what do you think, professor?" asked a bearded stranger, sitting opposite him at the table in Sócrates.

"You need to synthesize your hypothesis better," he said, using a line that always got him out of tight spots when he was distracted or didn't know where unexpected questions were coming from.

"Binary oppositions bother us," said the boy.

"Why?" said Renzi. "Binary oppositions are fine; I don't believe in the current fashion of posing so many alternatives that the convictions are watered down into a liberal jelly where all terms and categories hold the same value; we think on the basis of opposites, opposites are concise *a priori* judgments, they have multiple webs within them."

"I don't find binarism convincing," insisted the boy, "it's Manichaean."

"We are Manichaeans. In the Corominas dictionary, look up the etymological root of Manichaean and you'll see that Mani, the Persian prophet, was very agreeable."

"On the other hand," intervened Celia Gutiérrez, one of the members of the Colectivo, "Professor Renzi has brought up—"

"Yes," interrupted Renzi, "the notion of nostalgia as a way to open the memory/oblivion dichotomy, now what kind of memory or evocation does nostalgia involve? You have to think about that. Nostalgia involves a positive version of the past, not everything is ruins or tragedy and defeat, memory preserves and amasses splendid moments, there are joyous events amid struggle and conflict that one would like to relive. Nostalgia is on the order of the epic."

He went on talking a while longer but had already lost interest, so he asked Mónica to please pay the bill using the research funds. What do you think the university's money is good for? Not just for making photocopies or buying books but for having a banquet every now and then too, or isn't this place called Sócrates? So we hold a little banquet once a week; a modest one compared to what the Greek philosophers ate and drank to sharpen their wits. We're austere by comparison. Now then, Patricia, ask for the check, and keep the receipt with the financial documents for the university. He got up and, after a swift and general goodbye, went out into the street and stopped an empty taxi that was heading along Pedro Goyena toward downtown.

†

He had the cab stop in front of the Atlas movie theater on Avenida Santa Fe, up by Ayacucho, around the corner from his office, but he preferred not to go and leave his things there, so he entered the theater and sat down to watch Tarantino's *Pulp Fiction*, which had premiered the week before; his youngest friends were enthralled by the discovery of a *peli*, as they call them, made by a cinephile who was reinvigorating the Seventh Art. For Renzi, films were the only things that allowed him to stop thinking about the classes or lectures he'd given, which always left him agitated, unable to stop thinking, stray ideas, persistent reflections, things he could have said and didn't say, had they slipped his mind? He taught classes with a few notes and references written on a sheet of white, letter-sized paper, a summary table of the topics that he planned to present, but he was never able to consult it and generally improvised, trying to hold the audience's interest, not lowering his eyes to look at the notes because he would quickly lose his focus, and in this way he would be left paralyzed on the way out of a class, unable to stop turning over the same subjects unless he entered the dark aura of the cinema, which carried him off to another dimension, *cinema is the poor man's divan*, who said that?, was it Sartre?, no, it wasn't Sartre, the French philosopher's name escaped him, it was going . . .

He liked the title, which referred to cheap magazines, made from paper pulp, particularly *Black Mask*, where Hammett, Chandler, and Goodis had published their short stories; as paid advertisements and trailers for the next movies were going by on the screen, he recalled Joseph T. "Cap" Shaw, who had run that pulp magazine and who never wrote a line yet was the true creator of the hard-boiled crime genre. The lights in the theater had come on and then turned off, creating anticipation for the dark, imaginary ritual that was about to begin, and Renzi found himself seeing the sentence he was thinking as if it were written before his eyes: "And that, no doubt, is what Hammett recognizes in dedicating *Red Harvest*, his first novel, to Shaw."

The film didn't have much to do with the history of the genre; it wasn't a remake in the style of *Chinatown* but rather part of a new series, the neo-noir or *polar*, it wasn't about framing it within the genre, thought Renzi with the left side of his brain, while with the right side he was hooked by the movie and was feeling the violence of the action with a variety of emotions. Surprise, satisfaction, serenity, and seriousness as well. The dialogue, for example, was very good, he would think later, as he left the theater, talking to Carola, his wife, whom he'd meet at Babieca, on the corner of Riobamba; she never went to see movies that were in vogue and even less often to see stories manufactured by Hollywood to produce universal effects in an audience with the mental, emotional, and sexual age, she would say a bit later, commenting on the film over dinner, of twelve or fourteen, whom American movies were made for, since TV, and now the internet and cell phones, were pulling the audience away from films, not to mention rock concerts and their lighting effects, with sparklers, explosions, and mannequins disguised as counterculture musicians. She'd smile, unstoppable and beautiful, drinking Coca-Cola with bitters at the bar where they'd planned to meet after Emilio left the theater. "On principle, I don't go to any movie unless you have to be over eighteen to get in. Soon they're going to prohibit anyone under twenty-two from seeing the films of Godard, Cassavetes, Tarkovsky, and Antonioni." It was true, Emilio would agree, that at the theater, at Ozu or Bergman retrospectives, they'd run into other veterans like them in the lobby of the San Martín, old friends, great people who belonged to a forgotten culture.

But Emilio was hooked by the movie, and the best part so far was the handling of dialogue, which almost escaped him even though he could follow it perfectly in English and skip over the subtitles; he didn't have time to read because the conversations in Tarantino's film flowed at such speed, so gracefully, and were so inventive and brilliant that, so far, twenty minutes into the film, they were what had impressed him most. It wasn't dialogue to explain the action; rather, it set out from a very intense and extreme narrative situation—for example, two hit men were on the way to kill a few disloyal accomplices whom they would massacre—toward an act of maximum violence. In the meantime, the dialogue flowed freely, and they, the two killers, went on talking as they drove over to the place, and then, even as they entered the building and went up in the elevator, called at the door and entered the apartment and killed everyone, they were keeping up a conversation about hamburgers, mentioning the names and ingredients in quick, very entertaining dialogue.

If the dramatic situation is laid out well, the dialogue is secondary and works like background music; it has no direct function and is as free as if it were occurring to the screenwriter in a delirium, free-associating with no restrictions because the action is so powerful that it has no need for language. A preverbal film, yet very oral, with continuous and brilliant dialogues that have no narrative function and are beautiful and unforgettable as a result. The technique of the dialogue comes from Hemingway, Renzi would later decree, giving his version—not his interpretation, as he would clarify emphatically—of the film *Pulp Fiction* when talking to his friends at dinner; the narrative tension is so forceful that what is said doesn't matter, doesn't interfere with the action, and the language is very poetic and free as a result. It all comes from *The Killers*, where two gangsters who are going to kill a Swedish man in a bar are talking about the food that's served in the very place where they're waiting for the victim, and the whole story revolves around the various possible dishes yet in such an extreme atmosphere that the things they say about bacon and fried eggs carry a charge of danger that nothing can surpass. The technique of threat, Renzi thought in the theater as he watched how the men, continuing their jokes and wordplay, massacred the condemned men who'd stolen or held onto a briefcase of heroin.

The motivation was frontal and direct, nothing psychological or social, pure violence without emotion or sense, and that also went for the detective genre, which Renzi sometimes called paranoid fiction; in the movie, all of the characters were at some point in danger and were condemned to death by the powerful fat black gangster, who functioned as a deadly and omnipotent divinity. That is, the motivation was very weak and very clear, and all of the little stories that constituted the film, like a collage of isolated scenes, were being run by the malevolent and arbitrary spirit of the powerful and almost invisible lord of this microworld of crime. For example, the boxer, who refused to let himself be defeated in order to fix the fight, as the gangster had instructed him to do in order to raise the stakes, was being pursued by an efficient and malevolent assassin and then the story shot off toward an extreme sadomasochistic scene in which the black gangster, who was chasing down the boxer to kill him, was overpowered and raped by a policeman, humiliated and sodomized in a plain, secondary action within the film.

The boss's wife was taken away and accompanied by a young contract killer who, following the boss's order and will, had to entertain and amuse her, which led to a fantastic and very retro sequence in an

American bar where people danced in the gravitational pull of Elvis Presley, performed or replicated by a double who imitated him singing from a circular stage, while the tables were served by waitresses who pretended to be—and were identical to—Marilyn Monroe. This game of pop replicas was closed in the final scene with a robbery at a roadside restaurant, which actually connected to the first scene of the movie in which a couple was in the very same restaurant, planning the robbery that would be carried out—with paradoxical results—in the final scene of the film, at which point one realized that time was fragmented in the movie and didn't follow a linear order. The religious conversion of a ruthless killer who quotes the Bible from memory before executing his victims, thought Renzi as he left the theater, is typical of American film, which always finds a mystical-evangelical-psychotic way out, to explain—or hint at—the reasons or motivations behind serial killers and the extreme individual violence that is repeated in their movies, their television series, and their political reality. A religious impulse, he thought in the street; that is the basis of American tragedy. The night was cool, and the movie theater had once again helped him to return to reality and escape from his thoughts and his fixed ideas.

†

He was at Thelonious with Carola, Francine, Roberto Jacoby, and other friends, sitting at a favorite table, drinking champagne, all facing the piano, for that night Gandini was playing a concert; he'd been joking around with them and complaining about the acoustics of the room and also about the slow pace of his life. "Music is faster, it can be faster when it's good," he said, smiling, the slow movement was bothering him, and that night, in a lightning-fast action, he'd picked up a blonde woman, quite well put together, and had proposed to her on the spot; she was a fairly well-known singer; Gerardo had even hired her at the Centro de Experimentación at the Colón theater to sing several pieces by Charles Ives, accompanied by piano, and the performance had gone well but Gerardo had forgotten about her until that night when she came over to greet him as he was having a whiskey at the bar. He was on his own, Gandini, in those days; another woman had left him, protesting Gerardo's repeated absences, as he would leave and spend the night away from home, always under musical pretexts. "The ballerinas, oh, the ballerinas," he said, starry-eyed. He was always turning around and asking out girls from the regular cast in the theater's ballet section. The girl, Magda, had come to the concert that night to give Gandini an album of her songs and show him her admiration, and Gerardo took her hand, said he was going to read her future, and, after making two or three jokes about the future, asked her to marry him (which she indeed did some time later) because her destiny, as that delinquent Gerardo predicted, clearly visible on the palm of her hand, was to marry a musician.

With them that night was Francine, an old friend who taught at Berkeley and whom Emilio had known since the first time he went to the United States, in 1977. Francine was an Italian from New York and they brought her to listen to Gerardo, and she was very pleased with that immersion in the Argentine tradition that she'd been studying for years. She enjoyed music, Francine, and got to live the concerts and recitals that were presented every night in San Francisco. One night at the City Lights bookshop he'd gone with her to hear Miles Davis playing with his musicians, who, like him, had the air of metaphysical gangsters, and Miles played with his back to the audience, dressed in black, hunched over slightly with his trumpet pointing at the ground, and now Emilio and Carola had taken her to hear music from Buenos Aires. That night at Thelonious, Gandini was going to premiere his tango "A Don Emilio Renzi," which he'd already recorded in Germany but was going to perform for the first time—or, as Gerardo said, the way it should be—in Buenos Aires.

They were having a good time at Thelonious that night, and Gerardo came over to the table every now and then to have a drink with them, killing time until the hour of the concert. He sat next to Carola and told her about his emotional troubles. That night, between jokes, he made a bet that he would be married to the singer before the end of the year. Then he went back to the bar to resume his whiskey, and everyone watched him showing off and laughing with Magda, who was now with him at the bar, having a drink while, as Emilio observed, fixing her hair and putting on lipstick, facing the mirror that ran behind the bottles, leaning on the counter, standing there smiling as if she didn't realize that Gandini was kissing her hand. "I'm glad," said Carola. "I can't stand to see Gerardo all alone." Emilio had been concentrating on the piano; he only listened to music for piano and had a very important collection of piano pieces, versions of piano sonatas by Beethoven and Schubert and Chopin, and also recordings by Art Tatum and Oscar Peterson and Bill Evans and Erroll Garner, even by Nat King Cole from his days as a pianist before devoting himself to singing, and also by Mono Villegas and great tango pianists like Osvaldo Goñi and Horacio Salgán and Osvaldo Tarantino as well. It was a mania like any other, and in that respect he had a collector's mentality, not that he'd ever acquire the totality of music for piano, it was a pianistic obsession, he didn't have every version or every pianist, and on top of that he was losing seventy percent of the music he had been able to hear—including what he'd listened to before a passion for piano came upon him, almost overnight; it was a way to have a coherent classification of music, a way to restrict his purchases of CDs or even vinyl records, on which he had old recordings of Friedrich Gulda, for example.

That night at Thelonious, Renzi was going to take part in the concert with Gandini, and he was going to be the introducer, would say a few words before Gerardo sat down at the piano in a position that Emilio had seen many times, a pose in which the pianist would first relax his wrists and let his hands hang loose, as if out of his control, and then lean over the keyboard; he resembled a gnome, a hunchback, leaning over the piano, and the music seemed to emerge from his body, sometimes he could be seen murmuring silently, accompanying the music with unspoken words, for Gerardo improvised based on tango melodies, let himself be carried away by his private imagination and his musical knowledge. Because Gandini, from the impression that Emilio had, held all of the music inside his head. In the time when they shared a country house to spend summers, he'd seen Gerardo moving off among the trees in the park, alone, not speaking but listening, Renzi was sure of that, the music within him, and even at that time he was preparing for a concert in which he would play all of Schoenberg's pieces for piano but never rehearsed, never did preliminary exercises on the piano, and when he sat down that night to play the piano pieces, so difficult, by Schoenberg, he hadn't practiced at all, hadn't rehearsed except inside his head, yet played them with great quality and emotion. He wasn't an extraordinary concert pianist, he was, more simply, an extraordinary composer.

Renzi recounted some of this that night in Thelonious, introducing Gerardo amid jokes and an attitude of mutual understanding, of that spiritual, mental, and physical virtue that Gandini had when he sat at the piano. And then, to talk about Gerardo's post-tangos, which (for him) were simply improvisations based on traditional tango standards, first, Renzi recalled something that Gerardo once told him; in the days when he was the pianist for Astor Piazzolla, with whom he'd played all over the world, Piazzolla and Gandini were in a hotel room during the break between one concert and the next, listening to a recording by the Brazilian musician Hermeto Pascoal, a great pianist, and he'd hit a wrong note in one of his recordings while playing "El día que me quieras," hitting a minor second instead of a sixth, and the effect had made one of them say, Piazzolla or Gandini, that in that mistake, in that error while playing the melody, a door had been opened to renew the tradition of the tango. For both of them had seen in that mistake a future music, the potential to deliberately alter the emotion of the tango and, starting from that point, improvise a freer version following the unexplored pathways of the melody. That's what Gandini has done in his post-tangos, taking the music and moving forward by improvisation and free-associating toward new regions in the tango tradition.

To conclude, Renzi told a story that had fascinated him, which he'd read in an old biography of Carlos Gardel. One night, Tucci, the arranger and orchestrator who worked with Gardel in New York, took Gardel and Lepera to listen to the premiere of Schoenberg's *Pierrot Lunaire* and *Transfigured Night* at the Metropolitan Opera House. An extraordinary event, the tango singer attending the premiere of a work that would revolutionize contemporary music, and on the way back from the concert, crossing Central Park, Gardel had spoken with admiration about the music he'd heard that night. "The intersection or encounter of Carlos Gardel, the supreme figure of Argentine tango, and Schoenberg, the great innovator of classical music, that blending of Schoenberg with Carlitos Gardel, takes form in the post-tangos of Gerardo Gandini," and so Renzi completed his introduction amid laughter and jokes about Gandini, who was now seated at the piano, exuberantly attacking a version of Cobián's "Los mareados," which was Gerardo and Emilio's favorite tango.

✝

They'd gone out for dinner at La Cátedra, a restaurant on the corner of Cerviño and Sinclair, in the vicinity of the Palermo racetrack, an area once occupied by studs and racehorses, and for that reason, apart from academic jokes, the name of the restaurant referred to the experts—the "professors," as racing fans called them—who used to weigh in about the pedigrees of thoroughbreds and about the tips and hunches found in newspaper pages for betting on a "sure thing," and that was why there were so many framed photos of horses on the walls of the establishment. Renzi had been reeling off that history in tandem with the owner of the place, an opera lover who admired Gandini and had come over to greet the friends of the musician, gathered there to celebrate some uncertain anniversary that would be clarified over the course of the night, aided by the bottles of wine that had appeared on the table long before the food arrived.

Gandini had gotten to the place early accompanied by Magda, his very recent wife, who was already a couple drinks in when they all turned up at once, getting out of three taxis, each pair in turn, Emilio and Carola, Germán and Graciela, and also Roberto Jacoby and Kiwi along with Cecilia, Kiwi's sister, who came with José Fernández Vega, the vibrant official philosopher of the group (who'd done his doctorate in Germany with a thesis on Peronism and war). Gandini was amused because they'd added something to the menu in his honor and with his name, *Fettuccini à la Gandini*, and as soon as he saw Emilio and the other friends arrive, taking up their separate places at the large round table that had been prepared in a reserved room at the restaurant, he once again told him that he'd asked the owner to name one of the dishes after Emilio Renzi, but the chef and the maître d' had resisted, as Gandini said, because Emilio didn't quite make the grade for his name to be given to a house specialty. This immediately invoked the Cannelloni à la Rossini that several people had rushed to order, while Gerardo praised Rossini, a composer whom he placed "very far above Verdi." Cecilia had moved away from the table and was filming the restaurant and them from a distance, using a very lightweight digital camera, for a documentary called *Scenes of Argentina* that she was putting together for the Discovery Channel. She made a few loops around the place and then sat down with them, and from time to time she would take out the camera to film the faces and above all the hands of the friends who were eating at La Cátedra that night.

The conversation had started energetically, a musical andante that would last all night amid discussions and jokes and arguments revolving around the benefits and dangers of marriage. They were celebrating the anniversary of Emilio and Carola's marriage, which had been a great happening that had lasted several days and culminated in a party—unbridled, in Gerardo's words—at a beautiful, geometric art deco building that Germán had provided for the event. What was being honored, in reality, was the passionate decision of Renzi, who'd been a privileged bachelor for more than forty years and, as was his habit, had developed several raving theories on the celibate condition of the great artists and also, or most of all, the mythical private eyes or detectives in the crime genre who kept themselves apart from the conjugal institution, which was the basis, according to Renzi's reasoning, of capitalist society. He'd written many notable pages on the opposition between literature and marriage, posing the great celibates as examples, especially Franz Kafka. "Never get tied down, and so always be able to love women" was one of Renzi's favorite epigrams in his youth. In an interview for the newspaper *La Nación* years before, Renzi had argued the reasons why he would absolutely never and for no reason have children, first of all because that responsibility to biology, culture, state, and religion justified what he, in the interview, had ironically called "the madness of tying the knot"; people married in order to have children, and without progeny, marriage was an empty institution, a false step that an artist—and a revolutionary and conspirator (and for him all of those words were synonymous)—must never take. His rejection of fatherhood had provoked a wave of criticism on the part of the young writers who'd already been married before ever publishing a book, had made, as they say, a family and had children, descendants, heirs.

Germán had seen, in that unanimous, general, and journalistic rejection of this opinion from Renzi, a symptom of the fact that something had been disrupted by that defense of celibacy and that attack on the paterfamilias, most of all the fact of his saying it publicly, proof that society couldn't bear for someone to express a desire that diverged from the social norm. As a result, when the bachelor got married, there were great celebrations among Renzi's friends and acquaintances (who were for the most part married, with children) because, as Kiwi said, ironically, "Emilio had returned to the fold." He'd gotten married because he'd fallen in love and also because he'd decided to accept the professorship they'd offered him at Princeton University, and it was clear that in order to be a professor in the United States it was better to be a married man, as that would also simplify the process for Carola to come to North America with him. For the last few years he'd been a visiting professor, spending a few months teaching abroad and then returning to Buenos Aires as if he'd never left, but now the perspective of erasing himself from the toxic atmosphere of Argentine culture and "flying the coop," as Emilio said metaphorically, had led him to reconcile with the status quo of marriage.

He'd gotten married because he'd fallen in love with Carola; he'd known and been attracted to her for years but had maintained a platonic friendship with her because she was, in those days, the wife, the companion of his friend David, and he was determined not to repeat his adventures from the past yet again and yet again fall into an adulterous triangle, so that he started going out, as they say, with Carola only once she'd already separated from her evident companion, the intense, esoteric, and combative D. V., and yet, to reach that point, there'd been a chain of chance circumstances that their friends called "the miracle" and were celebrating on this night, 16 June, because it had been the day of that unexpected meeting, contrary to all logic and all terms of possibility—since the meeting had transpired in Paris—and this was also why, with a wink of mutual understanding and also a secret literary reference, that was the date—16 June—that they chose for their wedding and that now, just one year later, all of their friends were celebrating with jokes and truths at La Cátedra. What had happened, after all, on that day in Paris, the mythical origin of a series of events that took place one by one and were the reason why Emilio had ceased to be a bachelor?

Renzi had spent a few weeks in Germany along with other South American writers, going around to different cities, giving lectures and interviews and participating in roundtables, and, at the end of that rather exhausting cultural march, he'd continued, traveling to Paris by train to catch a bit of rest and visit his friends, especially Saer, taking advantage of a generous offer from his French translator, Antoine, to stay at his apartment while he was on vacation in the south of France, delighted by the weather forecasts that announced a sunny and pleasant month of June. And so he took his summer vacation early and offered Emilio his place in the Latin Quarter. One afternoon at Saer's house, when he was still living in his apartment on Boulevard Voltaire, after the meal, during the table talk, an Argentine friend invited him to dinner at her house the next day. Emilio accepted and wrote down the address on a scrap of paper along with a guide of the metro connections he should follow to make it in the early hours of the evening the next day to the house of Estela, an old friend from Emilio's university days who had traveled to Paris on a fellowship soon after graduation and ended up residing in France with a job at the École Normale as a psychoanalyst, an expert on Freud and Lacan.

That day, Emilio left the apartment on Rue Cuyas, Rive Gauche at 7:00 or 7:10 in the evening; when he reached the metro line 4 entrance from Saint-Michel to Porte de Clignancourt, he realized he didn't have anything to give his Argentine friend and so retraced his steps and bought two dozen red roses at a florist's, then made it back to the metro station at 7:30, took the line toward Pigalle, walked a block through the underground metro passageways, and went to the Barbès-Rochechouart station with a connection to Metro 2. He even paused on the platform to give a few francs as a tip to a Hindu girl who was plucking a sitar, sitting on the floor, playing Eastern music. Suddenly Renzi retraced his steps to pause a moment longer in front of the beautiful young woman and drop a few more francs into the wooden box that she had on the ground next to her. And so he watched two trains pass right in front of him and chose not to take them so as to go on listening to the captivating melodies of the sitar that vividly recalled Anton Karas's soundtrack to Carol Reed's film *The Third Man*, in the same way that a sense of urgency had led him to buy the flowers that he still held in his left hand, as he was left-handed. So it was that, at 7:50, he finally got onto the train that would take him to Porte Dauphine, where he could make the connection that would bring him to Pigalle and the house of his friend.

On the way he stood with the bouquet of red roses in his hand, feeling slightly ridiculous because all of the passengers were looking at him with benevolent expressions, understanding that Renzi was going to a romantic date. But it was another romantic date that fate had in store for him! He reached the station that opened a network of connections and had to pause to look for the route on the metro map. He pressed two buttons and two tiny light bulbs lit to show him the way, and so he left there and headed down the passage that flowed into tall stairways and followed the signs on the walls that showed him the correct direction. And along one of those paths, in a vast hallway full of people coming and going toward their destinations, he saw Carola coming, as if an apparition or a replica of his dear friend. It was really her, smiling to see him as if she'd been waiting. They stood there talking, and Renzi gave her the flowers. "I bought these flowers for you," he said, and she smiled with a warm and ironic smile because she understood the joke that fortune had laid for them. And he had stayed with her that night and now they were never apart and had married, choosing the very day of their fortuitous meeting as the date, 16 June, when they'd crossed paths by chance in the intricate, moving labyrinth of the Paris metro.

The story of that meeting was narrated by their friends that night, passing the word from one to the next so that Roberto and Kiwi, Germán, or Graciela recounted the parts of the story that they remembered best, adding details, specifying the facts, enthusiastic in spite of critiques from Carola, who attributed the merits of the meeting to herself, as if she'd spent all afternoon that day in Paris coming and going on the metro, convinced, she said, that somewhere within that hive Emilio was waiting for her, as if she were the queen bee over the individuals, the trains, which, in her version, performed the role of the workers in the honeycomb, preparing everything for the ritual meal, in which Renzi was no more than a being trapped in the queen's nest. In this way the night passed, a celebration of other events as well, which, although they weren't the topic of conversation, were present in an elliptical manner and were, ultimately, a way to honor what Jacoby called "the strategies of friendship." They said goodbye on the corner amid applause and jokes, and there, in the clear night, as if awakening, José pointed out with a look of concentration that the great philosophers too had been celibate and childless. "For example," he said, "Kant, Kierkegaard, Schopenhauer, Nietzsche, and Wittgenstein." Everyone looked at him in surprise and nodded with a distant air. And then they said goodbye and all took separate taxis and headed in different directions toward their homes until they were lost in the night like conspirators united in a secret cause.

†

We've been here for a week now and ever since I arrived, I've been wondering if we said goodbye on the night of that last dinner at the restaurant. You left suddenly, as is typical of you, with the grace of an avant-garde provocateur, something I hope you won't lose now that you're occupying an office once upholstered in red (I liked the part about the button hidden under the table, because it could also be used to communicate with the bodyguards), but I don't know if we managed to embrace as would be proper for two Argentines trained in the old tango tradition of friendship, whose greatest example was El Trolo Troilo.

Yesterday, once again in the chance way of reading, I came across a slightly enigmatic allusion that to me seems to refer to you (at least it refers to a possible "musical" explanation). Wittgenstein confided to Norman Malcolm that the slow movement of Brahms's third quartet had twice brought him to the brink of suicide. What is it about that quartet? Can we use it to kill our enemies? (I could use it to bring about the death of a character as a perfect crime in a detective novel . . . every night the character hears that music coming from the house next door and in the end commits suicide.) Wittgenstein was a bit exaggerated (a fanatic, really), but it seems to me a good metaphor for the powers of *la musique* . . . Here, in June, summer has arrived and everything is flourishing and we're getting ready to acquaint ourselves with a few beaches that are an hour away from Princeton and are, from what they say, a Yankee version of La Costa Azul (to the east).

While doing work for my seminar on the tango, I once again find secret information dedicated to you. There's a tango (from 1944–1945) with lyrics by the great Homero Expósito and music by Enrique Villegas (yes, the monk), called "Si hoy fuera ayer," and the lyrics are beautiful. I guess you can find the sheet music at SADAIC and include it on your album along with the tangos and post-tangos. I quite liked your statement à la Cage, a speech in the form of a piece of music (I hope you have a piano nearby), really, it's similar to the Lope poem we learned in high school ("A sonnet Violante bids me write, such grief I hope never again to see . . . "), and I see that lately you've been dedicating yourself to insulting *la musique contemporaine*, and the *avant-garde* (the ex-vanguardists are the worst enemies of the vanguard), and to defending *le sens commun* (I hope it isn't the influence of Horacio González, through Fito . . .). To me, it seems like a miniature congress in which everyone (except the musicians) in which everyone (except the musicians) is going to become an "expert" and an "artist," all of them cynical and funny and like they've seen it all before, except for the pretension of seeming *à la page* (secretly emulating Teodolina Villar, the heroine from "The Zahir," which you'll no doubt remember as a precursor to "*nouveau trilinguisme*" in Argentina).

All fine here, I'm living as though in a Swiss clinic à la *Tender Is the Night*. I'm watching squirrels gather nuts for winter and reading the existing versions of Nietzsche's life for the book, reminiscent of Macedonio (because of its imminence), of our future opera, *Lucia Nietzsche* (I like the title, it seems more operatic than *The Flow* . . . and it makes me happy to have another Lucía nearby to love). Between the hours I write little sketches of Lucia Nietzsche's conversations, seeking the tone to differentiate each character, and between the walls of my skull (on the line that connects my cranial plates) I can hear the reverberations of the epic music of the incest and the sarcastic replies from Nietzsche's sister (and from the wicked dwarf). I'm pleased with the story and sure that I'll resolve the scenes and the monologues quickly, I just need two weeks clear with nothing to take up my mornings, but first I have to get out from under all of my outstanding work because I'm getting ready for the courses that I have to teach this semester.

I feel like I'm a mixture of Dreyfus and Ruggierito, I'm the Bairoletto of Argentine culture, chased by the pack, fleeing on foot and staining the plains with blood, alone in the middle of the campus ("on campus, we're going to live on campus" . . .), at night I turn over in bed and write deadly responses that I've already forgotten by morning, I taught a class on Horacio Quiroga today and it seems to me that I really understood him for the first time: the man went off to live in the jungle in order to escape from Buenos Aires and the literate atmosphere, and he ended up talking to the little titi monkeys, and will that be my fate?, talking to monkeys? I don't think so. I'm disheartened and furious (a strange mixture that's sure to have some effect); I try not to play the victim, since the types who attack me and want to send me off to jail cultivate the poetics of the victim, the bastards who act like martyrs. But imagining that front page where I appear as an emblem of cultural corruption causes tall waves of fury that break against my past, and I start to go blind again, it's good luck that my friends (the best, not all) have reacted with great loyalty (you first of all), but suddenly I have the urge to flee, never again return to that sinister country, accept the offer from Princeton and grow old here among the poplars and the English language, the same syndrome is taking hold of me as took Puig, who left Argentina and never returned, not even for one day, the key is for me to manage to forget myself and maintain my calm (calm and violence, like a character out of Burroughs). I don't quite know what traces are going to be left over after all of this, but for now, as you can see, I'm outraged. As you might also guess, the last two or three weeks in Buenos Aires were very dizzying, what with the opera and catching up with friends and the Beat circus and that whole crowd. Since I came back to Princeton I've been feeling much better, I spend my time reading books by Nietzsche and books on Coleridge (now you can see why); I'm trying to start writing again but lose focus straight away, I nearly finished a second part for the story about Saint-Nazaire and I'm also making progress on Lucia Nietzsche, the Mephistophelian girl.

I was stuck thinking about what I think you said to me last time: putting the scenes from Nietzsche's breakdown back in, as it's like a completed work in itself—the horse, the boarding house, the letters to kings and emperors, the arrival of his friend, the theatrical entrance at the Turin station where the train departs for Berlin, the ten years he spends isolated with his sister in the house, which will later become the Nietzsche Archive where he's exhibited to the faithful who want to see him, and the ones in which Nietzsche, mute, does nothing but play an indecipherable (or twelve-tone?) music on the piano: all of this transpires between 1888 and 1900; that "theme" (like the theme of the Aryan colony in Paraguay, with the German aristocrats liberated by Förster, Elizabeth Nietzsche's husband, and the natives exploited by those racist colonizers, whose decadence and abandonment begins around 1888 and coincides with Nietzsche's insanity) attracts me very much but seems very difficult to integrate with the three central themes that we've outlined.

a) The mysterious two-story house in Adrogué, where a woman lives who claims to be a blood descendant of the philosopher and his sister, the lyric soprano Lucia Nietzsche, who hires the young pianist as hostage to her Wagnerian madness in order to compose a false opera that she, in fact, means to attribute to the author of *Ecce Homo*, while she is watched over by her father, who moves around (drunk or on drugs) in his wheelchair.

b) The father, Igor, a German musicologist, who has conducted musical experiments with recorded voices. The sound archive where one can hear the songs and the lament for defeat and killing, the story of the conquered who tell their secret and silenced version of events, a manifold and varied history (a chorus from the twentieth-century concentration camps?, or the story of a shipwreck?, or the story of a plague?).

c) The first act of the supposed Wagnerian opera by Nietzsche. The wedding party, concealing the defeat and killings suffered by the girlfriend's kingdom, which makes her a political hostage of her husband, the despotic and depraved conquering prince, culminates in the crisis caused by the incestuous brother's irruption into the bridal chamber with his dwarf jester, and in the girl's suicide (it resembles a telenovela by Andrea del Boca, but we'll treat it with the tone of Wagner–Shakespeare–Estanislao del Campo).

It all seems fantastic to me and quite operatic (in the next few days I'm going to see Visconti's film *The Damned*, and I'm also thinking about Sartre's *The Condemned of Altona* and Peter Brook's *Marat/Sade*), yet very complex and difficult to structure. I've been thinking that perhaps level b) could include Nietzsche's insanity, and I've also thought that I'll have to work, on the one hand, using the chorus (the voices in the story as a representation of Nietzsche's madness, that is, the voices Nietzsche hears inside his head, that's why he doesn't speak!, and that's why he only plays the piano, because he's trying to find music to accompany that chorus). In reality Nietzsche is hearing the future, not seeing it, listening to the lament of the twentieth century, and dies as that century in beginning. On the other hand, what to do with the sister? (screw her!, the prince's jester would say) . . . I've been turning over these ideas and these characters in my head, trying to construct the dramatic situations and come to Buenos Aires in December with a basic scheme so that we can work together in the cabin at Triste-Le-Roy, sober and ascetic, like monks, like German artists (since part of the opera has to be spoken in German). I hope to have a first draft of the book ready by mid-September so we can work on it together while you're in Princeton. Everyone is expecting you here and they'll send you the schedule for your residency soon. On Thursday the twenty-seventh

I'd like you to come to my seminar, "The tango in Argentine culture," and say something if you can (and want to) about the trend of the music and its "evolution" (De Caro/Pugliese/Troilo/Salgán/Piazzolla or whatever series you like. You could even analyze a single tango, for example "Los mareados" or one of your choice, and if you want you could just talk about Piazzolla as well). What's important is that they learn something about what sort of music the music of tango is (the best thing would be for you to bring a few recordings to listen to and analyze). The talk will be in Spanish and you need to speak for an hour, more or less. I guess Arcadio will invite you to the seminar he's teaching on "my work," and there, in a very informal way, you can describe the process of *The Absent City* and maybe show a few fragments from the video. On Friday the twenty-eighth you have the post-tango concert and there's also the possibility that the people from the university's music department will invite you to do a little workshop on your music. They'll confirm the schedule for you next week; everything, obviously, will be very easy and calm, and you can modify the subject to your liking. The important thing is for us to spend a week together, talking and drinking wine and wandering around the area. We have a car now, and in her red sports car Carola is one of the most famous (and also most feared) figures in Princeton.

We'll see what melodrama to make in these solitudes (where there's an abundance, really, of scholars and of melodrama like Peter Brook); for the moment I'm adapting, I've already bought a fax machine (as you can see) and in the next few days a supersonic portable computer is coming for me (by mail), on which I'll set up, among other things, an email account. I get up at six in the morning and the day flows (it really does) like life in the nineteenth century; I spend my hours in the library, which is perfect and infinite, and now and then we go to New York just to confirm that cities still exist (sometimes I think that I'm still in Buenos Aires and that I've gone insane and that in my delirium, shut away in my studio on Calle Charcas amid the violent murmurs of the metropolis, I only believe that I'm living in a peaceful town in the endless Manhattan suburbs). You'll see, it never rains in this town, the ducks are getting ready to migrate to warmer areas, the scholars are alcoholics or secret serial killers, and everything here seems planned out so that one will pass one's life in peace (which of course doesn't mean that one wants to spend one's life in peace), reading and writing on a kind of forgotten island. So I'm writing a first draft of the book for the opera and also a few short stories to include in the reissue of *Prisión perpetua* (in the last few days I've been writing a story called "Diary of a Madman," which is a meticulous transcription of my days in Princeton), and from Monday to Thursday I go to my office on campus, do my shopping at the supermarket, go to the laundromat to wash my clothes, and I've discovered a very good Chilean wine that causes no shortage of confusion with its name, "Los Vascos," and also, of course, we're missing our friends (just not all of them).

Meanwhile, I'm reading Nietzsche (in English), who writes like no one else and has a unique tone, a phrasing that reminds me of Hölderlin, of Novalis. What to do with all of this? (confide in the musician): think of a fixed structure, very clear, that might perhaps bring everything out of the image of the archive of voices, a kind of invisible prison where the voices of the condemned persist, a white room, soundproofed, where the father moves around in his wheelchair. I'm going in circles here and will keep you informed. I go to New York whenever I can, and in the city, as you know, all languages coexist, all currencies, the global currents intersect, I'm visiting marginal museums (the one on the history of television, the one on immigration, the Jewish museum) seeking (as the idiots say) "images" for the opera, but it seems like there's actually an excess of images and I need to start cutting and getting rid of "good" ideas, because works aren't made from good ideas but from a single idea handled well and in depth (example: a woman-machine). Today is Friday, and this letter has been written at different points over the course of the day, and, as you can see, my state of mind (and the vacillations of my prose) still persist. There are a few people I like a lot here at the university, they spend their whole lives devoted to a single subject (as is proper for lunatics). There's one, for example, who's the foremost expert on *Don Quixote* in the world and has done nothing but teach that novel for thirty years, and if you pass at any hour of night you can see the light on in his office and imagine the guy reading Cervantes's book once again, with a kind of foolish obstinacy, as if there were something more to learn. Sometimes I think I'd like to live like that, far away from the world, with a fixed idea (fixed on a single point): I just have to decide which book that is . . . but sometimes I think that a character like that (obsessed with something, fixed on a single point) could be Lucia Nietzsche's father, and the old lunatic in the wheelchair wants, for example, to transcribe the voices he's recorded (but that perhaps no one can hear) . . . It's nighttime now, you sent me another fax and I'm meant to be answering it. I hope to see you soon, we're expecting you, and in the meantime we can send a few more faxes (*unos fax más* has a good ring to it). We're sending a big hug to you and warm wishes, *cálidos cariños con Carola* (that's perfect alliteration) for both of you.

†

As he entered, he thought he could see Amanda, and off to one side he saw Inés talking to Julia, she was dressed in red and the other two in black. Could it be? All three together, thought Emilio, it's a conspiracy, but he continued forward with Carola, who conducted him toward the back of the gallery. The circulation of visitors around the exhibition room was part of the work; they formed the work itself, passing among the mannequins that León Ferrari had intervened on with handwritten inscriptions and sentences in black and red marker. Distracted and nervous, Emilio tried not to be seen by his exes. They were there, there was no way out. The exhibition, which was being unveiled that night, was indeed called "The Black and the Red," and the—more or less involuntary—participants, on entering the basement of the bar and restaurant Filo-Espacio de Arte, received alternating red and black ID cards; red had to enter the gallery to the right and black to the left. There weren't too many people there that night at the *vernissage*, but there were enough to cause an effect of confusion, an organized throng. The mannequins were the typical human figures with no heads, arms, or legs, that is, a very elegant torso of pale wood with a peak, or rather, a vertical umbrella handle, painted black. The mannequins caused a certain effect of sinister familiarity, resembling unfinished statues or frozen phantom figures. Through an incredible series of coincidences, the women he'd loved were converging toward him. He saw that Amanda had gone up to Julia and that Julia was introducing herself to Inés. Emilio tried moving to face the wall so as not to be seen. Carola stopped and looked at him:

"What is it, sparrow?" she asked.

Did she call him sparrow? Maybe he'd misheard. Inside the room the voices rose and fell in intensity like a psychotic chorus. *A chorus of lunatics in an insane asylum for art*, he thought.

"Nothing," he said. "I'm trying to understand the sense of randomness in the show."

In order to view the work in its entirety, you had to climb a staircase that led high up in the room, to a kind of loft that Ferrari had set up as a private observation deck over the exhibition. In turns of two people— one red and one black—the participants were granted access to the observation deck in an arbitrary order. León chose the ones singled out to enter the observatory at random. Emilio hoped the three women would go up without seeing him; he was red and Carola had black. Three pairs separated him from the three exes, who were now laughing in delight, as if seeing him and talking among themselves was the best part of the night. Emilio put on an expression of surprise and greeted them, gesturing and waving his hands, but they didn't respond and went on laughing and joking around as if they couldn't see him. Carola didn't see anything either and was moving along the route indicated. With his angelic and malicious expression, León Ferrari, dressed—or rather disguised—as a painter, wearing a pale gray smock stained with several colors of paint and holding a brush in his hand, was gesturing to indicate the pairs chosen to access the loft.

Emilio and Carola had gone up after greeting the artist with a hug and now, from above, through the viewpoints in the shape of binoculars, were contemplating the work. Only two people at a time could see, or rather construct, the work; the idea of an installation that functioned as a human machine was very appealing, and from above the mannequins and people formed a series in continuous and circular motion. Not everyone who entered the room could see the work, as the concept of dual and selective perception was the basis of the experience; the second interesting point, of course, was that it turned the spectators into the artistic material and a part of the work. What could be seen from above was a mass of slightly flattened and unreal people—an effect of the magnifying lenses of the little windows in the observation deck; on the other hand, the spectators became voyeurs spying on a confusing and rather surreal event. They went up two at a time because Ferrari wanted to include the duplicity and commentaries of the observers. But Emilio, instead of viewing the whole, was trying to follow the movements of Amanda, the only one of them to enter his perspective from above; maybe they'd planned to meet and had gotten together without knowing that he'd be there as well, had they become friends? Did they tell each other in chorus about Emilio's contrivances? Where did that word come from? he thought.

When they went back down, he couldn't see them; were they up above, had all three gone up together? The beloved Erinyes. He prepared himself to listen to León. "At first," he was saying, "what I created was a deformed writing, or, more directly, signs from invented alphabets. It was an incomprehensible word. In that form, I wrote a series of drawings that I titled *Letter to a General*, and it was the first time that I introduced the political and conceptual element into my art. But by 1964 I started to create normal writing, in the sense of its being comprehensible. It is possible to read the text, yet it is a drawing as well. I mean that I write things the word can't express, and I express things with words that I couldn't communicate in any other form."

Emilio saw the three of them in a corner; had they come down without his seeing them, were they now trading jokes about him, making faces? They seemed very amused, and Julia winked at him. Emilio concentrated, was he hallucinating? Seeing visions? No. They were there and making gestures toward him. Were they going to come find him outside? Now he could hear León's voice. "I left the abstract line and writing to create political art in a direct way. One of those works was rejected at the Di Tella: it was a Santería Christ, crucified on an American bomber plane. The work was titled *Western Christian Civilization*. It was up for two days and then they took it down. Romero Brest said it offended the religious sentiments of the people who worked at the Institute. I recognize that it was very shocking. I also think it could have stayed up, but anyway. The truth is, after that episode, I practically stopped making art until 1975, although I took part in the organization of several shows."

Emilio had seen the Christ on the plane at the Di Tella show with Julia. Ferrari made jokes "for the purposes of not wasting oil paint, acrylics, plaster, Styrofoam, and epoxy, which my artist colleagues need so much; the works that make up this eco-friendly exegesis in this eco-friendly show are themselves eco-friendly. That is, they renounce material to the greatest extent possible: they are pictures, sculptures, installations made only of words: the easiest material to renew."

The people were dispersing or sitting down to eat at the establishment, they made very good pizza at Filo, thought Renzi, for his three ex-loves were no longer there, had they gone?, or dematerialized? The phantom of women loved. Carola was at his side, talking to Roberto J. Emilio went over to León.

"Literature is delayed in relation to art; painters abandoned the easel and canvas, but we writers remain bound to the pages and the book," he said; "maybe the computer screen and email can allow us to shake off our lethargy. The use of previously written texts as material for new works would be one way."

"You must use what is already made," said León.

"Of course," responded Emilio, "literature must deepen its conceptual impulse and advance toward a synthetic, *a priori* art."

"And that in two senses. First, paring down the practice, seeking maximum concentration, saying everything in very little space."

"There are too many words in the world and too many pages written to ever be read, and so you must seek velocity."

"Brevity and immaterial circulation."

"We are dematerialized," Jacoby, who had come over, said in amusement.

"Of course," said León, "we're looking for brief, cheap, and ultracritical works."

"The other way is to invent a potential articulation that would allow the creation of future texts spoken or thought or conceived by imaginary writers."

"Well, Valéry already did that with *Monsieur Teste*," said Carola.

"He posited a non-empirical literature," smiled Renzi.

"And he came before Duchamp," she said.

"And you, what are you up to, Emilio?"

"Always the same thing, but your Stendhalian optical device made me think."

They moved apart and Emilio began to write mentally. *The diary he writes is a laboratory for potential literature to him. The final gravitational, vast work. It is an inorganic assemblage, in motion; all of the materials are real, the words have previously been lived through by him, and in this sense it is an anthropological document about the life of an earthling, which could be used by a reader from another planet in order to understand the ways of life in a specific and localized and precisely dated human community. The life or the lives of an individual who in his distant youth wagered everything on the written word. And in that respect, it is a work of nonfiction, a true novel, a real testimony, and a historical document. What he says is a description, not a value judgment.* He seemed to see the words written in the night air.

"Where are you going," Carola said to him, "where did you go? Fly back down, little bird," she laughed. "Big bird is more accurate."

"Right," he said, "you hit the nail on the head, perfect. That's how I feel, a big ugly bird struggling to fly."

✝

The Diaries of Renzi or *Book of Quequén*—so named for having been found in the vicinity of a port of the same name on the shores of the Atlantic ocean—was discovered by Armeno and his cousin Roque, two fishermen from the Chinese factory vessels, who, as they lay down to take a siesta at the base of a sand quarry emplacement, saw the book among the ruins, in a pit beneath a concrete beam. It is said that Armeno cast the book into the sea "because he lacked knowledge about the importance of the discovery" (*Xul News*). The sea brought it back to the beach, very damaged but intact, and the copy remained there in the sand under the sun until dusk. That's why some historians have designated it *The Book of the Castaway*. It isn't a bottle in the sea, but it is a message sent from an island many centuries before, an edition lost in distant times.

For the last several months the volume has been located in the restricted room at the National Library. For the moment, its conservation status—and the library's traditional scarcity of funds—is preventing the enigma of its date of publication from being resolved for certain. This temporal uncertainty seems to be part of the concept of fiction to which the book wants to ascribe.

Some historians contend that the book was written during the first decade of the twenty-second century, pretending to have been composed fifty years before. Others, by contrast, accept the proposition implicit in the book and believe that the diary was indeed written over the course of an extensive period, approximately spanning from 1957 to 2007. Whatever the elucidation of this dilemma may be, it remains one of the most ancient testimonies of literary practice during the age of expansion of the Web culture, prior to its abrupt shift and its crisis at the end of the twenty-first century.

Philological criticism—the trend now in vogue at the University of Buenos Aires's Department of Classical Languages—analyzes this trilogy as a testimony from the moment in which literary works were still being signed by their authors, though already besieged by the expansion of the conceptual writings of cyberspace, the widespread anonymity of blogs, the virtual identities of Facebook and Twitter, the free interventions and modifications of texts through interferences in RAM and Web connectors. Those remote technologies—which aspired to disclosure, automatic translation, and generalized writing—called into question the notions of authorship, individual creation, and originality. *Literature should be made by all, not just by one*; the line from the Uruguayan Lautréamont was the literary motto of the era.

For its part, the historicist trend of the Bahía Blanca school considers these stories to be ethnographic documents from an eradicated culture, and the names of its authors a simple register of the identities of the informers. The texts of the diaries—according to this theory—would have taken the form of the testimony, the autobiography, the journalistic report, the chronicle, to simulate literature in life and no longer—as in the mimetic realism of the twenty-first century—life in literature. The historiographers consider it the only surviving archive of a period of transition, a map of the moment at which reality—composed by media, technology, and the sciences—came to be an illusion. These twenty-first century accounts—according to the most radical theories—were potent fictions capable of *entering* "reality." A mutant, terrifying reality that included dreams, myths, delusions, virtual worlds, real catastrophes, and imaginary events.

Whatever position one adopts in the debate, it is essential to point out the importance of these texts, the period of which—at least in the Río de la Plata area—makes explicit reference to the second centenary of the Revolution of 1810. In the twenty-first century, democracy was a utopia that the young American states were achieving on Earth, but by the twenty-second century that reality had become anachronistic and the dispersion and disorder of those individual states had turned it into a memory. My grandfather—if you will forgive this personal interference—could recall having received from his grandfather, and he from his, the mythical account of the pageantry at the second centenary (2010), when great royal caravans passed along the asphalt streets of the city center bearing picture cards and figures from history. It began with the original towns and reached as far as that distant present. The homeland was only two hundred years old then, but it already thought itself proud and ancient even though, viewed from our axial distance, it was hardly a minute—or two—within the interminable hour of history. We look now with irony, but also with admiration, at the enthusiasm of those times. Nearly a million people went out into the streets to watch the performance. "It's better than watching it on television," said one eyewitness captured by the cameras—an awed young woman with blue eyes (*Xul History*)—and her words still move us all. Direct experiences were still possible then, although the anonymous girl's epiphany shows that they were starting to become surprising and scarce.

As I advance with the studies for this book, I have a premonition—with nostalgia, as if I'd already lived through them and forgotten them—of what those distant years were made from. I suffer the illness of historians; after so much time imagining what people were like in the past, I transform into one of them and feel disoriented and foreign in the interminable present. My modest proposal is to restore—to the greatest extent possible—the historical context and the references implicit in the entries from the diaries. In order to understand the secret message that has reached us from that distant era, it is fitting to navigate backwards along the river of time and view the writings up close.

The text that has generated the most controversy is "Diary of a Story"; many researchers contend that there are traces of this story in a book— now legendary—of the same title, which was published some years prior to the second centenary. No physical copy survives, but there is an old Web copy circulating on *Xul*, considered by young short-story writers of the twenty-first century to be a cult book. It is written in first person by a young student who goes to visit his grandfather, a colonel from one of the ancient wars, which is to say that the story narrates events that took place in the second half of the twentieth century. Some details should be clarified. Dunes, for example, were banks of sand, sometimes mobile and nomadic and other times fixed in place by hedges that bordered the beaches of the south. These disappeared after the great oceanic risings, but images survive from the region of Mar del Plata (cf. *Tlön*.9), which is also referred to in a story from this book that I will discuss at a later point.

The story of the narrator's youth produces the same temporal uncertainty; at that time fire was a real threat and groups of volunteers in uniform would patrol the streets in pumper trucks on a hunt for fires. The prediction that is calmly articulated in the sentence "The dead announce the future" could be the means of anticipating, in that story, the blazing—or ardent—time to come. We must not forget that the author (cf. *Tlön*.8) was one of the foremost experts on spiritualism and psychoanalysis of his era.

The story of the woman who refused to leave her house repeats the plays with time and is part of a text of the same name originally distributed on the Web. Gardel remains well-known to everyone and his voice is still improving; at this very moment I'm listening to him sing "Viejo smoking."

We will now consider a series of notes from the diary that avoid recording political events but narrate their consequences. Some historians of antiquity have pointed out that the description of the Buenos Aires urban sprawl at several points in the book is significant historical information. There are no direct references in the account, but theorists of *thick description* contend that the atmosphere of terror confirms the theory that the Peronist movement could only have been destroyed by an extraterrestrial intervention that engulfed the electoral belts of Greater Buenos Aires in biopolitical ruin.

The sensation of a lack of masses, an absence of crowds, and the disappearance of neighbors from the working-class neighborhoods—typical of that dark period—appears in the second volume as well, but in particular it defines the atmosphere in *The Plague Years*, in view of the fact that it registers artificial high temperatures, labyrinthine arteries, and abandoned buildings, and calls attention to the remnants of the city, "empty and organized [. . .] which no longer resembles Buenos Aires." Additionally there are its references to the extra-parliamentary movements of that period.

For its part, the chronicle of Book II, with its precise description of the urban wasteland, seems to respond to the aforementioned periodization as well. The reference to the sect of "The Twelve (or La Doce)" is a testimony to the struggles of the scattered groups from the so-called *Third Peronist Resistance*. Some analysts contend that the chemical addictions suggested in the text are an effect of social depersonalization during those hopeless times. All of these explanations are conjectural, because the stories, far from thematizing their political keys, narrate events from the "low" and "blind" consciousness of the subjects of history.

In short, these apocalyptic writings are indirect testimonies of a catastrophic time. It can also be inferred that, concurrent with the devastated region, there existed closed cities and that the country was being dominated by mutants that had finally succeeded in imposing their neo-republican liberal pretensions.

The touching love story for Lidia seems to reprise the English legend of an impossible adolescent passion and is a complex and effective reconstruction of those uncertain years. Artificial biological gestation, new repressive laws, and new methods for control and imprisonment are the scientific and legal framework for the absolute separation of the masculine and feminine sexes, which recalls the utopian politico-sexual divisions postulated by William Burroughs.

We will now consider the series of stories from the third book, which are—to my understanding—subsequent to the great crisis. The debate around chronology is repeated here: if written in the twenty-second century, they were close to the events; if written fifty years before, they prefigure them. That ecclesiastical debate does not interest us, nor do the theories of the ridiculous Doctor Anselmi with their malignant repercussions and methodological inconsistency. With the information we currently have about that period and the new archaeological findings, a relatively acceptable reconstruction of the events becomes possible.

After a period of long darkness there came about the change of the name of the Republic, and as a consequence the whole political geography was modified. Somewhere around the second centenary, the social-democratic government—faced with the global crisis and the galactic rise of international financial demands—decided to transport the Argentine Republic and its institutions to the island of Martín García. The nation-state, with its three branches of power installed on the island, had to honor the legal commitments acquired over its history, whereas the vast continental territory began a new phase under the name of the Republic of Río de la Plata, now free from external debt, from its tragic past, and from the preexisting treaties to which peninsular Argentina now had to respond.

Thus began a new era in the southern provinces that the annals of history have recorded as *The Reverse Secession*. The Argentine nation was displaced to an island with its past intact, leaving behind an empty territory, in which history started over again, giving way to a new era free from debts (in every sense) and without the weight of inheritance received from prior governments. And so began a process of historic construction starting from zero that lasted until the end of the twenty-second century. The rest of the diary entries must be localized inside that situation and are chronicles of the new times. The Argentine tradition began to be told in another way; it was reformed and adapted to new ideas, and the heroes changed as well as the facts.

The state of the language employed in these accounts seems to conform to the rules of Spanish written during the period of unified grammar, prior to the great lexical and syntactical transformations of the High Web period, and I have subjected this report to that language. I have set and regulated it using the automatic translation methods of the Quain sensors, to which my eventual readers may also appeal in case of doubt around the meaning of any line in the chapters of this trilogy. We have preferred to preserve the original language of the text with its multiple archaisms—and its remote syntax—so as not to alter the scattered Río de la Plata dialects that constitute it.

The initial prologue, signed by Emilio Renzi, was the text most affected by the book's sojourn in the waters of the sea. Only a few isolated lines have survived.

We live in a time that is blind to the future, and for that reason it is auspicious to read these . . . And then, further down: *For us, utopian defenses are* . . . Finally, at the end: *I'm writing this prologue in Temperley on the eleventh of June of* . . . That's all that has remained of the text, but we wanted, nevertheless, to reinstate the name of the author so that this *Xul* reprint might preserve the frame of the original book. It will also be a way to recall this forgotten author, of whom only the memory of his friendship with the Uruguayan writer Amalia Ibáñez has endured; in a footnote from one of the countless theses dedicated to that author, it is established that the *Emilio* from her legendary poem *Tekhnai en Luján* was him, Renzi (or so he called himself).

†

Confused, he awoke, where was he?, or, where could he be?, or rather, where had he been?, was he him?, he'd been dreaming of *The Book of the Castaway*. One never knows how long dreams last; in dreaming, time becomes fragmented and accelerated and concentrated; the image of a grain of sand in the palm of your hand could contain an entire life, he thought; he could remember the dream better, more clearly, than his experience of the last few hours.

He was with Junior at an Irish pub on Calle Viamonte, down at the end, near Filo, they were coming from some place, Emilio and Carola, from the unveiling of something, the millennium had changed and nothing had happened, and he was talking about that with Junior, who was with Monique, his French girlfriend, his *darling*, it was fine to call his clandestine lover *darling*, his *kept woman*, he said as well. Was that her condition, the French girl? She'd been sent there by *Le Figaro* to report on the new century in the distant south.

It took him a while to realize that he'd been woken up in his study by the sound of ambulance sirens. Also the Sirens whose song seduces the traveler, the women with fish tails were seducing him and leading him down the wrong path, but who is the speaker in this case? *Siren song* is also used to refer to the final days or final footholds of what is imaginary and no longer in use. The siren song of Peronism, for example, said Junior, in the Irish bar.

Then he remembered a scene from the dream, the only vivid, virtual, visual, vital scene that he could recall with the unmistakable clarity of the things seen in dreams; the beach at Quequén, the resort where he'd spent a few summers, had been transformed, in his imagination, and was now a gully of wreckage, buildings in ruin, facing the Atlantic Ocean, the memory of a summer on the sea had been transformed, in sleep, into a lunar landscape from a future time, but how did he know, in the dream, Emilio, that the image came from the future? It was the undeniable certainty that one has when dreaming, needing no explanation. A book was taken out of the waters, it resembled an animal, mythological, malevolent, marine, or rather maritime. A book that the sea's waters had cast up onto the planet's penultimate sands.

Without getting out of bed, Renzi took a pen and, on the final page of the book that he had on the nightstand, *The Craft of Fiction* (New York, The Viking Press, 1959), on the blank page, he wrote: *a remote beach in an axial time*—the word *axial* came to him from his memory of the night—*and the damaged but unbeaten volume was the very one I'm writing.* He was able to read it, and, in fact, a large part of the dream had been the reading aloud of the prologue to the book of his diaries; he heard voices, do lunatics hear voices in their sleep as well? The daytime remnant of it, he calculated, had been the fierce and alcoholic discussion that he'd had with Junior about what was to come of his hope.

From the luminous numbers of the clock on the portable computer he saw that it was 5:00 in the morning, 5:00 a.m., as the North American clock on his iMac said, he managed to think, confused, before immediately falling back to sleep. An airy dream, with no images save for the words he deciphered, without seeing them, from memory: *A damaged but unbeaten volume*, was that how it would be?, or it wasn't like that, it never was. He'd woken up in his study, it took him a while to realize it, there in the room that he used whenever he stayed to sleep downtown, a divan bed, a nightstand where he'd left his portable computer turned on, he'd finished a piece of writing at 3:10 a.m., in other words he hadn't returned home, he'd caught a taxi and, drunk, had given the exact address on Charcas (ex-Charcas) without thinking, on Marcelo T., and straight away had fallen asleep in the car, and the driver had woken him, honking the horn like a madman, a crazed horn, a siren song, as a signal that his head wasn't running "entirely right," as he'd been told by the driver, whose name was Roco Armeno, he managed to read the driver's identity on the certificate, on a plastic card with a photo and everything, like a mugshot, that was hanging from the front seat, and so the dream had preserved that name and given it to the fishermen (Armeno and his cousin Roque), he managed to understand, happy about the discovery, in the half-dream that he'd fallen or relapsed back into.

He'd started a foolish argument with Junior in the Irish pub about the future of financial capitalism and Argentina, "the homeland," as Junior said to Renzi's indignation, and also about the future of Peronism and also about Emilio Renzi and his project, which is to say that they'd gone in descending order from totality to particularity, in rapid and confused steps. Junior, who was a real Peronist and also a journalist, cornered Emilio and criticized him for abandoning the battlefield since Renzi had, in the end, accepted the offer to take on a literature professorship at Princeton University beginning in September. For the best, while Emilio was spending the semester as a visiting professor in the spring of 1995, Junior had a romance with Clara, his ex, and had installed himself inside the apartment where Emilio had lived with her for several years and where part of his library was.

Carola and Monique had grown weary of the furious repetition of the subjects that Emilio and Junior discussed and their nighttime walks around the city, the two putting their arms around each other and sometimes stopping to mutually express their friendship and admiration, and then, in an abrupt change of channel, challenging each other to a fight on a street corner, under the streetlight, pulling off their jackets and glasses, squaring off, insulting each other and throwing punches in the air like two ridiculous dolls whom the girls observed, now tired of the masculine comedy of Argentine friendship, "which always ends badly," as Junior's friend noted in her strong Parisian accent. At some point while the two had gone back to holding onto each other and were walking unsteadily toward the next open bar, on Calle Córdoba, Carola and Monique called them ridiculous and repetitive and reactionary children and then the two of them left in the same taxi, which immediately roused the two competitors, who, standing on the corner, criticized them for being insensitive and dogmatic feminists from the old guard, with outmoded notions about masculinity, they complained in chorus before moving apart and looking into each others' faces, both a bit unsteady on their feet, before implying, both at once, that the girls were going to be together, not just in the taxi, but in bed as well. "It wouldn't be the first time," said Renzi, "that they've gone off to bed together, those girls."

Perhaps it was that alcoholic speculation that caused Emilio not to sleep at home that night ("so he wouldn't be in for a surprise"), and also because, just after three in the morning, an idea came to him for resolving a part of his diary that he was transcribing on his computer, and perhaps that was why he told the taxi driver the address of his studio.

And so Emilio and Junior went from bar to bar that night, discussing senseless matters seriously, for example, does literature have a future?, how much money would you need to go off and live on an island in the Tigre?, or what does it mean to go and teach in the United States?, or is Peronism a sentiment or is it a mafia?

Finally, at some uncertain hour of early morning, they parted ways, neither of the two able the next day to remember whether they'd said goodbye while fighting to the death or assuring one other, in turn, that each was the other's best friend, the closest one but also the most difficult and spiteful and unstable, at which point they'd go back to arguing heatedly about, for example, the afternoon when Junior went to Ezeiza to pick up Renzi, who was returning from the United States in a fury because his friend had thought of nothing better than to go and live with Clara and take over the apartment with his usual disorder and disregard, something that sparked another fight between the two friends that night.

He'd arrived at the office at three in the morning, not understanding how he'd ended up there; memories came like bolts of lightning and he saw images and places and felt dizzy from the alcohol. On the way in he'd picked up the copy of the newspaper *La Nación* from the floor, meaning that he hadn't come in to work that day, and sat in the armchair that he used to read and recapitulated what had happened. He ran into Junior on the way out of an exhibition and they went to get a few drinks at an Irish pub in Bajo; the day had started, in his memory, for him, at that moment, and he didn't remember what he'd done prior to being in the pub with Junior at midnight. He was seeking a way to forget, and the whiskey had erased an entire day of life from his head. He was a blank. He dozed off at intervals, holding in his hand, on his lap, the newspaper from June 16, 2000, open to the first page. "Ministry of Justice Project. Those who commit crimes for their addictions would not be imprisoned." Good news, I got off, he thought. "The Hebrew word for days can easily be confused with the one meaning years." He'd underlined that sentence in the book that lay at his side. Was he reading it yesterday? And why? His sense of time, disturbed. Now he recalls isolated fragments, lacking continuity. A street corner in the city, the white glow from the neon lamp, he and Junior crying in each other's arms, in the middle of the street; they want to hail a taxi and go together to the cemetery where Horacio was buried. But no car stops, even though they make exaggerated gestures trying to signal for them to pull over, and on the round clock at the corner of Córdoba and Florida it's 2:00 in the morning. Junior waves a white handkerchief but the taxis keep going, swiftly, and are lost in the darkness.

He doesn't remember how he ended up at the office instead of going to Malabia, they were already alone and drunk, Carola and Monique, Junior's French girlfriend, had left, tired of the drunks and their idiotic little speeches. Renzi saw Carola, who turned away with a gesture of annoyance and said something that he couldn't quite make out, although the expression "idiotic little speech" remained, floating around in his head, like a gleaming sign. Anyway, once he and Junior were left alone, they'd continued their tour around the bars until a short while ago, glad not to be facing down the watchful and caustic eyes of their beloveds.

He had to call Carola, but not this early, he felt terrible and parched, ashamed by what he couldn't remember, remorse is a destructive form of memory, always returning to the same place, the desolate events of life are repeated in the imagination, and it changes or modifies them; a simple change in tone is enough for the memory, persistent and terrible, to alter its course. The memory can't be forgotten but it can be changed, though that is a task that takes days and days. He remained in the armchair, sunk in a confused stupor, and after several failed attempts he managed to open his laptop, although he couldn't remember how he had managed to find it amid the disorder of his apartment, had he brought it with him?, or was the computer on the armchair where he sometimes sat to rethink his tiresome and insistent and inconvenient emails? *One confuses the past with remorse*, he wrote, with remorse, he thought, and pictured a machine grinding the flesh of memory; he kept turning over an event and couldn't escape from the jaws of remembrance, why didn't he keep Horacio there that day and help him get out of that false step? He'd always used his friends—he now described—as his *body doubles*; they did the dangerous actions for him, it wasn't just leaping into the void to escape from the fire that burns in life's mistakes, in imperfect murders—he liked that expression and typed it on his device—*imperfect murders*, that is, ones that hadn't been carried out, just as someone had to take the leap from the fifth-floor window toward the tiny circular net that the firefighters were holding in the street. I threw myself down for you, sang Emilio Renzi, exhausted and ghostly, in the armchair. *I threw myself down for you*. How many of his friends had thrown themselves into the void for him. In his imagination they did the things he'd never dared to do—or didn't want to admit he'd done. Letting oneself fall, for example. Junior had said as much to him, the two of them standing in the middle of the street, on the corner of Córdoba and Florida: "You live vicariously, *viejito*." Don't alliterate at me, don't screw me around with your five-cent interpretations. But he was right, he'd thought it many times, criticizing his friends over things he'd done himself. *Getting out of myself*, he wrote, *friendship as other possible lives*. That is, what was weighing on him, what he couldn't forget, was Horacio's death. He couldn't conceive of the idea that someone who had lived his life in another dimension, in a parallel, mirrored, symmetrical world, could have disappeared and left it behind in flesh and blood, could have retired from the stage. He couldn't bear the fact that he hadn't been able to reveal that truth to his brother on that afternoon at the cabin. Each of them unfurled an unlived aspect of his life. And he began to write his personal, private, secret list of the doubles or phantoms that had been with him and allowed him to keep going forward as if he hadn't sacrificed dozens upon dozens of moments and emotions that, in his imagination, others experienced for him. He made notes: *Cacho, or The Life of Adventure*; *Ramón T. and Political Violence*; *Horacio, A Quiet and Predictable Life*. They lived through the lost experiences of his life for him. But why lost? *So that they could be written*. It was too high a price. Was that their price? His own pound of flesh. And the women he'd loved? They were part of his reserve, his reservoir of emotions. Through them he had experienced—or seen, glimpsed, perceived, like a voyeur—the arc, the register of possible emotions. Each of his divine women sustained an emotion: Inés, jealousies; Julia, tragedies of the soul; Vicky, emotional fantasy. Amanda had been sexual passion, the girl who, in order to please him—he now realized—did striptease and served drinks in a *boîte*. And the redheads? They were all as one to him. In the engrossed lucidity of insomnia and alcohol—and the lines of cocaine that Monique had "shaved off," as Junior said—he saw the figures in his life as a succession of living pictures, presenting themselves before him with the unbearable clarity of wicked dreams, and he felt despondent and yet happy at the same time, as sometimes happened to him when he surmounted an invisible electric barrier. Dizzy, unwell, almost alive, I write words once wept in the city where I've loved, he recited in an elegiac tone, and felt better. He would go down, *would leave, at that uncertain hour when those who've died return, led by their watchdogs, their guides, faithful messengers, from the shadows*. He read what he had written and concluded the page; he couldn't forget, couldn't erase the still unthought thoughts from his mind, nor could he kill an old pawnbroker, better to laugh life off. His own miserable and comic life, or—to put it that way—life in general, this existence, diaphanous and abstract, meaningless, which takes the form of a diabolical joke? He didn't quite know what the matter was, but he was mortally gloomy, although at the same time he could see himself as a poor specimen, stretched out in an armchair, desperate, *but still writing*. That figure amused him; it was comical. He needed to go outside, feel the crisp early morning air and return to the city like a lone wolf. A dreadful anxiety, said Remo Erdosain, and so it was, it was already going to happen, what could he do? His life hadn't appeared before him like a movie, as described by survivors who, before death, witnessed private shows in which were presented the principal events from their lives, condemned and condensed. He saw nothing of that on his mental screen, but he did, in the end, have his annotations, his little notebooks, his miserable little speeches, and he could do nothing to alleviate the pain in his left side (in his chest), for, he remembered, it had been on his left side only a bit farther down, a few degrees further south, where Christ had received the stab of the lance. Such details made him delirious; for example, the detail with no function, the scene with the Roman soldiers who cast lots, at the foot of the Cross, for the garment shrouding the crucified man. I, the crucified, Nietzsche had written, and he'd also written, I am all the names in history, which, more or less, was what Emilio had said: I am Horacio, I am Cacho Carpatos, I am all the names of my friends and the women I have loved.

He was raving a bit by this stage, Emilio, as he went down in the elevator, watching his figure in the imaginary mirror: he'd wrapped himself in a black coat, his body dressed in light blue pajamas, when had he put them on?, had there been a woman who helped him remove his clothes when he reached his office in the early morning?, had he picked up a working girl and taken her to bed? A couple times in his life he'd woken up with a woman in bed, not knowing who she was and not remembering how that'd come to that situation. Junior had insisted that they go to a brothel, that wasn't the name, they just had to go to the bar on Córdoba and Reconquista and leave with two women, and walk arm in arm, the four of them, to the hourly motel in the cul-de-sac of Tres Sargentos. They'd done something like that many times, Junior and he, in the past.

But he was alone when he awoke in the morning, though he didn't understand how he'd managed to undress and put on his pajamas unassisted. Had he come in with a woman? The horrible feeling continued in that way. Oh, who could forget, erase the sins of the world from his soul. He laughed to see himself in the mirror, talking to himself and dressed like a lunatic escaped from the psychiatric ward dressed in the regulation pajamas but covered in an overcoat and barefoot.

Because he was barefoot, Renzi, that early morning as he came out of the building, half naked, disheveled, without glasses, wrapped up in a dark overcoat. Why had he left? He didn't know, didn't remember, and that made him feel like crying. But he didn't cry, he wasn't going to cry, he hadn't cried in front his brother Horacio's dead body. *Too late for tears*, he said aloud, and then, with the melody of "Jugo de tomate frío," he intoned *too late for tears*, singing as he turned down Ayacucho toward Santa Fe, looking for an open kiosk where he could buy a bottle of mineral water to quench his thirst. *We have thirst and animal patience*, he recited, with thirst and animal patience, take care of us. He'd crossed Calle Ayacucho and headed toward Santa Fe, looking for a corner market to buy water and quench his thirst. But what sort of thirst was it?, he wondered as he reached the gate of the church of the Misericordia, which was right in the middle of the pathway of his life, halfway between Marcelo T. and Santa Fe, on Ayacucho. Then he saw that the door of that temple was open and let himself be drawn on by a blind and atavistic impulse and entered the house of God, and immediately as he entered, a feeling of peace and calm overwhelmed him. He was alone inside the great nave, facing the altar crowned by a suffering

Christ, on the Cross, wearing a crown of thorns. In the stillness of the church, sitting on the wooden pew, he began to cry without realizing it. Between tears he saw a woman in a long leather coat get up from the confessional, and, as she passed, she made a gesture toward him, a slight inclination of her veiled head, to say that it was his turn. "It's my turn," Renzi said to himself, and he moved toward the elegant and discreet box of dark wood, within which a priest could be glimpsed, and he kneeled at the prayer desk and raised his head toward the round, latticed window. "I'm barefoot, Father," he said, in a falsely serious voice. "I was educated at a Catholic school in Temperley, but I lost my faith, and now I'm very disoriented." From the other side, something like a groan came to him, or perhaps it was a question or simply a sigh. Emilio waited a moment and then said: "I have sinned, Father, I think, or maybe I've been won over by the spirit of Satan, as if I made a deal with the devil to be able to write." A voice now reached him, weary and calm, and asked: "How long has it been since your last confession, my son?" At first Renzi didn't quite understand the question and answered without thinking: "I just spent the night confessing my misfortune to a friend . . . " It didn't seem appropriate to him to give Junior's name, he was on the point of doing so; then, as if to cover up the void of his friend's name, he began talking about his responsibility for his cousin Horacio's death. "I feel like a criminal, I have a death on my conscience, sometimes I talk to him, I don't know if that's a sin, but the conversation with the dead relieves me, because he answers me and talks to me with words only I can hear and calms me, saying I have nothing to worry about, although I don't know if that's exactly what he's telling me because he speaks in a very strange language, without verbs, Father, is that a sin?, talking to the dead can be viewed in different ways. Why is that death weighing on me?, my sorrow is permanent, and now I'm seeking respite in the peace of the temple." He went on in that style, growing a bit delirious and lamenting his inability to avoid remorse. The father, whom he never saw, followed his train of thought until a certain point when, as if suspecting that this guy was pulling his leg, as it occurred to Renzi while the priest was bringing the confession to an end, he told him to say three Hail Marys and three Our Fathers. "*Ego te absolvo*," he added, and closed the little window with a dull thud. Emilio stood and, as he passed before the altar, made the sign of the cross, crossing himself as he'd done so many times in childhood. Then he left the church, without making the prayer of the penitent, and walked along Ayacucho to his office. He was serene and at ease and felt pure and safe, navigating the broken flagstones of the sidewalk, walking barefoot toward his hideaway.

III

DAYS WITHOUT DATES

Private Eye

Monday

I spend the night at Princeton Hospital. As I sit in the emergency room awaiting my diagnosis, I see a man enter who is barely able to move. He is a recovering alcoholic who's had a relapse; he spent two days wandering from bars to bar in Trenton. They have to detox him before they can return him to the rehab clinic. His son, a shy young man wearing a baseball cap on his head, arrives a while later and goes to the desk to fill out some forms. The man doesn't recognize him at first but finally stands up, lays his hand on his shoulder, and speaks to him in a soft voice from very close by. The boy listens to him as though he is offended. In the diffusion of languages that's typical of these places, a Puerto Rican nurse explains to a black orderly that the man has lost his glasses and cannot see. "The old man has lost his *espejuelos*," he says, "and he can't see anything." The wayward Spanish word shines like a light in the dark.

Wednesday

He said he'd been in prison for fraud, and he told me that his father was a picker at the track and had bad luck at the races. He reappeared two days later and introduced himself again as if he'd never seen me before. He suffers from some uncertain defect that alters his sense of reality. He's muddled up in a continuous motion that forces him to think in order to hold confusion at bay. Thinking isn't the same as remembering; you can think even if you've lost your memory. (I've known it in myself for years: I only recall what is written in the diary.) All the same, he hasn't forgotten language. He can find anything that he needs to know on the Web. Knowledge is no longer a part his life. A new kind of novel, then, would be possible. "We need a language to express our ignorance," Gombrowicz said. That could be the epigraph.

Sunday

I've finally met a private detective. Ralph Anderson, Ace Agency. Kathy hired him to track down her mother, who abandoned her when she was six years old. Ralph tracked her down in Atlanta, Georgia. The woman had changed her name and was living downtown in the city, working at a fashion magazine. Kathy couldn't bring herself to go and see her mother, but she did become friends with the detective. Many of his clients seek out their lost relatives and then decide not to meet them.

Ralph lives in an apartment near Washington Square. Downstairs, in the building's entryway, a control panel on the door, a metal detector, cameras. Parker is waiting for us when we step out of the elevator. He must be thirty years old, with dark glasses and a face like a fox. He lives in an environment of high ceilings, an almost empty space with picture windows looking out over the city. On a vast desk he has four computers placed in a semicircle, always running, with open files and several active websites. "There's no need to set foot in the streets anymore," he says. "Whatever you're looking for is on there." He smokes one joint after another, drinks ginger ale, lives alone. He is investigating the deaths of three black soldiers from an infantry battalion posted in Iraq, in which a majority of the officers and non-commissioned officers were from Texas. A group of the family members of African American soldiers has hired him to investigate. He is certain that they were murdered. If he succeeds in proving it, they will take it to court. He shows us the photos of the young soldiers, the desert in the background. Then we go out for dinner at a Chinese restaurant.

Thursday

Strangely, no one seems to have noticed that T. W. Adorno wasn't the first to establish a relationship between the future of literature and the Nazi death camps. In 1948, Brecht, in his "Conversations with Young Intellectuals," had already posed the problem. "The events in Auschwitz, in the Warsaw ghetto, in Buchenwald would doubtless not bear any literary description. Literature was not prepared for such events, nor has it developed any means of describing them." Adorno later referred to the same issue in his 1955 essay "Cultural Criticism and Society," where he writes, in his usual cautionary tone: "Cultural criticism finds itself faced with the final stage of the dialectic of culture and barbarism. To write poetry after Auschwitz is barbaric. And this corrodes even the knowledge of why it has become impossible to write poetry today." Brecht, of course, doesn't accept that condemnation of poetry; he is only referring to the technical difficulties posed by the relationship between politics and literature. Some years earlier, in his "Work Journals," on September 16, 1940, he'd written: "It would be unbelievably difficult to express my state of mind as I follow the battle of Britain on the wireless and in the awful Finnish-Swedish papers and then write *Puntila*. This intellectual phenomenon explains both that such wars can exist and that literary works can still be produced. *Puntila* means hardly anything to me, the war everything; about *Puntila* I can write virtually anything, about the war, nothing. And I don't just mean 'may' but truly 'can.' It is interesting how remote literature as a practical activity is from the centers where decisive events take place." Adorno's thesis met with rapid diffusion among cultural critics, always ready to accept the metaphysics of silence and the limits of language. Brecht, by contrast, astute and free from illusions, never wondered whether what he was doing was permissible; he was only interested in knowing whether it was possible.

Monday

Faced with the proliferation of books found—in computer archives—among the papers of famous dead authors (Bolaño, Cabrera Infante,

Nabokov, etc.), a group of writers has decided to earn their living by writing posthumous novels. After several meetings, they decided to write Samuel Beckett's posthumous novel, *Moran*, a continuation of the trilogy. Along with the manuscript itself, they must invent a way for the novel to have been discovered. Beckett brought the novel to his psychoanalyst, Bion, who advised him not to publish it. Relieved, Beckett walked down the stairs precipitously and forgot the manuscript. Years later, a young researcher from the University of California at Irvine discovered the novel in Bion's unindexed archive. They negotiate directly with the heirs and, after agreeing on the advance, submit the book, etc.

Saturday

Every day I see the old man as he leaves his house and walks slowly through the snow to the edge of the lake. The haze of his breath is like a fog in the transparent air. We've spoken many times when passing each other on the entry road; he taught physics here at Princeton in the fifties but is now retired, lives alone, his wife died last year, he has no children, his name is Karl Unger, and he's a German in exile. As the wild ducks arrive, the first thing you hear is a faint noise, as if someone were shaking out a damp cloth in the sky. Almost at once you begin to hear their honking and see them as they come, flying in a straight line and then forming a V above the far end of the woods. They make two loops above the lake before launching themselves toward the frozen water, and when they dive, they skid along with their wings spread open and necks against the ice. They walk back awkwardly, sliding, and some stand still, their legs like dead bones in the frost. They live in the pure present and are surprised every morning when the crash into the ice. They've lost their sense of direction. They seek the temperate waters of the lake when they should be starting their migration toward warmer lands. When I see the old professor leave his garden, cross through the snow, and reach the lake to feed the wild ducks dying of cold, I know it is the beginning of another day that will be the same as the last.

2

The Blind Dog

Monday
It is pointless to go on, my mother said. No resignation. *It is pointless.*
As if she could choose the moment. My grandparents' house bore her
name, and her name was the first thing I ever learned to read. "Ida, do
you see?" she would say, pointing out the letters over the doorway. She
was wearing a blue dress. Her image in my memory is clearer than the
light of this lamp. She was always happy. At the end, slight delirium,
drifting off. She asked, what did you say? and smiled, just before she
died. And I wasn't there. Oh mother . . .

Wednesday
I need to call my mother, I think suddenly. Stray thoughts, nightmares. (I
dream that I'm a blind dog. Little movements in fright, snout in the air.)

Sunday
Gato Barbieri played at the Blue Note last night. Lots of people, all very
intimate. I hadn't heard him since '77, when I saw him at a concert in
San Diego to present *Ruby Ruby*. I'd like to make a documentary on jazz
in Buenos Aires with some friends. Gato at the origin of free jazz; in the
mid-sixties he recorded *Symphony for Improvisers*, pure improvisation
with almost no standard tunes. Steve Lacy was caught stranded and
broke in Buenos Aires, in 1965 or 1966, and he played at Jamaica, where
Salgán and De Lío used to play as well. I was going to hear him with

Néstor Sánchez, who at that time wanted to bring improvisation into prose: *Siberia Blues*. Strangely, in literature, jazz was always connected to an oral style (Kerouac, Boris Vian, Cortázar, etc.).

Tuesday
Carola has a facility for making friendships, the way someone might say "I make a work." Each of her friends, defined by a specific quality, has a slight distinguishing touch. The Hungarian who leads courses for civil servants in the United Nations to quit smoking; the young Brazilian who dedicates herself to discovering unexpected art galleries in the Bowery for collectors, who pay her for tours; the middle-aged woman, a former professional tennis player, who only sleeps with black men.

Friendship among women can take the form of a closed society where there are no secrets. Of course there aren't any secrets, Carola tells me, neither secrets nor private life. You have to live in third person. She looks out through the window. The squirrels thrive around here because there aren't any stray dogs, she says. They should import street dogs, etc.

Friday
A long conversation at the bar in Lahiere's with James Irby, a legendary translator of Borges into English and an extraordinary poetry professor at Princeton. We discuss a few poems by Lezama Lima, among them "Ode to Julián del Casal," on which Jim has written a long essay that he still considers incomplete. You should write a book about that poem, I tell him. Are there any books devoted to a single poem? We recall Butor's book on one of Baudelaire's dreams. The verses are like the waking remnants of a dream, a fabric of broken images, of lost memories and words. Calasso has now published a book on the same one of Baudelaire's dreams, Jim tells me, but without citing Butor.

The key to Jim's work is that he analyzes poems written in foreign languages. The reading is always uncertain, and the words seem like stones in a wall: meaning depends upon the weight, the placement.

We call this mode of reading *concrete criticism*. In the same direction, it makes me notice that the end of *Target in the Night* alludes to the anaphora in Rubén Darío's poem "Metempsychosis," which I've read many times over the course of time, although I wasn't thinking about it while writing the novel. Jim recites it with an air of irony, marking out the smooth scansion of the hendecasyllables and the stanza break:

> *I was a soldier who slept in the bed*
> *of Cleopatra the Queen. Her whiteness,*
> *her starlike, omnipotent gaze.*
> > *That was all.*

> *And her spine creaked in my arms;*
> *and I, a freedman, made her forget Antony.*
> *(Oh her bed, her gaze, her whiteness!)*
> > *That was all.*

And after a pause, now placing emphasis on the metallic rhythm of the verse, he speaks the final stanza: *I was taken to Egypt, with a chain / around my neck. One day I was eaten / by the dogs. My name, Rufus Gallus. / That was all.* I forgot a couple of the stanzas, he says, as we're heading out to the street. Sometimes one forgets in order to improve the poems, I say. That wasn't the case here, Jim smiles. Outside it is already night. You know they're shutting down this bar, no? he says.

As I was making a note about my conversation a little while ago with Irby, I remembered that metempsychosis—the word Molly doesn't understand at the beginning of the novel—lies at the origin of Joyce's *Ulysses*. Bloom is the reincarnation of the Greek hero. That conception defines the intrigue.

Auden is correct in noting that artists change their vision of the world in order to renew their poetics. That was how he explained his adherence to Marxism, and also Yeats's later passion for spiritualism or Eliot's conversion to Catholicism or Tolstoy's populism. The writer doesn't invent the ideology but finds it already formed and uses it as a working material. Before critiquing a writer's thoughts, you have to analyze their technical function. Hamlet's doubts serve to slow down the action.

Friday
David Simon, creator of the series *The Wire*, is a great social storyteller. He incorporates current events into the police intrigue (Bush's adjustment economy, the manipulation of political campaigns, the legalization of drugs). In the pilot episode of his new television series, *Treme*, which I saw the other night, the setting is New Orleans after Katrina: disasters are never natural, that is Simon's position.

Social narrative shifted from the novel into film and after film into the series, and now it's moving from the series to Facebook and Twitter and online networks. What grows old and loses currency ends up becoming loose and free: when the audience of the nineteenth-century novel moved toward film, the works of Joyce, Musil, and Proust became possible. When film is supplanted as a massive medium by television, the cineastes from *Cahiers du Cinéma* rescue the old artisans of Hollywood as great artists; now that television is starting to be replaced massively by the Web, series are being valued as an art form. Soon, with the advancing of new technologies, blogs and ancient emails and text messages will be exhibited in museums. What logic is this? Only what expires and falls "behind" becomes artistic.

Tuesday
On the corner of Witherspoon and Paul Robeson a man dressed in jeans and a plaid flannel jacket holds up a poster in support of the Republican candidate for the congressional elections. Onto it he attached a little American flag, a signal that he belongs to the nationalist right. He takes advantage of the slow traffic light to spread propaganda. I'd never seen a proselytizing act done by a lone man before.

Here, everything is individualized. Political attacks work in that way as well. Lee Harvey Oswald; Martin Luther King, Jr.'s killer; the man who shot at a Democratic congresswoman in Arizona. They are only the acts of a disturbed, *singular* individual. This extreme personalization is "the purely aesthetic appearance" of the social world, as Marx said in talking about Robinson Crusoe. The social struggles aren't seen, but their absence is expressed allegorically: a postal worker, in Ohio, fired from his job, goes up into a tower and kills the people passing on the street.

Another example is the ruling by the United States Supreme Court, which approved the law (Citizens United case) that compels us to consider powerful economic corporations as individual citizens. Utopia for North American capitalism is to have power groups and social forces considered as isolated persons. All of the individuals would be equal, each a Robinson reading the Bible on his desert island.

3

Tolstoy's Advice

Monday

I'd stopped drinking alcohol and had slight disruptions that produced strange effects in me. I couldn't sleep, and on nights of insomnia I'd go out to walk the streets. The town would appear deserted, and I'd advance into the dark neighborhoods like a specter. I'd see the houses in the clarity of night, the identical gardens; I'd hear the rustling of the wind among the trees.

Tuesday

I emerge from such states half-blinded, as though I've been staring too long into the light of a lamp. I wake up feeling unusually lucid, vividly recollecting certain isolated details—a broken chain on the sidewalk, a dead bird, a sentence from a book. It's the opposite of amnesia: the images are fixed with the clarity of a photograph.

Only my doctor in Buenos Aires knows what is happening, and, in fact, back in December he forbade me from traveling. Impossible, I'm going to teach classes. If the symptoms followed me, I'd have to get myself looked at. He's a great doctor and a good-natured man, always serene. According to him, I was suffering from a rare ailment called "arborescent crystallization." Accumulated fatigue and a slight neurological disturbance were causing me to experience little hallucinations.

Thursday

There's a beggar who spends his nights in the parking lot at Blue Point restaurant, at the end of Nassau Street. He has a sign on his chest that reads "I'm from Orion" and wears a white rain slicker buttoned up to the neck. From a distance he looks like a doctor or a scientist in his lab. Yesterday, as I was returning from one of my nocturnal walks, I paused to talk with him. He's written that he comes from Orion in case anyone else from Orion appears. He needs company, but not just any company. "Only people from Orion, monsieur," he tells me. He thinks I'm French, and I haven't denied it because I don't want to alter the course of our conversation. After a while he goes silent and then leans back under the overhang to sleep. He has a shopping cart where he carries all of his belongings.

Friday

Whenever I feel constricted, I go to New York and spend a couple of days amid the multitudes of the city, not calling anyone, not showing myself, visiting anonymous places and avoiding bars. I stay at The Leo House, a Catholic guesthouse run by nuns. It was created as lodgings for family members visiting the sick at a nearby hospital but is now a little hotel open to the public (although priests and seminarians are given priority).

In Chelsea, I found a video store, Film Noir, which specializes in detective movies. The owner is a fairly nice guy; they call him Dutch because his parents were from Holland. He has a few hard-to-find treasures, Edgar Ulmer's *Detour*, for example, an extraordinary movie, filmed in a week with almost no budget; long close-up shots of a car trip, conversations off-screen, lights in the night. It tells the story of a desperate man who goes hitchhiking and gets lost in the detours of the road. It seems like a psychotic version of Kerouac's *On the Road*. Everything he encounters by chance along the way is destructive and fatal.

I'm actually looking for *Section des disparus* by the French director Pierre Chenal, based on a novel by David Goodis and filmed in Buenos Aires in the forties. A mythical film that no one has seen. The Dutchman assured me that he can locate it, but I have to give him time; he thinks there's a copy in one of the bootleg hangars in Lima, Polvos Azules: duplicates of all the movies ever filmed in the world can be found there.

Monday

Yesterday it was close to midnight by the time I made it back home. I found some overdue mail in the box, but nothing important, unpaid bills, advertisements. I watched TV for a while; the Lakers were beating the Celtics, Obama was smiling with his artificial air, in a Toyota ad, a car was sinking in the ocean, on one channel they were showing Curtis Bernhardt's *Possessed*, another of my favorite films. Joan Crawford appears in the middle of the night in a Los Angeles neighborhood and wanders along its strangely lit streets. I think I dozed off, because the telephone woke me; someone who knew my name and called me Professor too insistently was offering to sell me cocaine.

When the phone rang, I thought it was a friend calling me from Buenos Aires and turned down the volume of the TV. When the dealer made himself known, I thought the whole thing was so extraordinary that it must have been real. I refused and cut off the line. It might have been a prank caller, an idiot, or a DEA agent monitoring the private lives of Ivy League academics. How did he know my last name?

On the screen, the silent figures of Geraldine Brooks and Van Heflin were embracing under the pale light. On the other side of the window I saw my neighbor's house, lit up, and in the living room downstairs a woman in jogging clothes who was doing Tai Chi exercises, slow and harmonious, as though floating in the air.

Wednesday

Recently there have appeared what we might call defensive utopias. How can we escape surveillance? An impossible flight strategy, for there is nowhere to go. A few months ago, we put together an anthology in

Buenos Aires and asked twenty writers from different generations to write a story set in the future. The texts, more than apocalyptic, were defensive fictions defined by loneliness and escape. Utopias that tend toward invisibility, attempting to create a subject outside of control.

Saturday

The women who go out to smoke in the doorways of the buildings in New York have a furtive appearance, something unsettling. You see very few men smoking in the street, fewer and fewer. Women come out of their businesses and light cigarettes in the freezing air, resolute because of the urgency and seductive flair of the addiction. A weak vice, if you can call it that. Junkies still hide it. I can feel that I've quit smoking, when I see them. After a while, as though continuing from what she'd said before, Carola says: In this era, for the first time in history, literature has more writers than readers.

Thursday

After so many years of writing in these notebooks, I've started to ask myself which verb tense should be used to situate the events. A diary registers incidents as they are taking place; it doesn't remember them or organize them narratively. It tends toward private language, toward idiolect. As a result, in reading a diary one encounters blocks of existence, always in the present, and only in reading is it possible to reconstruct the history that invisibly unfolds over the course of the years. Yet diaries aspire to story, and in that sense they're written in order to be read (even if no one reads them).

Tuesday

I'm working on the prologue for an edition of Tolstoy's last stories. He wrote them in secret, hidden even from himself, and they are, of course, excellent, as good as Chekhov's short stories.

After the conversion that had led him to abandon literature, Tolstoy decides to dedicate his life to the peasants, to become another person, to be purer and simpler. He renounces his property, wanting to live on manual labor. He decides to learn how to cobble shoes, for a pair of well-made boots is, he says, more useful than *Anna Karenina*. The town shoemaker—afraid of the count's dangerous eccentricities—teaches him his old profession.

Tolstoy wrote in his diary: *Writing is not difficult, what is difficult is not writing*. That line could be the motto of contemporary literature.

4

The Piano

Monday

Following the earthquake and tsunami in Japan, Carola is only reading Kawabata, the same way a rabbi would read the Torah in a time of crisis. In her case, it isn't a way of asking for sympathy but a way of being personally affected. I'm affected, she says, and reflects on the meaning of the expression. She thinks the word defines the affections—and the affects—of a true experience. Of course, it's also used to dismiss writers whom she finds to be *affected*. For example, that insufferable Murakami!, she says. Dreadful! She left for New York on Friday, very troubled about the crisis of the nuclear plants, and I've been alone at home since then.

I wake up early and go out for breakfast in town. The day is clear and cold, one of those luminous winter mornings of the northern hemisphere. I walk around downtown, buy papers at the newsstand in Palmer Square, and finally go to Small World Café.

I order a double espresso, a croissant, and orange juice. At the tables nearby, girls and boys are drinking mineral water or green tea, intent on their laptops, their iPods, their BlackBerrys, wearing headphones, isolated in their space capsules but connected to exterior reality by cell phone. In the *New York Times*, for the last two days, news about the reactors in Fukushima has replaced coverage of the military intervention in

Libya and the conflicts in the Middle East. At the same time, the military operation and the nuclear risk have lately replaced the local news.

As always, actions of control and aggression are made in defense of those being controlled and treated with aggression. If you call some public agency on the phone, a mechanical voice appears announcing: "For your security, this conversation is being recorded." In this case, the CIA has decided to bombard the civilian population "in order to protect the civilian population."

As I'm reading the sports section, my cell phone rings. It's Carola; she's at Park Avenue and 50th Street. She always needs to locate herself before speaking. I'm right in front of the record store where we were the other day, she says. She and her friends have formed a kind of agitprop brigade and are participating in protest circles and marches in front of the Japanese embassy. They are going to contaminate the oceans, she says, emphasizing the plural. Radiation is coming by sea. Whatever you do, don't eat fish! She wants us to go and live in Berlin because the Greens have power in Germany and it's possible to fight against the destruction of nature.

Thursday

For years I've been turning over the idea of making a history of painting based on the titles of paintings. A series of very long duration. Sometimes they're a narrative; sometimes they seem like a lost line from a poem: Fragonard's *Coresus Sacrificing Himself to Save Callirhoe* and Matisse's *Luxe, Calme et Volupté*. Some show the uncertainty of representation: Rothko's *Light, Earth and Blue*, which can be viewed as *Light, Earth and Sky* or as *Bright, Brown and Blue*. Others are very precise: Vermeer's *View of Delft*, Hokusai's *Thirty-six Views of Mount Fuji*.

The names improve as paintings cease to be figurative. Monet's *Impression, Sunrise* (1872) is a foundational title (for impressionism). And we could say the same of Malevich's extraordinary *Suprematist*

Composition: White on White. Or the Duchampian title of Xul Solar's *To Judge*. Being descriptive, they tend to seem enigmatic because the images they represent aren't easy to name. As a result, many painters have ended up working with description degree zero, like Pollock with his *Number 32* (1950).

The key, of course, is that the title depends on the painting; in a sense it describes it, and in any case it names it. The tension between *mostrar* (showing) and *decir* (telling), upon which Henry James founded his theory of the novel, determines the tension between the words and the image.

They define a particular function of language: what is named is there. (In literature, what is named is no longer there.) Something is fixed in language; it would be better to say: language is fixed in an image. It depends upon it even as it denies it, as in Magritte's famous *Treachery of Images*. To describe what the work deals with isn't to say what it means, and what it means doesn't depend on the title.

Photography, by contrast, seems to need language in order to signify. Everything is so visible that what is needed is what Jean-Marie Schaeffer calls *lateral knowledge* in his book on photography, that is, certain information that does not arise from the image itself. Like dreams, the photo needs language to find its meaning. We could say that it needs a title. It would be better to say (in a Freudian way): the title of the photo is its interpretation.

We live in a culture in which interpretation defines images. Hyper-explanation is the mark of culture today, circulating through the media, on blogs, on Facebook, in tweets: everything must be clarified. Series in the United States like *Lost* or *The Corner* are interpreted and discussed almost at the very moment when the episodes are broadcast, and the viewers have a complete understanding of what they're about to see.

The same thing has happened in football, the great narrative spectacle of the masses; the commentary on the games is accompanied by a very sophisticated analysis, explaining the strategies and the meaning of the game. It is narrated and interpreted at the same time.

Tuesday
I give a lecture at the University of Pennsylvania on the writer as critic. Then I have dinner with Roger Chartier, Antonio Feros, Luis Moreno-Caballud, and other friends at the White Dog restaurant. Madame Blavatsky, the founder of the Theosophical Society, once lived in this house; they say that the piano in the main hall sometimes plays on its own in the night. A very entertaining conversation about superstitions and American academic culture. I spend the night in Philadelphia and in the morning, before returning to Princeton, I manage to see the Roberto Capucci exhibition at the museum. An extraordinary show. Illuminated with white light in the penumbra of a circular gallery, the dresses and fabric sculptures look like mutant women from a parallel world. These bodiless feminine figures should be added to the history of the representation of women, which John Berger reconstructed admirably in the TV series *Ways of Seeing*. Capucci designed the dresses for Silvana Mangano in Pasolini's film *Teorema*.

Literary criticism is affected the most by the current situation of litera-ture. It has vanished from the map. In its finest moments—with Yury Tynyanov, Franco Fortini, or Edmund Wilson—it was a reference in the public discussion about the construction of meaning in a community. Nothing of that tradition remains. Today, the best—and most influ-ential—readers are historians, like Carlo Ginzburg, Robert Darnton, François Hartog, or Roger Chartier. The reading of texts passed on to become an issue of the past or of the study of the past.

Wednesday
Carola is waiting for me at Princeton Junction and, on the way home, we stop at The Home Depot. The hardware store is enormous, with

tools, machinery, and equipment covering the space like the pieces in an endless disassembled workshop. There are no customers or employees; the place is empty. It's the crisis, she says. We walk along the numbered aisles between large red objects and mechanical drills. I have the sensation of still being in the museum in Philadelphia. A masculine museum, Carola says with irony. It's a fantasy of the toolsheds from old houses, she says, but expanded to the point of delirium. The cash registers are locked and covered. At the end, a girl is working at the only functioning counter. No one is in line because no one is there. I buy a snow shovel, a pair of canvas gloves, and some pliers (to open and close the windows). A snowstorm is forecast, maybe the last one of the winter.

5

The Bear

Tuesday
A bear has been seen in the woods, on the edge of a gully, not far from here. It was a blot among the trees, a haze. It wended its way along and turned up in a vacant lot on the side of Mountain Avenue. Rearing up on two legs, irritated by the noise of cars, with a murderous gleam in its eyes, it circled around and finally moved off toward the undergrowth.

It reminded me of a bear from a traveling circus that had set up camp on an empty piece of land behind my house in Adrogué when I was a boy. I watched it for hours from the privet hedge. Tied on a chain, it too moved around in circles and could sometimes be heard growling in the night.

The circus ended its program with theatrical performances, shows adapted from costumbrist plays and popular radio dramas. The actors had asked my mother if they could borrow some furniture for their set. When I went to the performance, the pale wooden chairs from the garden of our house that appeared onstage would not allow me to believe in what I was seeing. This bear prowling around the vicinity of the campus has the opposite effect on me.

Wednesday
I'm reading Saul Bellow's *Letters*. Written between 1932 and 2005, the letters can be seen as the history of a writer who constructs—or invents—his own tradition.

Bellow is the first translator of Isaac Bashevis Singer into English (the story "Gimpel the Fool," in his translation, is published in *Partisan Review* in 1952), but he moves away from the realist portrayal of victims (the shlimazl) and gray defeated men from the Jewish tradition à la Bernard Malamud.

"Somewhere in my Jewish and immigrant blood there were conspicuous traces of doubt as to whether I had the right to practice the writer's trade," Bellow says. The moment of rupture was *The Adventures of Augie March* (1953), in which he finds his voice and discovers that he has no reason to force himself to write "following the rules of our dear WASP establishment, like an Englishman or a contributor to the *New Yorker*?"

The hero in his great novels is an intellectual: what's important isn't the way in which reality constructs the characters' consciousness, but rather the way in which the characters' consciousness defines—and gives form—to reality. *Herzog* is the highest point in that line.

Among us, the one to accomplish that operation of rupture is Roberto Arlt: he wrote against the central tradition and thus opens up a new way of creating literature. His daughter, Mirta Arlt, defined him clearly: "My father was friends with Güiraldes, who was a very posh fellow, but my father never aspired to resemble posh people, whom he despised deep down. Among other things it was because, to these posh people, a son of immigrants seemed suited not to be a writer but rather a prison guard."

Thursday
I started going to the gym. Boxing categories aren't defined by age but by weight. I used to be a lightweight (66 kg), but now I'm a middleweight (72 kg).

The guys who train here are fourteen- or fifteen-year-old boys preparing for the Golden Gloves. Some, however, come to strengthen their arms for fastball pitches in baseball. They practice jabs and cross punches against the sandbags and exercise the thrust of their shoulders and the rotation of their bodies so they can throw a ball at a hundred miles per hour without tearing a muscle. Their exercise routines follow the rhythms of a match: three minutes of rigorous training and one of rest.

The coach is an old Cuban exile who claims to have been a featherweight champion in some socialist boxing championships far away in Moscow. A very laid-back, mixed-race man, he's a fan of Kid Gavilán and Sugar Ray Leonard. In a boxing match, he told me, style depends on eyesight and speed, in other words something he gives the "scientific" term of instant vision.

Everyone suspects that I came here to write an article about gyms, and they tell me their stories. Several say they're acquaintances of the author Joyce Carol Oates, who's written a fine book about boxing, and they all affectionately call her Olive because of her resemblance to Popeye's girlfriend.

Friday
I'm rereading Stendhal's *Journal.* I recall my visit to the library in Grenoble with Michel Lafon. In the basement level I was given access to the original copy of the diary. The woman in charge of the manuscripts was a Stendhalian figure, a severe and attractive woman, with an icy eroticism, who brought out the notebook on a red velvet pillow. I had to wear a pair of white latex gloves to touch the pages, all the while sensing the French woman's breath over my shoulder.

Stendhal includes drawings and sketches alongside the scenes he narrates in his diary. He describes a dinner with friends and then makes a tiny illustration of the room and the arrangement of the guests sitting around the table. He had a spatial, cartographic imagination. You need only recall the panoramic view of the town of Verrières at the beginning of *The Red and the Black.*

He writes in his diary, on August 23, 1806: "That's what makes me hope that I'll have some talent. I observe better, I see more details, I see more accurately, even without centering my attention on a thing . . . " Stendhal's diary, another exercise in "instant vision."

Saturday
The first translation of *Don Quixote* into Chinese was the work of the writer Lin Shu and his assistant Chen Jialin. As Lin Shu didn't speak any foreign languages, his assistant visited him every afternoon to relate episodes from Cervantes's novel. Lin Shu translated it based on that account. Published in 1922, with the title *The Life of the Bewitched Knight*, the work was received as a great event in the history of literary translation in China. It would be interesting to translate that Chinese version of *Quixote* into Spanish. For my part, I'd like to write a story based on the conversations between Lin Shu and his assistant Chen Jialin as they are working on their imaginary transcription of *Don Quixote*.

Sunday
The suicide of Antonio Calvo, the Spanish language lecturer at Princeton University, has caused a commotion in the academic community. Three days before his tragic death, Calvo had been dismissed by the administration, which not only decided that his classes be immediately suspended without providing any explanation, but even sent a security guard to block him from accessing his office, as if he were a dangerous trespasser.

To reach their decision, the authorities used the observations and opinions spilled out in some of the letters of evaluation that the administration had requested from Calvo's students and colleagues. What's at play in this terrible incident isn't the content of these letters—which habitually circulate in the evaluation processes, numerous and Kafkaesque—but in the way they are read. Over Calvo's ten years of work at the University there wasn't a single event that would justify that decision: it was basically an issue in the interpretation of cultural metaphors, expression, and styles.

The academics tasked with reading the letters behaved like the peasant from the classic tale who interrupts a play in the theater to warn the hero that he's in danger. Antonio Calvo was a young Spanish intellectual, educated in the debates around his country's transition to democracy. Nothing explains his suicide, and nothing explains the arrogant decision made by those charged with judging colleagues who belong to different cultural traditions from those that dominate American academia.

Heroes in classical tragedy paid for the mistaken interpretation of prophetic words with their lives; at present it is others who tendentiously read the texts that encode personal destinies. The signification of the words—as one of the Wittgenstein disciples that abound on campus might say—depends on who has the power to decide their meaning.

Monday
The pianist who lives opposite, on the other side of the street, practices Schubert's last sonata every evening. He advances a little, pauses, and starts over. A sensation like a window taking a while to open. Today I saw him under the yellow light of the streetlamp, standing in front of his car, the hood raised, in a state of repose. From time to time he would lean forward and listen to the sounds of the running engine. Then he would straighten up again and remain there, motionless, in an indecipherable and tranquil waiting.

6

Scott Fitzgerald's Bar

Monday
I can only do one thing at a time. Slow. I barely move. My life is ordered into discontinuous series. There is an invisible persistence of habits. The series of bars, readings, politics, money, love, music. Certain images—a light in the window in the middle of the night; the city at daybreak—repeat over the course of the years.

I'd like to publish this diary in sequences that follow these series: all the times I've run into friends in a bar, all the times I've gone to visit my mother. In this way, it would be possible to alter the chronological causality. Not one situation after another but rather one situation *equal to* another. An ironic effect of repetition.

These ideas arise as I'm teaching my final classes at Princeton. A seminar, "Poetics of the novel." Another possible series: all the times I've entered room B-6-M in Firestone to teach class over these fourteen years and the things that have happened afterward.

Wednesday
I go with Arcadio Díaz Quiñones to visit the Latino New York exhibition at El Museo del Barrio. The relationships between Latin America and New York, from the seventeenth century onward.

Arcadio is one of the first to have called attention to the importance of the extralocal condition in the Puerto Rican diaspora and in the history of the city. Just as Juan Goytisolo has highlighted the Arab presence in the galleries and neighborhoods of Paris, Arcadio has registered the marks of Latin culture on New York and—conversely— the way in which migration into the United States has defined the artistic practice and national tradition of Puerto Rico. His books *La memoria rota* and *El arte de bregar* have established a new notion of Latin American culture.

On a corner in the neighborhood we see children getting out of school, parents coming to get them. Black, Latino, Korean, Arab children don't go around the city on their own. A woman covered in a veil walks with her five- or six-year-old daughter, also veiled; they wait for the traffic light to change, the girl holding onto the mother's robe with her hand.

Thursday
The discussion around the Antonio Calvo case continues. Good statements from Paul Firbas and Luis Othoniel Rosa-Rodríguez. They raise the need to politicize the matter. Why don't professors' unions work? Why is there no student center? Conflicts are made personal and there's no place to turn to in the case of firing.

Saturday
My brother and I go to Atlantic City to gamble in the casinos. The outlying neighborhoods full of darkened and burned buildings; images of warlike disaster in the poor areas of the city. Then the luxury hotels, the boardwalk, the neon signs lit during the day. We lose all that we brought with us in roulette, but one of us finds a credit card in a wallet despite promising to leave them at home. We go back in, make back our money, and win a few dollars more.

On the way back, we take a wrong turn and get lost. We end up in an unknown town, no one to be seen in the streets; finally, in an empty supermarket, there is a Korean or Chinese woman pushing a vacuum along the large illuminated aisles. She doesn't know where Princeton is or how to get back on the highway. We make a few loops through the dark suburbs before finally finding the freeway, and we get back in time to have dinner at Blue Point.

Sunday
A few months ago, Alexander Kluge came to give a lecture at Princeton, but a small winter accident forced him to postpone it. He couldn't speak because he'd hit his face and broken an arm. Kluge appeared in the hall, wearing a cast, and nodded in greeting with a kind of Chinese courtesy. That was all.

In his narratives, there's always a surprising event—a contretemps—that alters the temporality and assembles multiple meanings. In German, a surprising occurrence is *unerhörte Begebenheit*. The unexpected incident lies at the origins of the *nouvelle* as a form. And the middle-distance story is the model for the narration in Kluge.

In his story collections—*Attendance List for a Funeral, New Stories, The Battle*—the protagonists' short lives are glimpsed through the plot of historical events. Kluge works like no one else with the difference between the sense of experience and the impersonal void of information. Literature as historiography.

Tuesday
We spend a couple of days—with intermissions—watching the nine hours of Kluge's film on Marx's *Capital*. In reality it's a narrative essay about the phantasmagorias of capital, its ability to create new realities. On one hand, it picks up the caustic potency of the *Communist Manifesto* (the manifesto form as the emergence of a new critical vision). On the other hand, it renews the discussion around the concept of commodity fetishism and analyzes the illusory quality of the real within capitalist society. Very fine use of signs, written slogans,

and posters as verbal images, in the vein of Russian constructivism. A lesson in political pedagogy and didactic art, in which Eisenstein's montage and projects, the catechism chapter from Joyce's *Ulysses*, and Brecht's poems all coexist. A new historical dramaturgy in the era of advanced technology.

Thursday

After seeing Kluge's film, Carola has decided to travel to India with two friends. Not a familiar trio. They are going precisely in search of absolute defamiliarization. They're thinking of going to New Delhi and then spending some time in an environmentalist, semi-deserted town (barely a million inhabitants). All of the people are vegetarians, medicine only uses natural products, plastic and polyester are prohibited. Carola and her friends are going in pursuit of distancing, *ostranenie*, the v-effect. Most likely, I tell her, you'll all turn into objects of attention. We're also going for that, she says.

Monday

The students from the seminar give me a Kindle as a memento. To update the way you read, professor, they say with irony. With it they include the complete works of Rosa Luxemburg and Henry James. I spend several hours studying the numerous possibilities of the digital device. A reading machine, more dynamic than a book (and colder).

Do we read the same way in spite of change? What is it that persists in this practice of such long duration? I tend to think that the way of reading hasn't changed beyond the changes in the medium—papyrus, scroll, book, screen—and in the position of the body, the systems of illumination, and changes in the layout of text. Reading has always been the passage from one sign to the next. That motion, like breathing, hasn't changed. We read at the same speed as in the time of Aristotle.

When they say that a picture is worth a thousand words, they mean that the image comes more swiftly, the acquisition is instantaneous, whereas reading a thousand-word text, whatever it may be, requires a different time, a pause.

Language has its own temporality; rather, it is language that defines our experience of temporality, not only because it thematizes it and incarnates it in the conjugation of verbs, but because, in use, it imposes its own duration. In order to be at the level of velocity at which new technologies circulate, we would have to abandon words and move on to an invented language, made from numbers and mathematical notations. Then perhaps we might be at the level of the fast machines. But it's impossible to replace language, all Esperanto is comical. The system of shorthand abbreviations on Twitter and in text messages accelerates the time of writing but not of reading; the missing letters must be replaced—and their desolate syntax must be reconstructed—before the meaning can be understood.

Saturday
I go to the bar at Lahiere's, which is going to close permanently in a few days. Scott Fitzgerald came here. I order a whiskey on the rocks after nearly a year without drinking alcohol.

Monday
Last class. Group photos. I'm going to miss the students.

A meeting in Palmer House with my colleagues from the department. Greetings, memories, speeches, gifts.

Tuesday
An interview at the Retirement Funds office to discuss the salary I'm going to receive after I stop teaching classes and become a professor emeritus. The meeting is in a beautiful place, maybe the most elegant office in the university, facing the woods and the lake. The receptionist in charge of the matter is young and smiles automatically after each of her sentences. She's a kind of soulless, cheerful killer. "How

many years do you estimate that you and your wife will live?" she asks, reviewing my private file on her computer. That amount of money must be divided into the number of years of the "beneficiary's" life. She speaks of the matter naturally and efficiently, even showing me statistics and graphics that show the life expectancies of retired professors from the university. It appears that the ones who last the longest are the mathematicians and physicists (eighty-five years on average). Literature professors usually die very young here (average seventy-six years). "There are exceptions," she tells me, smiling, "but the estimate is important because the amount of the pension depends on it." Well, I defend myself, my mother and my grandmother were very long-lived, I tell her, they surpassed the average of the mathematics professors. She listens to me, serious but smiling. She also advises me on where to invest the capital. If there's risk, the interest increases; if the investment goes to covered bonds, of course, she tells me, smiling, the earnings are less. She also asks, as if in passing, how many years Carola will live. I look at the beautiful landscape visible through the large picture windows and feel a bit disheartened. Estimating how long people will live in order to calculate how much money they can receive each month is the purest example of the ethics of capitalism. There are no ideological veils or false hopes; one is confronted with reality itself. In the end I propose a deal, preferring not to put a limit on my life. In that case, she says, you can take out a life insurance policy and receive a stipulated salary. It's a wager, like Pascal's Wager. If I live long, the joke's on the retirement fund; if I don't, the joke's on me because the rest of the money, which will continue to make profits after my heartfelt passing, will then transfer to the federal funds. I'll start earning the income in January of next year; now we'll see how long the salary lasts.

Wednesday
Andrés Di Tella came for the Princeton Documentary Festival and takes this chance to film while I'm vacating the office, returning books to the library, taking down pictures, emptying drawers, filing papers. In him I have my own personal Big Brother.

Thursday
We get dinner with Arcadio, Alma Concepción, and Sarah Hirschman in the legendary—for me—Chinese restaurant in the shopping center at the end of Harrison Street. We bring our own wine. I drink too much because I don't like goodbyes

Kennedy Airport. Journey to Buenos Aires.

7

What Cat?

Friday

I land in Buenos Aires in the morning after months of absence. I go in circles around the house, open windows, make some calls. In my office, the day on which I left is crystallized as if I'd fled. In the armchair a newspaper, *La Nación*, from the month of May; note cards, diagrams, and loose notes stuck to the wall (*Men in white overcoats, with dark glasses, threaten her. The girl thinks: If I look at the guns I'm done for*). On the table, books I might have been reading: *The Setting Sun* by Osamu Dazai, *Terrorism and Modern Literature* by Alex Houen. *El amparo* by Gustavo Ferreyra. What was I up to back then?

Carola has stayed in Philadelphia and expects to go on to Los Angeles and then to Tokyo. She travels without luggage. "I'm only going to bring my camera and sleeping pills," she says.

Saturday

I spend Christmas Eve alone in the empty city. There are no cars in the street, few lights, the shops closed, a strange half-shadow. I head down Corrientes looking for somewhere open where I can eat and finally end up at a makeshift grill at a shop with tables on the sidewalk. In the background, behind the Obelisco, a play of lights seeming to come from the river. Here and there explosions and fireworks. One by one, the place is filling up with the castaways of the night, people on their own,

Germans, Belgians, North Americans, travelers like me, out looking for somewhere to eat. I order a grilled strip steak with salad and a bottle of wine. After a while I get into a conversation with an Englishman sitting at the next table. He's from Liverpool and came looking for—he says "fishing for"—soccer players from the minor leagues. I end up trying to explain our soccer to him with the footballing, physical, creative identity of Enrique Omar Sívori, Ricardo Bochini, Diego Armando Maradona, and Lionel Messi: the kickoff, the feints, the fake outs, the curve shot. "They were very similar," I conclude. And the Englishman notes down what I tell him on the edge of the white paper that serves as our tablecloth. Meanwhile, high in the night ring out sirens, whistles, crashes, distant and out of phase.

Saturday

Writing by hand is an archaic practice, prior even to oral language. The instruments have changed over the course of the centuries, but the motion remains the same: the more skilled hand is used to trace the letters and the other for occasional assistance. I'm a lefty who was forced to convert; I use my right hand only for writing and the left for everything else. The unforgettable Señorita Tumini, first-grade elementary teacher, forced me to write with my right hand. I can see myself in the empty classroom, copying words with the furor of a deranged little dyslexic.

Wednesday

In the past I was constantly getting into public polemics. Now I find no sense in the incessant babbling of opinions and predictions. Nevertheless, sometimes, even now, in the early morning, in the shower, I write imaginary outraged letters to the newspapers in response to idiotic arguments. As soon as I emerge from the water, these retorts fade away.

A homeless woman killed another in the poultry market at Plaza Once because she stole an apple from her.

Thursday

In an old issue of *The Magazine of Fantasy and Science Fiction*, I read about the persistence of the tiger in English literature: W. Blake's tyger burning bright in the forests of the night, Rudyard Kipling's Shere Khan, Hilaire Belloc's tiger of the Yucatan, Ian McKenzie's dappled tiger on the plains of paradise, and then I think that the tiger has also been stolen from the libraries by the blind creator who wanted to dream of them, but unsuccessfully, for the tigers came out "looking more like a dog or a bird."

Friday

I'm writing a prologue for Sylvia Molloy's novel *Certificate of Absence*.

When we say that we can't stop reading a novel, it's because we want to continue listening to the voice that narrates. Beyond the plot and the peripeteias lies a tone that determines the way in which the story shifts and flows. It doesn't have to do with the style—the elegance in the arrangement of words—but rather the cadence and intensity of the story. In short, the tone defines the relationship that the narrator maintains with the story he or she is narrating.

She sends me her emails from the BlackBerry: short phrases, slogans ("Water the plants!")

Monday

I go out to buy the newspapers. On the sidewalk of Calle Cabrera, a woman is talking to a little cat high up in a tree. The cat licks his paws, indifferent. The woman is trying to make it come down. "I don't want it to live a filthy street life," she says. The mother cat had given birth to her litter in the hollow of a fork in the trunk, and yesterday she took the other kittens away and abandoned this one. When I pass on my way back, the woman is gone but the cat is still there. I get a bit of ground beef and milk from the Korean supermarket. The cat comes down and I bring him home with me.

I had a cat many years ago in Mar del Plata, when I'd just finished secondary school. In March I left to study in La Plata and asked my mother to look after it. I came back home for the winter holidays and didn't see it. I asked my mother: What about the cat? She looks at me with her beautiful, ironic eyes. "What cat?" she said.

The Russian neighbor. I met her in Princeton, where she'd settled in 1950. She'd left Russia via Finland in 1937, when Bukharin fell out of favor, and had gone into exile in Paris. Over the last few decades she has published two volumes of a monumental biography of Tolstoy and is working on the final volume, tentatively titled *The Conversion.* She has already traveled twice to the former Soviet Union to work in the secret KGB archives recently made accessible in Moscow.

Saturday
I'm interested in the distinction that Sartre establishes in *Being and Nothingness* between being dead and being "retired" (*"être mis à la retraite"*): in the first case, the past does not exist; in the second, there is nothing else.

The ex-boxer, the ex-fighter, the ex-addict, the abandoned lover. The one who is retired (I myself, retired from Princeton). The line from Hemingway's *In Another Country,* which F. Scott Fitzgerald considered one of the most suggestive and unsettling in the English language (*"In the fall the war was always there, but we did not go to it anymore"*), accounts for that nostalgia for an intense experience that persists as a *place* one cannot return to. It could be translated into Spanish, literally, like this: "En otoño la guerra estaba todavía ahí, pero nosotros ya no íbamos más hacia ella." An alternative: "En el otoño, la guerra seguía ahí, pero nosotros ya no íbamos hacia ella." A sentence that is clear yet strange due to its slight syntactic displacement and twisting of pronouns.

On the other hand, the experience of there being no past refers to the figure of the *living-dead,* one who has no history and knows nothing of the past, who has drunk from the waters of the River Lethe. "Ask the historians! Go to them, and then come back. It's so long ago. How can I be expected to keep it in this overcrowded brain?" says the hunter Gracchus who wanders through time and the Black Forest in the incredible story by Kafka ("Here I am, dead, dead, dead").

This is the site of enunciation and the ironic tone that Beckett takes from Kafka in order to define a new type of narrator. The first story he wrote in French, "Le calmant," says at the beginning: "*Je ne sais plus quand je suis mort. Il m'a toujours semblé être mort vieux*" ("I don't know when I died. It always seemed to me I died old"). Stories that narrate the experience of living outside of life, in a perpetual present. Thus their contemporaneity, etc.

There's something of that figure in political culture today. The notion of the witness as the deceased in Walsh's *Operation Massacre* ("One of the executed men is alive"), which sets out from that figure to restore the truth. There is also the case of the secret prisoners who've survived inside Argentine concentration camps (the disappeared who returns) and are key witnesses in the reconstruction of events for the *Nunca más* report and the current trials of the military officers.

The witness as survivor of an extreme experience. Perhaps this is the only case in which the equation *only one who has lived it can tell it* has value, because, beforehand, it seems impossible to survive that situation. Call me Ishmael, I am the survivor of the Pequod, I am the hunter Gracchus, I am Molloy, I am Malone.

The detective novel situates truth in the place of the dead. (The classic scene of a dying man who doesn't quite manage to say . . . who the murderer was.)

Chekhov, in the same vein, defines the plot of a story (which, I believe, he never writes): "*A man whose madness takes the form of an idea that he is a ghost: walks at night*" (*The Note-Books of Anton Tchekhov.* Published by Leonard & Virginia Woolf at The Hogarth Press, Richmond, 1921). "Un hombre cuya locura le hace creer que es un fantasma: camina en la noche."

Two more from Chekhov: "I wake up every night and read *War and Peace* (If I had been by Prince Andrey I should have saved him)." And while reading Turgenev's *Fathers and Sons*: "Bazarov's illness is so powerfully done that I felt ill and had a sensation as though I had caught the infection from him." The doctor's reading.

Monday

The cat adapted quickly to his new life. Immediately he settled down on the patio and set to observing the birds that flew over the vines. ("Investigations of a cat"). He looks fixedly into the air, absorbed, as if perceiving something no one else can see.

8

Low Tide

Carola cut her trip short and returned last night. She spent several weeks between Philadelphia, Princeton, and New York. She refused to continue to Los Angeles, outraged by her treatment in American airports. "They treat you like a political prisoner," she says. During a layover in Dallas they confiscated her camera and returned it two hours later with several images erased. She's been taking photos of the security cameras for years. "They don't like it when you photograph *them*," she says.

Monday
At midnight, when the heat abates, we go out for a walk. We cross the city, which grows old as we draw near to the river to the south. In Bajo, the shorefront is beautiful. There are open-air grills with tables beneath the trees. Fishermen on the jetty, backs facing the city, with their rods and rigging. An amusement park with colorful lamps and slightly run-down games. This is the world of *Alrededor de la jaula* and *En vida*, two of Haroldo Conti's finest books. The distant lights of ships crossing the river are the only horizon of those stories with no way out.

Often the most lyrical writers, those most attentive to the landscape, narrate the river. Several masterworks have been written in that vein: Di Benedetto's *Zama*, Saer's *El limonero real*, Conti's *Southeaster*, Wernicke's

La ribera, Briante's *Hombre en la orilla*. They seek slowness; they tend to narrate things already past in the present tense. Some of Conrad's novels move in that direction: the dead calm is the motivation for the story. In *Heart of Darkness*, while they wait for the tide of the Thames to rise, Marlow tells the story. The deeper the stillness, the more intense the narrative. The dispersion of time's flow is stemmed, and the ebbing soothes it; the swell that never arrives becomes a metaphor for the art of writing.

Tuesday

I go to the dentist. He advised me to wear a dental guard. It's a line of transparent—and very hard—acrylic that replicates the upper row of teeth. With that, I won't keep grinding my teeth when I sleep. Grinding and chattering were signs of terror in the comic strips and adventure novels I read as a child. At night I sleep peacefully and dream that I'm traveling on a trolley.

Thursday

Fernando Kriss, a lifelong friend, comes over; an inactive philosophy professor, or, as he says, deactivated. He brings two bottles of white wine. We buy Middle Eastern food at the restaurant on the corner and sit down to eat on the patio. Without getting into the current style in which people act like experts and swirl the cup several times under their noses before drinking a little wine, we set into a delirious discussion about the difference between Chardonnay and Chenin. We could, Fernando says, halfway through the first bottle, apply fuzzy set theory to the difference between the wines. It is a type of logic that attempts to introduce imperfect syllogisms, that is, uncertain and diffuse knowledge. The reasoning is based on experiences that are similar but not identical; imprecise, we might say. He has married four times. A month ago, his latest wife went on a trip and returned a week later without Fernando having noticed her absence. He calls these incidents an experience with fuzzy sets. Some of the intellectuals who supported the Falklands War during the military era have now put their names on a paid announcement defending Great Britain's position. They're not opportunists, my friend laughs, they're just fuzzy. We open the second bottle of wine. In the open air, the night is magnificent.

Sunday

I read in Brecht's *Diaries* (8/9/1940): "On abbreviation in the classical style: if I leave out enough on a page, I receive for the single word 'night'—for instance in the phrase 'as night came'—a full measure of imagination on the part of the reader." Identical to Hemingway's iceberg theory: except that in Brecht's case what the reader knows is left out and in Hemingway's case what the reader doesn't know is left out.

In *A Moveable Feast*, referring to one of his first stories, Hemingway writes: "It was a very simple story called 'Out of Season' and I had omitted the real end of it which was that the old man hanged himself. This was omitted on my new theory that you could omit anything if you knew that you omitted and the omitted part would strengthen the story and make people feel something more than they understood."

Walsh's story "That Woman" belongs to that first category. All—Argentine—readers know that the woman, who is never named, is Eva Perón. By contrast, García Márquez's "Tuesday Siesta" belongs to the second. The central scene—the woman going to the cemetery with her daughter under the accusing eyes of the town—is never narrated, and the reader must imagine it. In both cases what is subtracted defines the story.

Tuesday

Giorgio Mara is putting together an exhibition in Madrid and Buenos Aires of works by Eduardo Stupía along with fragments from this diary. Eduardo uses my notes as a pretext to advance in his investigation into the manifold possibilities of constructing an image. We discuss the possible registers of a diary. We already know that its only condition is to be chronological and aleatory. It's about a register that only abides by the succession of the days. A diary records what is not yet, I say. Eduardo laughs, "Too metaphysical," he says. Giorgio opens a few boxes of books that he's received. Among them is the second volume of Beckett's correspondence and several books on Lee Krasner. "It seems her husband painted as well," Eduardo says.

Wednesday
The Russian neighbor. Now, when I recall those months, I think that if I did manage to stay relatively sane it was thanks to Nina Andropova, my Russian neighbor. She was of an uncertain age between eighty and ninety years old, a period during which some women flourish once more before coming to a glorious end. Slender and slight, with steely eyes and hair of a luminous white, she exhibited such animation and such grace that, instead of seeming actually old, she had the appearance of a young actress playing the role of a lady who was getting on in years.

Friday
In October 1921, Kafka gave his notebooks to Milena. ("Did you find something decisive against me in the Diaries?") Tolstoy does the same thing with Sophia, his future wife (and she never forgives him for it), and Nabokov with Véra as well. Pavese thinks about that possibility at various times ("Why write these things that she will read?"). In my case, the women who've lived with me not only read these notebooks but also write in them. Sometimes there are corrections on the content (*We actually spent the night on the train*) and others on the form (*what horrible syntax!*). I never hide these notebooks because there's nothing to hide. And whoever contributes to them only wants to make it clear that they've read them.

9

The Island

Friday

We spend several days at the house of some friends on an island in the Tigre. While navigating along the branches of the Paraná river, I, like so many others before, think that there is no other city bounded, as Buenos Aires is, by an archipelago of remote islands that move away to become lost in the tranquil waters of a river so slow that the locals call it "the slow-winding path."

This landscape recalls the atmospheres of Conrad, and that resonance can be found in one of Borges's finest poems, "Manuscript Found in a Book of Joseph Conrad," which is, all the same, a clear image of the heavy summers in the Delta.

> In the shimmering countries that exude the summer,
> the day is blanched in white light. The day
> is a harsh slit across the window shutter,
> dazzle along the coast, and on the plain, fever.
>
> But the ancient night is bottomless, like a jar
> of brimming water. The water reveals limitless wakes,
> and in the drifting canoes, face inclined to the stars,
> a man marks the limp time with a cigar . . .

(and I can't recall now how Borges's poem ends).

Saturday

I go down to the river and swim out, letting the current carry me to a backwater on the Rama Negra. After a while I feel a strange vibration in the water and, diving down, I find, in the muddy riverbed two meters below, a ringing cell phone. Someone threw it away or lost it, but the most incredible thing—or most disturbing thing—is that the telephone is still responding to calls with its metallic voice.

One could make an encyclopedia of the things that still persist in the transience of the present. Everyone here has Wi-Fi and internet and they write emails and tweets, yet still the mail boat passes —as it always has—in the early morning and late afternoon. On the way out they leave the correspondence on the docks, tied onto a plank, and on the way back they collect the letters that island residents have left hanging over the river on the end of a rod.

Sunday

I went out to row; there was some sloshing about as I got into the boat, and the neighbors—islanders from three generations back—looked at me with sarcastic smiles like countryfolk, out on the land, observing a cocky outsider mount a horse.

Monday

Tranquil nights, conversations on the open balcony that looks out over the river, the balsamic scent of mosquito coils in the still air. Amusing to realize that the myth of a return to nature has immemorial antecedents. In his excellent book *The Artificial Savage*, Mexican anthropologist Roger Bartra points out that in 493 BC the play *Savages* (*Agrioi*) by the Greek dramatist Pherecrates was performed for the first time; the work, of which only a few fragments have survived, relates the history of two Athenian misanthropes who flee from the confusion of the city and take refuge in a primitive setting, seeking a natural existence divested of the bustling evils of civilization.

Wednesday

A very fine translation of Dante's *Inferno* by the poet Jorge Aulicino has just been published. Some time ago, an important version by Robert Hollander was published in English. The classics must be translated again every so often because language changes. It would be better to say that there is a change in each era's model of literary style, which the translator implicitly obeys. Therefore a history of translations would be the best path for a story of literary style.

The first translation of the *Divine Comedy* in Argentina was done by Bartolomé Mitre, a politician and officer who became president of the Republic. Lucio Mansilla, an important writer and the only Dadaist dandy of the nineteenth century, had an appointment with Mitre but the man made him wait. When Mansilla entered his study, Mitre told him he'd been delayed because he was working on his translation of Dante. "But of course, General," Mansilla said. "You have to work hard on those gringos."

Thursday

The cat I found on the streets lived peacefully in the house. He adapted quickly, staking out his territory on the patio, walking around among the rooms, going up onto the terrace, and when I was reading he would come up to me. He liked watching TV but couldn't stand the channel Animal Planet. He slept in a shoebox, and he disliked electric light. The veterinarian told me he was healthy; I was going to have a cat for a while. When I went to the Tigre I put my neighbor in charge of taking care of him. He seemed to recognize me when I came back. He immediately stationed himself on the armchair as though waiting for me to sit down and read. Yesterday I went out to eat with some friends and when I returned the cat wasn't there. I supposed he was out walking along the rooftops and didn't worry. This morning he still hadn't returned, and when I went out to buy the paper, I found him in the hollow of the same tree on Calle Cabrera that I'd rescued him from a month before. He returned to the fold, as Gramsci said of the intellectuals. He prefers being a street cat over spending all day among books.

Friday

We go to see W. Herzog's documentary *The Cave of Forgotten Dreams* about the rock paintings found in the caves of Chauvet-Pont d'Arc in the southwest of France. The images are close to 40,000 years old and may be considered the beginning of figurative representation in art. One of the rocky walls of the cave, which opens onto to the River Ardèche, collapsed, covering the entrance and preserving the figures like a time capsule for thousands of years. The paintings and drawings in the cave have the quality of a Sistine Chapel from the Paleolithic. There's a bestiary of powerful animals on the walls and, in one wing, an extraordinary group of horses with heads of a surprising lightness and beauty. Traced on the slant of a rock is a woman with her legs apart, joined to a bison. As Herzog points out, this figure seems like a distant echo of Picasso's series of sketches *Minotaure et femme*. "In a way they are like traces of forgotten dreams that have later surfaced in modern art." The experience of the film is unforgettable and unsettling. What we call art was given from the beginning in all of its perfection. The cave paintings seem to confirm Aby Warburg's theories: there is no evolution or progress in the history of images. The forms can be compared to one another, unmediated, in an open constellation of representational styles shared beyond centuries of difference. Looking at these figures, I thought about the theory of the spirit as creator of symbolic forms, from Ernst Cassirer, a thinker somewhat forgotten today but widely read in the days when I was studying at the College. We must recall that Cassirer worked for many years at the Warburg Library and was in fact the "house philosopher." His influence is very clear in Panofsky's book *Perspective as Symbolic Form*. Iconography had begun to replace authorship and chronology in the conceptual analysis of art. A certain Kantian Platonism will always be welcome in the study of forms and artistic processes of creation.

Thursday

It's very hot in the city. I'm walking back at noon, and by a construction site I pass two boys talking in the shade of a tree. As I pass, I hear one of them tell the other, speaking of an absent friend: "He found the girlfriend in his bed with *un flaco*." A perfect story in ten words. The best part is the displacement of possession from the woman to the bed and the sympathy in the final utterance describing the intruder.

10

A Perfect Day

Friday

Someone recalled that sunset did not exist as a poetic theme for the Greeks. All merit was given to sunrise and its many metaphors: daybreak, dawn, awakening. Only in Rome, with the empire's decline, did Virgil and his friends begin to celebrate sundown, twilight, the end of day.

Are there, then, writers of sunrise and writers of twilight? These are the kinds of lists I'd like to make. But on the other hand, now that night has fallen and an old lamp is giving me light, I'd like to call to mind a feeling bound to the sun's setting. How could we define a perfect day? Maybe it would be better to say: how could I narrate a perfect day?

Is that why I write a diary? To capture—or reread—one of those days of unexpected happiness?

Tuesday

Sánchez Ferlosio explained in *La forja de un plumífero* how he wrote his novel *El Jarama* . . . "My turn came in the militia in Morocco; naturally my compatriots were from the most modest classes, and I began to develop an interest in popular speech. Once discharged, I began making a list of everything I remembered from the militia,

351

which kept on expanding with all manner of words, turns of phrase, 'idioms,' constructions, or syntactical twists—with double, triple, even quadruple negatives—that I noted down systematically. Those terribly long lists were the warp on which I wove *El Jarama*, even in terms of the plot. Often, certain conversations—or situations—*were invented with no other motive than to make space for one or another item from my lists."*

Monday
"The Polish Immortal" is a chess game—by the master Miguel Najdorf—considered to be a work of art. In 1922, in Warsaw, the young Najdorf sacrifices several pieces and achieves checkmate in twenty moves through a brilliant and insane assault on the king. All very well, but (in art there's always a but) some contemporaneous opinions from the time when the game was played "doubt" its authenticity, and they suggest that in reality the game played was *similar* to this one, so that, in short, what we know is only a lovely *post factum* analysis that retouches and improves the play of white and black; obviously nothing can be proven or denied, "but" it is true that there are certain blind spots; for example, it's unclear which tournament it was played in. We might think that it was only an analysis and was never actually played, or that it was only played to make that gameplay famous (something which was achieved, since the combination has found eternal life). It's obvious that, if it hadn't been presented as an actual game, it would've been hard for this analysis to have any repercussion, for who remembers a brilliant analysis?

In 1939, Najdorf sought refuge in Buenos Aires, where he'd come to play in a tournament, and he became an Argentine citizen and won best board in the Chess Olympiad in which Argentina came in second after the Soviet Union.

Najdorf and Gombrowicz were friends and sometimes met in the afternoon at the café Gran Rex, on the top floor of a cinema on Calle Corrientes, to speak Polish for a while and play chess.

Sunday

There's a tradition of incomplete books, having no ending, never finished, projects that take a lifetime; the works of Macedonio Fernández, Kafka's novels, *Bouvard and Pécuchet*, *The Man Without Qualities*. They represent the most radical attempts to alter the traditional logic, which views the key to a good narrative as being in the equilibrium of the form (that is, in the elegance of the ending). Written precisely in order to rupture that harmonious order, or written with a will toward an impossible totality, these unfinished works are read by us with fervor, as if they could make visible the impossibility of closing the meaning; the draft understood as a constantly rewritten and unstable text, poorly dated, lacking an end.

Some works have been written by following that same perilous and ephemeral criterion: Valéry's *Cahiers*, Connolly's *The Unquiet Grave*, Rilke's *The Notebooks of Malte*, even Borges's wonderful book *The Maker*. They seem to have no form or to have no form other than disorder and fragility. Pavese's *This Business of Living* is a special case: his suicide is the deliberate ending to the diary ("not words. Action. I shall write no more"), giving it the quality of an inevitable conclusion.

Tuesday

A few years ago, in Jujuy, far to the north, my friend Héctor Tizón and I visited the ruins of the old Marquisate of Yavi, the site of what had once been the main residence of the marquis Feliciano Fernández Campero, who, during the Wars of Independence, joined with the patriotic forces and was defeated and captured by the royalist army at the Battle of Yavi on November 15, 1816—because, from what Tizón told me, he was too fat to run away. We visited the library, which occupies a rather modest house, and the librarian—a slender and kindly woman, with the look of a Salvation Army lady—opened the door and let us in. The room, with high ceilings of straw and wood, was filled with books from the illustrious marquis. And then, off to one side, in a simple display cabinet, we saw the first edition of *Don Quixote*. The aura of art awaits us in the most

353

unexpected places. We leaned over the open pages of the book, which the marquis, a famous bibliophile and collector, had bought at the end of the eighteenth century, in his distant youth, and had transported to these remote provinces . . . Touched, we said goodbye to the woman and went out into the crisp air of the afternoon in the empty country.

We walked toward the car in silence, and I felt a procession of dark thoughts inside me, never confessed to Tizón: to come back alone a while later, to bring chloroform for the librarian, to open the display cabinet, *to leave a replica of the original*, to open the glass box and steal that magical novel for myself; to have the book at home and never show it to anyone; to read it, late at night, a solitary, sacrilegious, surreptitious reading. The idea that I would know I had it, that no one would ever see it, filled me with a turbulent emotion. I got into the car, thinking: Wouldn't that private secret forever change my life or my character, or at least my way of reading? We left by a windswept dirt road, seeking the provincial route that led up toward La Puna and the Bolivian border.

11

The Fall

Thursday

Today I had another fall, always a surprising and stupid event, and struggled to get up again. In bed, devilish trouble trying to sit, then I go to get my pants from the closet and fall as I'm turning around. Carola raves, the porter comes up. "Don't worry, Don Emilio," he says, bringing with him the young servant who receives clients for Deborah, the cross-dresser who works on the fourth floor. Between the two of them they help bring me back to life.

Tuesday

Dying is hard; there's something happening to me, it isn't an illness, it's a progressive state that alters my movements. This won't work. It began in September of last year, I couldn't fasten the buttons of a white shirt.

Monday

I'm selling my library, I need space. I'm keeping just five hundred books, the ideal library, with that quantity it's possible to work.

I've started to decline unexpectedly. No use complaining.

Saturday 5
My life now depends on my right hand; the left started failing in September after I finished the TV program on Borges. It happened to me at that moment, but not because of it. The doctors didn't know what it was due to. My first symptom was an inability to make fine movements, my fingers no longer obeyed me.

Monday
My right hand is heavy and uncooperative, but I can still write. When I can no longer . . .

I feel as if a hive is growing inside my body, a hatchery. I want to be certain before I write it down. Scrupulous until the end.

I always wanted to be only the man who writes.

I've taken refuge in my mind, in language, and in what is to come.

I can no longer dress myself, so I've had to get a cape or rather tunic tailored for me; it covers my body comfortably, with two cords to fasten it. I have two outfits; while one is being washed, I wear the other, they're made from blue linen, I need nothing more.

The madam nurse can enter the room at any hour, while I, between the folds of the bed, look at the city through the window.

The parrot in a cage.

The wheelchair, the mechanical movement, the metallic body.

Sickness as a guarantee of extreme clarity.

A passing illness.

So as not to despair, I've decided to record a few messages spoken aloud on a little digital recorder that rests in the upper pocket of my cape, or is it my carapace?

If you have use of your body, what you say doesn't matter.

Genius is disability.

ABOUT THE AUTHOR

RICARDO PIGLIA (Buenos Aires, 1940–2017), professor emeritus of Princeton University, is unanimously considered a classic of contemporary Spanish-language literature. He published five novels, including *Artificial Respiration*, *The Absent City*, *Target in the Night*, and *The Way Out* as well as collections of stories and criticism. Among the numerous prizes he received were the Premio de la Crítica, Premio Rómulo Gallegos, Premio Bartolomé March, Premio Literario Casa de las Américas, Premio José Donoso, and Premio Formentor de las Letras.

ABOUT THE TRANSLATOR

ROBERT CROLL is a writer, translator, musician, and artist originally from Asheville, North Carolina. He first came to translation during his undergraduate studies at Amherst College, where he focused particularly on the short fiction of Julio Cortázar.